THE
MONEY
RUSTLERS

Self-made Millionaires of the New West

Paul Grescoe and David Cruise

VIKING

VIKING
Penguin Books Canada Ltd., 2801 John Street,
Markham, Ontario, Canada L3R 1B4
Penguin Books, Harmondsworth, Middlesex, England
Viking Penguin Inc., 40 West 23rd Street, New York,
New York 10010 U.S.A.
Penguin Books Australia Ltd., Ringwood, Victoria,
Australia
Penguin Books (N.Z.) Ltd., Private Bag, Takapuna,
Auckland 9, New Zealand

First published by Penguin Books Canada Ltd., 1985

Typeset by Jay Tee Graphics Ltd.
Printed and bound in the United States of America

Canadian Cataloguing in Publication Data

Grescoe, Paul, 1939-
  The money rustlers

ISBN 0-670-80207-7

1. Capitalists and financiers - Canada, Western -
Biography. I. Cruise, David, 1950- II. Title.

HC112.5.A2G74 1985 338'.04'0922 C85-098662-1

Reprinted 1985

To my mother, Christina Grescoe, the first entrepreneur I ever knew, and to my wife, Audrey

P.G.

To my mother, Claudia Cruise, who always knew I was really a writer

D.C.

Acknowledgements

We would like to thank Don Smith, Pat Gareau,
Lois Hammond, Gillian and Terry Stewart, the Colberts,
Julie Ovenell-Carter, Tom Harrison, Roger Newman,
Dr Michael Goldberg, Donna Grescoe and all the Rustlers
who gave their time.

Contents

THE
MONEY
RUSTLERS

Introduction

> Rustle: (a) to bestir, to shift, deal with rapidly; to acquire or get together by one's own exertions.
>
> Rustler: (a) a cattle thief, (b) an energetic or hustling man.
> — *The Oxford Universal Dictionary*

The people profiled on the following pages are Western Canadians who together own over $5 billion in assets and directly employ fifty thousand people. Some of the individuals described here have glided to the top with regal ease and style, while others have grasped and groin-kicked every inch of the way. We call them the Money Rustlers because the title hints at the cunning, ruthlessness, ingenuity, energy and creativity we found at the heart of these people and at the core of their various enterprises.

The obvious question is how the Money Rustlers were chosen. Hundreds of promising names were culled before the final sixteen people were picked. Some were interviewed before being eliminated from the final list because they just didn't quite meet the criteria.

The first requirement was that each of the people must be self-made, having inherited neither wealth, influence nor business. The only possible exception is the Ghermezian family of Edmonton, who brought to Canada from Iran an unknown portion of the family wealth. Even so, Jack Ghermezian, the father, was without influence in Canada and his four sons made their fortune in construction and land development, a field far removed from the family carpet business. The second criterion was that each of the Money Rustlers must be worth at least $1 million. Thirdly, they must be owners, not employees — and preferably owners of the entire business. Manitoba resource merchant John Doole was an employee for most of his career, but he purchased the Winnipeg company he worked for. He is included because his metamorphosis into an entrepreneur gives considerable insight into the qualities required for success. Finally, the Money Rustlers must not have been extensively profiled elsewhere, particularly in books. This requirement disqualified household names like Jim Pattison of the Pattison Group in Vancouver, Jack Gallagher of Dome Petroleum in Calgary, the Belzberg brothers of First City Financial Corporation in Vancouver, and so many others who leap readily to mind.

Dealing with business, particularly in the West, can be a risky thing for the writer: no sooner do you settle on appropriate subjects than one of them loses everything or moves to Borneo. In three cases, profiles were dropped when the individuals inconveniently went bankrupt. The people in this book, however, are representative of their kind throughout Western Canada.

Three groupings of people are missing from these pages: Money Rustlers from Saskatchewan, once-successful risk-takers who are now on the financial skids, and women entrepreneurs. Although Saskatchewan Rustlers exist, their numbers are still relatively few and the ones we might have chronicled are not representative of a group in their province. Currently unsuccessful risk-takers, no matter their previous wealth and entrepreneurial triumphs, do not conform to the definition of the Rustler as someone on the way up, not down. Nor do any women meet the criteria of the Rustler: many were self-made, a few were millionaires, but not one was a truly self-made millionaire. To complicate matters, comparatively few women who are visibly successful like to talk about their wealth or divulge specific financial information about their businesses.

In a few years, all of this may well have changed. Saskatchewan is at a fascinating juncture in its history having shifted from its recent socialist past, when private enterprise was de-emphasized, to a Conservative administration that is attempting to encourage individual entrepreneurship. Before long, other researchers may be able to choose from a host of flourishing Rustlers. Soon, too, there may be fresh and optimistic chapters to write about the trio of formerly prospering losers we mention here. And certainly in a decade or less, Western women who meet the criteria of the Rustler will be filling a volume this size; there are many now in the West on the verge of multi-million-dollar success.

Saskatchewan — The Co-op Province

Saskatchewan is the prototypical Canadian home of those original Western entrepreneurs, the farmers, whose energy and initiative we celebrate in the first of our portraits. The farmer as entrepreneur is represented in spirit by Brian Heidecker, the farmer-rancher from Coronation, Alberta, near the Saskatchewan border. But the reality is that the farmers of Saskatchewan are less rigorously Rustlers than their counterparts in Alberta. Fierce individualists though they have always been, the men and women of this province — which until recently bore the nickname Next Year Country — had to band together in the early years for sheer survival. Barn-raising bees begot wheat pools, then credit unions and other cooperatives on a scale unmatched in the rest of Canada. As a consequence, Saskatchewan's contemporary farmers have never been as purely entrepreneurial as those in other provinces, in the sense of breaking the mould, embracing new and exogenous ideas, actively seeking growth, and operating like bucolic business executives.

The same qualities of cooperation that fuelled the Saskatchewan farmers also resulted in a different kind of entrepreneurial activity in the towns and cities of the province.

Because of its long history of CCF and NDP administrations, Saskatchewan has been a North American crucible for the concept of government entrepreneurship. In its first term alone, during the mid-1940s, the CCF opened a brick-manufacturing plant, a shoe factory, a box factory, a provincial bus company and a sodium sulphate mine. Its business-minded bureaucrats later created the first government automobile insurance plan in Canada, Saskatchewan Power, Saskatchewan Oil and Gas, and the Saskatchewan Systems Corporation. Their developers were entrepreneurs of the public sector, but government enterprise lies beyond the breadth of this book. And Saskatchewan has only a handful of publicly traded companies, which is symptomatic of the fact that it has spawned relatively few risk-takers who are truly Money Rustlers.

The Losers

The recent recession hit the Western provinces especially hard; hundreds of entrepreneurs were ruined during the early eighties. But three losers in particular stand out: J. Bob Carter, Nelson Skalbania and Murray Pezim. They were the very cowboy capitalists and eccentric millionaires who typified the West's freewheeling, go-for-broke image. And more than any others, the media portrayed them as *the* Western entrepreneurs. They were the flamboyant, heedless men that many would-be risk-takers used as models. And, though none of the three is broke, all have lost what they wanted most in life — which definitely was not money.

In Carter's case, what lies shattered is his hard-won reputation as a respected businessman. John Arthur Charles Patrick (J. Bob) Carter of Vancouver is larger than life in all things. He stands six-foot-four in his hand-tooled cowboy boots, weighs a slightly puffy 250 pounds, and the speed and magnitude of his ascent is matched only by the resounding crash of his fall. From the obscurity of a minor-league hustler, he emerged on the national oil scene in 1977 as the organizer of the then-biggest oil deal in Canadian history — a complicated $522-million purchase of the producing properties of Hamilton Brothers' Petroleum in Denver. Since then, he has amassed a personal fortune of $75 million using tax loopholes and legions of accountants to buy other producing oil companies.

But in 1983 Carter poured $2.4 million down the drain trying to salvage the luckless Vancouver Whitecaps of the North American Soccer League. (Both the team and the league have since folded.) After purchasing a 50 percent share in the team, he charged in and announced the state of the Whitecaps' debt ($4.5 million), which promptly sent creditors scurrying to cash in their notes. Two years later, after Carter resigned from the Whitecaps board, John Laxton, a prominent Vancouver lawyer and director of the club, commented, "He will hardly be a lost asset."

Carter resigned in the wake of highly publicized sex charges, the details of which painted a sordid and pathetic picture of his not-so-private private life. The first charges were rape, buggery and gross indecency involving a woman, and indecent assault against a man — allegations that Carter has been fighting since 1980. In another case, in November 1984, a haggard Bob Carter, claiming he couldn't remember anything because of a drinking problem, pleaded guilty to gross indecency charges involving a $2,000 sex session with two female prostitutes, aged fourteen and seventeen. The Crown said Carter instructed the girls to take off their clothes and provided them with a leather harness and whip. The older one donned the harness and lay on the floor while Carter took the whip and struck her two or three times on the back of the legs and buttocks. Carter then instructed the youngest to whip the older girl before she performed oral sex on him.

During the trial Carter announced his decision to resign from all publicly held companies and sell the major assets of Kelvin Energy Limited, a deal worth $35.5 million. Nonetheless, he still controls Carter Oil & Gas of Vancouver and has the resources to cushion his fall from grace. After being fined

$3,000, he declared his intention to cure his alcoholism at the Betty Ford Drug Rehabilitation Center in California, at $2,500 a day.

Nelson Skalbania's big loss was his magical image, that devil-may-care aura that always illuminated him. "He is Canada's first full-fledged Gonzo capitalist," Peter C. Newman wrote in his 1981 book, *The Acquisitors.* Skalbania rode the torrid 1970s real-estate market with the verve of a surfer mastering a giant wave. By decade's end he was flipping — buying and quickly re-selling — hotels, apartment buildings and office towers from Vancouver to Quebec City, from Kamloops, British Columbia, to Corpus Christi, Texas. He controlled 51 percent of the Indianapolis Racers of the World Hockey League (signing Wayne Gretzky to his first major-league contract), held a $500,000 mortgage on the World Hockey League Edmonton Oilers and had a 10 percent slice of the Vancouver Whitecaps. At various times his sports empire also included the Montreal Alouettes football club, the Calgary Flames NHL team, and the Western Hockey League New Westminster Bruins. He was still president and 48 percent owner of the firm where he'd begun as a structural engineer. The poor Polish-Canadian boy born in Wilkie, Saskatchewan, had grown up to fashion himself a life out of a Harold Robbins novel, with a million-dollar jet, a 173-foot diesel yacht, two Mercedes 450 SLs, four Rolls-Royces, and eventually a $4 million, 17,000-square-foot Greek-style villa — which he began building on 1.7 acres of residential land after tearing down a perfectly good mansion owned by department-store heir Chunky Woodward. But he never finished the house, which was meant to fulfil the dreams of his new wife, Eleni: the recession and his misfortunes with sports franchises toppled him off his wave and sent him crashing onto the rocks.

As interest rates soared, Skalbania's earlier boasts about never borrowing were lost in a welter of bank loans supporting his various enterprises. Then the bottom fell out of the real-estate market and he collapsed under his holdings, many of which he had purchased at the height of the market. In 1981 his jock dreams dissolved. The Calgary Boomers of the North American Soccer League were $2 million in debt, the Alouettes had lost $4 million and were the laughing stock of Canadian football, the New Westminster Bruins were sold for $300,000 after losing $150,000. In all, it amounted to a litany of debts and lawsuits.

Shortly before the 1981 meeting of his creditors brought the persistent rumours of money problems to a head, Skalbania threw an enormous party in downtown Vancouver. The purpose was to declare publicly his love for, and tearfully beg for the return of, his wife Eleni, who had left him just a year after their marriage, telling friends she was tired of the spotlight that Nelson's antics threw on her life. The gesture was tasteless, almost embarrassing, but it worked: Eleni took him back and the creditors, apparently as moved by Skalbania's words to his wife as by his pleas to them, allowed him to keep his beloved Rolls and an annual salary of $90,000, while he worked to restore his shrivelled assets. (He owed $45 million, with assets of about $18 million.)

Nelson Skalbania's current deals are paltry caricatures of those he cut while on top. In 1984 he bought into Circus World near Orlando, Florida, acquired a string of recreational theme parks operated by Malibu Grand Prix Corporation, and got involved in a mobile-home park under construction in Coquitlam, British Columbia. He has also mentioned vaguely that he was considering opening a coal mine in northern British Columbia — ignoring the world coal glut — and hinted at involvement with the Philadelphia Eagles of the National Football League. It's a little like an aging film star reduced to soap commercials, talking bravely about a new screen career.

Murray Pezim has built his career on a series of comebacks. He has always hungered for that colossal score that would transform his image from that of an opportunistic promoter into that of a financier. He almost made it. But just when he got the really big one — the Hemlo gold field in northwestern Ontario — his massive ego kicked it all away.

Pezim, who used to work in his father's butcher shop in

Toronto, stormed into Vancouver in 1963, and the small, conservative financial community has never been the same. He rented the Lord Stanley Suite in the Hotel Vancouver, stocked it with food and booze and invited women of doubtful virtue, and started a nonstop four-month-long party attended by senior bankers, company presidents and cabinet ministers. Pezim's charm was soon pulling even sceptics into his endless, oddball, get-rich-quick ideas — Vita Pez rejuvenation pills, Minnie Pearl of Canada (a fast-food chicken franchise), the Pez chocolate bars, a three-wheeled Pezmobile, monogrammed apples. Inevitably, as investors lost money on his schemes, people began wondering whether Pezim was a crook. In fact, he isn't. He exaggerates, and his schemes are so complicated that no one else can understand them. But he's simply bigger and better at what most other promoters do more discreetly. The RCMP have also decided that Pezim isn't a crook: at least five thousand taped phone calls, three years of videotapes of his bedroom and bathroom, and Mountie surveillance did not turn up any evidence of stock fraud.

The way Pezim likes to tell it, he single-handedly brought in the massive Hemlo gold field, located two hundred miles east of Thunder Bay — all the while battling valiantly against stubborn and stupid Torontonians. "We spent a couple of million bucks before discovering Hole Number 76 in May 1982," he states grandiloquently. "Everyone was against us." In truth, two of Pezim's associates in Vancouver, Doug Collingwood and Nell Dravogan, first brought Hemlo to Pezim's attention as early as October 1980; he wasn't the least bit interested. By the time they badgered him into full involvement, there were already sixty-five holes drilled with decent results. From there, Pezim's story of persistence in the face of long odds has some truth.

In 1983, inflated by Hemlo's extraordinary success, Pezim embarked on a crusade to buy control of BC Resources Investment Corporation because he didn't like the way the board was running the company. His takeover attempt lost him $2 million. His next major disaster was Pezamerica's production of cassette greeting cards with tacky, semi-funny messages recorded by broken-down stars. Instead of testing the waters, he cannonballed in, spending $250,000 to renovate a warehouse to produce the cassettes, hiring ninety employees and eating up $4 million in manufacturing and promotion costs before the sheriff nailed the door shut.

An accumulation of bad investments, margin calls on the stock he'd bought at $7 that was now $2 a share, and shareholders' revolts in key companies plunged Pezim from a 1983 paper value of $40 million to about $9 million by the end of 1984, according to his business associate, Peter Brown, president of Canarim Investments. It was the first time Murray Pezim had been solvent after a crash, but he'd lost control of International Corona, his ticket to becoming a big-time financier — a once-in-a-lifetime opportunity for a hustler who was already a very old sixty-three.

Western Women Entrepreneurs

Throughout Western Canada, there is a second generation of women entrepreneurs on the rise. They are still small in number, but they exist as a different breed from the women who came before them in the 1950s; women who hesitated before dipping their toes into the frigid waters of self-employment. When members of this first generation eased themselves into the pool occupied almost entirely by men, most stayed in the shallow end, risking only small businesses — bakeries, clothing boutiques, interior-design firms. But their successors, better-educated, more self-assured, are plunging into entrepreneurship with both feet. No longer feeling out of their depth, they operate companies that are more androgynous in nature, such as multi-outlet exercise centres. And many of them have broadened their businesses in size and scope; an enterprise that began by selling women's clothes through home parties became a multi-million-dollar network of budget boutiques in three Western provinces; a one-office temporary-personnel agency grew into the West's largest.

Throughout Canada, the number of women entrepreneurs is steadily increasing. About two-thirds of the estimated seventy-five thousand Canadian businesses launched in 1984 were owned by women. If, as the Canadian Federation of Independent Business suggests, small business produces at least 70 percent of all new jobs, then women are creating the majority of new employment in Canada.

In Western Canada, the energy level of risk-taking women is particularly high.* As early as 1978, the Association of Independent Business Women was meeting in Vancouver (it soon had sixty members), and a year later, the first formally organized women's network in Canada was founded in that city. In Winnipeg, the Human Development Centre, a private consulting and training firm owned by two women, originated a study of self-employed men and women in Manitoba; it resulted in an informative and inspirational guide for prospective women entrepreneurs called *Minding Her Own Business.* That study of one hundred male and female entrepreneurs considered the major factors that people judge important to business success. The factors highest-ranked by both sexes were positive attitude, commitment and personal energy, and the least important factor was luck.

A cross-Canada study of 1,989 new businesses by the management consultants Laventhol & Horwath found that only 25 percent of the firms led by men had survived after three years, but 47 percent of those led by women were still operating successfully. Two years later, 40 percent of the female-led firms were still alive, which compares to a survival rate of 25-30 percent over five years for business generally.

---

* In contrast to those in the Maritimes, where women are only beginning to step out of their economic ghetto. Lois Stevenson, a commerce professor at Acadia University in Wolfville, Nova Scotia, says the business world has accepted women there more slowly than in the rest of the country. Three-quarters of women entrepreneurs in the Maritimes have been in business for less than a decade. Their image as financial incompetents is deeply rooted, as she points out: "In Nova Scotia until 1968, married women could not own property or enter in legal contracts in their own right."

The Quintessential Rustler

Our basic research involved hundreds of hours of personal, in-depth interviews. In some cases, getting the interviews required as much work as the research. Edmonton financier Donald Cormie and the Ghermezian family, for instance, have never before given lengthy interviews. And the last interview about his entire career given by Edmonton developer and investor Charles Allard was in 1971.

From these interviews, most of all we wanted to know why and how the Money Rustlers achieved their success. We wanted to know what parts luck and stubbornness, arrogance and diligence played. If everyone has warts as well as strength and conviction, the Money Rustlers differ in degree; their warts are often mountains, their convictions Ulyssean.

The Westerners in this book are distinguished by their creative flair and by their passion for innovation, and they are clearly virtuosos. Every one of them is a true Westerner, which is mostly a state of mind; in fact, many of the Rustlers have roots in other countries. The most obvious characteristic of all of them is intrepid risk-taking. Their state of mind includes a regional bias that at times expresses itself as virulent antipathy towards Ontario, sometimes to the detriment of the entrepreneurs or their businesses.

Typical Western businessmen, they have long memories. They refuse to forget that it wasn't until 1930 that the federal government deigned to transfer ownership and control of natural resources to the provinces. As Ralph Hedlin, a Western-born, Toronto-based economic consultant, notes: "The three Prairie provinces went into the depression and drought of the 1930s in a terrible financial situation as a result of the public debt they built up while Ottawa was looting their land and resources."

Most Money Rustlers have achieved success at the expense of or in spite of the eastern establishment. John Buhler, a feisty farm-machinery manufacturer in Winnipeg, complains: "We are producing grain and oil and minerals and putting the money in the bank — and the money goes down east." The good-humoured oil tycoon Nick Taylor speaks of "they" and "them" when talking about Ottawa. And Ed Alfke, who created Rent-A-Wreck in British Columbia and has since franchised it across Canada, makes a distinction between what he perceives as his own bedrock Western ethics and those of easterners: "Right and wrong is quite simple for me: [something is] either right or wrong. The easterners have a lot of trouble with this. It's hard when those guys come back trying to negotiate a franchise, which is a non-negotiable document."

The Rustlers are as much visionaries and castle-builders as they are money mongers; what ties them all together is their obsession for control of their dreams. John MacDonald of Vancouver's MacDonald Dettwiler gloried in the atmosphere of the Massachusetts Institute of Technology. When he was unable to find its match in the Canadian West, he re-created the environment himself with a $21-million corporation. Donald Cormie was thriving as the innovative partner with Edmonton's leading law firm, but he craved more control than he had as a legal consultant. Dreaming of a pool of Western capital, he set about fashioning it with the Edmonton-based Principal Group conglomerate of financial companies.

The Money Rustlers are also vigorous, vibrant people, and in most cases are such egoists that accumulating money isn't quite enough — they must perform on a larger scale. Motivated by more than bottom lines (the concern of most businessmen), these men have not only a need to achieve but also a compulsion to be recognized for their achievement. Alberta oilman Nick Taylor made his millions by investing in long shots, but success in the financial area wasn't sufficient. He became the quintessential showman, and rarest of politicians, an Alberta Liberal. Even Dr Charles Allard, almost a recluse, is not above seeking a slice of the limelight: he once owned the very public Edmonton Oilers and is now the owner of Superchannel — possessions that hardly guarantee anonymity. Umberto Menghi became a book writer and television personality. The personal flamboyance of Vancouver rock manager Bruce Allen sometimes garners as much publicity as the bands he manages. Brian Heidecker, the entrepreneurial farmer-rancher in Alberta, has turned to politics and is an increasingly influential ranching spokesman in the Conservative party. John MacDonald revels in his profile as a guru of high tech and spends more time gadding about, consulting with dignitaries and the scientific élite, than he does at the drawing board. The Ghermezians, abhorrent of publicity, built the shopping colossus called West Edmonton Mall, one of the loudest and lushest signs of wealth and prosperity in the West.

Many of the Rustlers are not altogether likable. Controlling millions of dollars and thousands of jobs has inured some of them to the individual human repercussions of their decisions. Although Donald Cormie is a courteous and generous man, he projects a chilling intellectual aloofness. But if Cormie began worrying too obviously about the effects of his actions, he might lose his entrepreneurial touch — just as a trapeze artist is finished when he starts thinking about how far it is to the ground. Menghi the restaurateur plays the jovial clown when it's to his advantage, but he is merciless in cutting others down to proper size when they encroach on his territory or fail to meet his exacting standards. Brian Heidecker does not allow sentiment for his land, machines or employees to interfere with his decisions. Even Nick Taylor, Liberal and humanist, says bluntly that shareholders who don't like his penchant for gambling with their money can sell their stock and go somewhere else.

Modern Heroes

The Money Rustlers are fascinating because wealth, like fame or beauty, is fascinating to the majority of us who don't have it. But these rich people are especially important because, as distinctive as they are from one another, they are all classic entrepreneurs. And, increasingly in North America, this is the era of the entrepreneur. Our culture is in the midst of a love affair with financial innovation. The CBC, never before considered a friend of business, introduced a new weekly television series in early 1985, "Venture," which virtually canonizes Canadian risk-takers. At about the same time, the publisher of *The Globe and Mail* took space in his own newspaper to collaborate on an article urging a societal shift to encourage the creation of businesses, notwithstanding the perils involved. *Time* anointed as its 1984 Man of the Year the organizer of the Los Angeles Olympics and declared him the definitive entrepreneur, a lofty example of a breed that must be nurtured. *Esquire* proclaimed business success to be the religion of the eighties. In his new book, *The Spirit of Enterprise*, George Gilder — President Reagan's favourite economist — celebrates the entrepreneur as the forgotten hero of capitalism.

The governments of Western Canada, recognizing this trend, have been making halting but real attempts to encourage entrepreneurs. Manitoba has quadrupled its funding of a $1-million pilot program called Venture Capital Companies. Saskatchewan and Alberta have created new venture-capital schemes that encourage investors to finance small firms. In 1985 Alberta also took a dramatic step to promote the growth of entrepreneurship by eliminating its 5 percent small-business tax and establishing the lowest corporate tax rate in Canada — 5 percent on all manufacturing and processing income earned within the province. In British Columbia, the government has assembled a volunteer board of high-powered corporate executives to oversee its $5-million Discovery Enterprise Fund, designed especially to vitalize businesses operating outside the province's traditional resource-based industries.

Sadly, however, despite all the entrepreneurial hoopla from academics, corporation presidents, the government, the media and those who've already made it, the optimism hasn't yet filtered down to the general public. As we criss-crossed the Western half of the country interviewing and observing our cast of characters, we talked to dozens of other people with walk-on parts: the lonely middle-aged waitress in a deserted airport, the taxi driver in his snowbound cab, the Friday-night drinkers in a cowboy bar, and general-store owners in the middle of nowhere. Inevitably — for we were bursting to talk about these Rustlers after being with them for days on end — the conversation turned to entrepreneurs. With rare exception, the audience was enthralled, hungry for detail, parched for assurance that someone was still fulfilling the rags-to-riches Western Canadian dream. And, after the warm glow of each anecdote faded, many a listener added the wistful comment: "That's great, what he did. But you sure can't do that any more, not here anyway."

From British Columbia to Manitoba, we found the same defeated attitude. It was as if Westerners believed their place in the sun had vanished. And, because it is still a young region and a seemingly fragile one — old wealth and established success have no permanent home there yet — confidence, the stuff of which the West was supposedly made, froze quickly in the chill of the recession. The young insisted that entrepreneurial ideas couldn't work anymore, as if the people we described existed in another time and place. But the Money Rustlers *are* of their time. Inflation, interest rates and unemployment have all nibbled and sometimes gnawed at their progress. What propels these people is the very quality of confidence missing in others. None of them have doubts about their ability to outrun the demons at their heels. Superficially, it's an inexplicable characteristic in a group of people whose obvious goal is making money, more and more of it. If that had been their only goal, however, the recession would have cut them down like so many others. But because they are entrepreneurs with a creative zeal as well as an avaricious one, their immovable and often arrogant confidence has allowed them to cope, alter, shift direction and prosper as never before, even during a downturn.

Pondering the contradiction between what we'd learned about our subjects and the general assumption that such success was now impossible, we started to realize that the Money Rustlers, in addition to being profoundly interesting, were symbolically important: symbolically important not because their lives necessarily shine with professional merit or personal rectitude, but because they are entrepreneurial heroes — a rarity in Canadian popular mythology. Heroes are critical to every nation, as Donald Creighton, the distinguished Canadian historian, has pointed out: "Heroism is not a memory of the past. It is the virtue by which a nation can preserve its identity and fulfil its destiny." Contemporary visible heroes in this country are hockey players and rock stars. While every child in the western world has these kinds of idols, there has to be something more to replace them when the young grow out of baseball cards and school dances. In the United States, industrialists — often admirable, frequently reprehensible — have provided a template for enterprise, ingenuity and hard work. They are part of the heroic culture of the nation which, although usually distorted, feeds the brash confidence of today's American capitalists, large and small.

Lately, any entrepreneurial heroes Western Canada produces, or the media discovers, tend to be long on style and, as we found when the recession hit, very short on substance. Before land prices dropped by 50 percent and interest rates shot up to 21 percent, the Western entrepreneurs we read about or saw on television were the high-rollers who flipped real estate, rode on the backs of sharks, held parties in private jet helicopters and spoke movingly of astral travel. They were the stock promoters who dropped their pants in public, and the oil men who struck it rich and rushed out to buy massive steer horns for their stretch Caddies. More than anyone else, Vancouver property speculator Nelson Skalbania seemed to personify this type of feckless entrepreneur. "There's something wrong with this world where you work your ass off and your kids get it or the charities get it," he told us in 1978. "Well, I want to taste it now, spend it now."

The media ate it up. Eastern magazine editors asked for comic-relief profiles of Western go-getters while the serious meat of business journalism emerged out of Ontario's Golden Triangle. When their pages needed tarting up, these editors fell back on a cowboy capitalist from Texas North or an eccentric character from Lotus Land. Even Westerners have accepted this warped image of themselves while ignoring real success. When Umberto Menghi opened his first American restaurant in Seattle in 1980 — a coup in a business where the restaurant trade normally moves from south to north — it went virtually unnoticed in Vancouver papers, while the Seattle press treated it as a major event.

Certainly the Skalbanias have their place in the mythology of the West: their reckless risk-taking is basic to Western entrepreneurs, and the flamboyance they embody is evident, to some extent, in all the Money Rustlers. But their lone example leaves the impression that style is more critical than ability, that idiosyncrasies are more important than character. When these frail reeds, the lightweight Western success stories, were mowed down by the recession, many despaired, not realizing that they were only a part of the fabric, not the whole cloth.

The sixteen Money Rustlers portrayed in these pages delineate the true dimensions and character of the Western entrepreneur. No matter what you think of them, these and the hundreds more like them are people who through their own energetic and hustling efforts have bestirred themselves to form new businesses, rapidly dealing with their problems as they came along and acquiring great wealth — and not incidentally stimulating the Canadian economy.

1

The Resource Merchants

From the first, the Western economy has been rooted in its natural resources. In the late 1600s the adventurers of the Hudson's Bay and North West companies came in search of its treasure-house of furs. The discovery of gold, first in the sandbars of the Fraser River in 1857 and later in the creeks of the Cariboo, helped transform a colony into the province of British Columbia. By the turn of the century, pioneers were descending by the thousands on the Prairies, the "Last Best West," lured by the land and its sweet promise of becoming the world's bread basket. And half a century later, a seminal oil well at Leduc, Alberta, thrust Western Canada into post-war prosperity.

Out of the cornucopia of Western resource industries — including forestry, fishing and mining — this chapter focuses on agriculture and petroleum, and on resources refined from their raw state into building materials. Farming brought the first boom to this half of the country, and oil resulted in the most recent concerted expansion of the economy. Both instilled pride in Westerners, a sense of achievement and confidence.

A Federal Finance Department discussion paper argues that Canadian farmers generally (and roughly half of them are in Western Canada) are nine times as well-off as the average Canadian, citing the net worth of the average farm as $508,000 — $417,000 of it free of debt — compared to the average family's net worth of $47,000. The average farmer pays only 4 percent of his income to the federal and provincial governments compared to 14.9 percent for other businesses and 15.6 percent for salaried workers. Even the level of bankruptcy among farmers, which reached a disheartening high in 1984, is just one-fifth of the total for business generally.

But, at the same time, net income received by farmers has been shrinking steadily for years to 1.17 percent of GNP in 1984 from 1.35 percent in 1980. Farm bankruptcies are climbing higher every year, even faster than the record-breaking collapses in 1982. The most dramatic example is in Western Canada, with Alberta reporting a 50 percent increase in farm failures in the first five months of 1983 over 1982. The farmers who not only survive but prosper are those who run their businesses the way any of the citified Money Rustlers run theirs: with an imaginative intellect that capitalizes on such new technology as computers and gets them involved in lobbying governments to make the rules of the game fairer — always with a weather eye fixed firmly on the bottom line.

As recently as 1980, Alberta was the most prosperous of provinces, its health based on the petroleum industry which, directly or indirectly, employed nearly half the population. Albertans then had the highest average income in Canada, the lowest unemployment rate, the highest per-capita budgetary spending and the lowest provincial taxes — all thanks to oil and natural gas. The mood was irrevocably optimistic, as Dan Mothersill, a former communications coordinator for Esso Resources, explains: "The banks certainly allowed people to borrow on ideas, on ideas at that time that seemed good, that should have panned out. Everybody was making money. There was great excitement about the possibilities and the potentials . . . it [the opportunity for success] was there, just for the asking." And then it wasn't. A combination of the recession and the federal National Energy Policy burst Albertans' ballooning wealth and left them staggering.

What the resource merchants have in common is an enormous capacity for endurance. Farmer Brian Heidecker is a primary producer, oilman Nick Taylor is a middleman, and John Doole is a retailer. All three realize that they are in fields that must continue to develop in sophistication to survive.

The traditional finding or growing or selling of raw natural resources is no longer enough in Western Canada; adaptation, diversification, innovation are critical. Dr Michael Goldberg, associate dean of economics at the University of British Columbia, sounds the warning about those still stuck in the old ways of resource entrepreneurship. Calling them Darwinian survivors, he says: "It didn't take a lot of brains to make a lot of money in natural resources up through the seventies. You sat back and picked the trees off the landscape and dug the ore out and collected your profits. And the resource people of the past are not willing to accept that the environment has changed." This frontier style is ruinous, he says, "because it tends to degrade education and the need to really get out and look for new ideas — be an entrepreneur."

The message is inescapable: the natural-resource roots are still strong, but creative entrepreneurs must graft new branches on the main trunk if the West is to flourish. Entrepreneurs with the versatility and vision of Brian Heidecker, Nick Taylor and John Doole.

Brian Heidecker
— The Dryland Millionaire

Farmers were the original entrepreneurs, tough, aggressive men with little to lose who pushed their way westward undaunted by the natural hazards that defined the West's harsh character. Innovation wasn't a marketing device, it was a matter of survival: if they didn't have the proper tool or spare part they had to jerry-rig an alternative; if the creek flooded out the only bridge, or a prairie brush fire gutted the barn, another had to be built. There were no alternatives like crop insurance, emergency aid or subsidized loans. It was all a matter of determination, enterprise and adaptability.

But farmers have lost their way. Addicted to the government programs they inwardly despise, they've lost the sense of themselves as innovators and self-made men. Once the pioneer breaking new territories, the jack-of-all-trades, the canny trader who took pride in taking a neighbour in a deal, the farmer now sees himself more closely allied with organized labour than with the ranks of the entrepreneur. But there are exceptions.

At the age of forty, Brian Heidecker of Coronation, Alberta, is one of a rare breed — a rancher who treats farming as a business, views his land as an asset and feels in control of his destiny. Starting with nothing in 1970, he's parlayed his business skills into a net worth of over $5 million and a ranching, trucking, fertilizer and feed mill empire that grosses over $6 million annually. (In comparison, the upper one-third of Canadian farmers have an average $891,000 worth of land and buildings.) Heidecker's feats are all the more impressive considering two facts: that his twelve-thousand-acre Drylander Ranch, one of the largest spreads in the province, is in Alberta's dry belt, one of the most difficult growing areas in Canada, and that farmers, in general, are losing their slice of the pie.

"Most farmers think the world is out to get them," says Heidecker disdainfully. "Everything is everybody else's fault; the banks, the CPR or the government. Hence the crying farmer image. We're not poor. Successful farmers have a lifestyle and standard of living better than any other occupation."

Brian Heidecker lives in a world of weathered faces, deep-seated traditions, long drawn-out silences, tangled generalizations and chronic pessimism. Yet his smile is quick and unforced, his eyes are bright with enthusiasm and his thoughts spill out in lean, crisp sentences. Though his short body is powerfully built and his hands battered by the elements, his forty-year-old face is as unlined as a schoolboy's and he walks as if he can hardly wait to arrive. While his contemporaries are fatalists, casting their fortunes in nature's lap, hoping for the best, expecting the worst, Heidecker relies on long-range planning, careful record-keeping and computer-assisted predictions. And, if he doesn't like the odds, he bends them to his advantage.

Heidecker also cannot be called parochial, a label that

keeps Canadians from taking farmers too seriously. He reads widely — Milton Friedman, *The Financial Times*, weekly news and business magazines, Ayn Rand and, of course, a plethora of farming publications. He also collects quotations. A favourite comes from William Jennings Bryan: "Burn down your cities and leave our farms and your cities will spring up again as if by magic, but destroy our farms and the grass will grow in the streets of every city in the country." Heidecker is a man who knows his worth.

Heidecker's drive to be the best in his business is a deeply ingrained element of his personality. "I had an assignment in high school to write about what I wanted to do," he remembers. "I put down a smart-ass answer and said I wanted to be a millionaire. I was told being a millionaire wasn't an ambition — I got zero for that assignment. But it was true, that's what I wanted." According to his wife, Gail, who has known him since high school, Brian was an inquisitive, searching youngster, always "a little different" from the other farm boys. Even so, there was little to distinguish him from other aspiring farmers, as much prisoners of their fate as the animals they raised for slaughter. It took a specific incident in 1968 to focus his curiosity and zeal and make him realize that there were higher stakes and more excitement in farming than simply surviving from season to season. "I was selling some calves to a crusty old rancher," he remembers, the sting of the incident still vivid on his face seventeen years later. "I made some derogatory remarks about the price. He turned to me and said, 'You're a bloody fool to be selling those calves. Look around at the people who are making money. They aren't selling, they're buying.' He proceeded to tell me how he made money and I realized I was operating a pretty shabby outfit."

The old rancher humiliated Heidecker by stripping him of his comfortable preconceptions about the traditional farm cycle of breed, feed and sell. Heidecker woke up to the fact that profit lay in predicting market whims and manipulating his product to fit the peaks and troughs of pricing. That winter, he attended a short course in farm management. Heidecker looked around the classroom and saw that "they were all working cowboys and not professional meeting-goers," and he learned as much over beer as he learned in the classroom. It was all a revelation. "I realized that the system was very open to those who weren't kicking it," he remembers. Heidecker vowed to learn as much as he could and, as a consequence, he formulated his first business strategy. "Running with the winners and dropping the losers," he calls it in retrospect. The winners had information; without it, theories about forecasting and bending the market to your advantage are just so much rhetoric. The winners, he discovered, were also deeply involved in cattle politics. Heidecker quickly became active, too, and his philosophy is to understand the implications of government action and minimize damage to his business instead of flying into impotent rages at unwanted intervention. In 1974 he was elected as a regional representative of the Alberta Cattle Commission and between 1978 and 1983 served as a national director of the Canadian Cattleman's Association (CCA) with a major role as its chief economic strategist. Heidecker is extremely proud that through CCA lobbying, Allan MacEachen, the then federal minister of finance, revised fifteen of the most offensive provisions of his 1981 budget.* Currently he is the powerful national beef representative working to turn beef production into a cost-competitive, export-oriented industry where the promises of profit increase dramatically. Politically, he is a self-described right-winger ("If they think Lougheed is a free trader, they haven't talked to me."), but he speaks with quiet amusement of government stupidities and foibles; his attitude is that government is just another cost of doing business.

* The CCA is not to be confused, at least in Heidecker's hearing, with the six-thousand-member, and to his mind socialist, National Farmers Union. The NFU is a high-profile lobby group that has garnered considerable publicity by slaughtering a calf on Parliament Hill and by stalling miles of highway traffic behind convoys of tractors travelling at five miles per hour. Heidecker despairs at this connection between labour and farmers, feeling that there is little they have in common. "I don't consider myself a worker, a stiff on the street," he says. "I'm a businessman operating my own business. I don't go to union meetings to find out how to run my business."

So successful has Heidecker's beef politicking been that it was only a matter of time before he launched himself into the electoral fray. Early in 1985 he announced his intention to chase after the federal Conservative nomination for the Chinook riding. While some look upon politics as a duty, and others view it as a personal challenge, Heidecker makes no attempt to hide the fact that he thoroughly enjoys locking horns over a deal — be it political, financial or personal. Two years ago he attended an Ottawa conference to discuss amendments to the Debt Moratorium Act. After hours of listening to threats, whines and expostulations from both sides, Heidecker made a speech that "laid the wood on them good and proper and got the bill killed." There is some family precedence for Heidecker's public feistiness; his mother was the no-nonsense mayor of Coronation from 1980 to 1983.

Unlike other modern mega-ranch owners with backgrounds in retail clothing chains or breakfast cereal, Heidecker actually has farming in his blood. It comes as a bit of a surprise, since the father-to-son tradition is part of what keeps so many farmers deeply rooted in the past. His German-born grandfather, Henry Heidecker, settled on a quarter-section (160 acres) near Coronation, Alberta, in 1907. His father began farming in 1938 and one of his three brothers, Ron, currently works a 3,200-acre spread just down the road from Drylander. Heidecker was thinking seriously about farming when he was seventeen. He tried to buy a neighbour's 2,000-acre ranch for $20,000 but the deal collapsed because his father refused to co-sign the loan. From Heidecker's current perspective the deal was small potatoes but his father, whose own ranch was only 1,600 acres, thought his son was reaching too far. "He doesn't believe in borrowing money," shrugs Heidecker. "And he was just plain chicken. Don't forget, I was still four years under the age of majority then." Thwarted, when Brian Heidecker finished high school in 1963 — his graduating class numbered four — he took off to spend a year working on oil rigs, which in those days was a romantic, adventurous job peopled with two-fisted beer drinkers. It was also profitable and he was making nearly $1,200 a month

— a fortune to an eighteen-year-old in 1963. That same year, higher education also had a small appeal to him, so in the fall he left the dirty, sloppy grind of the rigs for engineering at the University of Alberta. At first he was swamped by 450 bright, urban-educated students in his class; by the end of the year, he stood a credible sixty-ninth. He left with no clear goals and an abiding dislike for academe: "It was a cultural shock. I couldn't adjust to the system. Besides, I've found that the longer the words, the less people know." He drifted for two years, and in 1966 he married. With $500 in their pockets he and his wife, Gail, began doing what he had always wanted to do: farm. They rented 2,600 acres from his grandmother, just three miles down the road from his father.

Their tiny two-room farm house, really just a shed, was barely worthy of the word shelter. There was no indoor plumbing, and heating was supplied by an old pot-bellied stove. The wind whistled off the prairies, hardly pausing as it whipped through the cheesecloth-like walls. "The only time I was warm was when I was shovelling furnace coal," remembers Heidecker. After a year of discomfort they moved into his grandmother's house, palatial by comparison. Still, there was no sewer system and only cold running water, but they lived in it for six years. Hired help was unimaginable and during those first years Gail Heidecker kept up her full-time job, ran the tractor and baling machine and battled the dust and dirt which continually seeped into their home.* It was a barely perceptible first step towards an empire. Expenses in 1966 amounted to $7,500, producing a net loss of $5,200. The only thing that kept them going was credit and Gail Heidecker's $200-a-month bank-teller's salary.

Such hardships are common with every farmer who works the land from scratch. Small wonder, then, that rural sentimentality is as foreign to Heidecker as it is to an urban corporate executive. If you have fond images of bronco-busting

---

* While Brian Heidecker is indisputably the businessman, Gail Heidecker is integral to the operation of Drylander. She handles the books, accounts receivable and the investments and has taken over the same duties for the Paint Earth Fertilizer and Feed Mill.

cowboys rounding up cattle and serenading them with "Giddy-up Little Dogie" on the long trail to market, forget it. Modern beef production, at least the successful kind, is a highly mechanized business and Heidecker is as attached to his animals as any other businessman is to his inventory. "When I look at a four-legged animal with black fur, I see a carcass with loins, steak and roast," Heidecker states.

Heidecker's emergence in the role of farmer as businessman, scientist, and political activist roughly coincided with the worst years farming has seen since the Dust Bowl days. In 1982-83, while others were crying in their cider, Drylander Ranch had a record year: the combined beef and grain operation grossed $3.8 million, 69 percent higher than in 1979. (For all Canadian farmers, 1982 receipts were just 6.5 percent higher than in 1979.) For Heidecker, the bottom line varies between a loss of 5 percent in a disastrous year to a net profit of over 20 percent when everything comes up cherries. A net of 10 percent is average. In contrast, most farmers today are feeling lucky if they can just break even.

Grain and beef receipts, however, are really just the fuel that keeps everything going. Land is the heart of farming. It's the good fairy and the bad fairy all rolled into one; it's the albatross and the lucky rabbit's foot hanging around every farmer's neck. Put two farmers together and if they aren't talking about the weather, they're probably cursing or praising the dirt beneath their feet. Land value is always difficult to pin down, particularly in the bull/bear market of the recent past, but Heidecker's ranch, located 150 miles south-east of Edmonton, is worth between $6 and $7 million, including equipment, inventory and livestock. In 1982 he diversified by buying out a fast-growing feed mill and fertilizer operation, which grosses $2 million annually.

In 1970, Heidecker took the first step in assembling his land empire; it was also the first sign of his bargaining acuity. He traded some breeding cattle and an old, likely uncollectable, debt for a half section (320 acres). That same year, he showed the daring side of his still-raw business instincts by importing six head of French Limousin cattle, a choice European breed whose import had previously been banned in Canada, mainly because of distrust of foreign cattle. The cost — $5,000 to $7,000 for one calf compared to $300 for domestic varieties — was staggering for any rancher, let alone one who'd yet to make a profit, but Heidecker was betting on his developing ability to forecast the future. Three years later, trading on the Limousin's curiosity value, short supply, and its 3 percent higher meat-to-fat ratio, he sold a calf for $16,500 and a cow for $29,000. Similar profits on the remainder provided the cash to begin acquiring land in earnest.

Among other farmers, Heidecker cultivates the image of being just one of the boys jawing over coffee, but if they watch carefully enough, they will notice that he listens rather more attentively than it appears (particularly when the subject of land comes up), and that he casually asks far more questions than he answers. His antennae are always out for any hint that someone is thinking of selling, be it an illness in the family, a string of bad years or simply a tinge of ennui in a farmer's voice. And once he's on the scent of opportunity, he has the salesman's — or, some would say, the con man's — gift of leaving the other guy certain that Heidecker got the worst of the bargain. His biggest single purchase, seven quarter-sections of prime land bought in 1976, is a beautiful example. He caught wind of that rare chance from an idle comment made by a farmer bellyaching to an audience in a coffee shop. That afternoon, Heidecker returned to the store, found the farmer, alone, and closed the deal. Heidecker's strategy is simple: meet the asking price if it's at all reasonable, and then, while the other farmer is feeling puffed up about the sale, negotiate tough terms, almost as a throw-away gesture. The seven sections changed hands for a minuscule 10 percent down with the balance carried by the farmer and spread over fifteen years at 9 percent. Heidecker even enjoys the fact that his neighbours, including the original owner, still believe he was the chump. "So what if the vendor brags that he got $15 an acre over the market if his terms allow me to self-finance the land," he points out. Heidecker's skilful assembling of twelve thousand acres, much of it when land prices were highly inflated, makes a lie of the myth that farmers and nonfarmers alike are fond of reiterating: that it's impossible for young people to start farming — land, the saw goes, is too expensive, you've got to inherit it.

Drylander Ranch, which took Heidecker only fifteen years to accumulate, is easily the biggest in an area where lack of moisture and poor soil reduce per-acre yield and necessitate large-scale operations. The average farm in the region is 2,000 acres, compared to the Alberta average of 887 and the national average of 540. The scenery is far from lush: annual precipitation is only thirteen inches, and in a near disastrous year like 1984, it can drop to two-and-a-half inches during the growing season. The land is comprised of #3 soil, sandy loam capable of growing a crop most years, and #4 soil, mainly clay and primarily suitable for grass. A small misstep like overfertilizing or overcultivation can turn a tenuously productive field into a sandy waste in one year. The infamous Saskatchewan Dust Bowl region is only eighty miles away.

Heidecker strives to run his operation in a business-like manner, but there are some quirky problems unique to ranching. Cattle-snatching and grain-rustling are not unusual. Occasionally someone will drive out from the city, pick out a prize steer, shoot it, load it on the pickup and have it butchered, packaged and in the freezer before you can say "Let's form a posse." It is also a simple matter to drive a tandem up beside an isolated granary — in most cases they are unlocked — axe a hole in the side, hook up a power loader and pump it dry. A grain rustler can be on the road again in less than an hour with $5,000 to $10,000 of grain in the truck bed. Once it's on the road, the grain is no longer identifiable; it is very difficult to brand a seed of wheat. Another scourge is the four-inch, doughnut-shaped tread protector, many of which litter oil sites on Drylander. Heidecker rents out the sites, but he would trade that revenue for release from these livestock hazards. At best, they result in festering, swollen hocks and knees; at worst, the animal will break a leg and have to be destroyed. Then there are odd, unexplained deaths. Sometimes, the hands come across a steer dead in the middle of the prairies for no discernible reason.

Heidecker's dispassionate view, teamed with his knowledge

that the winners in his industry are on the leading edge of technology, allows him to introduce both business and scientific techniques into his operation with amazing results. For example, a few years ago it took twenty-four months to take a calf from birth to market. Heidecker has reduced the time to thirteen months through the use of feed lots, a system of pens where cattle live and are fed a carefully calculated and controlled diet of feed, growth hormones and antibiotics. Daily weight gains vary from 2.75 pounds to four pounds, compared to the 1.25 typical for range-fed cattle. Naturally, the less time his product takes to get to market, the better the margin. Science is evident in minor ways as well. Heidecker inserts fly-repellent ear tags in the cattles' ears. For $3 a head, he increases the animal's overall weight gain by 20 pounds because the strip eliminates the tail-swatting, head-jerking aggravation caused by insects — excess movement that burns up precious calories. A small thing, perhaps, but 20 extra pounds on two thousand head adds up to an extra profit of around $32,000 at market time, for a cost of only $6,000.

Heidecker, building on the hard lesson of the old rancher's scathing criticism in 1968, takes great pride in his ability to predict the ebb and flow of the cattle market, selling the maximum poundage of meat at the highest possible price. It is this acumen that more than anything has turned the Drylander into a big-time operation. In 1977, for instance, when cattle prices were very low and others were selling in a panic (the same thing that Heidecker was doing to earn the old man's tongue-lashing nine years before), he started building up his herd because he anticipated a boom market in 1979. He slowly enlarged the herd from one thousand to three thousand head and then, with exquisite timing, hit the jackpot by selling the entire lot within a week precisely at the market's peak in February 1979. That year, Drylander Ranch Ltd. had a net profit of $412,000 on sales of $2.2 million.

Heidecker usually spreads his cattle production and sales over the entire year to guarantee the highest possible average sales price. But when all the right factors coalesce, he moves with the skill and daring of a professional gambler going for the grandslam. In January 1982 he had three hundred steers at market weight, but the prices were very low. "I was completely confident the market was going up," says Heidecker, "but I couldn't extend the steers far enough,* so I rolled them into another class of cattle that would be ready later." He sold the three hundred head at a $45,000 loss, a loss he faced in any case, and immediately bought seven hundred 500-pound heifers (cows that haven't calved) at 52 cents a pound. He put them in the feed lot, and sold them three months later at their finished weight of nine hundred pounds for 85 cents a pound, yielding a tidy $353,000 gross profit.

Heidecker's sharp-shooting business abilities haven't entirely erased the farmer from his personality. He still loves to pull up a chair and talk. "I'm probably the worst bullshitter in the country," he admits. And though his conversations start with ritualistic statements about the weather — usually rain or lack of rain — it doesn't take him long to get around to his favourite subjects: diversification, increasing efficiency, enterprise analysis, computerization and tax planning. While Heidecker is primarily a beef producer, he does grow eighty thousand bushels of wheat annually, partly to keep his hand in that side of the business, but mostly because it improves the ranch's efficiency — a word that resides as a kind of deity over the Drylander spread. "We can raise two hundred head just on the salvage after harvest," he boasts.

A few years ago, while mulling over ways to increase profit margin, Heidecker realized that only two-thirds to three-quarters of most farms, his included, is productive land. The remainder consists of bush piles, depressions and rocky spots, usually cursed as a nuisance and an obstacle to ploughing. Heidecker decided to try reclaiming these traditional waste lands. Today, he develops two to three quarters annually by bulldozing trees, burying rocks and levelling holes,† netting 30

---

*Heidecker can and does manipulate the growth rate of his cattle by adjusting their ration-mix or putting them out on the range for a period. This allows considerable latitude in picking an opportune time to go to market.

† He's even trying to rehabilitate sterile alkali slough by planting a special salt-tolerant grass.

to 40 acres from each quarter at a cost of $100 an acre. (The same land would cost him between $300 and $350 an acre on the open market.) This reclamation and redevelopment yields 20 percent more arable land, decreases equipment wear and speeds up planting and harvesting. Before development, it took six and a half hours to cultivate 130 acres. Now it takes only five hours for 160 acres. What's more, the reclamation work can be done in slack time, allowing better use of manpower and equipment. Not incidentally, the overall value of Heidecker's land is dramatically increased. His satisfaction comes as much from doing something unique, even revolutionary, as from upping marginal productivity. Other farmers, beginning to see land redevelopment as a way to increase their margin, are clearing land in a haphazard way, but "Nobody goes as crazy as I do," Heidecker insists.

Maintenance is a vital link in the success of Drylander. Heidecker deplores the careless way most farmers, insensitive to insidious deterioration, treat their valuable equipment. The romantic image of farmers hunkered down by the fire, sharpening blades and painting shovel handles while winter rages without, is just a matter of good intentions on many ranches. Inevitable breakdowns by neglected machinery are viewed as one of the inherent frustrations of farming, but Heidecker condemns the waste as tantamount to flushing money down a toilet. Heidecker plans his maintenance schedule a year in advance to get best use of his manpower during the winter. He could no more go to Florida for the winter while his equipment depreciated and buildings stood empty than he could rely on aching bunions for a weather report.

Back-ups are vital to Drylander: the most important machinery must have stand-ins primed in the wings in case of unforeseen breakdowns. A 6,500-square-foot Quonset hut stores his $550,000 worth of machinery and a 2,000-square-foot insulated and heated shed is used for repairs and the endless maintenance régime that prolongs life and increases value. "A combine shedded over the winter will sell for $10,000 to $15,000 more simply because it looks better," he claims. The shed is equipped to handle welding and fabricating as well as routine maintenance. Naturally, the best care can't anticipate every breakdown, so Heidecker keeps a large parts inventory to avoid costly downtime: a delay of as little as six hours could be disastrous in the race to beat frost to the crops. His trucks are also radio-controlled, so if something breaks down and no parts are available on site, his wife can be radioed to dash into town to pick up what is needed. Most of the Drylander equipment is no more than six years old — unusual in an area where 1949 Maple Leaf Chevys aren't uncommon and where farmers hang on to machinery until it collapses. He depreciates his equipment $100,000 annually, but turns the tax savings directly back into updated and improved models.

Tucked beneath Heidecker's sophisticated talk of trade-in value and depreciation cost is the boyish zeal of a gadget fancier. In 1983, he bought a $50,000 state-of-the-art airseeder/ fertilizer that looks like a Rube Goldberg concoction of tubes, pipes and valves. It has a $5,000 computerized depth-control mechanism that can plant seed or band fertilizer accurately below the ground to fractions of an inch. (Seed set an inch too deep will cut the yield by 50 percent, and fertilizer laid too shallowly cuts its effectiveness by 30 percent.) But even cosmic gadgets can't obscure Heidecker's attention to the bottom line. This particular gizmo allows one man to seed 4,200 acres in twelve days; the same job used to take two men eighteen days.

Ironically, in spite of Heidecker's seemingly callous attitude to the good earth, Drylander is rapidly approaching the self-sufficiency only dreamed of by back-to-the-landers. Heidecker spent $100,000 on a fully automated feed mill that mixes the cattle's grain rations and ensures he neither has to pay nor wait for someone else's service. Drivers pull their truck into the mill, select the required combination of ingredients and load up without even leaving the cab. To feed, they simply drive between the cattle pens and fill the feed bunks with a power dispenser. Again, the gadget easily pays for itself in time saved. The feed mill allows Heidecker to eliminate one full-time job and feed his cattle more quickly. Today, 3,500 head are fed in five hours — the same job used to take forty-five hours.

Managing labour is also part of the Drylander operation. Typically, a farm needs extra help at certain key times: harvesting, planting and cattle marketing. The quandary faced by most farmers is that they all need help at the same time and naturally, good experienced hands are in limited supply. Heidecker solves the problem by relying as little as possible on seasonal labour. He keeps four full-time employees* completely occupied in winter with non-peak time duties like fertilizing, recovering land and vehicle repairs. Heidecker also has a full schedule of fence maintenance and road upgrading; he tries to replace completely two or three miles of fence a year rather than simply patch up weak areas.

The never-a-slack-moment system works well, if he can keep the crew apart after work. "It's the one disadvantage to being so isolated," laments Heidecker. "After work, the men and women meet socially, and then all hell breaks loose." After a few notable donnybrooks, Heidecker, no more a sentimentalist about manpower than cattle, spread the housing to the far corners of his land. Nonetheless, Gail is as much occupied with employee relations as she is with the books. "My job is to keep the wives happy. It's so different here from a town. Farming can be all day and half the night, and the wives get bored and restless, and all kinds of petty jealousies develop."

Having created a uniquely successful business, the Heideckers have no intention of letting it fall apart when they die. The problem of inheritance drives many farm children into other careers, creates tremendous animosity within families or results in the division of land into uneconomically small units. Heidecker sketches a typical scenario: A farmer dies and leaves his land equally to his four children. One son

* Heidecker likes to keep good workers, so he pays them an average of $1,000 a month — more for one who's been there a few years and less for raw recruits — and throws in free beef and accommodation in various houses and mobile homes on the ranch.

may have invested twenty years of "sweat equity" into the land yet receives only the same 25 percent share as the others. To continue farming, he is faced with assuming a large debt to buy out his siblings or else he must fork out 75 percent of the profits to them.

Incorporating in 1978 put the Heideckers into an élite group of farmers — only 3 to 4 percent of farms are incorporated in Canada. The move also ensured an orderly inheritance. The company's sophisticated corporate structure allots all class A shares to Brian and all class B shares to Gail with provision for future classes for each of their children. This setup allows Heidecker to disperse the ranch's earnings throughout the family and pay a minimum of taxes. Drylander Ranch Limited offers all the corporate tax advantages common to any other business; but most important, it solves the inheritance conundrum that plagues Canadian farmers. Each of the Heideckers' four children, Shelley aged seventeen, Bill aged fifteen, Brenda aged twelve and Lee aged eleven, will automatically receive 25 percent of the shares in the corporation, but only those actually working the land will have voting rights. Further, the board — Brian and Gail — will reward those children who begin working the ranch before inheriting, by voting additional shares.

The Heideckers are great believers in rewarding their children when they achieve and withholding perks if they don't work for them. They provide cash awards for good grades at school; if one of the children ends up with nothing, they may agonize about it privately, but the child still receives nothing. The children all manage their own allowances, paid by Drylander, for chores. The older children invest in cattle, which they show in 4H Club competitions and then sell at auction. There are no advances on allowances, although there is a brisk trade in interest-bearing loans among the siblings. "You should have heard her bitching when interest rates went down," Heidecker says proudly of Shelley. If any of them get into difficulty over foolish purchases, the only avenue to liquidity is additional chores, so they manage what they have carefully. Billy, who has been driving a harvest tractor since he was eight, is showing signs of becoming a wheeler-dealer: in 1983 he bought an adult neighbour's $600 computer and video game accessories for $250 when the farmer ran into a little financial trouble.

Computers have pulled the only inefficient, labour-intensive part of Drylander into the high-tech age. Planning and meticulous book-keeping are an integral part of the entire operation, but doing all the calculations by hand used to be slow dog's work. Each element of the operation, from beef production to the grain harvest, is now analysed and a monthly statement prepared by a $12,000 Vectorgraphic computer and farm-related software, which Heidecker has modified. Heidecker can determine the break-even point of every element of the ranch in minutes. He can, for instance, calculate the daily cost of the feed lot down to the penny and then relate that figure directly to the weight gains of the cattle.

The computer is critical to the complex decisions associated with crop selection. Each field is different and Heidecker can produce a maze of possibilities by juggling market prices, yields and seed costs for various grains. "I can pound numbers into the machine and play the 'what-if' game," he says, relishing the ease of permutations that once took days. Most other farmers decide which crops to plant in the spring, but Heidecker charts the layout of his fields at least a year in advance. His plans are coupled with the results of his annual fall soil analysis — another unusual practice — to design a fertilizer program that ensures optimum yield per dollar of fertilizer for each crop grown. (Despite the increasing sophistication for soil analysis, only 20 to 30 percent of Canadian farmers do it regularly.) Nothing is left to chance or, if he can help it, to the vagaries of nature.

In 1985 $80,000 worth of fertilizer was applied on Heidecker's property, so it pays to maximize its benefits. Heidecker bands, or spreads, it in the fall, because lower demand means it is considerably cheaper then, and because research shows that there is a 10 to 15 percent better utilization rate when fertilizer sits on the field all winter. And the early application saves storage costs and gives work to his permanent four-man staff during an otherwise slack period. Heidecker takes pains to record the history of each field in intricate detail, including type of soil, fertilizer used, annual rainfall and the resultant crop yield. His system uncovers some interesting facts. "I couldn't understand why I could never grow anything on one quarter," he reveals. "But when I got a soil analysis it showed that the field had only ten pounds of nitrogen per acre." It takes ninety pounds per acre to support a wheat crop.

The truest test of Drylander's sophistication is when Heidecker takes off his rubber boots and brings the bankers to him. Traditionally the scapegoat, along with the railways, for all farming's ills, bankers are as beloved in the country as bankruptcy trustees in a recession. Too often, farmers wait until they are in desperate trouble before they go, cap in hand, to the bank for money. Heidecker knows that he will have $300,000 invested in his crop by the time it's harvested, so he arranges a $200,000 revolving line of credit at half over prime even before the fields are seeded.* When it comes to capital expenditure, like the purchase of his feed mill, he switches roles with the banks. Instead of knocking on their doors, he draws up a budget and prospectus and sends it to the banks for bids. "They kick like hell," he says with a smile. "But they do it. After all, if you are renting a lawn-mower you haggle over the terms. Bankers are in the rental business, too."

Having reached the point in farming where others eagerly solicit his advice, Heidecker took on a new entrepreneurial challenge in 1982 by spending $100,000 to buy a local feed mill. It was a logical step in his diversification process, but ego and curiosity provided stronger motives. "I wanted to see if I could do the same things in business as I have in farming," he admits. "I didn't really understand many aspects of business — like the tax system — so I thought I should find out." Heidecker's first step was to widen the mill's base by building a $150,000 fertilizer plant beside it. He then instituted a

---

* Cash flow is managed just as carefully: all bills are paid on term, and cash receipts, such as cattle sales, are couriered from the auction to the bank.

unique payment policy, really just old-fashioned barter, that allowed cash-strapped local farmers to trade their grains at the mill for fertilizer. They can also deliver the grain to his mill on the ranch. Sales at the feed mill promptly jumped, and Heidecker saw his market share rocket from 20 to 60 percent almost overnight. He increased his profit margin again, from 10 to 25 percent, when he borrowed an ancient shipping maxim: "Never return with an empty load." He began back-hauling his own and bartered crops to market in fertilizer trucks that had previously been deadheading to the mines.

Brian Heidecker's approach destroys many of the fanciful myths of farming, and to some it may seem brutally callous. But he is one of the few Canadian farmers who haven't inherited their land and are making their operations pay in proportion to the time and money they invest in it. Heidecker loves the farm life, takes enormous pride in high-quality beef production and high crop yield per acre but, in the final analysis, his yardstick is the bottom line. And that's what sets him apart from the herd. "Money isn't everything," he concedes, "but it's so damn ahead of second place it doesn't count." The Brian Heideckers — the farmers who know their true worth — are few and far between, and perhaps it's just as well. If they weren't, you could be damn sure Canadians wouldn't have the world's lowest food costs.

Nick Taylor — The Liberal Oilman

It is Calgary's eighth annual Leadership Prayer Breakfast — a curious gathering * at the Palliser Hotel in late 1984 of three hundred achievers: the oil industry's élite, key professionals and the politically important who bask in the opportunity to

---

* The antecedents of prayer breakfasts are vague, but they have been held in Ottawa for twenty years and in the United States probably date back to the days of the Nixon White House, when Billy Graham was a frequent visitor. They are non-denominational and, in the words of the accompanying brochure, "A public affirmation of the privileges and responsibilities of a nation under God, sponsored by concerned government, business, labour and professional leaders." Taylor, however, who seemed to know everyone else, couldn't point out any labour types.

rub shoulders with their peers. They are all present to give thanks for their past year's success, reaffirm commitment to their fellow man, espouse civic responsibility and then be back in the office by nine — making money. It's a dignified gathering and there is a pleasant conversational hum in the air, with a distinct undertone of Houston twang. The men are genial, polished, well-travelled, mostly over forty-five but decidedly *not* slick — slickness hints of the East and Bay Street and that is to be avoided, studiously. Women are rare and they belong to the men; attractive, intelligent, immaculately groomed women. When they begin to sit after the prayer, practised hands move quickly to ease in their chairs.

But the smooth proceedings are slightly ruffled by an odd stir among the gathering. A surprising number of people are contriving, before, during and after the session, to speak with one man. He is craggy-faced, with deep creases running horizontally down both cheeks. His hair is whitening and there is a ruggedness about him that speaks of riding, roping and mending fences. He is one of them: a family man with nine children; a farm boy who, through hard work and native intelligence, has made a $10-million-dollar fortune in the only game in town that really counts, the oil business. Best yet, he is a genuine maverick in an industry that prides itself on individuality. He's a gambler who has played long shots on every oil frontier in the world — Vietnam, Ghana, Egypt, Malaysia, Fiji, Cyprus, the North Sea, Pakistan and Italy — and a few of them have even come in. His peers approach tentatively, bashfully and, if possible, inconspicuously, for they have come to apologize, to offer their excuses.

The people feel guilty. Many are Liberals (federally) and not only did they not vote for sixty-two-year-old Nicholas Taylor, Alberta provincial Liberal leader, but they didn't work for or contribute to his party.* These people are his

*Alberta is resolutely and, some believe, irrevocably, a province of the right. The Conservative government holds seventy-five of the seventy-nine seats, the NDP has snared two and the remaining two are held by independents who find even the Tories a little too leftist for their tastes. In the 1982 election, the Tories had an incredible 62.8 percent of the popular vote, the NDP 18.75, and the Western Canada Concept, a quasi-separatist party, 11.76. Nick Taylor's Liberals scraped up an embarrassing 1.81 percent.

natural constituency and though most privately concede that he's a superior candidate, they still don't support him. The problem is that liberalism in Alberta is seen by many as akin to communism. Their reasons for shirking their duty laughably resemble the prevarications of a schoolboy with unfinished homework. "I would have voted Liberal," insists one, "but you had a crazy man running in my riding." Another blamed his lack of support for Taylor on Trudeau, conveniently ignoring the fact that the former prime minister wasn't running. And so the litany goes, with Taylor politely acknowledging each statement, like a priest hearing confessions, all the while knowing deep in his heart that the failure to gain the support of this, his natural constituency, makes him at once one of Canada's most enterprising and successful independent oilmen and a magnificent failure as a politician.

Nick Taylor's personality has always had many sides, something that explains the Western oilman/Liberal enthusiast dyad running rampant throughout his professional life. His past is a seductive combination of bucolic roots, adventurous risk-taking and successful wheeling and dealing, all of which would make him a political folk hero — that is, if he could ever get elected. Born in 1927, the oldest of five children on a dryland farm in Bow Island, Alberta, 150 miles southeast of Calgary, Taylor is an extraordinary blend of hard-headed prairie practicality and flamboyant romanticism. By the time he was eight years old, he was routinely performing a full slate of farm chores, including driving and repairing the tractor.* His curiosity extended beyond the farm into books. By night he devoured the robust and romantic works of Kipling, Tennyson and Byron, and it doesn't take much prompting — in fact no prompting at all — to get him

* Nick's father, Fred, a great horseman, was afraid of the family tractor. "He was secretly convinced that motors were possessed by the devil," says Taylor. "He didn't understand them and he wanted nothing to do with them. He would try to use the machinery and if it didn't work he would throw his hat on the ground, sometimes throw rocks at it, kick the tires and call it awful names. 'Piss-complected son of a bitch. Northern Ireland son of a whore.' " As a result, the eight-year-old Taylor started "monkeying around on the motors. I'd patiently try things and nine times out of ten, I'd get it going again."

to break into verse, escaping on imaginary, swashbuckling adventures to the far corners of the globe. Taylor's father, Fred, a shy contemplative man and early member of the CCF, was much given to philosophizing around the general themes of individual rights and being one's own boss. He felt financial sacrifice was a small price to pay for running your own show. His mother, Louise, an avowed Conservative politically, was a forceful, energetic person. "If you trod on her toes you better be ready for a fight," remembers Taylor. Throughout his childhood Taylor often incurred his father's wrath for his irrepressible exuberance. Once he earned a licking by holding a stampede, with his father's calves headlining as the bucking broncos. All the neighbouring boys were invited; "If the calves didn't buck, we'd run along behind with a whip." Another episode involved taking his father's wagons apart so that when pulled by horses, they resembled chariots. (Taylor presided as Ben Hur.) On another occasion, he carefully piled snow on a board sitting across a haystack and boobytrapped it to avalanche down on the hired hand when he dug for hay.

Every father with a rural childhood has stories of walking barefoot to school. Taylor actually did it, not because his farm family was poor, which it was, but because in those days before gravel roads, "It just felt nicer walking on a country road in the summer." However, much as he savoured the feel of mud between his toes, Taylor was careful to always have his shoes on when he arrived at school. "It was an awful thing to get in a fight with another boy with a big set of boots on."

Taylor didn't go looking for fights; they were an inevitable outcome of his precociousness. He was always younger than his classmates in the Bow Island one-room school — Taylor was five when he entered school, six in grade three, fifteen when he graduated from grade twelve — and diplomacy was a skill he took some time learning. "I was always a teacher's pet. . . I think I was a teacher's dream. My father was a strict disciplinarian, so I was polite. I was also curious as hell. I would do my work in no time and I would be listening to all the other grades. And I could recall the teacher turning to me and asking questions. I used to get looks of dire hatred from the older students: they were set to croak me." Fortunately, Taylor was husky for his age, seldom forgot to wear his shoes and believed, as his freedom-loving father used to say, that "It's better to take a licking than to take shit." The older boys soon learned that they'd get their share of lumps for their efforts and Taylor discovered that a bit of judicious misbehaviour and a few strappings were his ticket to becoming one of the gang.

In 1942, Taylor had to leave his family and move to Medicine Hat, several hours away on rough roads, in order to attend grade twelve. The Taylor family couldn't afford room and board, so Nick got his first real job at an Ayreshire dairy, milking cows before and after school and cleaning the barn at night. He was paid $15 a month and accommodation was thrown in — an unheated lean-to that he shared with a far older farm worker. The drudgery of the work coupled with an eight-mile bicycle ride to and from school was too much even for Taylor, and he jumped at a chance to be a bell-hop after school in downtown Medicine Hat.

Taylor's mother arranged accommodation for Nick with an old acquaintance, blissfully unaware that the woman was offering more than simple room and board. "It wasn't exactly a bordello, and to this day, I don't know whether the ladies were professionals or very enthusiastic amateurs," laughs Taylor. Whatever the occupation of the ladies at his rooming house, the professional credentials of women who worked at the Assiniboine Hotel during his four to midnight shift were indisputable. Each night, in addition to his legitimate duties as bell-hop, Taylor mingled with the prostitutes and pimps, delivered alcohol for the bootleggers and provided room service for the highstakes card games. During the day, he was taught by tough nuns at St. Theresa's Academy, a convent school. "It was an entrancing year," Taylor remembers fondly. "It blew my horizons wide open. It gave me an appreciation of people. The prostitutes were as interesting as the people sitting on the front pew." His Catholic education wasn't all starched hats and prayers: one of the nuns taught him how to box.

Taylor cut a dashing figure around Medicine Hat: he was known as the one-eyed bell-hop because of a pink patch he wore to protect a pink-eye infection. Ironically, and perhaps fortunately, he had little opportunity to push his curiosity about life to its natural limits. The whores, he says, "watched me like a hawk. I led a sheltered life that I don't think even a convent could have offered. Talk about surveillance — I think a British spy in Nazi Germany would have been better off." The loose folk at the hotel were the back end of society, but the whores checked his report card, * the pimps protected him from rambunctious servicemen and the Assiniboine's ancient and cantankerous old cook saved him extra food. And they celebrated when he got good marks — albeit in his absence.

The fanciful nights and busy days weren't enough to dim Taylor's aptitude for books. Teachers and classmates, among them Bob Colborne, later to become president and owner of Pacific Western Transportation, remember him as a bright, single-minded and hard-working student who was mature beyond his years.

After graduation in 1943, when still only fifteen, Taylor lied about his age so he could enlist in the navy. He was already taking basic training at the Esquimault naval base in British Columbia when he was caught, a couple of months after enlisting. "The only embarrassing part of that was I was dating a twenty-year-old Wren and I had told her I was nine-teen. She was working in the CO's office when I was called in. I should have known what it was about because she just glared at me and hammered away at the typewriter, muttering something about robbing the cradle." The military didn't send Taylor home: he was allowed to re-enlist as a "probationary bandsman" and to enrol in the officer training school at Royal Roads, just outside Victoria.

When he was demobbed in 1945, Taylor had no clear idea of what he wanted to do, but he wasn't yet tired of the books. He headed back to Alberta and studied electrical engineering

---

* One woman, who took a particular liking to him, talked a rancher "friend" into opening, and paying for, a charge account for him at the local book store.

at the University of Alberta, until he discovered it had little to do with his love of tinkering with motors. After a stint in min-ing engineering, he eventually settled on geological engineer-ing — a profession peopled by bush-lovers and man-boys who loved to get mud between their toes. Summers were exciting times spent working in Yukon gold mines and on seismic and exploration crews travelling by dog sled and canoe through the Arctic and Northwest Territories.

Taylor met his wife-to-be, Pegi Davies, a refined ballerina from Llanelly, Wales, on the Edmonton-to-Calgary student train at Christmas, 1948. She remembers him as fun at the time but otherwise says he didn't particularly stand out from the others on the train, who included Don and Peter Lougheed. But Taylor's determined courting led to their mar-riage in early 1949. Although Taylor speaks proudly about his father as an early feminist who talked approvingly about careers and independence for women, his own relationship with his wife is a very traditional one. She is unquestioningly his helpmate, organizing the family's six-thousand-square-foot home in Calgary's Mount Royal district to provide the kind of stability upon which enormously successful men often depend. He gets up at 7:30 every morning, runs three-quarters of a mile (sometimes Peg walks while he jogs circles around her), takes a shower and then tinkers with his collection of old cars * until 9:00, when Peg calls him to breakfast over the in-tercom he installed in his workshop. From 9:00 to 10:00 he eats breakfast and returns media calls (before politics, this was a time when he and Peg could be together). He arrives at his office anywhere from 10:30 to 11:00. Lunch is invariably eaten on his desk because "everyone who has had two mar-tinis wants to tell me how to run the party." † From 6:00 to 9:00, Taylor is back home; these are the sacred family hours and until his nine children started leaving home he insisted that everyone be home for dinner. Then Peg goes to bed and

---

* Taylor's collection includes three MG's — a 1947 T.C., a 1951 T.D. and a 1955 T.F. — and a 1954 Model R Bentley.

† The combination of Taylor's success and his political convictions has not made him universally popular in the oil patch. Carl Nickle, an outspoken Calgary

Taylor heads back to the office where he stays, usually until midnight, and often until 2:00 or 3:00 A.M.

Taylor graduated from college in 1949, about the time the Leduc oil field was discovered, and it was the beginning of a new kind of gold rush. Once-impoverished Albertans began their steady climb to the status of blue-eyed sheiks. It was a time of opportunism, expansion and investment in the fledgling oil industry. Taylor and his new wife decided to try his new degree out in Calgary, and in the space of one day they were delightedly considering job offers from Imperial Oil, Union Oil and Canadian Cities Service Petroleum. The Taylors gambled a little and decided on Cities, a small American company, with more potential for rapid advancement. The company, attracted by his summer bush experience, immediately shipped him to Peace River to supervise seismic crews. In those days, the oil industry was mostly dominated by Americans from warm climates who worked feverishly throughout the short summer and slacked around all winter. With a prairie farmer's disdain for sloth and those who can't take a little chill in their bones, Taylor set about changing all that. Drawing on his farm experience, he soon acquired a reputation for getting things done. He devised an ingenious method of moving around on the muskeg. He'd clear the ground of insulating snow with small Caterpillar tractors, allowing frost to penetrate deeply enough to support the big cats needed for hauling drill equipment. Other innovations included rigging exhaust hoses through water tanks to keep them from freezing up and mixing salt with drilling mud to keep it liquid. Taylor and a handful of other Canadians revolutionized oil drilling in the North; so much so that now virtually all drilling is done in the winter rather than summer.

In 1953, thanks to his success in the Peace country, Cities promoted Taylor to chief geologist, a real plum for a twenty-six-year-old, and transferred him to Calgary. "They loved him at Cities," remembers Joe Badyk, who worked with him at the

---

oilman, has disparaged him from time to time. "Let's face it, his initial success came because an American oil company paid a sizable price for a piece of property he had in the North Sea. But he's made a political career out of criticizing the oil industry, the industry which has made his fortune."

time and is now president of his own company, Prudential
Steel. "He's one in five hundred geologists, a natural oil-finder
with an ability to sniff it out." Just two years later, Cities
offered Taylor a vice-presidency not just of the Canadian
division, but of the entire company. To get the promotion,
Taylor had to complete a management-training program and
then move to Bogota, Colombia. A man with strong roots,
Taylor didn't want to leave Calgary. "I was quite happy in
corporate service," he says, "but when I turned Cities down,
they became quite sulky. It was as if I'd turned down a chance
at heaven."

In those days, jobs for experienced oilmen were plentiful
and Taylor wasted no time in moving over to the massive
Honolulu Oil Corporation, which was delighted to find a
chief geologist content to be in Canada rather than in exotic
locales. The Taylors started settling in earnest: they bought a
modest house, Nick ran for the school board and the young
couple produced children and more children. Still only thirty-
three in 1960, Taylor was already among the élite, his salary
was over $30,000 (equivalent to about $75,000 in 1985) and he
was starting to think rather well of himself. "I was very successful in the corporate world, so I was on the invitation list
for golf tournaments, fishing tournaments and curling tournaments. Friends would take me out to dinner. I was lulled
into the sense of thinking I was a great raconteur, a great
dinner companion." But that year, Honolulu Oil sold out their
Canadian division to AMACO for $55 million. It was a stunn-
ing price for a company that Taylor estimates only had $8
million invested in Canada. Furthermore, Taylor believed
that the company's success was largely attributable to his own
oil-finding skills. With the sale, and his inflated confidence,
Taylor thought seriously for the first time of his father's words
about independence and self-employment, and struck out on
his own — but he wasn't quite ready to be an entrepreneur. "I
was going to be a consultant and advise people. I thought I'd
be good at it. I thought there must be all kinds of people out
there with capital who would love to have someone like me
advise them about where to put it in the oil business."

In 1960, using his handsome savings of $30,000 and another $10,000, Taylor formed N.W. Taylor Management. It was a dismal failure. Within six months, social invitations dried up and friends disappeared as Taylor discovered that his previous popularity was less a reflection of his brilliant personality than of his ability, as an executive with a large corporation, to dole out contracts. But fickle friends were only part of his problem. Contrary to all his expectations, the consulting business barely limped along, and by late 1962 the Taylors' financial situation was desperate.* Taylor developed a serious stomach ulcer and there were no consulting contracts waiting reassuringly on the horizon. Suddenly they only had enough money left for three months. Frantically searching for something — anything — he remembered an oil lease in the Swan Hills area 150 miles northwest of Edmonton that no one would touch. Taylor took a look at it, read the seismic reports, and felt in his gut there was oil. "Shell had the land and were willing to farm it out to anyone who would drill it in return for a 50 percent interest." Taylor snatched the opportunity and pounded the streets approaching eighty-four different companies, including every hole-in-the-wall outfit with enough cash to buy letterhead. The three months were almost up and at last he got a nibble; Dome Petroleum was willing to gamble. He cut a brilliant deal with them. In return for finding the property and bringing the principals together, he received an option to purchase a 6½ percent working share after the second well had been drilled. In other words, Dome took the risks and Taylor didn't have to spend a penny until the second well went in. It was a beautiful deal that uncovered, in addition to Taylor's intuitive sense of where the oil is, a gift for striking deals — the flesh and blood of the high-stakes oil game.

The oil business is a little like detective work, and prospecting often begins with a few facts, a few feelings and a lot of

---

* The Taylors' income was so low that they actually qualified for assistance to pay their medical insurance premium. Taylor was too proud to apply, but it was a devastating blow for a man who was on top of the world just two short years before.

hunches. Say, for example, a competitor makes a strike in the North Sea. That stirs a memory about another location you prospected twenty years ago, which turned up nothing, but the geology is similar. In the oil business, that's called an "idea" and that in itself can be worth money in the hands of a canny salesman. But you decide to hang on and the process starts. After preliminary investigations, perhaps buying another company's surveys or flying over to get a feel for the property, you could have as little as $20,000 invested. By the lease stage you may have $100,000 at stake and up to $1.5 million before the well is actually drilled, with absolutely no financial return. The cost of drilling a well can be astronomical; one well being drilled by Taylor and Texaco in 1984 in the Beaufort Sea has already cost over $12 million. And there is no guarantee that you're going to find anything but mud. Taylor estimates that the odds against finding anything of commercial value range from 3-to-1 for drilling around already established fields in Canada to over 100-to-1 on the frontier. So typically, small companies bring in majors to act as operators: doing the actual drilling and carrying the bulk of the costs.

There is a crucial point in the early, risky period to bring in the big guns — the point where you can maintain the highest possible share and at the same time offer an enticing enough deal to get the right terms. The earlier you go after a deal, the less risk for you and consequently the smaller share; the later the deal, say at the pre-drilling stage, the more money you have invested and the greater risk. Even with a sure bet, it's easy to run into trouble if you try to hang on too long and end up financially strapped. The majors can sniff out an overcommitted company and force acceptance of bad terms. All this amounts to some pretty hairy shuffling of money and resources. Taylor uses the risks to motivate himself. "A lot of people in the oil business are happy to build a company big enough to sell out, and make a million dollars. They're not going for it. I've always eschewed the short-term gain for the really big one."

The Swan Hills deal was a coup for Taylor, who played all the hunches just right. He'd known from the beginning that he could find oil, but Swan Hills gave him the confidence to begin taking the risks himself — to become an entrepreneur. When both wells came through, Taylor hotfooted it to the bank and borrowed the $20,000 necessary to buy his interest; if the holes had been dry, he would have just walked away, with no financial outlay. Henceforth he owned a considerable percentage* of an operating well.

Between 1962 and 1965 N.W. Taylor Limited grew slowly as Nick Taylor continued making small deals similar to the first one. By 1965 he was netting as much as he had at Honolulu Oil, and from that point on his fortunes leapfrogged as he showed a flair for anticipating the future. He brought together a group of Edmonton and Calgary lawyers, bought up the patent right for plastic beverage cups and formed one of Alberta's first petrochemical firms. In 1968, he had a hunch that potash had a big future in Saskatchewan and bought shares in defunct railroad companies, which incidentally owned a generous allowance for mineral rights. He bought the shares for less than $100,000 and resold them for $500,000 to the Saskatchewan Potash Corporation in 1969. That same year, Taylor's net worth was $3 million.

In the late sixties the oil industry was approaching its zenith. It was a time of enormous expansion and vast fortunes accrued to those with the capital to go further and further afield. Taylor was enjoying his success and he was hooked on drilling wildcat wells. He wanted more, and the quickest way to get them was to go public. In 1969 he folded his private companies into Lochiel Exploration Limited.† The move did

---

* A hint of the kind of rewards possible even with a small percentage is Taylor's interest in the Buchan Field area of the North Sea. His company owns a minuscule .907628 percent working interest of a well, a share that translates into 260 barrels a day. In 1984, that share, less than one percent, generated nearly $3 million of income — almost 25 percent of his company's total revenue in 1985.

† The company is named after a forbear, Cameron of Lochiel, a general for Bonny Prince Charlie in 1745. Taylor can trace his genealogy back to 1793 in New

more than give access to public capital, it allowed Taylor to take advantage of the tax loopholes then available to public companies, and to reward employees by giving them stock options.

Since then, Lochiel's growth has been phenomenal. By 1984 Calgary's authoritative *Oilweek* magazine ranked Lochiel as Canada's seventy-first largest oil company out of five hundred, with $50 million in assets. Despite the impressive figures, Lochiel hasn't been a bonanza for shareholders looking for a steady return. Profitability has been sporadic and occurred in only three of Lochiel's sixteen years of operation. "He's stuck his neck out very, very far in high-risk areas," points out Rob Jennings, one of the principals of the Calgary financial consultants, Carson Jennings & Associates. "He'd have a stronger company if he'd stuck closer to home." Taylor, who owns half of Lochiel's twelve million outstanding shares, agrees with the analyst's assessment that he puts too much into long-shot, wildcat drilling, but he's totally unrepentant. "You want to try and please the shareholders," he says. "But if they don't like what I'm doing, they can move on to something else." He believes in dividing Lochiel's capital into three areas: conventional, low-risk development where the pay off is as high as one in three; exploration in the United States and Canada and, finally, frontier or foreign exploration — the big ones that pay off once in every one hundred tries.

An important element of Lochiel's current success is Taylor's flexibility. "Business is nothing more than economic ju-jitsu," he says. "You take advantage of the laws that are in the marketplace and turn them to your advantage. Rockefeller made millions in China by giving away free lamps. Everyone was tickled but they had to buy his oil to put in them." Taylor used economic ju-jitsu to take advantage of

---

Brunswick. On holidays and on business trips he often finds time to browse for hours in cemeteries, tracing the bloodlines and migration patterns he finds on the tombstones. A particular coup is to find a Taylor that fits in with his lineage. "I know where I can find him if he disappears on holidays," laughs Pegi. "He'll be in the cemetery."

both the federal Liberals' 1980 National Energy Program and the Conservative provincial government's responses. In 1985 alone, a combination of programs initiated at both levels added $3 million to Lochiel's revenues.

Taylor still hasn't hit the big one, but he points out that the odds are in his favour. He plans to work for another fifteen years, and the fact that he's kept Lochiel stable while gambling so much indicates that when the jackpot shows up he'll be in a position to take full advantage of it. He could, of course, easily show a bigger profit if he put his priorities on safe investment by drilling more inexpensive wells, closer to home. But without the risk there would be no point, at least to Taylor. "It's all curiosity. I get fun out of the newness of something, the originality. Making a profit, quite often, is just doing the same deal over and over again. That's boring." *

While Nick Taylor has been very successful in business, his political career has been anything but. His interest in politics began in high school, when he followed his father as a supporter of the CCF. But Taylor was impressed by the skilful handling of the war economy by C.D. Howe, the Liberal prime minister during the Second World War, and the young man began thinking of himself as a Liberal. "I didn't come out of the closet until 1957," says Taylor, "and I should have taken it as an omen." It was the year of the Diefenbaker landslide and Taylor worked during the disaster as a poll captain for an unsuccessful federal Liberal candidate. To complete the augury, Taylor returned home election night to find that heavy rain had collapsed the roof of his home. Since then, Taylor's political ambitions, never quite getting off the ground, have limped along much like his early consulting business did.†

* Considering Taylor's penchant for "rolling the dice," his big hit in the North Sea was more a case of following the leader. "I got going in the North Sea," he admits, "because lots of people were buying stocks. Everybody [investors] wanted to know if you had land in the North Sea." Taylor sent a man over and told him to "get some yellow on our map," any yellow. Lochiel took what it could get, essentially the leavings. The geology was poor, but they struck oil on the first hole, The Buchan.

† Although the Liberal party hadn't been a provincial power since the thirties, they were still the dominant federal party in Alberta. Diefenbaker changed all that by

In fact, despite twenty-five years of trying, the only elected
public office that he's held was his stint as a trustee for the
Calgary Public School Board from 1960 to 1964. He ran for
Calgary City Council in 1964 and was roundly defeated. In
1968 he got close as a federal candidate for Calgary Centre but
narrowly missed by 307 votes. He tried the same riding again
in 1972 but this time suffered a 3,000-vote shellacking by
Harvie Andre. There were more losses: first in the Calgary-
Glenmore provincial constituency in 1975 and 1979, then
another narrow loss in a 1980 byelection in Barrhead, followed by another drubbing in 1982 when he lost Barrhead by
an impressive 1,500 votes.

No one can say Taylor isn't trying. He played the Trudeau-
mania to the hilt in 1968 with a bevy of attractive female cam-
paigners called The Dynamiters. They wore buttons with
T.N.T. on them (Try Nick Taylor) or (Taylor and Trudeau).
The second and only other political victory in his career was
in 1974, when he won a hotly contested battle for the leadership of the provincial Liberal party.* As leader, though
neither he nor any other Liberal has a seat, Taylor watches
dutifully from the speaker's gallery and then has to hustle outside and walk several blocks to his rented office to give the
press a reaction to events in legislature.†

Just why Nick Taylor is one of the most unsuccessful Canadian politicians ever is hard to understand, at least super-

---

destroying the old federation of provincial Liberal organizations that Mackenzie
King first established and carefully cultivated during his twenty-two-year reign.

* Why it was hotly contested is impossible to imagine. Liberals hadn't formed the
official opposition since 1959. There were no Liberals sitting in the legislature. The
last Liberal M.L.A. had resigned four years before and party coffers were empty.
What's more, Peter Lougheed's Tories had just won the 1971 election and looked
like they were settling in for a long stay. To complicate matters, there really was no
provincial Liberal party and the national party, organized and funded directly
from Ottawa, played footsie with the Social Credits, called the shots and dispensed
the patronage.

† Because he has no seat in the legislature he isn't allowed to speak during session,
and because he has no office in the building he uses his Lochiel offices as headquarters.

ficially. Many serious political observers, even Liberals, see him as too glib. "He comes across as a bit of a goof," says a former Liberal campaign manager. Glibness would seem an asset but it is this very skill, Taylor's mastery of one-liners, that has buried him. The media, voracious for a colourful counterpoint to Peter Lougheed's bland Conservative government, give coverage to his witticisms, but rarely mention his platform. Taylor is aware of this failing but the jokes still slip out. "The Southam press thinks Lougheed was born in a manger." . . . "The oil industry is so tightly regulated, the care and feeding of oil companies has become a national sport." . . . "The oil economy is as up and down as a toilet seat at a mixed party." . . . "Peter Lougheed likes oil wells because they are phallic symbols."

Though overshadowed by the clever remarks, Taylor's political platform has always been sexy, perhaps too sexy for the meat-and-potatoes politics of Alberta which, in the end, always seem to come down to keeping the Ottawa looters and rapists out of the province's living-room. Taylor's message has changed little over the years: don't overindustrialize, build renewable jobs from nonrenewable resources, build a highly educated cultural society and export brainpower and technology — not just resources. Would Alberta be further behind, he asks, to leave oil refineries unbuilt, export the gas instead, and use the money to foster brain-based industries like petroleum and computer technology? He points out that one set of drawings for a satellite generator can bring as much money into a community as a year's worth of petro-chemical production. "Around here people get elected by being against Ottawa," he fumes.

But Taylor knows it, has always known it and his excuses for not getting elected seem feeble and a little naïve. First there's the albatross theory. Through the late seventies, Taylor feels his problems were simple. "I was always branded with Trudeau. He was a colourful bugger. The premier and the media goaded everyone into paroxysms of fury about him: you'd just have to say 'Trudeau' and everyone would turn purple and start to boo and spit." Ironically, Taylor didn't like Trudeau any better than other Albertans. "I found he was superior intellectually to anyone else I met in politics and inferior, you might almost say retarded, emotionally — very childish, spiteful. If he didn't get his hand kissed, or get sucked up to, you got cut off." There's also the Tommy Douglas Syndrome. "I'm probably the best-liked politician in Alberta," he boasts. "People love to hear me speak. I can fill a hall any time, but I just can't get elected."

Although Taylor has doggedly flown the Liberal banner since the early sixties, he's received few favours for his efforts. He's always had trouble getting his phone calls returned in Ottawa, and has consistently been overlooked by the dispensers of patronage. The Trudeau government did dole out some goodies but the Senate seats, public-relations contracts and government jobs went to defeated federal candidates and previous provincial Liberal leaders rather than to Taylor or to the people who were currently supporting the provincial party. Even in 1984, after the Liberals were so convincingly defeated by the Conservatives, federal leader John Turner couldn't find time to say hello. Prior to the eighth annual Leadership Prayer Breakfast in Calgary, Taylor was astonished to learn, by reading the Palliser Hotel's schedule of events, that Turner was meeting with Alberta Liberals.

Taylor complains frequently about the Ottawa cold shoulder, but he doesn't help himself much. He's a skilled impressionist who wickedly and accurately caricatures his political friends and enemies. His John Turner impression is deadly. Instantly, he is Turner: jumping up, careening around and bobbing like a hyperactive wind-up toy, eyes blinking spasmodically — with jerky steps and back and bum slaps. Even the voice is good. "Hi, I'm John Turner. Let's have lunch sometime." Taylor also does a good imitation of a grumpy and petulant Pierre Trudeau and a sulky Peter Lougheed, invoking God.

Even Pegi Taylor isn't sure why, despite her own urgings to the contrary, her husband hangs on to his political hopes — always seeing opportunity just a little way off in the future.

But Taylor's urge must be linked to his love of wildcatting around the frontiers of the world. Politics for Nick Taylor is just one more longshot waiting to come in.

John Doole —
The Reluctant Entrepreneur

Of all the people appearing in these pages, John Doole was the most reluctant to become a true entrepreneur. For more than a quarter of a century he was content to work for Winnipeg Supply and Services Limited as an employee, drawing a salary, never dreaming of owning the company, and not taking the hint when the owner first suggested that Doole buy the business from him. Yet he is among the most imaginative of them all: a man of modest renaissance sweep who values the excitements of the mind, the peculiar delights of culture, all the while maintaining that his most imaginative acts revolve around his life as a businessman.

He is sixty-one, a bulky six-footer who wears glasses and is losing his hair; his mustache is greying, the chin below his long oval face has doubled, and he has a paunch. An accountant and a general manager, since 1982 he has been the owner of Winnipeg Supply, the largest independent building-materials supplier and residential mechanical-services company in the Manitoba capital. His two building centres, a fuel-oil division, and a mechanical division that provides plumbing and heating services and installation, have combined annual revenues of $12 million.

When he bought Winnipeg Supply, John Doole bought an institution, not just a business. Every town in Western Canada has an umbilical relationship with its major building-materials company, the source of the lumber and concrete and other resources that keep it alive and growing. Winnipeg Supply has been more of a life-force than most. It has been an integral part of the city since 1904, when it began as a fuel dealer delivering coal and wood in horse-drawn wagons. At one time it was the largest retail coal dealer in Western Canada, and before the Second World War it had expanded into heating equipment, building materials, lime and fuel oil. And when the demand for heating oil dwindled in the face of cheaper, more efficient natural gas, Winnipeg Supply diversified again, into residential mechanical services, ready-mix concrete, even land development. John Doole oversaw it all, changing gears as he switched hats, handling it creatively with more than an accountant's touch. He went beyond the role of a salaried employee; if anything, he was a corporate entrepreneur.

He has since acquired a bookstore that has also long been an institution in Winnipeg, and hopes eventually to turn Mary Scorer Books into a chain. The interest in books is more than passing: John Doole is also a part-time poet who in 1983 published a selection of his thoughtful and whimsical works in a book entitled *Pith And Vinegar.* He illustrated the work with his own satirical drawings, for he's an amateur artist who has held shows and sold his paintings. In one section of the book, the subject is music — not surprisingly, because he was a trumpet player who played professionally with dance and jazz bands in England.

"Historically," he says, "businessmen have been tremendously underrated with regard to creativity. The idea of the typical businessman being a plodding, unimaginative money-grubber is crazy. Yet businesspeople themselves don't consider themselves creative. I've been involved in the classical creative endeavours and I believe that to successfully run a business takes far more breadth of creativity than being a musician or artist or writer. Because to be successful, you've got to have an enormous range of abilities, most of which can't be taught, most of which is instinctive. One minute you're worried about advertising; the next you're dealing with unions, and then the phone rings and you're handling an accounting problem."

He was born in 1923, an only child, and raised in Ipswich, the county town of Suffolk in eastern England, a port on an estuary of the North Sea. There was never a lot of money in the working-class Doole family. John's father was a marine engineer, travelling the world to install oil engines that furnished electricity on the Ivory Coast, in Spain and the Sudan. John was closer to his mother, grandmother and an uncle than he ever was to his wandering dad; he remembers nothing but fights in the house when his father arrived home. "I hated the smell of oil on him and found stories about engines incredibly boring," he says now. "So why am I running a company that has an enormous mechanical department?" His wife, Iris, sees other signs of his father in him: an obstinacy, an obsessiveness.

The Doole household was a matriarchy. His mother and grandmother worked at home as tailoresses for the whole neighbourhood, from six in the morning till ten at night. They knew how to enjoy themselves too, taking Friday nights off and sending John down to the local pub to bring home a bottle of Segavin, a pre-mixed cocktail. His relationship with his mother was loving but never overly intimate. "I appreciated that sort of distanced relationship — love without being smothered," he says. Iris describes him as an icily objective man, "seeing things as they exactly are, not embellished, and making a decision fairly quickly and then not changing his mind."

An independent, self-contained child, John indulged himself in two passions: birds and music. He bred budgerigars for show in his postage-stamp backyard. Although raising budgies was a hobby, he discovered that it could earn him decent pocket money. Doing things he enjoyed would continue to prove profitable for him. At thirteen he bought his first trumpet from a pawn shop for 30 shillings, and a Salvation Army cornet-player taught him to read music. For the next twenty years, the trumpet would handsomely supplement his income.

At fifteen, without taking his matriculation exams, John left school. He was earning money in a jazz band by then and wanted to be his own man. He went to work as a mail clerk in the accounting department of a large Ipswich agricultural-implement company, Ransoms, Sims and Jefferies Limited. It was the better of two evils — he was desperate to stay out of the foundries where others of his age and limited education wound up — but even when he became a junior in financial accounting, he found the work excruciatingly boring.

He found his pleasure in the evenings, playing trumpet for jazz bands, and when war broke out in 1939 and the professional musicians were called up, his humble talent was suddenly in demand seven nights a week. But in 1941, his musical career was cut short when he turned eighteen and was drafted into the Royal Navy. The day he left home, his mother didn't see him off at the railway station; typically, in her reserved manner she waved goodbye to him from the front bay window of her home.

He had an active war, serving on two aircraft carriers, making raids on German shipping along the Norwegian coast and patrolling the Mediterranean. His only injury was a burst eardrum from swimming off Malta. Near war's end he was put ashore in Scotland, where he met Iris at a camp dance. "She had the shapeliest bum in bell bottoms in the Fleet Air Arm," he recalls, his face warming with the memory. She was an intelligent Irish girl, a dark brunette from Armagh, a foot shorter than he was, and she disliked this tall, cool man on sight. But he was persistent; Iris soon learned that he liked books and music as much as she did, and bit by bit her opinion of him changed. During their six-month tour together, they decided to get married. For one frigid weekend in February, they honeymooned in the seaside resort of Felixstowe — Doole, all the while, hopping in and out of bed to put sixpences in the gas heater.

For the first three years of their marriage, Doole doubled his regular salary back at Ransoms, Sims with his night-time trumpet work. But he was increasingly aware of the fact that he was no more than a mediocre musician, and when his son, Christopher, was born, he realized that his future would be dim if he continued to play second fiddle in a large accounting department. He enrolled in a correspondence course in cost accounting and for five years worked eighteen hours a week on the course, nine hours a day at the office, and three to five nights a week with his band. At the end of it, he found he was considered too valuable to be transferred to a better job, and other companies in Ipswich had a gentleman's agreement that they wouldn't hire anyone away from an influential firm like Ransoms, Sims. He was stalemated. At the time, the drummer in Doole's band was planning to emigrate to Canada. *If we've got to sell up in Ipswich,* Doole thought, *why not consider the world?* He began reading about Canada. "Feeding my wife and child has always been paramount," he says today. "That's why I'm not a typical entrepreneur." Figuring that most emigrating English would head for Montreal, Toronto and Vancouver ("I figured most of those cities were pissed off with Englishmen," he remarks dryly), he settled on Winnipeg, in the middle of the country, a city he had heard was short on professionals.

In 1957, the thirty-five-year-old Doole came to Canada with his wife and six-year-old son. He felt little fear for his prospects in a foreign setting; an egotist convinced of his own qualities, he had not the slightest doubt he would find a good job. The original plan was to use Canada as a way-station on the road to South America and Australia. For Doole, Winnipeg's worst characteristic was its lack of sophistication: he-men didn't attend the ballet in those days, and because he didn't know much about the supposed aphrodisiac effects of Canadian rye at first, he'd order a sherry in a restaurant and feel as if "everybody was backing away in case I touched his bum." For Iris, however, the scale of this new land, the expanse of the Prairies, proved much more upsetting; the two of them soon agreed that moving on to yet another country would be needlessly traumatic. Canada would become home.

He had sold his trumpet in England to help pay for the trip. The sale had symbolic overtones of a re-commitment to his family. His part-time musical career had meant that in ten years of married life he had never enjoyed a Saturday night or holiday evening at home with Iris and Christopher. Over the years he'd miss the trumpet but would compensate by becoming a knowledgeable student of jazz and classical music.

During those early years in Canada, there was no time to regret his loss. While still in Ipswich, he had obtained the name of the secretary of the Registered Industrial Accountants Association in Winnipeg, who told him, within days of his arrival, that there was a position open in a business called the

Winnipeg Supply and Fuel Company Ltd. The company was looking for a cost analyst with statistical experience; while none of the Canadian accounting courses then included statistics as a specific topic, Doole had received high marks in the subject in England. Going through the job interviews, he eventually met Alex Robertson, the president of the business that had been in the Robertson family for three decades.

The company, Doole was to discover after he got his $300-a-month job, was a local institution. Since 1904, it had touched the lives of Winnipeggers in myriad ways. It was the major distributor of residential heating oil; a leading independent retailer of building materials and plumbing and heating services; and a key supplier of ready-mix concrete and concrete products to large contractors throughout Manitoba. It had its own gravel deposits and, although the mining and sale of coal was no longer its prime business, the company still owned substantial coal reserves.

Within two weeks of joining Winnipeg Supply, Doole was called in to the president's office to double-check calculations in a proposal to supply concrete to the Inco nickel-mining operation in the northern Manitoba town of Thompson. "It was a little nerve-wracking," he recalls. "I was a fifth-rate clerk from England working with the president on a multi-million-dollar proposal." He impressed Alex Robertson, an aggressive, intelligent man who believed there was a logical, defined way of doing things. Within a year Doole was assistant to the president. "I never realized how tough you had to be in business — to the point of being obnoxious," Doole says. "I found there were times when you had to be goddamn unpleasant. But beneath Alex's veneer of The Iceman Cometh was a heart of gold. Alex couldn't fire anybody. I could." Between 1960 and 1964 the building-materials division was doing large volumes of contracting business (as opposed to its residential-supply trade), yet making no profits. Doole — becoming a corporate entrepreneur — hired a couple of university students for three months to conduct time-and-motion and truck-utilization studies, then did a one-year cost analysis — all of which showed that the division was losing money on its contracting work. Within a week he fired fifteen

employees involved in the business, earning himself the
epithet The Axeman.

Along with other senior staff, Doole once saw an industrial
psychologist at Alex Robertson's behest. When the psychologist told him he had no empathy with other people, he
replied: "Bullshit. I can walk into a city-council committee
meeting with fifteen people sitting at the table and within
thirty seconds of making a presentation, I can smell whether
or not I should back away or whether my proposal's going to
be passed."

"That isn't empathy," the psychologist replied. "That's
powers of observation. Empathy is when your friend bleeds
and *you* hurt." He then looked up a chart and said: "Do you
know that 97 percent of Canadians have more empathy than
you do?"

Despite his coolness, he was gaining a reputation within the
company as a flexible trouble-shooter who could fit into any
slot; he got regular raises without asking for them. Between
1959 and 1972, Winnipeg Supply expanded into residential
construction and land development, becoming a 40 percent
partner in each of three companies formed by some long-time
local developers to create a prestige Winnipeg community
called Tuxedo Park: about three hundred houses that, if built
today, would be worth about $300,000 apiece. Doole was the
project administrator, and the partners, who wanted maximum returns with minimum effort on their part, were content to let him operate independently — once they'd decided
he had the persistence of a bull-terrier in controlling costs. "It
gave me some insight into the fun you can have with business
and making money; the profits were disgusting," he says. Not
that he tasted the financial fruits of the project. His own ambitions were always contained, and involved little risk.

In 1971 he was forty-eight, a happy man, satisfied with his
position as executive assistant to the president and with his
salary (no more than $1,500 a month), when Neil Baker
bought Winnipeg Supply from the Robertson family. Baker
was John Doole's first close encounter with a significant risk-
taker. Fifteen years younger, Baker was a high-flying financier and stockbroker, an archetypal Western entrepreneur

whose priorities, when he took the company over, were to make sure it performed first for the bank, then for him, and only incidentally for the continuing economic vitality of Winnipeg Supply. "It was strictly a financial play; I didn't know anything about any of the products," he recalls. To ensure its performance, he depended on John Doole, whom he made his general manager. "My first impression was that John was a classic English-trained, detail-oriented jack-of-all-trades cost accountant. But unlike most with that traditional English background, he wasn't fixed in his ways. He was gregarious — in fact, really a North American."

The unwieldy company Neil Baker bought had grown to seven different divisions, in locations from Thunder Bay to Victoria, with annual sales of $22 million. But after two bad years in a row (mostly because of losses in the northern division's road-building operations), it had run up almost $10 million liabilities. In a quick assets strip, he sold off several separate operations to repay the bank; among them, the industrial minerals division, which wholesaled lime and silica sand, and the industrial products division, which wholesaled fibreglass and contractors' materials. John Doole helped his boss liquidate debt by getting rid of millions of dollars' worth of property in the land-development division and streamlined the company by reducing overheads, sub-leasing expensive head-office space, and refocusing on the building-materials and services business.

As Baker told the trade magazine *Western Construction and Industry* in 1974: "If a homeowner wants his chimney cleaned, we have a chimney sweep. He can call us if he needs concrete for his driveway; his furnace fixed; central air-conditioning installed; one of our roto-rooter men to unblock his toilet or sink; or even if he just needs advice on painting his home or building a fence. The homeowner, contractor, commercial or industrial business concern . . . can call on us for anything required in the building-maintenance or service field. Concrete, concrete blocks, gravel, lumber, nails, shingles, plywood, as well as materials required or the complete installation of electrical, plumbing, roto-rooter, heating and ventilation for a home, warehouse or industrial manufacturing plant."

Within two and a half years, there was $2 million in the bank: the new management team had performed an astonishing $12-million turnaround in liquidity.

Within four years, Baker was so impressed with John Doole and his flourishing entrepreneurial instincts that he made him president of the entire company. "With Alex [Robertson] we were a medium company that had visions of becoming a big one," Doole says. "We had a bureaucratic style; we wrote lots of memos. But with Neil it was 'Cut out the bullshit; let's make some money. And if you need to know what I'm doing, let's get together at eight o'clock in the morning for a few minutes.' I enjoyed it. If we were talking about buying five trucks, I'd get somebody to do the analysis and then make a decision in about three minutes."

John Doole was as contented with his lot as ever; he was working for a man he thought of as a friend; his business life was more interesting than it had ever been. In December 1981 it became even more exciting. Neil Baker, who had become a partner in the Toronto stockbroking firm of Gordon Securities, announced to him one day: "Look, I want out. Make me a proposal." The fifty-eight-year-old Doole, because he had never contemplated the possibility of buying the company that had employed him for twenty-seven years, misunderstood him ("I guess I had a mental block — the whole concept was so far out of my range of thinking"). Baker had to suggest on two more occasions that perhaps his employee would be interested in acquiring Winnipeg Supply. Even when he understood, Doole resisted: "I'd received a paycheque all my life, a paycheque I was always comfortable with. So why aggravate yourself?"

But Baker was quite serious about the offer ("I forced it on John," he says), and the more Doole considered it, the better it sounded. After all, he knew the company's cash-flow situation well and he could project potential profits reliably. "Price wasn't a sticking point," he remembers. "Once we had agreed on a principle of evaluation, it was just a matter of double-checking figures. We'd taken inventory just before we started negotiations, so then we added the subsequent purchases and reduced inventory by the number of sales." The only problem was Doole's ability to borrow money. Of the three banks he approached, one agreed to finance the purchase if Doole put up his personal guarantee. He balked: "My wife would have a hemorrhage if she thought her dining-room could be whipped out from under her if things didn't go well in the business." (In fact, Iris knew nothing of the deal until it was consummated; "I'd probably have waffled for weeks anyway," she says.) At that point, Neil Baker suggested that he would provide all of the financing; banks, he says, have a way of interfering between an owner and other lenders.

Baker sold the sizable concrete ready-mix division to other buyers and closed down two paint-and-glass locations that were unprofitable. In March 1982, Doole bought the most publicly visible side of Winnipeg Supply: the building-materials, fuel-oil and service divisions — about 40 percent of the holdings — for $2.8 million (at the time, they were grossing about $9 million). "When you're suddenly on the hook, you either fold under pressure or you blossom," Neil Baker says. "John loves it. He blossomed."

Doole slashed his head-office staff by seven, down to an absolute minimum of 12. His personal secretary looks after the payroll for the 110 employees, does all the typing, and doubles as company secretary. There's one accountant. Doole initials every single purchase order and accounts payable of the hundreds processed every week. He handles all the marketing himself, including the writing of radio commercials. He raised the volume of advertising by 20 percent and, because Winnipeg Supply's building materials had a high-price image, increased the number of loss leaders and introduced the slogan: "Nobody beats our prices." While the company remains the largest supplier of fuel oil in the city — it took over the accounts once handled by Shell and Imperial Oil — the dwindling demand has spurred Doole to build up the range and volume of the other divisions. He opened a second building-materials centre (twenty-eight thousand square feet, including warehouse, compared to the original twelve-thousand-square-foot centre) which has new specialty flag and gun departments. He placed renewed emphasis on the installation of hot-water heaters (and now rents as well as sells them), and began offering insurance policies for furnace and air-conditioning-unit breakdowns. The mechanical division has a plumbing department and 25 servicemen, the most of any Winnipeg company, installing and repairing oil and gas furnaces, sweeping chimneys and power-cleaning residential ductwork. The manager of each department runs it like a small company and, through an incentive scheme, can earn an annual bonus of up to three months' salary.

With $12 million in sales a year — $3 million more than when he bought the company — Winnipeg Supply has been successful beyond John Doole's expectations. By the end of 1985, he expected to pay off his loan to Neil Baker without having to go to the bank.

For an hour or two each day, he sequesters himself in his split-level office on the second floor of Winnipeg Supply's building-materials centre on Portage Avenue. He entertains guests there over lunch ("I'm also the world's greatest salad chef," he says, flashing a toothy smile), serving them from the well-equipped kitchen and fully stocked bar. He stage-managed the redesign of the office and now takes overt delight in the surprise with which most visitors greet his private space. It could double as an artist's studio: two enormous skylights illuminate the white brick walls hung with his own works, from capricious sketches reminiscent of the line drawings of the English cartoonist Ronald Searle to three-dimensional collages of mixed-media acrylics using such found materials as cork, cardboard and tissue paper. Sculpture, stained glass and hanging plants further soften the surroundings; high-tech shelving and fancy directors' chairs offer a slight pragmatic edge. A Mitsubishi compact-disc system provides an upscale Muzak backdrop with passages from Bach or the classical trumpet-playing of Wynton Marsalis. *Stereo Review* and *Gramophone* magazine share the shelves with *Fortune* and *The Financial Post Magazine.* "I only come in here for fun," he says.

As he thrived on the creativity involved in running his own

company, he discovered that he had less energy to apply to the painting he'd done since 1962, when Iris bought him an $8.50 oils set for Christmas. Self-taught, he'd sketched idly for his own pleasure all his life. Coming home from the high pressure of work, he would spend hours at the kitchen table on his art, inspired by the cubism and collage of Picasso and the disciplined geometrics of Paul Klee, but never by what he saw as the more emotional Old Masters. As in all pursuits, he focused on art with what Iris calls his binocular vision, taking lessons at the Banff School of Fine Arts one summer and becoming good enough to sell his works for $150 to $200. ("The purchasers were always engineers or architects, which I found flattering because people like that have a better appreciation of proportion and design than the average guy on the street.") When the intensity tapered off after he bought Winnipeg Supply, he replaced painting with writing while he watched television with his wife. He began by scribbling limericks, then a series of rhyming poems about birds that smacked of Ogden Nash, and graduated to more serious blank verse:

nothing words of wit
strung out in sentences
like noisy beads of glass
have never yet
and never yet will give
one secret of the hows and whys
we live
        and questions
        if you have to ask
        don't matter
            not at all

Putting it all together in book form, and illustrating it with his own witty line drawings, he offered the manuscript to several Canadian publishers, none of whom was interested. Always fascinated by the publishing business, a regular reader of the trade journals *Quill and Quire* and *Publisher's Weekly*, he decided to publish it himself under the name Rondo Books.

Each of the thousand copies cost him about $4 to print; about half have sold locally at $14.95. Recently he began a second book of poetry.

When it's published, he will have his own book-store in which to sell it. Relaxing in his office one day in May 1984, he heard on CBC Radio that Mary Scorer Books, the oldest independent in Winnipeg, had failed after twenty-five years in business. John Doole decided to leap into one of the least predictable of all businesses. Although a relatively minor bit of risk-taking, it was one that he wouldn't have even considered in his more security-conscious, cost-accountant days. But in taking over Winnipeg Supply and within two years turning it into a personal profit centre, he had been bitten by the bug of entrepreneurship; approaching his sixth decade, he had turned his back on the fiscal caution that he'd pursued throughout his career — limiting his life adventures to the realms of arts and culture. He tries to rationalize the decision: "In some ways, there was a common thread: Winnipeg Supply since 1904 has been a household name in Winnipeg for service and reliability. And Mary Scorer, in the book business, had exactly the same sort of reputation. I *am* stretching it. But if it had been a cheapjack, quick-buck operation, I wouldn't have even thought of it."

Owner Jack Oleksiuk showed him the store's audited figures for the past ten years, which convinced Doole that modest profits could be made in a bookselling operation. He sold some of the inventory to pay the receivers and paid the former owner a few thousand for the rest and for the Mary Scorer name. He also made Oleksiuk the manager of the relocated store (double its former size) in a downtown site between Eaton's and The Bay. The major expense was the $100,000 worth of stock: a catholic collection of books as well as compact discs and pre-recorded cassettes of classical, jazz and easy-listening music, recorded books and plays.

"We want to make money out of this store," says John Doole. "After I've established that we have the right inventory and appeal to the right segments of the market, then I'm wide-open." With a smile of delight, he talks of Mary Scorer bookstores in other Canadian cities, of getting into the book-distributing business, and somehow he no longer sounds like a reluctant entrepreneur; he sounds like a man who gets as much of a kick out of running his own business as he once did from blowing his horn.

2

The Money Mongers

The money mongers of Western Canada all have breadth of vision as well as several traits in common with their counterparts in the East: they buy and sell companies and property the way the rest of us use and discard Kleenex; they wield cash not merely to make profits but because they enjoy playing and winning the real-life game of High Finance; they relish that special frisson of calculated risk; and they want to create personal kingdoms. But, with rare exceptions, the self-made empire-builders of Eastern Canada are more single-minded and much less visionary than four Westerners whose scope and style sum up this breed.

The most telling example of their prescience is the manner in which many of them have embraced technology. At sixty-five, the enigmatic Dr Charles Allard of Edmonton — after having created one diversified corporation — is centring his new conglomerate on technology. The former surgeon now controls the Western pay-TV network, Superchannel, and was one of the founding directors and continues to be an 18 percent partner in the Canadian Communications Satellite System — Cancom — which beams commercial TV to remote communities across the country.

Joe Houssian is president of Vancouver's Intrawest Properties, which made its original millions as a development corporation; but he had no hesitation in broadening his sphere of activities when an opportunity arose to invest in Mitel Corporation. Houssian hired technical consultants to familiarize him with the Ontario telecommunications giant and to make him knowledgeable about the complex industry; soon he was digesting such detail as the significance of SX-200 digital telephone-switching systems. After six months' research, he choreographed a classy $27 million investment deal with Mitel.

A Winnipeg farm-implement factory is not the most obvious place to look for technological innovation, which is one reason president John Buhler has given pride of place to an advanced computerized lathe. His company, Allied Standard, makes such equipment as hay-bale elevators and front-end loaders for tractors. An automatic numerical control lathe that Buhler installed takes twenty seconds to make a cylinder headplate that once took a lathe operator thirty minutes to fashion. "My vanity told me to put the automatic lathe right up front near the office, where people can see it," he says. "I don't apologize; there's about $350,000 worth of engineering there."

The money mongers also share a restlessness of spirit, a curiosity of mind that take them into unknown territory beyond their immediate business concerns. Calgary-based Jack Singer, for instance, has spent most of his career as a conventional land developer, but has also promoted boxing matches and such bizarre, visionary schemes as a glass roof over a chunk of downtown Calgary. Well into his sixth decade, he took a flyer on the movie business and wound up owning the Hollywood studio once run by the renowned director Francis Ford Coppola.

Dr Allard was a superb surgeon at Edmonton General Hospital when he began dabbling in business. He became so successful an entrepreneur after twenty years that he left medicine. As a full-time businessman, he found it hard to focus his energy on any one industry. He was enamoured of airplanes, even though he hated to fly. (In fact, he took flying lessons and failed to solo — "probably because I was chicken.") And it was that love, not business acumen, that led him to found International Jet Air in 1968 and import the first Lockheed turbine Electras into Canada, to fly freight and passengers to the Far North. Even though the airline was a consistent loser, he wasn't dissuaded from meeting with Russian trade officials in an unsuccessful attempt to import their

Yak-40, a solidly built tri-jet that might have replaced the workhorse DC-3.

John Buhler has the same catholic approach. When he got a good deal on a vegetable cannery, he gave himself a crash course in the chemistry of canning. He felt confident enough to fire the general manager, who was also the cannery's food technologist. ("*I'm* a food technologist," Buhler told the media at the time. "I'm forty-five years old and I've been eating since Day One.")

Another general characteristic of the money mongers is their sense of place, which demonstrates itself in more positive ways than mere Toronto-bashing. Joe Houssian, after graduating from the University of Saskatchewan, had to choose between heading east or staying in the West; he chose Calgary and eventually Vancouver. Later, he decided to quit his job with Xerox in Vancouver, in large part because continuing with the company would have meant moving to Toronto or New York — and he believed he could build just as credible a career in Western Canada. John Buhler is another unashamed chauvinist: "I have a very strong feeling that if we're going to do anything in the West, we won't do it by fighting the East, but by doing our own thing here." Until the 1970s, the decision to do their own things at home could have meant financial sacrifice for Western businesspeople. As Dr Allard points out: "There's no doubt that throughout most of Canada's banking history — until, say, the 1950s — the periphery of the country suffered. There was no local authority to do any lending except in modest amounts. I sometimes think they built those tall towers in Toronto so they could go on the roof, and if they could see you, you existed."

Dr Charles Allard —
The Reclusive Giant

As the 1970s came to a close in Canada, the economic signals that Dr Charles Allard read all around him were disturbingly familiar. The sixty-year-old doctor, once the chief of surgery

at Edmonton General Hospital, was now a fabulously successful Alberta businessman. His conglomerate, Allarco
Developments Limited, had substantial real-estate holdings
throughout North America, and he believed that the inflated
prices of land and buildings were about to burst with the
inevitability of a soap bubble. The once-cautious Canadian
chartered banks were caught up in a frenzy of lending to all
comers. It had taken him only a single afternoon, from his
office in Edmonton, to borrow $150 million from a bank to
build a third methanol plant in Medicine Hat, and a mere five
minutes to add $25 million to the loan as an afterthought.
Given this sort of casual financing, he believed the Canadian
economy would either explode in hyper-inflation that would
significantly devalue the money supply, or the nation would
be plunged into a deep recession. Dr Allard felt the chilling
winds of the Great Depression he had lived through as a boy.
So after three decades of building a financial giant with 1979
revenues of $119.8 million and a net profit of $19.9 million, he
decided to divest himself immediately of Allarco Developments — all but its most interesting companies.

He found a willing buyer in Carma Limited, a Calgary-
based cooperative of 135 land developers that wanted to
expand beyond home-building. Carma had already bought
out his minority partner, Zane Feldman, and in July 1980 it
paid Dr Allard $130 million for his 50 percent interest in an
astonishingly diversified public corporation. Over the years,
financial analysts had found it difficult to grasp its breadth; as
The Financial Post reported in 1978, many experts "throw up
their hands in frustration at the complexity of it all."

Even Carma, the purchaser, was not prepared for the range
of holdings that came with Allarco Developments. Among
them were 40 percent ownership in Alberta Gas Chemicals,
the province's major methanol producer, with 1980 sales of
about $88 million, and a partner in a profitable methanol
plant with the New Zealand government; controlling interest
in North West Trust, Canada's forty-fifth largest financial
institution, and Seaboard Life Insurance of Vancouver, which
insured about five hundred thousand Canadians; 9,628 acres

of urban land spread throughout all the Western provinces, Hamilton, Las Vegas, San Diego, Phoenix, Atlanta and Puerto Vallarta, and 35,839 acres of farmland in northern Alberta and northern California; at least ten apartment buildings in Edmonton, Calgary, Red Deer, Medicine Hat, Vancouver and Victoria; hotels in Las Vegas, Edmonton and Fort McMurray; five Alberta shopping malls; two construction companies; Western Canada's biggest Chrysler dealership; Oliver's Restaurants in Edmonton, Calgary and Winnipeg, the Steak Loft in Edmonton, Lucifer's in Edmonton and Calgary, and the Beachcomber in Victoria; fitness centres in Edmonton and California; and uranium leases, an interest in a molybdenum mine in Idaho, and a moderately successful Alberta-based oil and gas exploration company (which even Dr Allard couldn't recall owning when he was first reminded of it five years later).

"To give you some idea of his diversified bag of assets," says Roy Wilson, Carma's president, "we ended up with a little bank, Northwest International Bank and Trust Company in the Cayman Islands; the Western Canadian distributorship for Suzuki four-wheel-drives; a travel agency; and half-interest in Allartic in San Diego, a finance company with a manufacturing arm that made a sophisticated $4,500 exercise cycle with a computer that programmed pictures of a million different trails. As late as the fall of 1984, we discovered some oil and gas leases we didn't know about."

Relieved of all that burden, Dr Charles Allard was free to pursue his current passions. Today, at sixty-five, he remains almost as hyperactive as he was before selling out to Carma. He is the creator and hands-on owner of Superchannel, the pay-television network seen across Western Canada, and ITV, an Edmonton station whose active production company taped the successful comedy series "SCTV" for North American distribution and currently makes TV movies and commercials for the U.S. market. In his complicated deal with Carma, he bought back ITV for a bargain-basement $15 million (some observers say it was worth $100 million), and kept his Murray Grey cattle, his ranch at Leduc, Alberta, and his nineteen thousand acres of developable land at his California winter retreat in Palm Desert, not far from Palm Springs. Every year he makes his one concession to age and comfort and winters in Palm Desert for a few weeks, far from frigid Edmonton. But from his 5,550-square-foot home on the fourteenth tee of the Ironwood Country Club he keeps in touch with his Edmonton broadcasting interests through a receiving dish pointed at the Anik B satellite. And at night he can stroll outside, gaze far across the Coachella Valley and point out two clusters of house lights that are many miles apart. "There," he says to a visitor, "the space between the lights that's black in the middle, that's all my land."*

Another passion has been the Bank of Alberta, which he founded in 1983 after dreaming of it for a decade and a half. Through his investment company, Cathton Holdings†, he put in $2 million and organized the shareholders, who now include Hokkaido Takushoku Bank of Japan with 10 percent ownership. He is also a partner with an engineer friend in a New Jersey high-tech company that is pioneering the use of powdered hydrogen to create, among other products, batteries that can run on solar energy.

The foundations of Dr Allard's financial colossus were laid during the twenty years he was a surgeon practising sixty hours a week at the Edmonton General. His business colleagues call him simply The Doctor, and he ran his conglomerate in the arrogant style of the brilliant chief surgeon he was, making his influence felt as much as humanly possible, given the number of companies he controlled. In most aspects of his life, he behaved like the martinet of the operating room. He alienated his partner, who eventually refused to talk to him, and neglected his family, which led to his divorce by the first of his three wives. His public image was that of an intensely secretive man who refused the media access throughout most of his career. Ultimately, by involving himself in the

---

* He has since sold half the land to the Nature Conservancy, which mounted a $2-million drive to purchase the Coachella Valley Preserve to save the habitat of the fringe-toed lizard.

† Named for his daughter Cathy and son Tony from his second marriage.

high-profile business of broadcasting — in the hearings for a pay-TV licence, in the first two years of trying to make Superchannel work — he could not avoid public exposure. But he would continue to seek control of the amount of detail disseminated and would never discuss his past, his wives, his feelings. He would remain the chief surgeon, in charge, operating by his own rules.

That consuming need for privacy was one reason he sold Allarco Developments to Carma. Running a public company, as he admitted when he broke a fourteen-year silence, was often worse than performing a serious operation on a patient: "People trust you with their lives; not so with their money."

But there was another, more profound motive for selling when he did. All his life he has been bedevilled by the Depression, which began when he was ten years old. His father, Charles, and mother, Ethyl Begin, descendents of seventeenth-century French settlers in Quebec, came West in 1912. Seventeen years later, at the time of the stock-market crash, his father was operating a general store in Fort Saskatchewan, north of Edmonton. He had extended too much credit to survive. The family moved back to Edmonton, where he became a travelling salesman peddling sweaters to retail stores. "He was never the same man again; the bankruptcy affected him the rest of his life," the son says. The Depression destroyed his father's entrepreneurial spirit, and his strongly Roman Catholic mother, taking in boarders to struggle through the thirties, became the backbone of the family of three sons and a daughter. Charles, the third son, was disturbed by the daily trek of the itinerant poor who came to their home for food or clothing, never to be turned away.

After winning every high-school elocution contest, Chuck Allard seriously considered translating his oratorical skills to a career in law. But as the Depression deepened, he realized that lawyers were much less well off than doctors. With security as his major motivation, and a $600 scholarship as one of the three best students in Edmonton, he entered the University of Alberta in 1937 to study medicine. There he earned more awards, one of them carrying him through his final three years. In summer during those wartime years, he was a timekeeper for a construction company and a crewman on a Hudson Bay river freighter that ran between Fort McMurray and Fort Smith, Alberta.

In fourth year, when he was twenty-one, he married a girl named Effrica; Betty to her friends. After graduating in 1943, he and his new wife went to the coal-mining community of Mercoal, Alberta, where he worked for six months as a general practitioner to pay for post-graduate work at the University of Toronto. By then he knew he wanted to be a surgeon: "It was a much more active, dynamic part of medicine. You have to make a lot of decisions quickly." He had ideal hands for the specialty — small enough to fit inside a modest incision. The following year he moved to the Montreal General as a resident surgeon, and spent a season at Boston's famed Lahey Clinic working directly under founder Frank Lahey. (In hindsight he suspects he was chosen because Lahey was a short man and the five-foot-ten Allard wouldn't tower over him.) The experience was invaluable: the clinic attracted specialized cases that a young surgeon normally wouldn't see, and the strict Dr Lahey insisted on discipline in the operating room, a quality that his protégé would later emulate. "I regarded surgery as a very important discipline," he says. "The operating room isn't a place to talk about last night's party."

Throughout these years he and Betty were having four children in quick succession: Cameron, Judith and twins Peter and Charles. But between his obsessive dedication to work and their shortage of money, the marriage was beginning to tear at the seams. Earning only $25 to $125 a month as a resident, Dr. Allard needed financial help. His parents were running an Edmonton shoe store for one of his brothers in the service and his shrewd mother had begun to invest in houses, fixing them up and selling them, and then in land — all of which gave her some spare cash to support her surgeon son.

She would help him again in 1948, when he returned home as a twenty-nine-year-old to open his practice. Finding no room in any of the few downtown medical buildings in Edmonton, he was forced to work from an office above a clothing-store. Frustrated at not being surrounded by colleagues, he decided to become involved in the first business deal of his life. He would build his own medical centre. His decision wasn't as foolhardy as it appears. After the Leduc oil well began gushing in 1947, Alberta experienced the beginnings of a boom. And Dr Allard had a well-located lot on the main street, Jasper Avenue, which his mother had bought as an investment. It became a bell-wether for him throughout his career. Like the grandfather in *The Apprenticeship Of Duddy Kravitz*, who advised: "A man without land is nobody," he would forever see real-estate investments as his amulet against the ghost of the Depression. Even at fifty-five, he unblushingly utters that truism about land: "They aren't making any more of it."

With his two brothers, Dr Allard imaginatively put together the $850,000 in necessary financing to raise the seventy-thousand-square-foot, seven-storey Northgate Building, the largest to go up in Edmonton since the 1920s. At first it was to be only three storeys high, and North American Life agreed to hold the mortgage, with the land itself as equity, and the Bank of Montreal giving the brothers a loan. But when Interprovincial PipeLine said it would like to move in as a tenant and required four more floors of space, the bank refused to lend any further money. Dr Allard went down the block to an Alberta Treasury Branch office, a provincially owned retail-banking operation, which agreed to advance the extra funds because there was a good tenant in the wings.

Although risking his mother's savings, he never had any doubt that his début as a businessman would work. In fact, the rents always covered the Northgate's mortgage payments. "The secret of real estate is to be able to carry it if you don't own it outright," Dr Allard philosophizes now, as if he were revealing a grand truth. "If you get over-extended, that's where you get hammered." The success of his first venture into capitalism emboldened him. On borrowed money he bought more land as a hedge against the financial ruin that always lay around the corner (if the experience of his father were to be credited). A parcel in East Edmonton cost him $25,000, but he traded it to the city, as a school site, in return for several lots scattered throughout Edmonton.

One of the lots was at 101st Street and 105th Avenue near the downtown. Like so many of his business deals, the development of the lot was happenstance. In 1950 the thirty-one-year-old Dr Allard was trading in a car at a dealership owned by Sam Belzberg (who would become the billionaire financier of First City Financial Corporation, based in Vancouver) when he met a salesman named Zane Feldman, three years his junior. "He told me his car was used as an ambulance, but I could hear the meter ticking," Feldman recalls. Allard had been driving an old cab. Amused by the zesty Feldman, the doctor returned to the car lot at the end of a day just to chat. Four years later he offered the salesman the opportunity to become a 35 percent partner with him in opening a car lot at 101st and 105th.

Here, the stories the two men tell start to diverge. Dr Allard says he gave Feldman his personal car to sell as an investment to start the business. Zane Feldman begs to differ: "That was supposed to be the money to start it, but the doctor needed the money so I gave it to him and he never put a dime in the company. To this day I can't figure out why we weren't fifty-fifty partners, because nobody put any money in." Feldman, who earned $75 a week that first year, took used cars on consignment from dealers in Alberta and Hamilton; that, he claims, is how the business grew into a Hudson and then a Chrysler dealership. Dr Allard, in his accounts of the rise of Allarco Developments, doesn't attribute its success to the cashflow from their Crosstown Motors. Feldman does: "If it wasn't for the car business, there would have been no Allarco."

Between the time Dr Allard had met Feldman and they started Crosstown, his first marriage had failed, weakened by years of neglect. He was divorced in 1952; Betty left with the children to live in Vancouver. Later that year he was remarried to a Nova Scotian nurse, Edna (Gillie) Gillingham, and they had two children, Tony and Cathy.* "Your family always gets neglected," Dr. Allard admits. "You really have your children backwards: you should have them when you're old."

Throughout the 1950s, he had little time for anything but surgery and business. In 1956 Dr Allard, recognized for his brilliance in the operating room, became chief of surgery at Edmonton General. "He was the best surgeon there," recalls one nurse. Her name was then Shirley Livingstone and she was in awe of him. One day when he was performing a rare operation, the tying-off of an artery behind the knee, she arranged for a student nurse to assist. "Why aren't *you* scrubbed?" an infuriated Dr Allard demanded of Shirley Livingstone. "I want a graduate scrubbed." The atmosphere was tense as he began to quiz her while doing the operation. "Miss Livingstone, what is the relationship between the vein, artery and nerve in the popliteal space?" She hadn't a clue, but she wouldn't dare tell him that. "Brother and sister?" she said quietly. The chief surgeon laughed; the tension eased. Twenty years later, the exchange would take on special significance when their paths crossed again.

In his business life, his investments with Zane Feldman continued to grow as they moved their car dealership around to centrally located lots where they would eventually erect such prominent local structures as the Devonian and Cambrian buildings. By the end of the decade, they had assembled five full blocks of choice land along Jasper. The partners would often meet over lunch in the basement cafeteria of the General. Dr Allard would oversee the business on his Wednesday afternoons off, at nights and on weekends. "He never had anything to look forward to; it was strictly business," Feldman recalls. Sometimes, he says, his partner would sink into fits of depression.

---

* Cathy (Roozen) is now vice-president, investments, for her father's Cathton Holdings in Edmonton; his other daughter, Judith, is a Vancouver housewife. Eldest son Cam is involved in real-estate investments in Edmonton. The other three sons — Tony, Peter and Charles (Chuck) — are practising law.

Although the men were then good friends, theirs was an unequal partnership, which Dr Allard does not deny. At first he agreed with Feldman's verbal deal: "I don't take out appendixes and you don't sell cars." But over the years it became apparent that the doctor, with his 65 percent share, was also the boss. It was he, for instance, who decided to take their company into the trust-company business in 1957. Two experiences prodded him into it. After he'd built the Northgate with his brothers, a supposedly experienced trust company came to him — a novice — to ask how many elevators and other features it should install in the building it was planning. And in dealing with another trust company, he had leased land on the understanding that he had an option to buy it, yet the company sold it without giving him the right of first refusal. If a trust company handled property management well, he mused, it should succeed. He had no intention of getting into the deposit-taking side of the business; the responsibility of looking after other people's money truly frightened him.

As much as he would have liked to control the day-to-day operations of North West Trust, he was locked into running a surgery and doing patient rounds seven days a week. He quelled his natural instinct to do everything himself and hired as president of North West Trust the skilled Adam Miles. Within a year Miles was taking deposits; property management never became a significant contributor to the handsome profits the company was soon making (when Carma bought it in 1980, North West had total assets of $445,725,000 and six-month net earnings of $6,760,000).

During the early sixties, the Allard-Feldman partnership flourished in diversification as the doctor came across businessmen who had deals to sell him. Mitch Klimove, a commerce graduate who had opened the Steak Loft in Edmonton, got the partners into the high-quality restaurant business with seven locations in Western Canada. He eventually became a vice-president of Allarco. When building apartment blocks in Vancouver, Allard and Feldman met a contracting supervisor named Ralph Redden, liked his style and set him up with a 45 percent share in a new company called Redden Construction, which pioneered high-rise apartments in Edmonton. Redden built the major shopping centre and a hotel in Fort McMurray, a community Dr Allard knew from his riverboat days in college and whose potential he recognized as the heavy-oil boom began there. The company also constructed the Chateau Lacombe, a prestige hotel, on the downtown valley-view site where Allard had lived in a rented house as a teenager. Allard and Feldman had acquired the land in a swap with the city. To finance the hotel, they sold the land to Great West Life for $1 million, who leased it back to them; eventually, they re-bought it.

Although he maintained a low public profile, Dr Allard experienced his first bitter fling with the media in 1960. An advertising salesman convinced him to start a weekly newspaper called *The Edmonton Free Press*. Unfortunately, the salesman became the editor and produced a racy rag that, as well as detailing rape cases on its front page, failed to reflect the doctor's decidedly right-wing views on the horrors of socialized medicine and closed-shop unions. "There's nothing as exasperating as having to put money into a newspaper you don't agree with," he says. It soon folded without a trace (his daughter Cathy, who works for him, didn't know of its existence) but it left the sour legacy of a company named Metropolitan Printing, which consistently lost money for eighteen years. Instead of hiring a competent manager, Dr Allard spent fruitless time on Metropolitan himself, fiddling instead of fixing. "We should have got rid of it ten years before we did [in 1979]," he says. "If you've got a variety of businesses, you neglect the ones that are running well for the ones that aren't. It's human nature."

Inevitably, his eclectic way of collecting companies and their sheer number led him into serious errors of judgment. Soon companies he and Feldman purchased during the sixties either had their problems or forced him into unwelcome public prominence. North West Trust had half-interest in the Parkland Nursing Home chain in Edmonton, whose employees much later went on a very high-profile strike for

three years, earning Dr Allard unnerving media attention as
the arm's-length owner. Vancouver restaurateur Jack Porter
won a $200,000 out-of-court settlement from him for alleg-
edly violating a ten-year contract to have Porter run three
Beachcomber restaurants in Edmonton, Calgary and Victoria.
"It can be very costly if you make snap judgments about people," the doctor says. "Over the years, a big weakness of mine
was to take people at face value."

In 1967 Dr Allard appeared before the Alberta
government's Kirby Commission, called to investigate charges
of impropriety in office by Welfare Minister A.J. Hooke and
former Provincial Treasurer E.W. Hinman. While there were
insinuations that he had profited from his friendship with
Hooke in borrowing $1 million from the Alberta Treasury
Branches, the commission absolved him in its report.

Two years after his well-reported appearance on the stand,
he felt compelled to open himself up to unrestricted scrutiny
by going public with Allarco Developments. In spite of the
fact that he had no experience of the problems inherent in
running a publicly traded company, he wasn't wary about the
move. And certainly Allarco could use the funds: although it
had sizable retained earnings and various personal loans
propping it up, the company had reached the point where it
required more capital. The first public offering of more than
$7 million, which sold within a couple of days, paid off all
bank debts.

But the fifty-year-old Dr Allard had to pay a higher price.
The underwriters insisted that, for the offering to proceed, he
would have to end his medical career and devote full attention
to the business. The decision drew blood. His twenty years as
a surgeon, most of them as a chief surgeon, had been the most
important experience of his life. "Every once in a while as an
individual surgeon, you do something that can save a life.
You really can't replace that feeling. Everything else is anti-
climactic. But I was at the peak of my career, which is always
a good time to quit. You shouldn't wait till you're a doddering
old idiot."* He knew as well as the underwriters did that

---

* In the late sixties he did a dozen operations on severely obese patients, shortening

running a public company would leave him little time for his patients. "To do justice to the practice, the best thing to do was quit. I regretted it; I didn't mourn it."

In 1970, with Allard as full-time chairman and president at its helm, the new corporation, Allarco Developments, reluctantly took over Seaboard Insurance of Vancouver, whose parent company had borrowed $450,000 from Allarco's North West Trust. When the parent, Cosmopolitan Life Assurance, ran into serious financial problems in trying to take over a financial conglomerate, North West and later Allarco ended up controlling Seaboard, a small, struggling life-insurance company. "We knew we weren't getting any bargain," Dr Allard recalls. "Seaboard had been getting drained of cash." He put his own management team into the company and held meetings of the directors in Edmonton once a month. Mac Burnett, an executive vice-president who became president in the takeover, says: "I'm not sure Dr Allard was a willing owner. He sent in some of his own henchmen. We had too many people; he eliminated positions where we were over-staffed in marketing executives and cut out some activities which were probably leading nowhere. We turned it around." They certainly did: between 1975 and 1979 alone, Seaboard's total assets more than doubled to $35.4 million.

Dr Allard was more interested in acquiring a television licence in Edmonton, which he had failed to do in 1958. Fifteen years later, he got his licence and in 1974 opened CITV, an independent station that, through his encouragement, became a Western Canadian pioneer in producing TV specials for worldwide distribution. While memories of his days as high school correspondent for *The Edmonton Journal* had fuelled his interest in the news and public-affairs side of television, it was sheer entertainment that had CITV making money by its second year. Promising a daily variety show as

---

the gastro-intestinal tract to curb their food intake. But there were unsettling complications which convinced him to reverse the procedure on all but two patients, who refused. In an unusual paper prepared for the Western Surgical Society, he detailed his cases — his failures, really — with the object of discouraging such operations.

part of its mandate, the station was soon bringing in talent from Los Angeles and New York and, with a brashness born of naïveté, began featuring such international entertainers as Tom Jones and Roberta Flack in concerts backed by the Edmonton Symphony. It would do fifty-five of these specials and distribute them in fifty-five countries — the most successful such series in North American television.

Less successful was CITV's attempt at a $3-million talk show featuring David Steinberg, the Winnipeg-born comedian whose irreverent religious monologues made him a *cause célèbre* on American television. He had completed only two of a scheduled 130 shows when Dr Allard fired him for vulgarity; one of the features that outraged him was a mildly suggestive song by two New York singers called *Wet Dreams*. Then, in an uncharacteristic gesture, the doctor defended his action publicly: "There is no way our station would show a program that wouldn't be shown in my own living-room." He invited members of the media to attend a screening of the two shows, but they refused him when he more characteristically insisted that station officials had to see their stories before they could be published. In an attempt to head off any suit by Steinberg, Dr Allard sued the comedian, later letting the legal action lapse. "I certainly have no regrets about the incident," he says ten years later, "except for not taking control of the creative part of the series" — like a chief surgeon in command of his own operating room.

He has more pleasant memories of those early days at CITV, among them the opportunity it gave him to invite such stars as Engelbert Humperdinck to visit his wife, Gillie, who was suffering from cancer. It began as a mole on her knee. "One day it started to bleed and I knew it had to come off," her husband says. "There were no symptoms for eight years, but by then it had really spread. I'll never forgive myself for not removing it." The terminal stage lasted only about a month; Gillie died in 1974. Zane Feldman, who says his former partner "has no empathy; he can't cry," admits that Dr Allard wept when his wife died.

One of the staff in the cancer clinic where Gillie Allard had been treated was Shirley Livingstone, the wise-cracking nurse who'd made Dr Allard break up in the operating room of the Edmonton General twenty years before. In 1976, two years after his wife's death, he was driving down the street when he spotted a woman tending a bandaged scottie dog on her front lawn. He slowed to help, then realized it was Miss Livingstone. They were married that year.

By the mid-1970s, Allarco was into a strong period of growth, powered in part by its chairman's investments in the petrochemical industry. A quarter-century before, Dr Allard had met a broadly educated engineer, John LoPorto, who was installing Imperial Oil's Strathcona Refinery in Edmonton. They became friends; the doctor, a chemistry buff (who still regularly reads *Chemical Week*), was as intrigued with the world around him as the engineer was. Now, in 1973, the two men were interested in a Russian method of processing natural rubber. "Anybody who says they've planned their life is a damned liar; it's a series of accidents," Dr Allard says, offering his petrochemical involvement as an example. After he commissioned the firm that employed LoPorto to do a $250,000 study, they learned that the rubber process required methanol, which was produced by only one small plant in Canada. This was a better idea: Why not build a methanol plant in Alberta? First they moved sideways, buying a plant in Houston that produced polystyrene instead — on the theory that it would generate funds to finance a methanol operation. It didn't. Neither man, so enchanted by science that they'd forgotten their business instincts, had bothered to investigate the polysterene plant thoroughly; it lost money and they closed it. Looking for a Canadian partner for the methanol plant, they approached Robin Abercrombie, a vice-president of Calgary's Alberta Gas Trunk Lines (later the Nova Corporation), who convinced president Bob Blair to invest $500,000 in common shares along with Allard and LoPorto and jointly float a $3-million loan to the new company, Alberta Gas Chemicals.

They spent $48 million to start up two methanol plants at Medicine Hat, Alberta, in 1975 and 1976, and a third large one came in under the budget of $150 million in 1979 (they didn't need the $25 million they had added to their bank loan as an afterthought). From the beginning, Dr Allard says, "they were money machines." Even before the first plant was on stream, the partners had made $1 million just buying and selling methanol on the world markets. When John LoPorto sold his share of Alberta Gas Chemicals in 1980, he received about $25 million.

Through all this, the doctor's minority partner in Allarco, Zane Feldman, stayed in the background, focusing on their several Edmonton car dealerships, some of which ranked among Canada's largest. But in 1976 he was a keen participant in their investment in the Edmonton Oilers, then a member of the ill-fated World Hockey Association. "It says in *Alberta Report* that it was Dr Allard's money behind it all," Feldman says. "That's a crock of crap, because I signed for as much as he did with the Oilers." As Feldman tells the story, a lawyer acting for four American players was insisting on some financial security against their salaries before he would allow them to play in Edmonton; Feldman, a hockey fan, pledged some of his shares in Allarco. Dr Allard says: "I only got into the Oilers to help them. I had no experience with a sports franchise and wasn't particularly anxious to have any." The partners each picked up a third of the team, with a third held by a friend. Dr Allard got into the spirit of ownership, wearing an Oilers jacket and even embarrassing himself once when he blew up at the media in the dressing room for criticizing the coach. But the franchise did poorly at the box office, so he was ripe to have Vancouver real-estate entrepreneur Nelson Skalbania take it off his hands; they lost $400,000, Dr Allard estimates. Feldman, who says their losses totalled several hundred thousand more, was upset about the sale.

For him, it was one of the final straws to break the back of their partnership. He had become increasingly angry at what he considered the doctor's autocratic control of Allarco. It rankled him when his majority partner butted into the business of the car dealerships. And one day when Feldman was at a Toronto meeting of the World Hockey Association, in his capacity as a WHA governor, Allarco vice-president Mitch Klimove and an Edmonton business colleague, Dan Pekarsky (currently president of the Belzbergs' First City Financial of Vancouver) also showed up at Dr Allard's request. "He sent them to take over," Feldman claims. "That was the beginning of the end. I just came back and told Dr Allard that I'd never set foot in the Allarco Building again." For the next three years, the bitter Zane Feldman never even spoke to his partner; in 1979 he sold his share of Allarco to Carma for $16.3 million.* "We had a falling-out," Dr Allard says, choosing his words carefully. "I suppose it was acrimonious, more on his part than mine. What happens to people over the years is that they get egos. Ego destroys more people than any other cause. These falling-outs are probably not one person's fault."

It was only a year later that he too sold to Carma. Allarco had just experienced its best year ever, with sales increasing 35 percent to $119 million, for a net profit of $19.9 million. But looking around him, Dr Allard didn't like what he saw in the Canadian economy. It reminded him too much of the Depression that had crippled his father. Better to batten down the hatches and wait out the storm of hyper-inflation or recession with a few comforting companies of his own. "And I was tired of a public company," he confesses. "You've got a terrible responsibility with a public company."

He took his $130 million from Carma and bought back his nineteen thousand acres of Palm Springs land and his Edmonton TV station. Roy Wilson, Carma's president, says: "The doctor had all his money and could have been very difficult, but he wasn't. He stayed on and ran the company till the end of the year." During those six months, Wilson got an appreciation for the Allard style of management. "In Carma, we don't have a one-man show, so we've run a more traditional organization. Allarco didn't have an organizational chart as

* He now owns West Edmonton Chrysler, the first Canadian car dealership in a shopping mall — the West Edmonton Mall, the world's largest (see Chapter Three, The Ghermezians). In less than two years, the dealership grew from a staff of forty-five to ninety-two to become the second-biggest in Alberta. And he still isn't talking to his former partner.

they teach at Harvard. The division of authority, responsibility and duties wasn't a textbook case. I was surprised at
the very hands-on management style the doctor used. It was
such a super-difficult task to manage this empire; I wouldn't
even begin to try to copy it. There's only one Dr Allard in this
world. And he was just running out of hours in the day."

The Allard lifestyle has now become much less hectic, less
regimented, although at sixty-five he certainly keeps more
active than most businessmen of thirty-five. He pays most
attention to his broadcasting interests. In 1982 the Canadian
Radio-Television and Telecommunications Commission
(CRTC) issued him licences to set up regional pay-television
operations in Alberta and Ontario. At the same time, the
federal regulator awarded a national-network licence to
eastern-based First Choice. But Dr Allard's movie channel in
Ontario attracted a stronger subscriber base than the national
service did. And when he eventually won licences for all of
Western Canada and launched Superchannel in competition
with First Choice, a brief battle ensued for the hearts of Canadian viewers. For two years the doctor was involved in the
business daily, fighting First Choice's estimated $80-million
budget during that period with only about $15 million. Super-
channel had certain advantages. One, he says, was that "First
Choice were a bunch of people spending other peoples'
money: Manufacturers' Life, RoyNat. They went through $11
million of their original $20 million before they got on the air.
With Superchannel, it was coming out of my own pocket." So
he concentrated on trying to provide a better service, retain-
ing a shrewd American film expert ("his whole life is movies"),
who runs the Z Channel, the most successful pay station in
the Los Angeles area.* "We probably could have killed them
off," Dr Allard says, "but they brought one of the Bronfman

* Not many viewers noticed any difference in the two Canadian channels. Film
critic Robert Fulford, editor of *Saturday Night*, said that both performed miserably: "Their films are poorly chosen, poorly scheduled, and incoherently advertised. They both have the odious habit of promoting movies that viewers have
already paid to see. Fools like me, who signed on for both of them, can't decide
which one is worse. Eventually one will fail and just possibly the survivor may
gather enough subscribers to fulfil at least some of the original promises about
[original] production."

family in." In 1984 the battle ended in a truce, with the two networks splitting up the eastern and western halves of the country and informally getting together to buy movies. Superchannel sends the up-link signal for both companies to a satellite from Edmonton.

In 1985 Superchannel had just turned the corner into making money, although it hadn't recovered its losses. Dr Allard was promising that all profits would be put into original production, and Superchannel had already done two TV movies: "Isaac Littlefeathers," a true story about a Saskatchewan Indian, with Lou Jacobi; and "Bridge To Terabithia," an adventure story with Canadian actors, which was shown on the U.S. Public Broadcasting System. It had also invested in "Louisiana" with Canadian actress Margot Kidder and "Blood Of Others" with American Jodi Foster. "For a while, I'm going to be very involved in decisions on every production, because you can lose your shirt," the doctor says. "There are a lot of flaky people in this business."

He has divorced himself, however, from any day-to-day involvement in the Bank of Alberta, which he opened in 1983. As early as 1967, when he first applied to Parliament for the bank's incorporation, he was saying: "I think the people of Canada will benefit by having more and smaller banks offering different specialties in banking." But it was really his belief that the eastern-based banks were insensitive to western interests that in 1982 prompted him to invest the initial $2 million in the venture. He then brought in a group of shareholders, the most prominent of them being Eugene Pechet. Pechet had been building hotels in Alberta and along the Alaska Highway for four decades and, with his son Howard, owned Edmonton's Mayfield Inn complex, which includes the dinner theatre Stage West.* The timing was ripe: Fred Sparrow, the chief executive officer of the Alberta Treasury

* The Pechets' Mayfield Investments was the largest founding shareholder, with 7.02 percent of the bank's 3.2 million shares outstanding. Another son, Harvard Medical School doctor Maurice Pechet, took another 3.12 percent. Dr. Allard, through Cathton Holdings, held 1.56 percent. Other founding directors included film producer-director Arthur Hiller (*Love Story*), a former Edmontonian, 1.56 percent, and Allan Jackson, president of Knowlton Realty, .78 percent. Currently the largest shareholder is Hokkaido Takushoka Bank of Japan, with 10 percent, followed by the oil-rich Samson Indian Band of Hobbema, Alberta.

Branch, had retired at fifty-seven and was willing to become chairman and chief executive officer of the Bank of Alberta. Dr Allard had long admired the Treasury Branch, which had financed his first business venture, the Northgate Building. The bank, which was immediately profitable, soon adopted some of the branch's concepts, such as the use of fifty deposit agencies throughout the province, in which the bank bonds a local businessman to accept term deposits and retirement-savings-plans funds on his own premises.

Seeing his dream of an Alberta-based bank realized was enough satisfaction for Dr Allard. His son Chuck is the bank's company secretary and keeps him posted on its operations. "I'm not that interested in spending a lot of time on it," the doctor says. "There must be twenty directors and that's really not my cup of tea. I'm more interested in things that I own myself."

With old pal Jonn LoPorto he has bought Energetics (they hold 38 percent each), a New Jersey company experimenting with various metal alloys that, on contact with hydrogen, form hydrides that can be used in powdered form. The company has already powered a truck with one of its special hydride containers, which became a fuel cell that can be energized by the sun. The hydrides also eliminate the dangers of gaseous hydrogen, which has to be stored under pressure. The potential delights Allard the science enthusiast, who sees its uses in vessels like submarines and perhaps space ships; Energetics has done work for the U.S. National Aeronautics and Space Administration.

"Obviously," Dr Allard says, "none of the past was ever planned. I have no plans now. I'm sixty-five and I suppose I ought to be getting sensible. But I wouldn't retire. Who knows? John LoPorto wants to do a lot of things and I may go along with him. There are resources in Western Canada that ought to be processed as fully as you can there, so that you're selling the added value by manufacturers. I guess I could get involved in something like that in the petrochemical industry. I'm like that South African bird that flies backward: It knows where it's been, but it's not quite sure where it's going."

His once-dark hair, combed straight back, is silver now. His stomach has slipped, his chin has doubled and his sun-spotted face is pouchy and red with broken veins. But even in his winter home in the security-guarded Ironwood Country Club at Palm Desert, California, he is on the phone throughout the day and watching his TV channels from Edmonton via his satellite dish. He spent two and a half months there in 1984-85, the longest he has ever been away from Edmonton, justifying the time with trips to Los Angeles to do Superchannel movie business. The doctor feels comfortable in his Palm Desert house that he shares with his wife Shirley and their fat black scottie, Teddy. It cost him well above the $529,000 that other homes are currently being sold for in Ironwood. There is the outdoor swimming pool and whirlpool, the five bathrooms, the adjoining Arnold Palmer-designed golf course (which he never uses), the grapefruit picked fresh for breakfast. And, whenever he feels the cool winds of the Depression breezing towards him, the doctor can step outside into the searing sun and look over the Coachella Valley at his thousands of acres of rapidly appreciating land.

John Buhler — The Turn-Around Man

In 1982 Renn Industries, a Western farm-equipment distribution company, collapsed owing Manitoba entrepreneur John Buhler $420,000. He flew to Toronto to confront two major shareholders of Renn's parent company, Anthes Industries: Donald C. (Ben) Webster, president of Helix Investments of Toronto, and a fellow Westerner, Richard (Bones) Bonnycastle, the scion of the Harlequin romance-novel fortune. The two men put their arms around Buhler and said that if he wanted to try saving Renn, he had their blessing and they'd give the company a $200,000 transfusion within a month. "If I turn it around," Buhler told them, "I'd like to buy it." He flew to Renn's head office in Calgary, fired the general manager and eventually thirty-five other people, then began phoning about 350 of the 440 creditors, who were owed more than $4 million. It took him two months, twelve hours a day, six days a week, to reassure them that they would soon get 25 percent of their account paid and the balance over twelve months, interest-free. The creditors — impressed that he was one of them, on the hook for $420,000 — delayed petitioning Renn into bankruptcy. Webster and Bonnycastle paid Buhler $100,000 for his two months' work, $10,000 to cover his expenses and the 25 percent down payment on what was owing him. They eventually settled with the other creditors and Renn stayed in business. "I'd still like to buy the company," John Buhler says.

Throughout the early 1980s, Manitobans were ripe for a hero who would express their frustrations and try to wrest control of at least one farm-implement corporation from Ontario and bring it to its natural home. A hero appeared in the unlikely form of Buhler, a country businessman who is small in stature, but not in aspirations. Within the past dozen years he had taken over four faltering mid-sized companies in the province and had breathed new life into their corpses while saving two hundred jobs.

He did it at a time when Manitoba was like a dowager long past her prime: fallen on hard times, dowdy and decaying, whatever fortune she'd once had now just a memory. The recession had rolled into Manitoba with devastating momentum and crushed business after business under its weight. The province, a poor relative compared to the rest of Western Canada in recent years, became paralysed by the general economic downturn; the population declined as people fled to greener pastures. In the capital city of Winnipeg, which for a few long-ago decades had flowered as the capital of the West, the major downtown thoroughfare of Portage Avenue felt as abandoned as a bomb site. Companies had closed their doors and there were no others to take their place. In the outlying towns and on the farms that fuelled the provincial economy, pessimism prevailed. Manitoba was dying.

The province was particularly resentful of its next-door neighbour, fat-cat Ontario, which even during the height of the recession survived well with its concentrated pool of population and its strong industrial base. The antagonism was almost tangible on the subject of those manufactured goods that Manitobans fervently believed could just as well be made in their province or elsewhere in Western Canada as they could in Ontario. The most galling of all those products was agricultural equipment. The majority of Canadian-built machinery for the farm was manufactured in the East, although, for instance, more than 90 percent of combines made there were used in the West.

Approaching his fiftieth birthday, John Buhler seemed impervious to the general malaise in Manitoba, neither wistful about the past nor thwarted because of the present financial climate. If he had heard of the recession, he'd misinterpreted it as an era of opportunity. While his business colleagues spoke of slow death and euthanasia, the enthusiastic Buhler was talking about life and growth and a future that meant more jobs for Manitobans. "He got a lot of press," recalls Dennis Anderson, a professor of marketing at the University of Manitoba, "because he's always positive, always saying he can do it, in a down economy. He waves his arms about a lot. And in cloudy times he has simple solutions."

But John Buhler proved that he *could* do it — that his solutions, simple as they sounded, did work. With his horse-trader's eye, he had bought each of his companies for a bargain price. Then, by cutting staff, changing product lines and taking advantage of a total of about $500,000 in government expansion funding, he had turned each of them around to profitability.

In 1970 he had taken over an ailing agricultural-equipment company, renaming it Farm King Limited; it would flourish in Morden, Manitoba, growing into an eventual gross profit of close to $2 million a year and a net income of $250,000. At 45, he contemplated retirement from the business world, but bought a vegetable-canning factory instead. In four years he transformed Morden Fine Foods' $500,000-a-year loss into a $60,000 profit before selling out. More recently he had acquired two other failing companies, Allied Farm Equipment

Incorporated and Standard Industries Limited, which manufactured steel components for grain elevators; both had
become profitable. By 1984 the combined sales of his companies were $12,310,000 and his net after-tax profits
$813,000. Small as the profit margin sounded, it was a
remarkable performance, given the perilous state of the industry: while this little upstart of a man and his pups of corporations were earning money — Farm King had its most profitable years from 1981-84 — agricultural veterans such as
Massey-Ferguson and White Farm Equipment were being
bailed out of bankruptcy. In fact, White Farm went into
receivership again in April 1985.

White Farm's Brantford, Ontario, operations were in
receivership for the first time in 1983 when Buhler, with an
$11.6-million bid supported by the Manitoba government,
tried to bring the Dallas-owned factory to Winnipeg. He
failed, but in making his nationally publicized attempt he
established his persona as an arm-waving Western patriot, a
performance that the eastern media noted with fascination. "It
bugs me," they reported him saying, "that every fridge and
stove, washer and dryer, every deepfreezer, every car, every
truck and anything automotive has to come from Ontario."
The following year he continued to get press with his offer to
take over the Manitoba government's debt-plagued transit-
bus plant, Flyer Industries, which symbolized the province's
belief that it could be home to heavy industry. In February
1985 he made a further proposal that the government was
seriously considering: he'd run Flyer for $1 a year for three
years with the option of buying it anytime during that period
at its current book value. At the time of the offer, he figured
the value was $35 million. "My job," he said, "would be to
bring down the book value to about $15 million [by stream-
lining operations]. If I don't, I'd lose my $50,000 deposit. But
I'm totally convinced I'd turn it around."

The press was bemused by this entrepreneur of many ambitions. An awkward boy who couldn't play sports, he was one
of five children of an impoverished immigrant Mennonite
family. His father, now deceased, always worked for other

men and never got ahead, and Buhler determined in childhood that he would someday control his world. In first grade
in the southern Manitoba town of Morden, where he learned
he had a head for figures, Buhler decided to become a
businessman. In sixth grade, sitting behind the son of the
town mayor, he promised himself that he would grow up to
be the mayor of Morden.* To control his life meant that he
must make money, and early on he vowed to be a millionaire
by the age of forty-five — when he would retire to become a
missionary who would give something back to the world, a
world that by then he would have mastered.

John Buhler was also a man of many contradictions. Successful as he was, with retained earnings of $3.9 million in
1984, Buhler also had long- and short-term bank debts of
nearly $9 million. Yet he almost revels in debt, in how it sym-
bolizes progress and risk-taking: "I like it; it doesn't scare me.
I've gone to the Bank of Montreal and said, 'Someday I'm
going to borrow $10 million from you.' " The same stubborn
negotiating line, the stinginess he adopts in taking over companies, also surfaces in his private dealings, where he buys
everything for cash — and at a discount. He embarrasses his
long-time girlfriend, Bonnie Buhler,† by bargaining in every
shop, even in the staid department stores. A Winnipeg real-
estate agent discovered this when Buhler bought a Fort Garry
house, overlooking a man-made lake, to live in with Bonnie
and her two daughters. The asking price was a reasonable-
sounding $139,000, which Buhler countered with what
seemed an absurd offer of $105,000. He had to insist that the
unwilling agent take the offer to the owners. From time to
time over the next few weeks, the agent would call Buhler
with new prices: $129,000, $118,000, $116,000. "You don't
know me," Buhler told the man. "When I said $105,000, I
meant it." And that, finally, was the price he paid for it.

His stubbornness arises even when it appears to threaten

* He would get elected to town council three times, but lost in his only mayoralty
bid.

† She had her name changed legally to his.

the most advantageous business deal. Buhler owns Valley Cable Vision Limited, which has about three-thousand cable-TV subscribers in five southern Manitoba communities. * In 1981 he agreed to sell to the Manitoba Telephone System all the underground cable that Valley had laid. The asking price was a little more than $1 million, or about three-quarters of a million more than he'd paid for the entire cablevision company. But he wanted to consummate the deal without the expense of hiring his own lawyers, a breed for which he has the Western entrepreneur's not-uncommon disdain. The telephone company's lawyers, however, insisted that they had to disburse the $1-million-plus payment to him through a lawyer, *any* lawyer representing him. He refused. The company's lawyers insisted. So Buhler responded, "Well, we'll just call the deal off." Fine, they replied. Whereupon he phoned the president of the Manitoba Telephone System to say: "It was a pleasure doing business with you; we almost made the deal." The next morning, the president personally handed him a cheque for the full sum.

A Cadillac-driving, diamond-ring- and gold-chain-wearing capitalist, John Buhler claims to lean to the NDP (which may be a politic statement, given the nature of his province's government). He speaks well of unions: "I wouldn't be here if it weren't for the unions; I'd be the peasant working in the field for some eastern Canadian lord." Yet a few moments later he says that if his unionized workers at the combined Allied and Standard plant went on strike, he'd close the place down and build his products elsewhere. Somehow, that seems closer to the unvarnished John Buhler, the man with a hair-trigger temper that hides under buckets of ingenuous charm. Still, as he proves on a walking tour of the 107,000-square-foot factory, he knows all one hundred men and women by name. Though he often wears a three-piece pinstripe suit, they realize he'll put on coveralls to work alongside them, as he did in erecting overhead steel beams; in doing so, he fell through

---

* In 1985 Buhler applied to the CRTC to serve fifteen other communities with his debt-free cable system, which was earning him an effortless $50,000 profit a year.

the roof and broke his wrist. While he wouldn't give them a pension plan because he believes that such schemes profit only the financial companies, in early 1985 he planned to introduce an employee-ownership plan that would give workers and managers in Winnipeg and Morden 10 percent each of his companies. "It may sound socialistic," he says, "but employee ownership is the way of the future. The problem of the country is management. What unions are asking for is some sort of participation. If management thinks they are some kind of god, that they're privileged, that's nonsense."

The contradictions continue. Although he photographs tall, he stands five feet, four inches and, as he says, that's cheating a bit. His wide face looks military with its broom mustache and strong jaw, but his demeanour smacks more of the farm. He calls himself a country boy and, in such things as eating habits and his unsophisticated directness of speech, he still is. Dining, he ducks his face to the plate and shovels in the food. In his relationship with Bonnie, he is not above announcing to her, "You should get a face-lift." He is a male chauvinist, a role he disclaims yet confirms by saying: "The only time I get angry with Bonnie is when the fridge is messy."* Born a Mennonite, raised in the Evangelical Church, he now bases his personal philosophy on the writings of such proponents of positive mental attitude as Wayne Dwyer (*Your Erroneous Zones*) and the TV evangelist Robert H. Schuller. He and Bonnie attend the United Church; to start the day she reads a daily devotional, and while driving to work he'll play a tape on positive thinking.

There is no paradox, however, in the fact that as a high-school dropout, Buhler is tickled about the regular invitations he receives from the University of Manitoba to lecture to business classes. "Students get excited by him," says Professor Dennis Anderson. "They tend to analyse things to death, and when they see somebody who can sum something up in two

---

* The first time he told her the fridge was a mess, she retorted, "Okay, clean it." Later, when they went to buy some gas at a self-serve station, he just sat and waited. She says she got the message: "I like to be treated like a woman; I don't want to fill the gas."

minutes and then move to action — and usually he's right — they find it refreshing. I find the guy refreshing myself. To the extent that people in the West are a little more down-to-earth — and he still has the Mennonite-kitchen cooking smell on his breath — people would label him as a typical Western entrepreneur."

All of this — his farm-community background, his unsophisticated life philosophy, his brevity of education, his height — help explain John Buhler's inordinate drive. But so does his mother, a woman who battled back from serious bouts of depression during her middle age to become forewoman of about eighty employees in a Morden poultry-processing plant. She was still there in 1985, in hard hat and coveralls, at the age of seventy-eight. Although she didn't need the money, Mrs Buhler also continued to clean the Farm King offices every night, where she got down on her knees to pray for the success of her son's companies; praying for each one by name — "that they don't go broke."

For her seventy-eighth birthday party John drove the one hundred kilometres south from Winnipeg to Morden (population: 3,886), a pretty town most noted for its innovative government agricultural station. In his two-toned Fleetwood with the sun roof, he drove down the streets where he used to deliver newspapers barefoot, past the elementary school where he failed first grade and performed so badly in sports. There is a barely contained glee when he comes to town today: he now owns about four hundred acres of land within Morden's municipal limits, as well as one of its three major industries.

His parents had come to southern Manitoba as a newly married couple in a great wave of Mennonite immigration from Russia in 1927. His father, whose grandfather had made wagons and farm implements in the Old Country, soon went to work for a Morden implement-maker named Adolph Krushel, who was to loom large in young John's life. The Buhlers were poor; John can't recall having had a bath in a tub till he was sixteen. Raising five children weakened his mother, and for a couple of years when she couldn't look after the family, he lived with aunts.

Those aunts and several of their husbands were at his mother's house in Morden on a January afternoon to help celebrate her birthday. In the kitchen, over coffee and a late lunch that Mennonites call *faspa*, they reminisced about John as a boy, laughing when he confessed to his mother that he used to insulate his pants with a kneeling pad when his disciplinarian of a father sent him out to fetch a stick with which to be beaten. "*That's* why I didn't find the pad when I wanted it," she said. An aunt remarked, "He has been smart from childhood." And shy. "I was so shy," John told his relations, "that when I walked in front of the class, I walked like this" — hunching his shoulders, lowering his head. The grown-up John Buhler brags that he worries about nothing. Did he worry much as a child? "He didn't have to — I do it," his mother replied. An old aunt smiled and said, "Worries are like a rocking chair: it gives you something to do, but it doesn't get you anywhere."

John's father was quiet, steady, unambitious. His mother, at forty-eight, went to work in the local poultry plant. She had always been enterprising and curious, qualities that influenced her children — one son became a United Church minister, another the successful owner of dress shops and a clothing distributorship in Calgary. John, the middle son, was slow in school and was forced to repeat his first year because he couldn't speak English. What's more, his eyesight was so poor that he couldn't see the blackboards. Nor was he good in sports. "I could never play ball. And in all your school years, that's the judge of how successful you're going to be." Convinced he was a dullard except in science and mathematics, he struggled through to ninth grade, which he also failed. During his mother's party, he recalled quitting tenth grade when his two-years-younger brother, Jake, caught up to him. At the time he left school, his mother was in hospital for an operation. "If I hadn't been in hospital," she told the aunts and uncles at her party, "he wouldn't have quit. I wouldn't have let him stop." The teacher told her it wasn't that Johnny didn't understand the lessons; it was that he was always busy with something else.

Everything else. By fourteen he was getting a piece of the action from three other kids doing paper routes in Morden and was driving taxi for a local garage, with cushions under his seat so he could see out the windshield. He also worked in the garage, where one of the owner's smart-alec sons would say, "We've got a white-collar job for you today," then have him clean out the washrooms. *Someday I'm going to own this company*, John Buhler promised himself. In 1950 he got his first job, as a seventeen-year-old assistant station agent with the CPR in Morden. Three years later he married Ruth, a deeply religious Mennonite girl, the daughter of Adolph Krushel, for whom John Buhler's father had worked. Krushel, by now the richest man in Morden, had made his fortune with a grain crusher he'd originally designed out of brake drums from old cars. John, after the first of his three children was born, had worked for a year in his father-in-law's factory, but it was not a fulfilling experience. Although he loved Krushel's curiosity, he grew impatient with his priorities — which included having five men rebuild an old steam engine even though the factory was losing money.

In 1957, when he was twenty-four, John Buhler was primed to go into business for himself. With $1,500 in CPR pension money, he and his father — his father who had always worked for someone else — bought the inventory of a small service station and auto-wrecking operation in Morden. They also bought the town's first wheel-alignment machine, with cash borrowed from a finance company. Within a year John was selling used cars, within five years he had sold 165 new Ramblers, and by 1969 had the town's Ford dealership.

Meanwhile, he was performing his first financial turn-around. In 1962 he convinced the North Star oil company (now Shell) to rent him a moribund gas station at the other end of town — for $1 a month. Business grew quickly and after two years, when the company decided to negotiate a better rental deal for itself, Buhler offered to buy the station instead. The company wanted $9,000, which it claimed was the value of the land. Buhler said a man had offered to sell him a similar piece of property just down the street for only $4,000. Prove it, the oilmen told him. He immediately drove off and returned with a receipt for the other lot (for which he'd paid only a $50 deposit). When North Star agreed to sell him its land for $4,000, Buhler then announced he couldn't pay any cash up front and would pay no interest on the monthly payments he would make. He got the garage, which became Buhler Motors.

In 1970 he heard from his father-in-law's employees that Adolph Krushel's plant, Standard Gas Engine Works, was on the verge of collapse. Suppliers wouldn't give Standard any steel; the banks wouldn't advance it any more money. Buhler had been secretary-treasurer of the company for several years and, with Krushel's approval, he borrowed $25,000 from the bank, put it in his account and, on the strength of that, bought some steel for the factory. The bank, meanwhile, put through all the cheques for Standard's creditors that it had been holding, a move that swallowed his borrowed $25,000. Buhler realized too late that he should have negotiated with the creditors for an orderly payment of debts.

"Ruth," he told his wife, "you can forget about me for six months. We're going to turn this around."

There was about $50,000 in payables remaining. This time he went to the creditors, asked them to check on the health of Buhler Motors and sent them twelve months of post-dated cheques — which included no interest — to settle their accounts. Within the year, he had managed Standard Gas Engine back into solvency. He was evolving his current management philosophy, which involves control over five variables: "You have to have a gut feel for how your accounts receivable are, for your accounts payable, for how much of your operating line you're using, for what you owe — your total debt (payables and bank) — and for sales to date. All this, within $50,000 — that's close enough." He still estimates his payables by keeping them in an accordion file, which he squeezes together every once in awhile to see how fat it is; he tells amused business-administration students that he's remarkably accurate.

Adolph Krushel had given his seven children the option of purchasing the company, and in 1972 Buhler convinced them to let him buy it. "I'm not going to work my butt off to increase the value of your share," he said in his characteristically blunt fashion. He gave them $5,000 apiece for their options and eventually paid Krushel himself $100,000 to acquire sole ownership.

A year later Buhler sold his garage and invested about $40,000 in the business, which he renamed Farm King (after one of the products). With the factory his own, he went after his first government funds ("I have competitors who can use them if I don't"), borrowing another $60,000 at nine percent from the Industrial Development Fund (later the Federal Business Development Bank). He was manufacturing crushers, grain augers, grinder-mixers, and hammermills that crush grain through screens. Buhler's companies now produce bucket elevators, drag-chain, screw and belt conveyors, grain-distribution systems and accessories, front-end loaders, grain augers, utility augers, snow-blowers, hydraulic cylinders, harrow drawbars and sections, rollermills, farm wagons, grain cleaners, fertilizer tanks, drill fills, and the Triumph line of woodstoves.

Buhler's self-taught management style is unpredictable; one week he chats up his employees, the next he chews them out. His foreman, Dave Bergen, remembers the day his boss criticized him aloud on the factory floor about men he felt were slacking off. Their argument boiled into a shouting match, with Bergen offering to quit on the spot. Buhler marched off to his office; ten minutes later, he called Bergen in — to apologize. He has never chastized Bergen publicly again.

Among Buhler's innovations at Farm King was an incentive plan that offered bonuses for productivity above the norm. Sales leaped from $290,000 to $1 million, the number of his employees from twelve to 114. In 1973, after the federal Department of Regional Economic Expansion agreed to give him 25 cents on the dollar to build a new factory, he went to an elegant dinner in the executive dining room of the Royal Bank in Winnipeg.

"How much money do you want, Johnny?" a senior vice-president asked him.

"A million dollars," Buhler replied.

"You've got your million."

Years later, Buhler would say, "It was then that I discovered it's easier to borrow a million than it is to borrow $10,000."

Of course, as security he had a five-hundred-acre farm that he, his father and a brother had bought in the mid-sixties for $125 an acre, a farm that sky-rocketed in value as Morden started to grow and the local council annexed some of the Buhler land into the town limits. "I wouldn't take $2,000 an acre for it now," he says. "Over the years the farm has provided security for bank loans; I never had pressure from the banks because they felt it was good security."

Throughout the seventies, Buhler expanded his operations three times. He added a line of agricultural snow-blowers and now sells more of them than any other Canadian manufacturer. Farm King, which spreads across a total of sixty acres, had 1984 sales of about $6 million, ranking it seventh among the eighty-five smaller-scale, so-called "short-line" companies in Western Canada that manufacture only small implements.* As Buhler's business expanded, so did his land holdings within Morden. He assembled ninety-eight beachlots

---

* The major companies for several years have been in bad straits; as farm costs rose and selling prices declined, the industry was appealing to hard-pressed Western farmers by heavily discounting list prices. Tough new competition has arrived recently from Japan, which is capturing a major share of the smaller-horsepower tractor market in Canada. As a result, 1985 saw an increase in the rationalization of the industry as J.I. Case of Racine, Wisconsin, took over the farm assets of International Harvester Co. of Chicago, which was expected to eliminate about four hundred of the two thousand Case and Harvester franchised sales outlets across the continent. This reduction affects the short-line manufacturers such as Farm King which depend on these dealers to distribute their products. Buhler's company supplies twelve hundred dealers across Canada; it sells about 30 percent of its products in the United States.

around a man-made lake within the town limits, which he intended to develop some day well into the future. In 1978, town council in a closed meeting cancelled his rights to create a subdivision on the lake, arguing that the development would pollute the local water supply (Buhler argued that it wouldn't and, in any case, he said he had no immediate plans to develop the land). Although he fought the decision in court and won both the original case and the town's appeal, the council foiled him by rezoning the land back to agricultural use only. Over six years he would spend $50,000 in legal fees, understandably gain the enmity of many townspeople, and in the end be forced to start selling the lots off as cheap agricultural land. Of the ninety-eight lots, he still had fifty-six left in 1985.

There was one outcome, however, that was more positive. When he began seeing his Winnipeg lawyer about the subdivision battle in 1978, in the office Buhler noticed Bonnie, the attractive blonde secretary with eyes as penetratingly blue as Paul Newman's. His marriage had weakened over the years, as he left any semblance of strict Mennonite ways forever behind. Ruth remained so devout that she refused to see *The Sound of Music* — movie-going was a sinful pursuit. Bonnie found John Buhler a sweet man. He was smitten. At first she refused to see him because he was married and had three children; she was the divorced mother of two. Buhler was also fourteen years older. When he persisted, they dated discreetly for nearly a year-and-a-half before a friend of his took him for a drive and told him he should be doing something about this girl he was seeing. In a typically unilateral decision, Buhler announced to Ruth and a son that he was leaving the marriage. Only then did he phone Bonnie to tell her and ask, "What do I do now?" They have lived together every since. As he and Bonnie were leaving his mother's seventy-eighth birthday party, one of the aunts wondered aloud when they would be getting married. "When I get my divorce," he promised. His own children, shocked at the abrupt way he walked out on his wife, have still not accepted Bonnie.

Her presence had been one factor in overturning Buhler's

decision to retire when he became forty-five in 1978. He had met his secular goal by becoming a millionaire; the little boy from Morden had made a success of himself. Because fifteen of his relatives were ministers and missionaries, Buhler had always thought he should work in the mission field with Mennonites in Mexico. "But," he says now, "you can't get your reward in heaven when you start fooling with girls who have Paul Newman eyes." Perhaps, he claims to have thought at the time, he could do something worthwhile by staying in Manitoba and creating jobs.

At about the same time he met Bonnie, the new Conservative government in the province had decided to rid itself of a vegetable cannery that the former NDP administration had bought in his home town. In each of the previous three years Morden Fine Foods had lost between $450,000 and $500,000. It seemed the perfect challenge; he bought the cannery six weeks before his forty-fifth birthday. The newspapers reported only that Buhler paid $1 million. He did, but it was a far better deal for him than the government would announce publicly. The cannery came free of all debts, it had $1.4 million worth of inventory and there were substantial accumulated tax losses that he could balance against future profits in Farm King. When his bank wouldn't give him the cash for the deal unsecured, he put up such securities as the subdivision land he still owned and his personal guarantees. In buying the cannery, he saved one hundred jobs.

With his usual abandon, he flung himself into the canning business. In what was supposed to be his first extended pleasure trip with Bonnie, he spent the train ride to Calgary reading books on canning. Although he immediately trimmed the obese management, including the general manager who was also the plant's food technologist, the cannery continued to lose money. "I did a 300 percent turnaround," he remembers with a smile. "It took me three years to lose half a million dollars." In the fourth year, it was an accident of nature that led Morden Fine Foods into the black. When a drought drastically reduced the cannery's own crop of green beans and corn, Buhler had soon tracked down kidney-bean supplies to produce pork and beans, which he found to be a more profitable line of canned goods. He also did some clever grassroots marketing of his products by meeting touring groups of senior citizens at the plant, giving them a little talk and samples of the pork and beans and telling them to go to their local Safeway and ask why it didn't stock *his* brand. Within two months of his pep talks, Safeway began to make unsolicited orders for Morden pork and beans.

His excitement about owning a cannery didn't last long. "I would like him to stay on one project until he's finished," complains the controller of Farm King, Jean-Guy Filion. "When he first bought the cannery, he was enthusiastic for the first six months. Then somebody else had to run the cotton-picking thing." Filion was elected. If some of Buhler's raw genius is in knowing how to buy, the rest is in knowing when to sell. In 1982, after the cannery had made its first profit, $60,000, he sold it to its manager and two others for about $500,000; within eighteen months, Morden Fine Foods was bankrupt.

A year before, John Buhler had already found another factory that was a more comfortable fit with Farm King. The hemorrhaging Winnipeg subsidiary of Allied Farm Equipment Inc., based in Chicago, was up for sale. Beyond his growing goal to create jobs, he had a more romantic reason for buying the plant: Bonnie was in Winnipeg and wouldn't move to Morden. The subsidiary was losing money, but Allied's president, Jim Kanter, proved to be a shrewder, smoother and more quietly hard-nosed bargainer than Buhler had encountered before: "Kanter knows what he wants and has the memory of an elephant. He has a way of getting a foot in the door and if there's a little crack left open, he keeps coming back." Milt Hayhurst, a controller whom Buhler brought in as a consultant (and who now manages the Winnipeg plant), recalls that Kanter was always placid while "John always gets up on the ceiling and stomps back and forth during negotiations." Buhler's hole card is his capacity to stand firm: "He has an uncanny ability to put a price on something and not move from it; his first price is always so close to what the deal winds up being." In the case of Allied, his price — and the price he finally paid for it — was $2.5 million, which was about $2 million less than Kanter was demanding.* In early 1985 he also acquired, for more than $250,000, the American company's Canadian distribution network, including warehouses in Moncton, New Brunswick, Pointe Claire, Quebec, St Mary's, Ontario, and Regina, Saskatchewan.

Once the Allied farm-equipment plant became a Farm King subsidiary, Buhler had to cope with the reality of an agricultural market that was in dramatic decline. To prevent any layoffs among the seventy-five employees, he approached the federal government to become the first Manitoba company to participate in Ottawa's Work Sharing Program. The company paid full wages for all days the men were on the job during a shortened work week; the Unemployment Insurance Commission paid 60 percent of regular pay for the remaining days. Buhler also insisted that his managers don coveralls and work half-days in the factory. The job-sharing eventually ended, but given their volatile boss, the executives remained on their toes. "I think John has fired me five times in three-and-a-half years," says Allied's general manager, Milt Hayhurst. "It usually lasts till the next morning. He hasn't fired me once in the past year, so we're making progress."

Allied † became Allied Standard in 1983 when a provincial economic-development officer tipped Buhler off that there was a nice little company in the Winnipeg area, a manufacturer of steel components for grain elevators, that was facing an immediate bank foreclosure. It looked like a good fit for

---

* Buhler says he learned more from the unruffled Kanter than anyone he has ever bargained against, although he also profited from seminars with Herb Cohen, the author of *You Can Negotiate Anything*, who negotiated the release of American hostages in Iran. "But my biggest enlightenment in life came from Wayne Dwyer," who writes books with such titles as *Pull Your Own Strings*. "He taught me not to allow anybody to pressure me; I want people to know I'm there because I *want* to be there."

† The original company still exists under that name in the United States, but acts only as a distributor of the products manufactured by Buhler and others.

Allied. Studying the assets and liabilities of Standard Industries, and deciding that the owner had nothing to sell, he offered him a kiss-off $10,000, which the man reluctantly accepted. The payables totalled $90,000; Buhler gave the creditors 60 cents on the dollar in cash. The largest creditor was the Royal Bank, which was owed more than $200,000. He quickly went to see the bank manager, who was still threatening foreclosure. "I'll give you a cheque right now," Buhler told him. He called his own bank to make sure it would honour the 200-grand payment, signed the cheque, shook hands all around and left. The manager later remarked to his amazed assistant, "You've just shaken the hand of a true entrepreneur."

Buhler also had to pay $240,000 to Royal Trust for Standard's building, a figure that brought the total cost of the deal to about $600,000. Within a year, the combined operations of Allied and Standard were earning a small profit, making agricultural implements and their components and snowblowers. He moved the two companies into a building once owned by International Harvester in the suburb of Transcona. The building's original price was $3.4 million, which dropped to $1.5; Buhler, who'd had his eye on the land for three years, bought it for $1 million. Within a year of acquiring the building and its thirty-nine acres of land, he sold four acres for $400,000. Later, when an American company wanted to buy the five acres the building was on, he struggled with his conscience. He could earn $400,000 clear profit on the deal and still retain twenty-nine acres. The only hitch was that he'd have to shut down his Transcona factory. "I lost a couple of hours' sleep for the first time in my life," he says. "But selling just didn't fit into my long-term plans. And a lot of people would have been put out of work."

His long-term plans were to employ more and more people in the province and he made a gallant run towards that goal in 1983, when he went after the bankrupt White Farm Equipment of Brantford, Ontario. He made his $11.6-million bid on the basis of $2.25-million in secured-loan backing from the Manitoba government, which he had stirred with his talk of bringing a farm industry to what he considered its rightful home. Manitoba's newspapers followed his campaign as if he were a bold knight riding to the princess province's rescue. But the receivers returned his $500,000 deposit on the deal when Borg-Warner Acceptance (Canada) Limited of Toronto, a subsidiary of the American industrial-equipment conglomerate, was successful in its bid of $13 million.

The outcome infuriated Buhler. He continued to vow that some day he'd have White Farm in Manitoba. On the window ledge of his office sat a metal model of a combine painted in White Farm colours, a visual reminder of his goal. It reminded him that he could create another two hundred and fifty jobs in his province. The poor, shy, awkward little boy from Morden who grew up to be a millionaire is determined to have a thousand employees by 1993, with or without White Farm.

Joe Houssian — The Dealmaker

The Lonsdale Quay Market deal that Joe Houssian presented to his regular pool of investors late in 1984 was uncommonly attractive. The land alone was an irreplaceable piece of prime waterfront in the heart of North Vancouver, looking across Burrard Inlet to downtown Vancouver. Next door, major bus routes converge on the terminal for the SeaBuses that ferry sixty thousand commuters and visitors a week between the two cities. Three thousand employees work in adjoining office buildings, which include the headquarters of the provincial government's B.C. Rail and the Insurance Corporation of B.C. Houssian's company, Intrawest Properties, had bought the land for about $3 million from the government's B.C. Development Corporation. The proposed project was exciting to even jaded investors: Lonsdale Quay Market would be a public food market the size of the crowded and profitable Granville Island Market in central Vancouver. It would also have specialty shops, restaurants, and a fifty-seven-room hotel with a night-club, pub and meeting rooms. The project architect is the award-winning designer of the Granville Island development, Norman Hotson, who had incorporated in Lonsdale Quay many of the best features of public markets throughout North America.

But in the depressed British Columbia economy of 1984, the specific nature of a real-estate deal, the essential quality of its smallest financial details, meant everything. The land could be strategically located, the development itself could be fascinating and the architecture remarkable. But if the terms of the deal were not exactly right, if there were uncertainties without safeguards, investors in the know would rather sit on their money than risk it. However, despite the lingering spirit of recessionary pessimism in the province, even the most cautious and gun-shy of them were eager to listen to the conditions of the Lonsdale Quay Market deal, because its creator was the president of Intrawest, Joe Houssian. The Dealmaker.

Houssian was only thirty-five, but he and his partner, Mohammed Faris, had a reputation among experienced investors as successful veteran developers of high-quality residential and commercial properties and ingenious packagers of fail-safe tax shelters. On Vancouver's Howe Street, where insiders traded rumours about them, the partners were legendary for their pipeline to Middle East money. Peter Brown, president of Canarim Investment Corporation of Vancouver and a fellow multi-millionaire, once predicted, "Joe's will be one of the big fortunes made in Western Canada."*

At first glance, Joe Houssian's Lonsdale Quay package sounded terrific. But, Joe, the potential investors wanted to know, how good are the terms? It was show-and-tell time. Show me why I can't lose. Tell me how much I can make. Joe Houssian was confident that the deal was exceptional: three

---

* In the incestuous, small-town waters of Vancouver's financial community, the sharks and great white whales among the money mongers keep bumping into one another on deals. Brown and Houssian have done several. Asked how long he has known Houssian, Brown replies, "Oh, I've forgotten. But he built MURBs for tax-shelter clients and we became a tax-shelter client of his. And he built lots of buildings for us."

officials of Intrawest, two lawyers and two tax specialists had
spent several hundreds of thousands of dollars and nine
months of almost continuous research and development on
the deal. The problem now was that the terms were so complicated and Intrawest had such a hard time compressing the
details into easily understandable English that it took an hour
to explain even the broad outline of the proposal. But for
those investors who had the time and patience to listen (and
many of Intrawest's regulars didn't), there were rewards.

Essentially, Houssian wanted to syndicate the $25-million
project among several investors. Given the financial convolu-
tions of the deal, the most reassuring detail to potential
investors was that Intrawest would be a partner. It wasn't just
building the market and then taking its money and running:
the company would be one of the participants for the long
term, helping to finance the development along with a bank
and fully managing it after construction. The project would
be owned by a series of newly created corporations that could
take advantage of such income-tax provisions as capital-cost-
allowance and interest-expense deductions. The financing
arrangement itself would allow investors sizable personal
deductions. So it was an inviting tax shelter. But Intrawest
would also provide securities to reduce the investors' risk. As
protection, there would be covenants — legal guarantees —
covering cashflow, interest rates and operational costs. Intrawest would, if necessary, provide loans to the project and
would guarantee financing rates. And with all that, the promised return on investment was surprisingly fast: the worst-
case scenario was that investors would get an after-tax
payback on their initial investment within four or five years.

In only eight weeks, excluding the period over Christmas,
fifteen investors — most of them from Vancouver, most of
them participants in other projects with Intrawest — became
members of the syndicate to finance Lonsdale Quay Market.
Construction had already begun and the market was scheduled to open on Valentine's Day, 1986, in time for Expo 86,
the World Exposition happening just across the inlet. Joe
Houssian, the dealmaker, had done it again: he had pleased
the customer.

Because Houssian and Faris abhor personal publicity, whatever low profile they have in the public consciousness centres on the activities of Intrawest, which manages more than one million square feet of rental properties that it has built in British Columbia, Alberta and Washington state, with a total value of more than $100 million. Few people know that Intrawest is also a significant investor in resource companies, and that it has done a $27.7-million deal with Mitel Corporation that gave investors in the Eastern Canadian telecommunications company an amazingly risk-free opportunity to make substantial and immediate profits.

Houssian is minutely more high-profiled than Mo Faris, since he handles Intrawest's millions of dollars of investment in public ventures like Mitel and the resource companies Roxy Petroleum and Asamera Incorporated. Still, even after the Mitel deal was made public, few if any investment analysts outside Vancouver recognized his name. Donald Whatley, who monitored Asamera's successful international petroleum and mining operations for the Toronto-based stockbrokers Alfred Bunting and Company, confessed, "I don't know him at all." And New York telecommunications researcher Francis McInerny of Northern Business Information, who appeared to know everything else about Mitel's finances, said, "Never heard of him."

Houssian is certainly no classic hustler in temperament. Faris — twelve years his senior — is even more serene and soothing a negotiator. Faris has a more patrician profile and a worldliness that prompts people to sit around with him and discuss global affairs. Both men sprinkle words like "moral fibre" and "ethics" throughout their cautious speech like holy water. "I don't mind saying Mo's a very moral, very trustworthy sort of person," Houssian says. "And that's probably indicated by the fact we've had a lot of investors in the Middle East and Europe trust us with their money." One stockbroker has estimated that they have access to a quarter of a billion Middle-Eastern dollars. In fact, while such funds helped get their company going in 1976, Houssian protests, "We don't have the ability to snap our fingers and get $250 million or even $2 million. We have people who have said that with the proper kind of business proposal and the proper kind of analysis, they'll look at a deal." In 1984 Houssian began travelling to London to raise capital in the European money markets. "If we can consolidate a European connection," he says, "there might be some synergy with the Middle-Eastern capital."

Intrawest Properties' earliest promotional brochure bore these words on its frontispiece, from Lebanese poet-philosopher Kahlil Gibran's *The Prophet*:

> *And he alone is great who turns the voice of the wind into a song made sweeter by his own loving. Work is love made visible.*

Both principals of Intrawest are also Lebanese. Houssian was born in Canada of Lebanese parents; Faris, his cousin, was born in Lebanon. The squat, dark-complexioned Houssian has a clown's wig of silvering tight curls, a six-o'clock shadow, and thick lips that only reluctantly turn up in a gap-toothed smile. Recalling their first meeting a decade ago, when Houssian asked him to help Intrawest design its real-estate tax packages, accountant Sandy Sheinin joked: "He's very quiet and contained, but he's a bit of a bulky guy; I didn't know whether or not he was going to kneecap me."

Keeping the customer happy was an important factor in the Houssian household when Joe was growing up. His merchant grandparents had come to Canada in the early 1900s from Lebanon. Joe was born in Brandon, Manitoba, and grew up near the Montana border in the Saskatchewan farming community of Rockglen (population: 500). His father, Hass Houssian, owned the only grocery store in town, a successful Red and White, as well as interest in stores in two other communities. Joe and his sister, a year younger, routinely worked in the store after school. "He always made the customer his number-one priority because that's what made business go round," his son remembers. "I saw a lot of situations where I thought a customer was perhaps being unfair, but my father always gave them the benefit of the doubt."

The Houssians were the only Lebanese family in Rockglen. Vanesa Mischkolz, who worked for Joe's father, says, "Most people liked him; he's a really easy-going guy." As a boy, he was a good student, and his high-school yearbooks reveal a kid active in basketball, hockey and curling. Joe can't recall ever discussing with his father the possibility of his taking over the chain of small stores some day; his father, a typical first-generation immigrant, wanted his son to get a higher education. While he never longed to live in a big city, Joe knew, like most prairie village boys, that he'd leave Rockglen after high school and likely never live there again.

His father's success in business inspired him to leave in 1967 for Saskatoon and the University of Saskatchewan, to earn his bachelor of commerce degree. There were no fireworks during these years: no professor who became a mentor, no critical development other than the growth of an intense interest in marketing. There was, however, a young woman, a sinewy Norwegian-Canadian girl with a full shock of blonde hair. They fell in love and, after Joe took a year off to work for an industrial-financing company in Calgary, he and Joanne Flaw attended the University of British Columbia. There he got his MBA and she her education degree; they married after he graduated.

During his master's year in a general business program, he thrived on a three-month course in decision-making. He learned that successful decisions result not only from the conception and analysis of all possible options, but also from the allocation of enough time to ponder them fully. Researching the Cuban missile crisis of 1962 — when the United States stared down the Soviets and the world felt it was on the brink of nuclear war — he was fascinated with the sophisticated negotiating and deal-making that had occurred behind the scenes. ("The decision-making process that went on," he remembers, "was certainly not the route that the U.S. military would have preferred to go.")

His early interest in marketing had continued; after graduation he actively courted that international marketing giant, Xerox. Refusing to wait for the campus recruiters to come by, he approached the company directly — which hired him to sell a new line of colour copiers from its Vancouver office. His immediate superior was Henry Saltiel, who wryly recalls, "Largely infatuated with our own success, Xerox decided that the only people who could go out and sell copiers were MBAs." Saltiel notes that "There is a certain defensiveness in Joe, a certain sort of protection, a cocoon, that he is very careful not to allow anyone to penetrate unless he is very comfortable."

Joe Houssian was a decent if untypical salesman. John Evans, who became a senior executive in Intrawest (one of three former Xerox employees Houssian has hired), worked with him: "Joe wasn't the sort who was able to generate a sales quota on a month-to-month basis. He saw some major opportunities with a couple of companies and would spend three months going after them" — a foretaste of his technique with his own company.

But Houssian's skills went beyond selling; he was soon made a product manager and then a sales manager, preparing marketing programs for the colour copiers. Saltiel, then branch sales manager, remembers sitting in his office with Joe "and in all of our conversations, I would usually wind up feeling that he really understood what *I* wanted to say to *him*. And *I* was the one who was supposed to be listening to the alternatives." The Xerox that Joe Houssian worked for was a corporate clone of himself: an intelligent, aggressive organization, which demanded analysis and discipline of its people — "a company that set very high moral and professional standards," he recalls. "And I suppose if you get exposed to those sorts of things, you carry them with you." Yet after three years with Xerox, the twenty-seven-year-old Houssian was ready to leave. Staying meant a climb up the corporate ladder that would require moving him and his family to the big cities of the East. He was still deciding whether he'd take that route when his cousin Mo Faris invited Houssian to join him in an entrepreneurial venture.

Faris, an engineer with a degree from McGill and his own company, had recently returned to Canada from work in the

Persian Gulf. Now he was looking for something different to do. The partners decided to take a different approach to real estate, a field that had just come through a couple of bad years, a field in which they were virgins. Faris had some of his own money and some from his contacts in the Middle East. "Mo's a guy you can trust with your life," Houssian says, "and when he came back to Canada again, he had some contacts who offered to provide financial backing for a new venture. It was very nebulous. Even when we opened the doors of Intrawest, there was nothing firm and concrete. It was more a case of 'You find something and we perhaps will fund it.' " With not much more than $100,000, Intrawest was born in 1976.

For the first year, the partners typed their own letters and answered their own phone. But they had picked their business wisely: real estate neither demanded millions of dollars nor had any barriers to entry. ("Everybody thinks they're an expert because everybody's bought a home," says Houssian.) The field had a universality to it with which money men in the Middle East and Europe could identify; it was Middle-Eastern funding that helped float Intrawest during its first two years. It took Houssian and Faris nine months of talking to others in the industry and studying the market before they targeted what they considered the most lucrative niche. Once they did, they soon had three projects on the go simultaneously, multi-family buildings in West Vancouver, Burnaby and Vancouver's apartment-packed West End; the first to be finished was a $4-million townhouse development in Burnaby. All were financed through the newly created tax shelters called MURBs (Ottawa's Multiple Unit Residential Building incentive) and ARPs (the federal-provincial Assisted Rental Program), which the partners had spotted as their likeliest opportunity. With these shelters, they could fashion a deal that would be as effective for their investors as it was profitable for themselves. They came up with their own twist, however. Most developers were syndicating their projects in small units among many investors. Accountant Sandy Sheinin explains the Intrawest style: "Joe came from a sales background and he said, 'Why the hell should I talk to a hundred people to sell a project? Why don't I just find one or two players to pick up the whole thing?' "

Not knowing anyone in the business in Vancouver, Houssian and Faris took an artfully simple approach to selling their projects. They visited national chartered-accountancy firms and such major real-estate establishments as the Vancouver-based Macaulay Nicolls Maitland and Company to ask if any of their clients would be interested in a real-estate deal that Intrawest was assembling. Macaulay Nicolls became one of their earliest and strongest supporters.

Not having the tax-shelter expertise, the partners decided to buy it. Because Daon Development was the most prominent of West-Coast companies taking advantage of these shelter schemes, they went after some of the same consultants Daon was using — among them Sheinin and lawyer Mitch Groper of Shrum, Liddle and Hebenton, which became Houssian's law firm. Intrawest developed medium- to high-quality multi-family housing, in one case using the stylish designs of big-name Vancouver architect Bruno Freschi. And it marketed its properties with panache, picking up a couple of graphics awards for their brochures. So far, the company has built about two thousand units and continues to manage all but two hundred of them for clients, who include three major chartered-accountancy firms. Typical of its residential developments are Pendrell 1,500, a $6.2-million high-rise encompassing a block of downtown Vancouver; One Arbour-lane, $12-million worth of luxury townhouses — 124 in all — with recreational facilities in Burnaby's Buckingham Heights; and Pacific Horizons, a $3.4-million apartment complex on Vancouver's English Bay. "They're all pretty successful," says Houssian, with typical understatement. Sandy Sheinin agrees, "Because the people who invested by and large have done very well, the position today is that people really go to Joe and ask him what he has, as opposed to him going out and beating the bushes."

As Houssian was learning, the specifics of the deal were everything. "To us," he says now, "building a nice piece of real estate isn't enough. It has to make some business sense. What's the tax treatment? What's the financing treatment? What are the long-term investment horizons? How do you make one plus one add up to three? You also have to look at what makes up a good project. The real estate is obviously one, the location, and a lot of our developers here have a marketing orientation; they're thinking as a consumer would think. And when we sell a project to an investor, we've sold him more than a piece of real estate; we manage and market it for him."

Their progress was not completely unrestrained. They expanded to Seattle in 1980, when they thought the real-estate market had bottomed out there. It hadn't, and wouldn't start climbing out of its pit for two years — which left Intrawest with some commercial and residential property sitting idle until they sold it. (In 1985, the Seattle market looked more attractive than Western Canada did and the company was seriously considering commercial projects there.) Late in 1983, Intrawest experimented with mass-marketing of a public-syndication MURB: Pacific House, a $14-million, 12-storey condominium in suburban Coquitlam, offering units at $10,000. All of the units sold, to more than one hundred investors, but Houssian admits, "It was a bloody tough job." They've also misjudged the complexity of some projects. When they attempted to develop a pier property on the downtown Vancouver waterfront, they didn't bargain for the political games that would be played by government; they wasted much of a year concluding a deal with Hilton International and working with architects on the design of a hotel — only to have the provincial government decide to shelve the development. The federal government took over the project as Canada Place, the Canadian Pavilion at Expo 86, which will later become the Vancouver Trade and Convention Centre. Intrawest re-bid, but was unsuccessful. In another setback, as the residential market softened in Vancouver in recent years, the company stopped building a showcase project called Monte Bre on West Vancouver's exclusive Caulfield Plateau. After selling twenty luxury homes designed by Canada's best-known architect, Arthur Erickson, it decided to sell off the remaining fifty lots to other builders.

Intrawest has now re-focused its energies on commercial development. It financed its own construction of a $25-million, 150,000-square-foot shopping centre with a nautical theme overlooking Calgary's Glenmore Reservoir, which opened in 1985; a financial institution has already expressed interest in buying it. In Edmonton, Intrawest and an international joint-venture partner were building a $24-million, 22-storey office tower near Legislature Park. Houssian and Faris were also looking for a manufacturing plant to acquire.

The two men hold equal shares, yet now operate different sides of their business. Since about 1982, Mo Faris has run Intrawest's real-estate operations, Houssian the outside investments. Houssian also acts as the corporate spokesman, which gives him the unwelcome attention he tries to avoid. For the most part, he manages to keep his personal life extremely private. He lives with his wife and three children in a West Vancouver mansion, gutted and refurbished in contemporary fashion, with the standard pool, outdoor Jacuzzi, sauna and tennis court. There's a plush ski place at Whistler. And a Mercedes, a Volvo for wife Joanne and a Porsche 930 for him. The Houssians travel — to New York and Paris, for example, and at Christmas to Hawaii, where they might take a group of friends and both sets of parents to spend a month with the grandchildren in Maui. But Joe Houssian doesn't go to night-clubs or play expensive practical jokes like his West-Coast peers. He's a moderate drinker, a non-smoker. He golfs infrequently (and badly). He doesn't charter a plane to take a ratpack of pals to Vegas; he'd rather head down to Seattle with his brother-in-law to catch the Dallas Cowboys.

Houssian became involved in the world of public corporations in 1982. Seeking a tax shelter for Intrawest this time, he bought $9.6-million of flow-through shares in Roxy Petroleum, shares that were targeted to finance East-Coast oil exploration.* With flow-through shares, the investment

* Roxy, which is 53 percent owned by Hudson's Bay Company of Winnipeg, has since had success with its oil wells in Alberta's active Peace River Arch area and has substantially increased its stake in natural-gas exploration.

money goes into a trust account for specific exploration work; as the funds are used, the investor gets ordinary common shares and can then deduct the cash expended. Intrawest wound up with about 1.5 million common shares, making it the third-largest shareholder after Hudson's Bay and Toronto-Dominion Bank. Its investment qualified for both a government incentive grant and a good tax deduction that Intrawest needed. The company also bought three million shares of Asamera Inc. of Calgary, a medium-sized resource company that explores for, produces and refines oil and natural gas, and mines gold and silver around the world. But Asamera was undervalued on the stock market despite strong new management. Houssian and Faris, believing the stock was worth triple its current trading price, became the second-largest shareholder after a consortium called Realwest Energy Corporation (which includes pals like Peter Brown). Since then, Asamera has made significant finds: gold in Washington state, oil in Indonesia. With the stock splitting three-for-one, Intrawest has made $24 million on the trade.

Early in 1983, Houssian was attracted by the 160 percent tax writeoffs Ottawa was offering investors in research and development in high-technology industries. He first identified Mitel Corp. as one of the stars in the firmament of North American telecommunications. A sideways approach through lawyers assured him that Mitel might be interested in a deal. *Might* be? As New York telecommunications consultant Francis McInerney put it, "The company is drinking cash the way people drink coffee in the morning." And Mitel had just seen a large research and development deal die on them. *

* In 1982 Mitel had sales of $204 million. With a combination of astute marketing and excellent products, such as compact microprocessor-controlled switching devices for telephone systems, they were competing handily with the giants in the American telecommunications market. But by that year there were also signs that development in this key market was slowing down and Mitel's share of the market had reached a plateau. What's more, the company was finding it more difficult to raise funding. Cash flow had been a continual problem. In recent years Mitel had financed little more than a quarter of its expansion internally, finding most of its money on the stock market through its high-priced shares. When that source began shrivelling during recessionary times, the company reluctantly had to approach the

In the spring of 1983, Don Gibbs, Mitel's executive vice-president of finance, didn't know who the hell Joe Houssian was. "We had to do considerable checking to validate his credentials. But the references came back that he follows through on his deals."

Joe Houssian, meanwhile, was putting together a package that would prove irresistible to investors who were seeking hundreds of thousands of dollars of tax shelter. Each unit of the deal was worth $630,000. For that, the investor could take a $1-million deduction on his tax return and get $500,000 worth of tax savings. So the net cost would be $130,000. But for his investment, Mitel would give him $540,000 in preference shares. These would bear a 6 percent coupon, furnishing about $33,000 a year in dividends — a nice return.

But Houssian was insisting on other nice touches — one demand was that, whatever happened to Mitel, the banks would guarantee that there would be enough money to buy back at least 60 percent of an investor's preference shares. That was the guaranteed profit. If an investor took his write-offs, converted his preference stock to common immediately and paid tax on the common, he would make an instant profit of $136,000 — after taxes — simply for signing his name to the deal.

The formula, originally designed by Mitel and Burns, Fry for the earlier research and development deal that fell through, included the current discount rate, present values, cost-of-living increases and the Consumer Price Index — among other variables. "We had a thousand minefields to walk through," said Houssian. The Mitel deal took six months and several hundreds of thousands of Intrawest's dollars in research; the uncounted man-years of assorted accountants and tax lawyers in Vancouver and of investment and telecommunications consultants in Toronto and New York; and a computer to prepare a complex formula of about five hundred

banks for $200 million. Now, with all those funds already absorbed, and the corporation's life dependant on fast growth and fresh markets, Mitel was out on the street again, seeking funding from investors.

pages to present to Revenue Canada — which eventually gritted its teeth and granted it a favourable tax ruling.

Where the true genius of Joe Houssian surfaced was in the astonishing guarantee that he had built into the deal for himself and his fellow investors. Under the generous terms of the agreement, hard-pressed Mitel was obligated to buy back their preferred shares within five years. The guarantee addressed their concern — potentially the only godawful glitch in the system — that Mitel might not still be around then. Their concern was legitimate. The corporation was the only major independent left in the shark-ridden waters of the North American telephone market. It was so vulnerable, analysts were warning, that it could be killed off, and both Mitel and the Canadian banks backing the corporation were taking a gamble with enormous risks.

But Houssian and his colleagues were not. They had an irrevocable letter of credit from the syndicate of five banks, led by the Royal, that guaranteed to buy back 60 percent of their shares even if Mitel went bankrupt. Looking at the total $27.7-million deal from the investors' point of view, the otherwise pessimistic New York consultant Francis McInerney said admiringly, "If their tax positions were right, and their accountants know what they're doing, and if this guarantee is solid, then the investors are laughing."

Before the deal went through, though, there were some harrowing weeks. Halfway through negotiations, IBM Corp. announced that, despite earlier plans, it would not be marrying its computers to Mitel's sophisticated new SX-2000 telephone switching system; instead, it bought into a Mitel competitor, California's ROLM Corp. "It scared the hell out of us," Houssian recalls. "We jumped on a plane and headed back east and started figuring out what was behind IBM's move. Was it because ROLM was that much better, or was there something negative about Mitel we didn't know about? We effectively started doing our work all over again to make sure we didn't miss anything."

He, meanwhile, was scaring the hell out of Don Gibbs, who said: "He's a very shrewd negotiator. He knows his detail and he's obviously done a lot of negotiating and plays all the psychological games." One of Houssian's games was to threaten, "We're going to walk away from the deal if we don't get what we want," then insist that Gibbs call him at home at a precise time — and not be there when a worried Gibbs called. (Houssian insists he simply doesn't use those tactics.)

Obviously, the detail that stuck most painfully in Mitel's craw was Houssian's demand for a bank guarantee in the form of a letter of credit. "We feel that we're a very credible company and going to be around for a very long time," said Don Gibbs, "and it kinda hurt [for Houssian] to question that fact and want absolute security for the money."

But it was that absolute security that so attracted investors. When Joe Houssian had approved the finishing touches to the first $20-million deal by the fall of 1983, it took much less than a week — Sandy Sheinin says only a morning — to sell every unit to fifteen investors. "I had clients who were disappointed that they couldn't get more," said Randy Zien, an experienced Vancouver tax lawyer who brought six of his wealthy clients into it. He and his excited colleagues at Ladner Downs and their learned friends at Shrum Liddle tried — too late — to form a syndicate to buy a piece of it. Peter Brown took about $4.5 million of the action. And Houssian himself, through Intrawest, invested $4.3 million and then another $7.7 million in a second agreement featuring most of the original participants.

Only one investor was unhappy enough to vow he'd never do a deal with Houssian again. He accused Houssian of not picking up about $10,000 worth of his share of expenses the dealmaker supposedly promised to handle up to the day the deal closed. Houssian claimed that this interpretation was a misunderstanding on the part of only two of the investors (and the one who complained was recently considering doing another deal with Houssian). Sandy Sheinin says that the issue occasioned one of only a few times he has seen Houssian raise his voice: "Some people threatened to pull out of the deal, and Joe said, 'If you're hung up about nickels and dimes, pull out!' " They didn't.

The sensitive Houssian would worry afterwards about all the publicity over the Mitel deal: "I don't want the thing to come across looking like Mitel gave the ship away, because that would be embarrassing." In fact, Don Gibbs said that Mitel didn't walk away empty-handed. He even suggested that he'd like to do another deal with Joe Houssian.

Gibbs never had the chance; he left Mitel in mid-1984 for "personal reasons," not long after the company reported a loss of $32.4 million, the first in its decade-long history. This was not long after he had been quoted as saying: "I'd like to go at Joe again because it's enjoyable negotiating against him. Like I said, he's very, very good."

It was praise that Joe Houssian's father, the popular storekeeper in small-town Saskatchewan, would have appreciated. The dealmaker had kept the customer happy.

Jack Singer — The Gambler

The March 1981 headline in *Variety*, the Bible of show business, read, "Coppola Rescue Spotlights Calgary's Megabuck Clan." The story began: "Thanks to an $8-million investment by Canadian businessman Jack Singer, Francis Coppola will finish *One From The Heart*. . . ." The article described Singer as an oil and real-estate tycoon, "the Canadian Howard Hughes." *Variety* pointed out that he was previously unknown within the film community.

And, until then, Singer was also virtually unknown outside his home town of Calgary. Soon the stories began to circulate throughout North America and even England, where *The Economist* called him "one of the largest real-estate developers in the five western Canadian provinces" (apparently annexing Ontario to the West). Inevitably the myths began to build too, becoming enshrined between the covers of Peter C. Newman's *The Acquisitors*. Newman mentions Singer and repeats the much-told tale that he had "invested $8 million with Francis Ford Coppola."

In fact, Jack Singer never lent Coppola more than $3

million. And the money was no high-risk investment in a new
movie or in the director himself, no high-rolling gamble on
creativity. It was simply a real-estate deal, a loan that Singer
had safely secured with a mortgage on the property where
Coppola had established Zoetrope — the old Hollywood
General Studios where Howard Hughes had once made
movies. The multitude of articles that appeared at the time of
Singer's involvement with Coppola never mentioned that the
Calgary businessman had a mortgage on the place and Singer
did nothing to correct that misapprehension — preferring to
revel in his image as a "white knight" rather than merely an
astute businessman. As Zoetrope publicist Max Bercutt said at
the time: "Singer's like all big men with a lot of money. They
don't shoot craps — not with *their* money. He hasn't gambled
one nickel; he's got the real estate."

But Singer *is* a gambler. In his sixty-six years he has also
been a boxer, a fight promoter and a racehorse owner.
Primarily, however, he's a developer for whom gambling has
paid rather well — his net worth is at least $500 million.
Together with his seventy-five-year-old brother, Hyman, Jack
Singer owns real estate throughout Canada and the United
States. Yet he is better known for a handful of strange
development schemes and his love-hate affair with
Hollywood than he is for his remarkable accumulation of
real-estate wealth. Singer masks his personal life and financial
career with the same kind of confusing stories that surfaced
with his début in Hollywood. In late 1984, for instance, the
troubled Bank of British Columbia, on the brink of losing its
charter, sold $110 million worth of its non-performing real-
estate loans — secured with hotels, shopping centres and
undeveloped land — for a bargain-basement $65 million. For
weeks, nobody knew who was behind the mysterious Ormskirk Investments Limited, the purchaser of the loans. It was
only unrelenting media pressure that forced the bank to admit
that Ormskirk's owners were Singer and his California-based
brother, Hymie. Their shares were held in trust by two company directors, a Calgary lawyer and his secretary. It was also
learned, to the astonishment of financial observers, that the

bank had loaned the Singers the $65 million to buy a piece of its own assets.

Jack Singer's major holding is United Management, of which he's chairman. He will pass on this mini-empire to Allan and Stephen, two sons from his forty-year marriage to Shirley, one of the Cohen family that owns the Western chain of Army and Navy department stores. (Allan Singer is now president of United Management, Stephen vice-president.)* United, through myriad smaller companies, owns hotels, apartment and office buildings and shopping centres throughout Western Canada. American holdings under the Singer control include a 355-acre residential subdivision in Tucson, Arizona, and 1,130 acres of expensive Bel Air, California, real estate that Jack Singer owns jointly with Hymie, his sister Rose and several other partners. Ashmont Developments Corporation is also a Singer company and it handles such Texas investments as the 2,500 acres bought in 1978 for $33 million — a purchase that was funneled through a Netherland Antilles offshore corporation. ("I would prefer if you didn't include that," says Bob Gibson, president of one of Singer's holding companies. "I don't like the term 'offshore corporation.' ") Commenting on that acquisition, *The Boston Globe* reported that Singer was "the builder of a $2-billion city outside Dallas." Actually, his company has so far developed only a handful of its residential lots in Plano, a Dallas suburb — hardly a city. Nonetheless, the Singer family was recently ranked fourth in the local *D Magazine*'s list of the top ten foreign landowners in Dallas.

United Management is a private company and its precise worth has been deliberately shrouded in secrecy, although Singer himself says its real-estate assets total $500 million. "He doesn't know what the figures are," says Bob Gibson. "I don't think he's very up to date. . . . Jack doesn't keep particularly current with what he's worth. I guess feeling that he's worth half a billion is sufficient to keep him comfortable."

* In 1982, Allan and Stephen donated $1.5 million to the city of Calgary on the condition that the Calgary Centre for Performing Arts Concert Hall bear the name Jack Singer Music Centre.

But Jack Singer was not always comfortable. He was born in 1919 into a family of classically hard-working Jewish immigrants. Abraham Singer and his wife, Bella, had emigrated from Poland in 1907. His father took a traditional route, becoming a peddler, hawking junk and old clothing door to door. Abraham bought a horse and cart in Toronto and travelled across Western Canada until settling in Calgary in 1910. During those first few years, the Singers' instinctive good sense about real estate manifested itself first in Bella. She opened a boarding-house in a rented building and within a few years owned three rooming houses. It was a harbinger of what was to follow in her sons. While Abraham stayed resolutely in the background, Bella became a local celebrity, almost a saint. Known to everyone as Meema Singer, Bella over the years sent Polish relatives steamship tickets to move to Canada, on the understanding that as they prospered they would bring others out of Poland. In 1959 *Time* christened her "the woman who cared" and quoted Jack: "It is at least three hundred she brought, and if you count their sons and daughters and the grandchildren, it is a thousand people who owe their lives to Mamma. Not one of the family that had to be left in Europe is alive today. They were killed or died." *

Abraham and Bella had four children. The oldest son, Hymie, left for Vancouver on a cattle car in 1931 at the age of twenty-one and quickly became an entrepreneur in the fickle entertainment business. He opened the Palomar Supper Club, billed as having the world's largest ballroom. Hymie served in the RCAF during the Second World War and on his return to Vancouver in 1946 opened the State Theatre, a burlesque house. In the mid-fifties Hymie finally made his base in California, adding to his fortune by buying packing houses

---

* In 1964, Jack and Hymie got into a nasty skirmish with Calgary's City Council when they tried to donate the site of Abraham Singer's original house to the city on the condition that it be named the Abraham Singer Park. When council hesitated — one alderman went so far as to suggest "that the lot was being offered free because it was unsaleable, in order to avoid taxes" — Hymie angrily announced that they would create the park anyway and put up a "plaque with the names of the aldermen who refused the gift."

and real estate. Like Jack, Hymie has had a fling with Holly-wood. In 1980, at the age of seventy, he returned to Calgary to produce his own low-budget movie, *Dante's Inferno*, described as a "zany comic satire" by its director, who had previously created the soft-core porn feature, *Dracula Sucks*. Hymie's *Inferno* was never released and altogether it lost bet-ween $1.5 and $2 million. * Although operating in different countries, Hymie and Jack invariably backstop each other's deals.

The two Singer daughters are Diane, seventy-one, who is married to Vancouver developer Jack Aceman, and Rose, divorced and living alone in the ninety-two-room Pullman House in the exclusive Hillsborough district of San Francisco. The house, built in 1900, is one of the largest private resi-dences in North America. Lucius Beebe, chronicler of America's rich, in his 1966 book *The Big Spenders* described the mansion as "an enormous country estate beyond her means to support." But not beyond the means of Jack Singer, who according to Diane Aceman actually owns the house.

Jack Singer, who now lives in the monied Mount Royal sec-tion of Calgary and has a place in Palm Springs, enjoys recall-ing his boyhood days in the twenties and thirties when he had to get up at three-thirty in the morning to deliver newspapers. "I swore some day I'd never have [to use] an alarm clock — and I don't. Back then, I'd have to pick up *The Albertan*, then run to school, then to Hebrew school, then to the Y for boxing, then to collect the rents. By this time my parents had two rooming houses. I remember one time when I'm, like, eleven, and this white hooker and this black guy are in bed and I says, 'Give me the 75 cents,' and she says, 'Can't you wait?' "

Inevitably, given his compact size, his Jewishness in an Anglo-Saxon community, and his hustling parents, Singer

* Another of Hymie's notable expenditures was his 1977 purchase, for $70,000, of the 391-foot luxury yacht the *SS Catalina* — because his wife had been nagging him to buy something larger than their 32-footer. At the time, Hymie announced that the *Catalina* — which had been the famed Great White Steamship that made the ferry run between Catalina Island and Long Beach — would be turned into a co-ed nudist colony.

was a competitor, a scrapper. Sports were one obvious route to success. He pitched for a local Jewish baseball team and, although a childhood bout of scarlet fever left him with perforated eardrums, he learned to box at the YMCA and became a good lightweight. Exactly how good is difficult to determine — Singer's boxing career is as murky as his financial involvement with Francis Ford Coppola. *The New York Times* said he was "once amateur lightweight boxing champion of Canada"; *Alberta Report* described him as "a former Canadian lightweight boxing champion"; and *The Boston Globe* remarked that he "could have been lightweight champion boxer of Canada." A Calgary boxing historian wasn't sure if Singer had ever won a title, which prompted Singer to acknowledge: "There are no records. Just say I was a boxer." A boxer, whose nose was broken enough to warrant later reconstruction. *

In 1937 at the age of seventeen, Jack Singer made his first real-estate deal. His partner was Abraham Belzberg — a relative brought to Canada by one of Bella Singer's steamship tickets — and they purchased the Foothills Building in Calgary with $25,000 of borrowed money as down payment. "We were partners for over thirty-five years," Singer says. †
(Belzberg's three sons have since built the Vancouver-based

* Even when he retired as an athlete, sports continued to preoccupy him. During the Second World War (which he sat out because of his ear problems), Singer promoted matches in Calgary and backed a couple of fighters, one of them a Canadian heavyweight champ. ("I can't remember his name," he said, "but he could *kill* this building.") Later he financed racehorses, among them Tyhawk, a world record-holder in the United States and a loser when Singer brought him to the shorter racetrack in Calgary more than two decades ago. Doug Abraham, *The Calgary Herald's* racing writer, was just a fan then: "Tyhawk was so fast he couldn't make the tight turns at all. I bet my last dollar on him."

† Abe Belzberg died in 1980 and Singer never developed the same closeness to Abe's sons — Sam, Billy and Hymie — even though they held about half the shares of United Management through their development company, Western Realty Projects Ltd. In 1969 the Belzberg brothers went public with Western Realty and four years later the British-based Capital & Counties Property Company bought it and developed it into Abbey Glen Property Corporation. The Belzberg boys were now out of the picture, so in 1976 Jack Singer acquired Abbey Glen's shares of United Management and full control of his company.

First City Financial Corporation into a multi-billion-dollar financial-services Goliath.)

Between 1946 and 1961 Jack, with Hymie usually acting as the front man and public spokesman, bought and sold apartment buildings, hotels, night-clubs and raw land in Calgary, Winnipeg and Vancouver. They were so successful that by 1961, they had a net worth of $20 million. When pressed for details on his early business deals, Singer is alternately vague and coy. Just when he seems on the verge of candour, he retreats to generalities and jokes — refusing to deal in specifics, first exaggerating then understating. He makes a big deal out of being broke in the late sixties. "I was overextended. I signed a note for someone and they called the note in. There was no money and I was in trouble. And when you're in trouble, there's nobody to talk to." He even had friends convinced of his dire straits. "He was bust out and starving," says Danny Baceda, a failed Vancouver night-club owner. "He knows what it's like to be there." In fact, Singer was only cash-poor — all he had to do was sell something to bail himself out.

Through it all, the Singer brothers, especially Jack, have earned a reputation as visionary developers — a reputation that arises from outlandish projects they've proposed and abandoned, or been forced to abandon, not from the hundreds of buildings they've actually constructed. In 1957 Hymie suggested that a subway tunnel, complete with bomb shelters, be dug to join Los Angeles and New York. Then in 1958 he proposed that the British Columbia government give him a ninety-nine-year lease on 1,700 sacrosanct acres of the University of British Columbia's Endowment Lands so that he could build a $3-billion city housing two hundred thousand families. In 1961 Jack and Hymie spent $40,000 developing plans for a $500-million-dollar luxury city on the North Bergen waterfront area of New Jersey, thirty minutes' commuting distance from Manhattan. The city was to house thirty thousand and feature marinas, a monorail transportation system, theatres and hotels. It was to be "a Venice of America," Hymie told the press. In 1971 the Singers announced a 190-storey hotel-retail-office building that would tower fifty floors above the Empire State Building and contain 6,500 suites and fifty international restaurants. In 1973 Jack Singer announced that he wanted to build a multi-billion-dollar diversified complex on a two-mile-long fireproof platform that would straddle Vancouver's False Creek and contain high-rise apartments and hotels. And in 1977 the Singer brothers offered to put a glass roof — at the cost of $1 million a block — over six blocks of downtown Calgary, an area where they owned extensive office and storefront space.

Jack Singer has had his share of losers, but they are even harder to track down than his winners. In 1981 he poured millions into Cornwall Petroleum and Resources of Vancouver, a junior oil and gas company with unexplored properties in the United States. Cornwall was just one of hundreds of hopeful similar companies and many questioned Singer's investment. "Who would put up that kind of money for an unknown?" wondered Vancouver financial reporter George Cross, who publishes the *George Cross Newsletter*. "The wells are not proven by any stretch of the imagination." Cornwall was a long shot, especially considering that the company's chairman was Harry C. Moll, a former West-Coast night-club operator who went bankrupt in 1976 and who had no known previous connection to or experience in the oil industry. Before Cornwall, he was peddling shares in a company that made plastic tire chains. Singer sold his Cornwall shares in 1984 and took what insiders estimate as an $8- to $10-million bath. "He gives me my youth," Singer says of Moll. (Maybe so, but a face-lift would have been much cheaper.)

Singer's involvement in the overheated world of movies satisfies the same need. The hype of Hollywood and its obsession with youth and glamour are attractive to aging businessmen. His fling with film didn't begin with *One From The Heart* and his track record has not been impressive. He's reticent about discussing the 1980 purchase of a small Los Angeles film company, which he renamed Atlas Warner/First International Pictures. "He doesn't like to talk about it because it didn't make any money," reveals one of his L.A. employees. Singer dismisses the experience, "I didn't know anything about the film business." He dumped $300,000 into *Surfacing*, the Canadian film of Margaret Atwood's novel, a movie that the critics denigrated. Although it was widely reported that Singer was planning a picture called *Gretta* starring rock star Deborah Harry and "has two other pictures in the can," Singer later admitted that the *Gretta* deal had fallen through and he had no pictures either completed or in production.

So Jack Singer's Hollywood connection remained his $3-million mortgaged loan to Zoetrope Studios. The way he tells the story, a Los Angeles real-estate agent he had met in Palm Springs knew Coppola's art director and invited Singer to take a tour of Zoetrope in early 1981. The art director introduced him to Coppola. "I had seen on television that he was in trouble." Publicist Max Bercutt tells a different story: "Singer called here out of the clear blue. I feel responsible for this. I was the guy that followed through and brought him to [Zoetrope's president]. We did not want to put up any more real estate, but he came at a crucial time." Making *One From The Heart* had almost thrown Zoetrope into bankruptcy when $8 million in tax-shelter money was withdrawn just before the musical went into production. Jack Singer's $3 million certainly helped, but much more was needed and Singer had announced widely that he'd be investing another $5 million.

Throughout 1981, Singer was like a kid playing dress-up with his mother's paste jewellery and evening clothes. He parked his silver Rolls next to musical director Gene Kelly's spot on the palm-fringed Zoetrope lot, sat in the three-room bungalow office that once belonged to Desi Arnaz, and grandly told visiting journalists: "I'm going to put Hollywood back together the way it used to be and then I'm going to leave them to kill themselves. I earned this seat; I earned this position." Stencilled on the canvas back of a folding chair in his office was "Jack Singer Producer."

At least he looked the part. He would smoke a cigar, gesturing lazily, hands adorned with large pinky rings. The requisite dark glasses were always present, as were the designer jeans, cowboy boots and the sweater cut to expose two gold chains on a grey-haired chest burnished by the Palm Springs sun.

The Hollywood Jack Singer could have been supplied by Central Casting. He even sounded like a typical L.A. huckster as he placed telephone bets with bookies through his sidekick, Harry Moll.

"Do you want to bet on the basketball?" Moll would ask.

"Give me Philadelphia," Singer would say. "Six thousand."

One afternoon when an attractive woman in her thirties walked by outside, Singer called out, "Hey, get that broad!"

Bewildered by the cries of encouragement from the old man in the window, the woman entered his office.

"Are you an actress?" Moll asked her.

"She's a book-keeper," Singer said.

"Actually," the woman said, "I'm a literary agent." And she walked out.

On another afternoon a slim-legged, 25-year-old actress, her hair in long ringlets, poured Almaden Mountain White Chablis for him as Singer wheedled to a producer on her behalf. "Bob, this lady who spoke to you deserves a shot. She's so straight and nice. Do me one favour in the world. . . ." On the phone again, this time to Joanna Carson, Johnny's ex: "I'm going to the Polo Lounge . . . I have a private number. Just a minute. It's so private I don't remember it. You keep well."

Then he and Moll headed for the Beverly Hills Hotel with their friend, Danny Baceda. Kid Flash, as the greying Baceda was once dubbed, was now living in Los Angeles after two of his Vancouver night-clubs had gone belly up and he'd failed miserably in his off-the-wall campaign to become mayor of Vancouver. As they left the office, Singer confided: "You know what I like about me? I have feeling." At the hotel's Polo Lounge, where the waiters wear white coats and bow ties and where Harry Moll gave the maître d' a $100 bill for a better table, Singer exposed that feeling to a young woman in a red dress and a sun visor: "I'm going to win the Academy Award." By early evening Singer was looking his age as Moll drove the Rolls Royce to the trendy Club Barrington with the parking brake on. There, over potato soup, Singer performed his producer monologue for a French starlet and admired the legs on a woman in a white dress at the next table. Again, he mentioned the Oscar that he personally would win for *One From The Heart.*

Zoetrope publicist Max Bercutt, hearing later about Jack Singer's braggadocio, would wince. For weeks, Singer had been milking his strictly financial link with Coppola, granting interviews to curious reporters. "I was the guy who came out of nowhere and took a shot in the dark," he told *The New York Times.* A Boston *Globe* reporter wrote: "The story is the rage of Hollywood. . . . Singer is the new mystery man of the film industry." Bercutt wondered aloud when the mystery man was coming up with that further $5 million he'd promised Francis Ford Coppola to finish *One From The Heart.* Singer had been telling anybody who would listen how he could put his hands on the money in five minutes. "I could get it with one call. I don't want to unless I do it in a different way. I've done the crisis part. I got the picture done."

"*We're* meeting the payroll now," Max Bercutt responded. "No thanks to him."

"I just want to sit and talk with them again," Singer said. But Coppola and Zoetrope's president weren't talking to him until he came up with the extra money. "I just want to change a few things. I saved this fucking studio." From time to time Singer would get on the phone and try to reach Coppola. "I want to tell these guys straight out: this would be a parking lot without me."

But Max Bercutt did not believe that Jack Singer was sincere. "The fact that he's still got $5 million waiting I think is a crock of shit," he said at the time. "I think he reneged on that a long time ago. As far as the $3 million [mortgaged loans] is concerned, I think he said something to the effect of 'I'll leave it in providing I get credit on the picture.' Well, if he still wants to get credit on the picture, he makes an investment — he shoots craps. In other words, if he wants to stay in on the basis of being a part of the picture, he can't do it without putting that $3 million into a different fund. He has to take it out of the security loan and put it into an investment loan."

Jack Singer never did.

The following January, 1982, *One From The Heart* opened

in New York with Francis Ford Coppola as director and Nastassia Kinski, Frederic Forrest, Lainie Kazan and Terri Garr as stars. Jack Singer was not on the credit list. At the opening-night press conference, Coppola confessed that if the film failed, he could lose his studio. Looking at the assembled critics, he said, "I really felt good when I was watching the film. And then I came in here. . . ." When asked about the financial contributions of the businessman from Canada, Coppola said bitterly that Singer had put in a "heavily colla-terized" $3-million loan. He added, "There was never any other Canadian money; he just kept putting his name in the paper." On top of it all, the critics were heartless about *One From The Heart*, and the movie that (including interest charges) cost $30 million to make has done little more than a paltry $1 million in business around the world.

Zoetrope was on the ropes. Coppola had to offer the 8.6 acres of studio property for sale for $20 million in 1982. But not one of the proposals to purchase was acceptable. Security Pacific National Bank then gave Coppola an $8.16-million loan. In October that year, when the studio failed to meet about $7 million in payments on its loans, Security Pacific foreclosed on the mortgage. The following July, the bank and other creditors forced Zoetrope's subsidiary, Hollywood General Studios, into involuntary bankruptcy. Two months later, an independent film producer and a mortgage broker agreed to purchase Zoetrope for $16.6 million. Suddenly, from out of the wings where he had been patiently waiting, popped Jack Singer. "No sale can be consummated until I give the okay," he announced as a creditor. "I'm not agreeing to the sale. Whatever they sign doesn't mean a thing." It didn't matter much in any case, because the prospective buyers were unable to secure financing to back their offer and did not pay the $175,000 required to extend their option.

Singer had his own scenario all along. Waiting for the inevitable bankruptcy auction, which occurred in the spring of 1984, he bought Hollywood General for $12.3 million cash. "The only thing I'm really interested in now is the studio," he said. He rented the soundstages and editing rooms to film-makers. His son Allan assumed the administration, starting with a renovation project that was to cost a few million dollars over eighteen months. Jack Singer no longer had to play-act. He now owned the studio that had housed such screen legends as Harold Lloyd, Mary Pickford, Mae West and Bing Crosby. He now owned the studio once run by another mysterious multi-millionaire entrepreneur, Howard Hughes. He now owned the dream studio of the man who had publicly scorned him, Francis Ford Coppola — but even that wasn't quite enough for Jack Singer.

In March 1984 Singer gave Francis Ford Coppola the *coup de grâce* by renaming his dream studio *Jack Singer's Hollywood Studio Center.*

3

The Idea Dealers

"Every successful enterprise requires three men — a dreamer, a businessman and a son-of-a-bitch." Thus spoke Peter McArthur, a rural Ontario columnist and humorist who published a paper during the early 1900s. (It failed.) At some point in the genesis of any business the dreamer, the businessman and the son-of-a-bitch must coalesce to produce the elusive variables of success. The businessman looks after the bottom line, the son-of-a-bitch makes the tough, often brutal decisions and the dreamer underlines and overlays it all with a vision of wealth, power, or fame. The entrepreneur has all of these characteristics, to a greater or lesser degree. But few of the people in this book are completely well-rounded and the trail of hard times in their enterprises directly corresponds to a weakness in one of the three areas. However, they do all share something vital — the idea. As integral to life as oxygen, the idea represents an indestructible embryo. Without the idea as inspiration, the dreamer, businessman and son-of-a-bitch evaporate into the legion of wage-earners. Not only must the idea exist initially as the foundation upon which everything else is built, but successful entrepreneurs keep the idea's essential nature inviolable over time. Certainly it changes as the entrepreneur adjusts to changing conditions, but the way an idea grows is the essence of both creativity and success.

To many armchair entrepreneurs, analysts and academics, the importance of the idea is a truism. Such pundits will offer the sage advice that good ideas alone do not an empire make.

But those same people fervently believe that the idea, especially in today's world, must be singular or extraordinary in order to succeed. Sometimes, of course, that is true. Some ideas are unique, like the Hooges' Love Shops (see The Entertainment Entrepreneurs), some are at the forefront of an expanding market like MacDonald Dettwiler and others resurrect an old-fashioned concept that most have discarded, like Don Cormie's theme of thrift for Principal Trust (see the Tomorrow Traders). But the implicit belief that the more original the idea the more likely one is to hit an instant jackpot is a pervasive misconception. In fact, research on entrepreneurs by I.A. Litvak and C.J. Maule of Carleton University indicates that new or unique ideas are the exception: most are adaptations of existing products, processes or functions. The three sets of entrepreneurs chosen for this chapter were selected precisely because their ideas are simple, even mundane, and because their stories show the range of possible paths an idea can pass along before reaching fruition.

Iranian immigrants Eskandar, Nader, Raphael and Bahman Ghermezian believed in the power of land to survive virtually all economic obstacles and to give them the sense of security they were unable to find in their home country. Their idea was to use their vast tracts of property to create self-contained shopping centres that would service every consumer need from food to cars and entertainment. It wasn't a new concept: thousands of malls — most of them dreary — exist across the country. What is unique is how the Ghermezians' idea evolved into the extraordinary magnitude of the $750-million West Edmonton Mall.

Before he created Rent-A-Wreck, Ed Alfke was an average businessman, a hard worker who had passing success operating a restaurant and selling jeans. The idea that unleashed his unexpected entrepreneurial flair was basic. He wanted to rent used cars at a price far lower than the huge new-car rental firms could match. Rent-A-Wreck itself wasn't even totally original: there was already a similar firm in the United States. But the force of Alfke's idea allowed him to carve a small empire out of a sector peopled by mammoth corporations and shifty car dealers.

It was more luck than any business sense that led Pete Nygard to the clothing firm he eventually owned, Tan Jay International. But once there, the creativity of his innovations and the astuteness of his basic idea — to take mid-priced clothing to middle-aged women — blossomed. Nygard's idea isn't on the scale of Jack Singer's plan for a $500-million model city in New Jersey nor in the league of Tomorrow Trader John MacDonald's dream of recreating MIT in Canada, but it demonstrates a remarkable ability to see gaping holes in a market that others think is saturated.

The experiences of these three entrepreneurs prove that a successful idea doesn't need to be either unique or earth-shattering in scope. What is important is the tenacity with which they have hung on to the essential nature of the idea, the skill, daring and raw energy they used to make the idea come alive and their unfailing belief that the idea was right. The process of taking a concept from the dream stage to the point where the businessman and the son-of-a-bitch have something to work with is fascinating. It's not unlike the magic of the birth of a first child, where every event is new, nothing is given or can be taken for granted. This is especially true of ideas that depend on something other than uniqueness for viability. Peter Nygard began in the already crowded marketplace of women's fashion. His success depended as much on his skill in carving a niche for himself there as it did on his idea to manufacture popularly priced clothing for the hard-to-fit. The Ghermezians took their dream of a super-mall into a city suffering from a shopping-centre glut; it was the way in which they realized the idea, not the idea itself, that has made them unique.

The idea dealers explore their ideas to the fullest, wringing the last drop of potential from them. The most common reason for small business failure is undercapitalization, but the second most common is inability to understand how far an idea can and should be taken. Not only are the idea dealers willing to risk everything when facing a crisis — expanding even when the bankers are beating the doors down and risking acquisition when the market begins to slip — but when times are good, they still push their ideas to the limit rather than revel in the complacency of relative success. Most people would have stopped once Rent-A-Wreck had become a very healthy business. By 1985 Ed Alfke was a wealthy man, yet he was exploring a modification of his original idea — renting new cars. Peter Nygard had his hands on something that worked, production of the kind of clothes everyone's mother wore — clothes for the perma-press, polyester set. He could still be concentrating on turning out middle-of-the-road labels. But he was convinced his idea had a broader potential and he had the nerve to insinuate Tan Jay into the viciously competitive arena of young women's fashion. It worked. Five years ago no one under thirty would be caught dead in a Tan Jay pantsuit. Now, separates with Tan Jay's Bianca label are frequently indistinguishable from the hottest casual fashions — except they are perma press and considerably less expensive. The Ghermezians, with $2 billion in assets and the world's largest shopping mall, have the security and community esteem they have yearned for, yet in 1984 they began fighting to build another of their shopping creations in Vancouver.

To put in perspective the accomplishments of the Money Rustlers in general and the idea dealers in particular, compare them with the general timidity of most Canadians to pursue even good ideas, let alone ordinary ones. Patenting inventions and innovations is one of the many steps people can take to become an idea dealer. The Japanese issue a hundred patents per one hundred thousand population. In Sweden the figure is forty, in the United States thirty-two. In Canada only eight people out of every one hundred thousand receive patents.

The process of turning dreams into reality and handing them over to — or learning to become — the businessman and the son-of-a-bitch is crucially important. Together the idea dealers in this chapter directly employ over 3,500 people and in the future, their dreams will be more important to a healthy economy than the Massey Fergusons and the Dome Petroleums, because, unlike monolithic corporations, the idea dealers are constantly searching for new ideas and opportunities. They are a natural resource, as are all creators, but like many artists and musicians with their private obsessions, the idea dealers protect their visions with powerful personalities — sometimes obnoxious, sometimes charismatic — and buttress them with ambition — sometimes enviable, sometimes repellent.

The Ghermezians — The Mall Makers

"We don't operate here as other businesses do," says Nader Ghermezian. "We" include his three brothers, Eskandar, Raphael and Bahman, and perhaps his eighty-five-year-old father, Jack. Tribal powwows are the hallmark of the Ghermezian style; to outsiders they seem a primitive, inefficient and even sinister way to conduct affairs. This in spite of the fact that the Ghermezians are one of Edmonton's most philanthropic families and there is no evidence of any dishonesty. But they take advantage of the tiniest loopholes to tie up deals so quickly and slickly that competitors are left gasping in their wake. The Ghermezians dream up developments few would have the nerve — let alone the imagination — to tackle.

Today the Ghermezians' holdings are close to $2 billion. With between twelve thousand and fifteen thousand undeveloped acres in their land bank — including five-and-a-half of them in downtown Edmonton — the Ghermezians are Alberta's largest private urban landowners and, through their various housing, construction and development divisions, the biggest housing contractors, too. Triple Five Corp., incorporated in 1972, directly employs two thousand people. The four brothers are all directors and the firm is authorized to issue up to forty thousand shares, but only four have, in fact, been issued — one to each of them for $1. Non-voting and

voting shares can be released as their sons grow up. Triple
Five functions as a holding company for the Ghermezians'
labyrinth of companies that own, in addition to land in
Edmonton, Calgary and Vancouver, numerous Edmonton
developments including West Edmonton Village, a 1,200-unit
rental complex; the Argyll Plaza Hotel and Ice Arena, containing GooseLoonies, a night-club and garish "playcentre";
North Town Mall; Convention Inn South, and two office
towers. Triple Five also shelters First Nuclear Corp., a mining
and oil company with Canadian and American holdings.·
Then there is West Edmonton Mall. Occasionally, partners
such as Rubin Stahl,† the bombastic president of West Edmonton Mall, are brought in on projects. Stahl says he is "highly
involved" with the brothers, but it's doubtful he owns more
than a small percentage of the mall.

The family's assets have grown from a small retail rug
outlet opened in Montreal in 1962 to Triple Five Corporation,
Alberta's dominant land developer, with nearly $2 billion
worth of land and income-producing property. Their prize is
the $750-million West Edmonton Mall, a consumer's nirvana
— 4.5 million square feet of noise, glitz and entertainment,
powerful enough to seduce the most adamant non-shoppers.
The Ghermezians are among Canada's few true billionaires, a
fact they jealously guard with security-conscious zeal. But
while they are shy about their wealth and personal life, they
sing out with the volubility of a vaudeville act when it comes
to their extraordinary creations.

One of the Ghermezians' greatest strengths is their ability to
function in each other's pockets. "We don't decide by vote but
by discussion," says Nader in describing the process. No one

* A rare glimpse into Triple Five's other assets came in 1981 when First Nuclear sold
a portion of its producing oil, gas and mining properties for $1 million to Canadian
Bashaw Leduc Oil and Gas Limited, a publicly traded company. The properties included producing oil wells in Saskatchewan and Alberta as well as a producing gas
well and pipeline in Utah.

† Stahl, who grew up in the vicinity of St. Urbain Street in Montreal, was in semi-
retirement when he joined Triple Five. He had already developed seventeen malls
in Eastern Canada but nothing remotely approaching the scale of WEM.

has ever seen the brothers argue, although they don't hesitate to harangue the media for errors and insults. They learned the parameters of business at their father's knee in Iran and they in turn are passing them on to their children by including their young sons in business meetings.* Each of the brothers has at least one area of expertise: Eskandar, the oldest, concentrates on finance and construction. Forty-one-year-old Raphael is the legal mind and also works on the company's financial affairs; he is dubbed the idea man by Nader. The youngest, Bahman, specializes in real estate and operations. Nader, who is thirty-nine, is also involved in real estate and is the company spokesman. No one talks to the press or government officials without Nader presiding. He's also the company voice in city council, knowing when to shout and when to shut up. "They call me the politician," he smiles.

Edmontonians have a Garbo-like fascination with the Ghermezians. They are Canada's most secretive businessmen, yet they can shock, surprise, thrill and appal with unparall-elled extravagance. Despite a legendary reticence with the press ("We don't usually talk to the media," Nader says several times during a hard-won interview) just about everyone in the city claims to know them or at least be privy to some cher-ished anecdote about them. A University of Alberta professor confides that they go everywhere in convoys of heavily armed limousines. (In fact, they drive their own late-model but nondescript American cars.) A government junior executive says she has seen them travelling with all the women crammed beveiled into the last car. (Since the Ghermezians are Jewish and veils are typically Moslem, it is likely that the last time the Ghermezian women wore veils was at their weddings.) Newspaper reporters assure you that armed sentries stand outside their houses day and night. (But three afternoons of hanging around their house turned up no sign of bodyguards.) And, depending on whom you talk to, the Ghermezians are Arab frontmen for Khomeini — or the Shah's family; Russian

---

* The Ghermezian women have nothing to do with the business and, from the way Nader brushes off the suggestion, it is unlikely they even realize the extent of the family's wealth.

capitalists; or members of the northern Mafia. On business row, those "close" to the Ghermezians say there are variously two, three or four brothers and that their father is still the boss.

The simple fact is that few know anything about these people and those who do guard their information. The Ghermezians go out of their way to foster confusion about their lives. Nader, slight and elegant with a thin, dark moustache, is unfailingly polite but he snickers a little at writers casting about for details. He is forever digging at Peter Newman for writing that the brothers sold second-hand clothing door to door in Montreal instead of new-clothing seconds. When a hitherto unrevealed tidbit is elicited, he taunts, "You're doing better than Newman," as if trying to prolong a guessing game. The reams of sparsely detailed media reports about the Ghermezians are full of contradictions and inaccuracies. For years the father was referred to as Jacob, but Nader insists the patriarch's name is Jack. The mother has often been called aging, but when she strolled through the Triple Five offices in November 1984, the tiny, hawk-faced woman, fashionably dressed in grey and recently coiffed, looked like anything but a doddering Bubby; Nader admitted she was only sixty-five. He has also said her name is Nenehjan but now insists, as if there had never been any question, that her name is also Mary. The family is deeply religious but won't confirm or deny whether they are Jewish despite the fact that at least one Edmonton rabbi believes it to be true, as does the brother's own partner Rubin Stahl, who mentioned it as a fact during a recent interview. "Did anyone say we are Jewish?" Nader quizzes in response to a comment. "Who? Was it confirmed?"

Nader has also said at various times that the family settled in Edmonton in 1963, 1964 and 1967; the last is true. At one point he claimed the brothers, except Bahman who stayed in Europe for several years, all attended McGill and graduated in commerce. Now he says only Raphael graduated. University records show Eskandar enrolled in engineering in 1960, took a year off, then switched to commerce for a year. Nader was a commerce student between 1961 and 1964 but did not graduate. Raphael was awarded a bachelor of commerce degree in 1967. Interestingly, both his registration and convocation records show his first name as being Rafi — but when that name is used today Nader becomes agitated and says it has never been his brother's name. "Academically Rafi was average," says Professor Laybourne of the Faculty of Accounting. "But I always thought he was much brighter than his marks reflected." Twenty years later all three brothers are still remembered by the university administration, but for different reasons. "We had a lot of trouble with them paying their fees," recalls the assistant registrar. "They were very attractive people and very persuasive, but they didn't seem to want to pay their fees."

Many believe the Ghermezians are Saudi Arabian or Turkish, but they are actually from Iran. Jack and his four brothers moved to Tehran at the turn of the century from what is now southern Russia. By 1950 the family had established a large business buying, selling, manufacturing and exporting handwoven and knotted rugs. For security reasons, the entire clan, numbering sixty-five, lived in a large five-storey building in central Tehran. The individual families lived in separate apartments, only meeting or eating together for holidays and other ceremonial occasions. Nader refuses to discuss their life in Iran and vehemently denies any association with the late Shah; unspoken is the implication that there are still Ghermezians in Tehran.

Like everything else the Ghermezian brothers do, their emigration was carefully planned. The three oldest arrived in Montreal in 1959 with their father to scout the territory and look for opportunities. At this time, the Shah's régime was shaky and the family considered it vitally important to find a safe haven for their assets. Part of the image the family likes to project is of impoverished young men selling clothing seconds and rugs door to door to finance their education. They did those things, but only for a short time; by 1962 the family company, ABNR, (the initials represent the brothers' names — A is the Arabic E) had opened a retail outlet in

Montreal on Sherbrooke Street. By 1964 there were sixteen offices in the United States and the Ghermezians were among the largest rug distributors on the continent. They still have a "substantial interest" in the rug business, according to Nader, but are no longer directly involved, that side of their affairs being run by Ellis Ghermezian, a cousin in New York.

The Ghermezians' first reconnaissance of Edmonton came in 1964, but they didn't actually move for another three years, when they purchased a small duplex where the four brothers and their parents eventually all lived. "We liked the resources," says Nader of their decision to live in Alberta. "Eighty percent of Canadian oil reserves are in Alberta and 80 percent of those are around Edmonton. I'm positive that it will become the best place in Canada." All four initially travelled back and forth to Montreal and throughout the United States, but Eskandar and Raphael soon concentrated on Alberta while Nader and Bahman were carrying on the rug business. Jack, then in his late sixties, stayed far in the background and was already turning things over to his sons.

The Ghermezians are rumoured to be conduits for Iranian money, escaping first the Shah and more recently the Ayatollah Khomeini. Considering that they are Jewish, it's unlikely that either the Shah or the fundamentalist Moslem Ayatollah would do business with them. In fact, the Ghermezians transferred the family wealth to Montreal by exporting carpets,* eventually turning them into an Edmonton-based land empire of twelve thousand to fifteen thousand acres, most of which was assembled between 1967 and 1973, when prices were extremely low. One of the reasons there is speculation about the source of their wealth is because public records show they borrowed relatively small amounts in relation to the kind of projects they were building. But they didn't need to borrow: escalating land values turned their initial purchases into an immense asset and a ready source of cash. In a nine-month period spanning 1979 and 1980, Triple Five sold

* The Ghermezians were one of the first to use this vehicle to export wealth from Iran, a technique that was used extensively prior to the Shah's fall.

seven parcels of land to the provincial government for a total of $22 million. Three of the parcels, totalling 119 acres, went for $5.6 million. The Ghermezians had paid $199,000 for the land in 1973. But not all the land was from their vast reserve. One of the parcels sold to the government for $5.4 million had only been purchased eight days before for $375,000.* These days, the Ghermezians short-circuit speculation about the source of their wealth by talking about their heavy borrowing at every opportunity — forcing it into conversations if it isn't brought up directly. "The bank owns West Edmonton Mall. We go to the bank just like everyone else," insists Nader. "We've got to build. We have to keep ahead of the bankers."

By 1974 the Ghermezians were the largest private land owners in Edmonton, but most people had never even heard of them. It wasn't until twenty-nine-year-old Raphael was wrongly accused of offering then-Alderman Alex Fallow a $40,000 bribe that they found an unwanted place in the public eye. † The scandal prompted the Morrow Inquiry, which spanned forty-four days in 1974 and 1975, called fifty-four witnesses and accumulated 3,966 pages of testimony and 184 exhibits. Throughout the inquiry, Edmonton was titillated by these mysterious strangers. The Ghermezians, abhorring publicity, sneaked out of hearings, faces averted. At the end of one day of testimony, the tall, volatile Raphael wrestled a photographer to the ground when he tried to take a picture. The event was captured by CBC-TV for their evening news and afterwards, upon leaving the inquiry, Eskandar and Raphael smeared grin-like grimaces across their faces and marched furiously past the cameras.

---

* Another example of the cash flow this land generates is the Donsdale subdivision of Edmonton. Between 1980 and 1985, Triple Five sold 350 lots at an average price of $35,000 for a gross of $12.25 million. The corporation owns another eight hundred acres in various Edmonton subdivisions.

† They had attracted fleeting attention in 1973 when they persuaded city council to rezone land for a proposed Westgate Mall — now the site of West Edmonton Mall. The bid enraged the powerful developers Western Realty Projects who had planned a similar mall nearby.

When the testimony was eventually untangled, Edmonton woke up to the fact that although the Ghermezians had only been active for six years, they were already a pervasive force in the city council. The inquiry unveiled a startling inter-relationship between the family and council members, nine of whom had been entertained at the Ghermezian home. Instead of being crushed, the brothers turned the tables and won sup-port with some devastating points. They testified that Fallow had been pressuring them for a piece of the family's Fort McMurray land, twenty acres worth $1.6 million.* They also said that aldermen had approached them for political dona-tions and had suggested development sites to them, only to vote against those same proposals in council. Public sym-pathy shifted to the brothers, whose English curiously evaporated during key moments. When Raphael was asked why they settled in Edmonton he replied, "Is a good. I like it here. First time I was here because I don't know. It was with that with the population I like." This from a man who Nader claims graduated from McGill, an English-language univer-sity. Raphael, the most vociferous of the brothers and, at this time, the family spokesman, was alternately enraged and con-fused during the inquiry. He complained to several reporters that if aldermen are bribed (something, he protested, *he'd* never do), everyone gets upset, but that because someone is a Liberal, he wins all kind of contracts with the federal govern-ment. His puzzlement is understandable in the context of Edmonton, a city that re-elected Mayor William Hawrelak in a landslide victory, four years after he was forced to resign over a conflict of interest.

When Justice William Morrow came to his lengthy conclu-sions, the Ghermezians were exonerated, although the suspi-cion that surrounds anyone offering politicians money, for any reason, still hangs over them. Morrow ruled that the pay-ment of $40,000 was made for past services and could not be construed as a bribe. He also admonished the city council for not policing their behaviour more ethically. Morrow even

* It turned out that the Ghermezians had only an option to purchase the land.

praised the brothers. The aldermen were "being lobbied by two of the most skilful, energetic and persuasive developers that this commissioner has ever had occasion to observe," he wrote. Despite the favourable outcome, the accusations of dishonesty still sting and today, when asked about it, Nader quietly commands, "You don't need to write anything about that."

The inquiry, while sometimes humiliating, didn't dent the Ghermezian style. The brothers blatantly cajole the media, elected officials and the public to achieve their aims. They still lobby individual aldermen, shout comments from the gallery, hammer the furniture with their fists, make impassioned entreaties and disrupt council meetings, insisting on being heard. On September 14, 1983, then-Mayor Cec Purves, in exasperation, accidentally referred to Nader Ghermezian as "Alderman Ghermezian" as he tried to quell a running debate between Alderman Olivia Butti and Nader, who was in the visitors' gallery. "They are expert lobbyists," says Purves.* "They really do their homework. Other developers expect to just walk in, state their case and leave with the approval. The Ghermezians leave nothing to chance. Council has been criticized for approving their projects so quickly, but the truth of the matter is that they do everything so thoroughly there are no questions left to ask."

The relationship between the press and the four brothers closely resembles the contortions of a lopsided marriage, with the Triple Five principals controlling the strings. They are wizards at turning the press into their own private public-relations agency. The media have gone from being cynical, suspicious and downright antagonistic toward the Ghermezians to being the bemused and often applauding observers of their endless conquests. Throughout the seventies and early

---

* Purves, who served as mayor from 1978 to 1982, was embroiled in controversy throughout his career. In 1981 a hue and cry was raised when he called Calgary Mayor Ralph Klein, asking him to meet with Triple Five and discuss development. Purves told Klein the brothers were "friends" and "good boys." A few months later the mayor met at the Ghermezian home to discuss a land swap. The next day the council approved the trade *in camera*.

eighties, columnists berated the city council for not standing up to these bullies. In 1981 *Edmonton Journal* columnist Frank Hutton, in describing the Ghermezians' influence, wrote, "Where else could you find a board of directors of a multi-million-dollar corporation the size of Edmonton making snap decisions while blindfolded?" But by 1983 the tune had changed. The same newspaper referred to the Ghermezians as "valuable citizens" and applauded them because they "don't sit back and whine. They fight. They win."

Between the conclusion of the Morrow Inquiry and 1980, Triple Five tackled two major projects:* the West Edmonton Mall and the Eaton Centre in downtown Edmonton. In 1980 Triple Five requested a special zoning permit for the $600-million five-storey Eaton's project, which would have been the biggest such development in the city and included a hotel, office building and residential towers. The proposal requested a density ratio of 19:1, nearly twice the existing limit. There was tremendous opposition to the project and *The Edmonton Journal* called the scale of it "monstrous, even for New York." At one point Nader startled council by showing up, without being on the agenda, with a scale model of the centre, arguing and pleading that he needed both approval and $9 million in tax concessions immediately or the whole thing would collapse. The request was passed after only one reading, the first time in council's history that had happened. Shortly after, Nader told council Eaton's was demanding better terms and he wrung additional concessions from the aldermen, estimated at between $5 million and $15 million. The council never saw the Eaton's letter that supposedly laid out these demands and Eaton's denied having written it.† The project stalled and was eventually shelved in 1981 when the

---

* "Minor" ones include the opening of the Convention Inn South ($37 million) and the incorporation of North Town Mall Investments Limited to finance another ($30 million) mall on the city's north side.

† The Ghermezian honesty was once again in question but Eaton's had erred and a letter did exist, although the brothers exaggerated the urgency of the demands.

store pulled out — a tremendous blow to the city's moribund downtown. It looked like the first significant failure for Triple Five. But it actually left the Ghermezians free to concentrate on West Edmonton Mall. They already had the vital rezoning permit for the downtown land and in the meantime they leased the property for parking, bringing in petty cash of $23,500 a month.

The Ghermezians are fond of calling West Edmonton Mall "the eighth wonder of the world" — it's nearly twice as big as the nearest competitor, Del Ama Fashion Center in Torrence, California — and its existence in Edmonton, a city with only five hundred thousand people, is astonishing. Calling West Edmonton Mall a shopping centre is like calling the Hearst Castle a big house. It's an indoor circus, a combination of Rodeo Drive, Disneyland and Radio City Music Hall. You don't go there merely to shop, you go to gawk, and visitors from Houston, Texas, to Dauphin, Manitoba, can be found wandering, dazzled, through a forest of sculptures, fountains, ferns and fish. Can't find Abercombie and Fitch? Turn left at the shark tank. The mall is non-stop action: around one corner the Edmonton Oilers hockey club is practising on the full-size ice arena and around another the Edmonton Symphony is warming up for a concert. The Fantasyland section includes a four-acre lake, diving cliffs, submarines, surfing, water-skiing, golf and, of course, seventy-one luxurious rides that bear little resemblance to their grubby carny cousins. Even the jaded confess West Edmonton Mall is like a child's first circus. The excitement is so pervasive that people often emerge, after only a few hours, dripping with sweat and complaining of headaches.

The genesis and growth of the mall's indoor amusement park portrays how the Ghermezians tackle decisions, using intricate research and intuitive guesswork, strict planning and a hair-raising habit of throwing the whole thing out the window for a better idea. The park started off "as an idea to have a kiddie train," according to Nader. By the time construction of Phase 1 had started in 1980 it had become Fantasyland, containing three ordinary fair rides and occupying ten thousand square feet. Three months later, when most project plans are long since set in cement, forty-three-year-old Eskandar attended an amusement-park trade show in Kansas City and was enthralled by what he saw. Nader still can't hide his amusement over the excited phone call he got one night from Kansas City. "We've got to make it bigger," Eskandar enthused and, when he told them what he had seen, the brothers quickly agreed. At six the next morning, Eskandar called an astonished Ronald McCarthy, the mall architect, and told him to expand Fantasyland to fifty thousand square feet* and, by the way, move the fifty-five-thousand-square-foot Hometown hardware store back 120 feet to accommodate the changes.

Another example of the Ghermezians' unorthodox style is the construction of the mall's Phase 2 in 1982. The brothers used the risky technique of fast-tracking to save interest costs, and because they weren't exactly sure what they wanted, they made design decisions one step ahead of the actual construction. It was enough to give architects, foremen and decorators heart failure, but they completed the additional one million square feet in twelve months, six months less than the normal time required.

The first phase of West Edmonton Mall, 1.2 million square feet, opened in 1981 to dire predictions of failure by economic pundits and to a chorus of distress by outside merchants, who said the mall would destroy their business. The mall was an instant success, and the chorus turned into a wail when the brothers pulled off a bargaining *tour de force.* Triple Five traded a sixteen-hectare (forty-acre) parcel of South Edmonton land, frequently described as "moose pasture" and "peat and bog," for a residentially zoned parcel of the same size adjoining the already operating mall. Triple Five said it

---

* McCarthy scoured Europe, making three trips, for the right rides. For the mall's first phase he settled on a $350,000-restored English carousel; each wooden horse is individually hand-painted and cost $5,000. The wave-swinger ride, basically a rotating top with chairs dangling on the ends of chains, cost $400,000 from a West German manufacturer. The ferris wheel, swinging-ship ride and two children's rides came from Italy and the bumper cars came from West Germany.

wanted the property for access and parkland "in harmony with and compatible to West Edmonton Mall." The city administration was vehemently opposed to the deal, maintaining that the city land would be used for expansion of West Edmonton Mall and consequently was far more valuable than the residential South Edmonton land.

Nader Ghermezian argued in a letter to city council that it was inappropriate to call the new Triple Five land commercial property because the corporation couldn't possibly use it as such: it already owned idle commercial land in the area, destined for Phase 2. The Ghermezians convinced council, in August 1981, of the wisdom of a straight swap. Two years later, the forty acres were quietly rezoned for shopping centre use and became the site of Phase 3. It was the deal of the decade. Realtors valued the forty acres the city received at only $2 million, while the zoning change turned the Ghermezians' new land into a $25-million property.

Phase 2 opened in 1982, making the $450-million mall the second largest in North America with three hundred stores. The hoopla and hyperbole were straight out of the excesses of Las Vegas. Advertising campaigns trumpeted about the biggest McDonald's in Canada, the biggest toy store in the world, the biggest indoor car dealership in North America, the biggest indoor amusement park, the biggest book-store in Canada, the largest display of oranges in the world — three thousand boxes of them — and on and on. Critics were silenced and rivals frightened as West Edmonton Mall bucked the current declining retail trend* and turned neighbouring shopping centres into little more than giant quick-stop convenience stores. Downtown Edmonton, of course, was poleaxed. Today the streets and stores are mere passageways to somewhere else and there seem to be more people waiting for the bus outside The Bay than shopping inside it. A city survey in 1982 revealed Edmontonians' devastating disinterest in the downtown core. Eighty percent of those questioned said they never visit, shop or browse downtown.

* Total Alberta retail sales dropped from $10.94 million in 1981 to $10.9 million in 1982.

By the time the specifics of the over two-million-square-foot Phase 3 were announced in 1983, competing developers and merchants were incensed at the mall's insidious and apparently unstoppable spread. This time city council took a firm stand when the Ghermezians descended on the city for further rezoning. The aldermen insisted Triple Five bear certain servicing costs, normally supported by the city. Nader, in fine style, threatened to drop Phase 3 and complained in a letter, "Triple Five constantly struggles to understand why its efforts to build in Edmonton are always opposed and always controversial. [Triple Five] has to fight and scratch for the ability to keep developing." Three days later he had the permit, without the extra costs for servicing, and a different outlook. "I have a good feeling for this city; I believe in this city," he announced to reporters.

The Ghermezian *modus operandi* is to nibble and nudge, taking as much as they can get and then going back for more. With the rezoning permit in hand, Triple Five announced its intention to construct an $82-million addition to Fantasyland. In order to do it, they wanted the city to hand over $20 million in tax concessions and, if that didn't demonstrate enough gall, similar grants from the provincial and federal governments. In the midst of general outrage at the request, they released a consultant's report saying that Fantasyland alone would reduce the province's unemployment by 3 or 4 percent and generate $430 million in construction income — a mainline injection into a crippled industry. The brothers also began quietly meeting with citizens' groups and individuals, soothing fears and promising park sites, noise berms and tree planting on streets that faced the giant mall. "We have respect for people's feelings," Nader says, pointing out that they built a noise berm in one community near the mall without being asked. *

Then they began appealing to Edmonton's ego. The glorious pleasure palace would be a 310,000-square-foot

* In one deal, Triple Five promised to plant one tree in front of every house facing the western boundary of the mall.

Fantasyland, six times the present size, with an indoor half-mile canal loop, a four-acre lake, five submarines specially built in Victoria, a giant wave pool for surfing, raft rides and water skiing, an indoor marineland featuring dolphins and sea-lion shows and up to four thousand marine animals. There would be water slides, twenty-foot diving cliffs, a sandy swimming beach and an artifical sun for tanning, a space park featuring a 360-degree theatre providing the feel of a space-shuttle flight and, of course, more rides. The mall would bring the number of stores to 720, making it the largest mall in the world.

Edmontonians were alternately aghast and fascinated by the mushrooming mini-city and its sensuous orgy of activity. The current mall was already open until midnight, with constant entertainment in its massive corridors. Those accustomed to annual getaways in Hawaii were starting to think how much further their vacation dollars would go spent on the beach at West Edmonton Mall. The Ghermezians took out full-page ads requesting Edmontonians to write with suggestions for the mall; seventeen thousand letters flooded in.

Opposition still existed, so the Ghermezians gently applied the stick. They told citizens' groups that if they didn't get permission to expand West Edmonton Mall, they would be "forced to use the land for multi-family dwellings," with higher density and increased vehicle traffic. Low-income housing is anathema in Edmonton, with most multi-family dwellings dumped in peripheral planned communities like Mill Woods. Established communities fight them bitterly. The Ghermezians wielded the benefits stick harder and sadly leaked hints that they couldn't afford to build without the concessions. Then Rubin Stahl joined the fray. "I'm not threatening, but I want to do this project. And if the Ghermezians can't raise the funds, I'll have to do it somewhere else." It was a bluff, of course; who else but the Ghermezians would even contemplate such an undertaking? But the non-threat added weight to the growing support from the public for the expansion.

Suddenly, in the fall of 1984, Triple Five called a press conference and announced the magical resurrection of the Eaton Centre concept for a pathetically empty downtown. The $600-million development would include two 550-unit apartment towers — the tallest in the city — with accommodation for three thousand people, a one-thousand-seat theatre, an Olympic-size swimming pool, a rink, and a health club. No date was set for the start of construction but the Ghermezians made it abundantly clear that continued opposition to the West Edmonton expansion would kill the Eaton Centre. They implied they were just as happy with their expensive parking lot anyway. It has been in the family's best interests to keep the downtown moribund — at least until they chose to move in. As long as the city centre was dying, they held a powerful trump. In at least one instance they went out of their way to maintain the status quo by killing a proposed pedestrian route between the Edmonton Centre mall and the Manulife Building across the street, scuttling a vital access for both.

Coincidentally, the Ghermezians chose this moment to open GooseLoonies, a multi-level, ultra-slick night-club and "playcentre." Everything about it was unexpected. It is located in the Argyll Plaza, six miles from downton, in south Edmonton, an area that looks like the backside of an industrial park. At the two-day opening, the devoutly religious Ghermezians, who rarely drink and whose women are traditional and self-effacing, entertained several thousand Edmontonians with muscle boys in a variety of extraordinary costumes, dancing girls in buttock-hugging Lycra, a $250,000 light system that comes close to being hallucinogenic, 360-degree gut-thudding music and an atmosphere dripping with sex and fun. At the opening, quaffing the limitless free booze, downing prawns, ogling the exuberant, suggestive dancers and glad-handing it with the Ghermezians were numerous aldermen.

The Ghermezians' final blow to Fantasyland opponents was typically ostentatious, almost vulgar in its excess. Triple Five announced that the new, expanded Fantasyland would be turned into a non-profit foundation with all the profits, "millions of them," said Stahl grandly, to be handed over to

The Northern Alberta Children's Hospital, the Red Cross, the Muscular Dystrophy Association, the Multiple Sclerosis Society and the Canadian Cancer Society. Nader estimates Fantasyland will generate over $3 million annually for charity. It was a fine flourish to end a fight that the brothers carefully played out with the panache of toreadors. Any further complaints died in tight-throated squawks — who could argue with millions for children and not be drummed out of town? In January 1985, Edmonton city council approved the $20 million in tax concessions.

The Ghermezians' personal eccentricity and profitable extravagance have not altered their paranoid avoidance of publicity. "We are not politicians. We don't run for public office. There should be a purpose when you go to the media," says Nader, baldly making obvious the fact that the family views the media as a tool and explaining that the family shuns publicity primarily for security reasons. The genesis of the Ghermezian caution dates back to Iran, when the clan of sixty-five banded together for safety. The family's longtime lawyer and sometime spokesman, John Butler, says caution is deeply ingrained and he relates a story of how the young boys witnessed a companion killed while they played a game because he accidentally hit another boy with a rock. "They also saw people taken right out of their midst by the police for no apparent reason."

It is impossible to overstate the family's fear of violence. During questioning about their personal life, the normally calm and very controlled Nader becomes agitated, with one of his feet jiggling uncontrollably. Each piece of information is weighed, considered carefully, and adjusted so it can't be fit into any discernible pattern. And when confronted with information he thought was unknown, Nader abruptly left the room to consult with his brothers. Several reporters have received midnight phone calls begging them not to reveal some scrap of information about the Ghermezians' personal lives.

Nader refuses to discuss how many children the brothers have or where they go to school, how many houses they own or where they take holidays. * He admits they like skiing, hockey games and water sports, but won't reveal where they do these things. They also enjoy hunting. "Tell them we like to hunt. We are good hunters. We have lots of guns," Nader stresses. He even hedges on such seemingly unimportant details as why the company is named Triple Five. "Can't you guess?" he coyly sidesteps, hinting at some great secret.

The Ghermezian house is located in a serene, old neighbourhood of wealthy residents including bank presidents, city aldermen and a few provincial cabinet ministers. It's a large, square, uninspired two-storey white building, clearly distinguishable from others on the street by the empty lot beside it and the tall, austere chain-link fence surrounding the property, completely out of place next to the neat, professional landscaping buffering other homes. The Ghermezians bought the house next door and tore it down, either to improve security or to build a larger dwelling to accommodate their communal lifestyle. No armed bodyguards are immediately evident, but Nader says video cameras and "other devices" are constantly vigilant. The house looks empty, inside and out, and even on an unseasonably balmy December day in the late afternoon when most schoolchildren are snatching the last few minutes of play, there is no sign of activity.

The Triple Five headquarters, on the top floor of a nine-storey building slightly removed from the main business district, is perched near the steep bank of the North Saskatchewan River. It sits, appropriately enough considering the sway the Ghermezians hold over Edmonton, near the provincial legislature, but outside the downtown core. Inside, their offices are both typical of the family's siege mentality and, in some ways, completely at odds with it. The corporation is armoured like a civilian military contractor's office. The door leading from the reception area to executive offices is camouflaged by paneling and controlled by buzzers operated from the switchboard. Individual offices are unidentifiable from the

* He also won't talk about the women in the family except to say that they are not involved in business, but the implication is that whatever the men do, so follow the women.

outside and each has a peephole. One gets the impression, walking down the corridors, of passing through a submarine ready to close bulkheads and crash-dive at any moment.

On the other hand, the reception area often looks more like the waiting room of a theatrical booking agent, a patent attorney or a union hiring hall than the holding area of a billion-dollar corporation obsessed with security. One man in grubby polyester walks off the elevator and says he wants to see Bahman. When asked if he has an appointment, he says, No, adding quickly, "But I've got something important to show him." The receptionist sighs in a brief break from phone calls, "I'll see what I can do," and motions him to take a seat, although all are occupied. One of the electronic doors opens quietly; a squat, dark, balding man barely over five feet walks out, summons the polyester-clad man and disappears. Bahman. Two other men waiting with boxes clutched on their laps are similarly whisked away by Eskandar, who is the same height as Bahman and Nader, but the most nondescript-looking of the four brothers. When asked about the array of visitors, Nader shrugs, "I get calls for megaprojects and letters from old ladies saying come and buy my house. We get inventors, too. They come here and we make arrangements with them."

Land developers often have as much integrity in the public eye as loan sharks, yet nobody questions the Ghermezians' generosity — calculated though it may be. It's a corporate virtue they are proud of displaying. In 1980 Triple Five donated one acre of land worth $200,000 to The Good Shepherd Catholic Church. * They donate all the coins in the West Edmonton Mall fountains (about $3,000 a month) to charity, † and they have given $35,000 toward a Canadian Islamic Centre, $25,000 to the Pope's 1984 visit, and seed money for the Edmonton Children's Hospital.

Neither is the family shy about proclaiming the good they

* Alderman Olivia Butti just happens to attend that church.

† The charities have to fish the coins out themselves.

are doing for Alberta and Canada. "We are changing the industrial base of Alberta," says Nader proudly, sounding more like a minister of tourism than a land developer. "We will bring in tourists and stop Canadians from always leaving the country for holidays." Already West Edmonton Mall looks like it might fulfil his ambition of eight million visitors annually. Before Phase 3 opened, the mall was attracting twenty thousand people a day and 80 percent of tourists stopping at the city's visitors' bureau were asking for information about it. A director of tourism oversees a staff of twenty and $5 million is dedicated to bringing in visitors from all over the world. In addition to many other incentives, that department employs a teacher for visiting school groups.

In 1984, the Ghermezians tried to bulldoze the city council of the Greater Vancouver municipality of Burnaby into *carte blanche* approval of a $900-million mall — presumably the ninth wonder of the world — that would draw shoppers from virtually every surrounding municipality. The council refused Triple Five the desired tax concessions, rezonings and land swaps. But the civic officials' and local businessmen's complacent, even smug assumptions that Triple Five's plans are dead eerily echo the attitude many Edmontonians had before West Edmonton Mall became a reality. Nader Ghermezian agrees. "We never give up," he states flatly.

There is no question that the Ghermezians are shrewd and sometimes ruthless businessmen, but there is an endearing quality in the childlike pride they take in their accomplishments. And their passionate pleas to city council that they are just trying to be good Canadians with their latest project ring of good acting, good business and a good heart. Their construction projects are far more to them than mere profit centres. Jack Ghermezian, at eighty-five, frequently wanders through West Edmonton Mall, tidying up after messy shoppers and sweeping up after special events. At the GooseLoonies opening, Raphael enthusiastically corralled guests, bragging about the lighting and sound system. When Nader walks through the mall, he can't resist checking for dust along the brass railings. And, when Fantasyland opened, the first in line, hooting with delight as he spun high up in one of the seats of the giant swing, was Raphael Ghermezian.

Peter Nygard — The Six Percent Man

When his alma mater, Glenlawn Collegiate in Winnipeg, called on him to address the high-school's graduating class, Peter Nygard quoted and generously borrowed from those self-help books that too neatly sum up other peoples' success stories or pass on uncomplicated formulae that are easy to express but horrendously difficult to translate into action. Ten years later, he had the insensitivity to present the entire simplistic speech again to a convention of Manitoba teachers, as if they needed the same advice their students did. In a lecture that brimmed with bromides about setting goals and radiating success, there was one key concept, one idea that has become Peter Nygard's personal credo: "Think about anyone who has achieved a mark in sports, in social work, in business or anything at all, and you will find them completely dedicated to their cause. They eat it, they drink it — they practise it constantly. You must become a professional in your undertaking. You must practise it so well that you know more about it than anybody else — everything else must come second."

In Nygard's career, every*one* else has come second to his own quest for competition, power, recognition of his peers, and money — in that order. "Peter goes through a lot of people, but the good ones stay," says his sister, Liisa Nichol, who operates her own $7-million-a-year retail clothing business from Winnipeg. Any price for his success has been paid by the men and women he bumps up against as he pursues his goals with self-confessed fanaticism.

This son of Finnish immigrants created Nygard International of Winnipeg, a $120-million-a-year business that is Canada's largest manufacturer of women's sportswear, and at forty-four he is living a lifestyle rivaling that of the movie stars he dates. Succeeding handsomely in all his objectives, he has gone far beyond his original good idea — and first real goal — of creating a competitive, powerful corporation that would clothe ordinary Canadian women in comfortable, inexpensive sportswear, no matter how odd their sizes and shapes might be. One of Nygard's early strategies was to offer the Tan Jay line that features compatible colours that blend from one year to the next, and clothing coordinates that, even if bought separately, mix and match easily into a complete wardrobe. His soundest tactic was to go after the half of the female population that is over twenty-five, women whom industry jargon dubs "the missy market."* In recent years, as he sought $100 million in sales, a goal that he reached in 1984, his base has broadened: he developed two high-fashion lines, Alia and Bianca, and escaped the economic confines of Canada. Since he set up a Los Angeles factory six years ago, Nygard International has become the third-largest supplier of women's sportswear in the United States, with projected sales of $50 million in 1985-86. Sales in Canada reached $70 million; he operates on a profit margin of about 12 percent before taxes, a more than respectable figure in his competitive industry.

In 1984, in a major new focus on marketing, he moved into direct retailing with three prototype stores in Western Canada that offer only single lines of his clothing (Tan Jay in Vancouver, which has a French farm-house atmosphere in the prestigious Oakridge Mall; and two Alia stores in Edmonton). He claims their revenues are double the sales per square foot of similar specialty and department stores carrying his merchandise. By the end of 1985 he planned to open ten more of his own stores, most of them in Montreal and Toronto. The decision to leap into the retail market was born of his belief that Canadian garment manufacturers will find it increasingly difficult to compete with low-wage factories in the Orient.

* *Certain* women over twenty-five. As one of Nygard's sportswear competitors in Winnipeg has said: "He doesn't design for my wife. She's thirty-one and has a nice figure. He aims at the woman over forty at a popular price and he's been damn good at it."

While his corporate headquarters and four of his factories remain in Winnipeg, where the company began less than two decades ago, he now owns his own plants in Thunder Bay and Los Angeles and contracts with other factories that do a major volume of work for him in Winnipeg, Los Angeles, Taiwan and Hong Kong. His design centre is in Montreal and he recently opened the showrooms, sales office and warehouse that comprise the company's national marketing headquarters in Toronto. In all, about one thousand employees work out of eighty Nygard offices around the world.

In earlier years detractors in the Manitoba fashion industry would downplay his contributions, considering him a renegade who refused to play ball with his peers and not the leader he should have been because of his ambition and the size of his company. Lately he has been in the forefront as an industry innovator in introducing computer technology to clothing design and manufacture — $2,000,000 worth by the end of 1985 — and the federal government chose him in 1984 as co-chairman of a fifteen-member task force struck to shape long-term strategy for the Canadian clothing and textile industries.* Yet antipathy towards him lingers even today. Ray Winston is executive director of the Manitoba Fashion Institute, an association of garment manufacturers. Because Nygard gets so much media attention, Winston is reluctant at first to talk about the position Nygard International holds in the industry. Pressed, he concedes: "They're one of the leaders; there's no two ways about it. They've gone in a very short time from a very small company to a very large one. Since he took over sole ownership, he hasn't looked back; his sales have increased tremendously." Peter Nygard, he says, is a superb merchandiser.

Some of the criticism directed at Nygard has been financial envy, some a moral tsk-tsking about his florid, storybook life

---

* The task force's final report was delayed by the change in federal government that year and by a lack of consensus on recommendations. "Making policy by consensus has to be one of the most frustrating and the least productive methods," Nygard says. "I don't have to deal with consensus much in my business. And now that I see how unproductive it is, I don't intend to deal with it."

as entrepreneur, athlete and womanizer.* In Winnipeg they've
called him a Viking Gatsby, and while there were never any
Finnish Vikings and F. Scott Fitzgerald's Great Gatsby made
his fortune in bootlegging, not women's clothing, there is a
certain sense to the forced comparison. Nygard has a Scan-
dinavian's sun-blond locks and sky-blue eyes, and like Jay
Gatsby he emerged from midwestern poverty to create a small
empire, surround himself with the handsomest of women, and
live like Hugh Hefner, the *Playboy* publisher whose name
comes up in his conversation. He radiates more of the volup-
tuary than the ascetic-looking Hefner: shoulder-length hair,
sensual lips, his six-foot-one body adorned with chunky gold
jewellery, blousy shirts open to the navel and soft jackets.
Unlike the reclusive Hefner, Nygard ranges the world, travelling to the Orient and Italy once a year and spending about
four months in Canada in total, two to three months at his
main residence in the Bahamas — where he has a ten-
thousand-square-foot mahogany-and-marble mansion on
Viking Hill near Nassau — and the rest of his time at his
American headquarters in Los Angeles. In three of those
places — L.A., Nassau and Winnipeg — Nygard keeps his
own Excalibur, that $60,000-plus reproduction of a classic
Mercedes-Benz roadster.† He used to have five racing
sailboats scattered around the world too, but sold them along
with the fifty-one-foot Morgan yacht he used to live on in the

*In 1980 Nygard was charged with the rape of an eighteen-year-old woman and
released on $7,500 bail, but the charge was stayed when the complainant later
refused to testify in court. Afterwards, Nygard said the police had used "poor
judgment" investigating the case.

† In *How to California* Jonathan Roberts describes what California auto dealers
euphemistically call high-end cars. Among them is the Excalibur, and Roberts
offers this rationale for buying one: "You're old-fashioned at heart, really you are,
and what could warm every fibre of your soul better than a nearly exact fibreglass
replica of a 1920s Mercedes SSK roadster? The historical purist in you will quietly
replace the Excalibur hood ornament (a sword) with a Mercedes crest (an
emasculated peace symbol)."

Bahamas. "I've settled down," he says, flashing his killer smile. "Now I've got *places*."

One of those places is in the raw reaches of Winnipeg, where he now spends a mere forty days a year. While there, he luxuriates in an office equipped to let him conduct eighteen-hour workdays — he quite literally lives in the office. The office space says many things about Peter Nygard. There is the obvious practicality of it all: the fridge, the sink, dishwasher, microwave oven, a stove to barbecue steaks; the conversation pit in the sunken living-room with a sectional sofa that pulls out to become a full-sized bed ("instant bed-room," as he needlessly points out). There is sheer efficiency: the bedside panel of buttons that controls the lighting, closes the drapes, turns on the TV and stereo and locks the door; the dusk-lit bathroom with sauna, shower and a phone beside the toilet; the four clocks that pinpoint times around the world. And the unapologetic hedonism: the Excalibur at his private office door, the well-stocked bar, thick wool and bear rugs on the heated floor, the salt-water aquarium, stone fireplace, cedar beams and fig trees, the sign quoting W.C. Fields, "Water? Never Drink It. Fish Fuck In It," and the mirrored tiles above the pull-out bed. Unasked, he takes a visitor on a tour of this — this office? boudoir? and when he hears the obvious comparison to the *Playboy* mansion, Peter Nygard replies: "I envy Hefner. He's gone one step further. That's the way to live."

He comes even closer to the Hefner style in his beachfront Los Angeles base on the Marina del Ray peninsula, one of the most exclusive pieces of real estate in the world. It's a refurbished three-storey house; actor Dudley Moore is his neighbour. Business is conducted on the first floor, guests stay on the second, and Nygard lives, amid spa, sauna and a retractable roof, on the top. The distinctive touches here are the lofty grotto that Nygard designed to run through the centre of the house — it's alive with a jungle of palm trees and waterfalls — and the $100,000 worth of rocks he had placed as rugged decoration on the third floor. "I've always been living on flat land," he explains, "so I created my own mountain."

In his L.A. office-*cum*-home he entertains the women who play a constant, if very secondary role in his life. "I've always hung around with the best — Miss North Dakota, Miss Manitoba, Miss Universe," he says. In recent years he has been dating actresses, including Susan Anton, the five-foot-eleven star of the movie *Golden Girl*, a former girlfriend of five-foot-four Dudley Moore. "Susan Anton was with me a few times in the summer, but I had to maintain my freedom," Nygard says with an audible sigh. His freedom comes in spite of the woman named Pat who lives in his house in Nassau and has borne his three children, a two-year-old boy, Kai, and two pre-adolescent girls, Bianca and Alia, for whom he named his better clothing lines. He is not married to Pat and prefers not to talk about her.

"He says he can't be faithful to one woman," explains his sister, Liisa Nichol. She says it forgivingly, in the tone a sister reserves for an admired older brother. They were unusually close as children, thrown together at the ages of ten and nine when their parents emigrated to Canada from Finland in 1952, fleeing the unavoidable presence of Russia, the neighbour next door. In Finland their father was superintendent of one of the country's largest bakeries and his mother was supervisor of a chain of milk-and-bread stores the bakery ran. They spent most of their money on the passage to Canada, but they were going to a land of opportunity. The elder Nygard's first job was as a baker in Deloraine, Manitoba, and the family had to live in one room and sleep two to a bed. The big city of Winnipeg seemed more promising; his father — who couldn't speak English — spent several mornings chasing after bread trucks to follow them back to a bakery where he could find work. *

Neither of the children could speak English at first; to this day, Peter has thick, Finnish-accented overtones in his speech. As close as they were because of their mutual language barrier, brother was not above practising his embryonic business

---

* Years later, Peter would help his parents buy their own bakery.

skills on sister: lending Liisa money, charging her interest on it and then sharing half the candy she would buy with the loan. ("I was a sucker," she says now.) As a twelve-year-old Peter contracted out four newspaper routes, collecting profits on each, and sold them two years later for $200 apiece to fathers who wanted their sons in business. The tendency toward entrepreneurship was inherent. "Our whole family history is competitive," Peter Nygard says. "Every one of our twenty relations in Finland — cousins, uncles and everybody else — is in their own business." The motivation was environmental: "With our parents," Liisa says, "it was always 'work hard' — not 'don't work too hard.' "

Peter was gifted with an athlete's frame and a winner's drive. At Glenlawn Collegiate he set jumping records and became a school champion in curling. "I was always a fanatic in whatever I did — in track or anything, I always did it with dedication and conviction." As an adult he remains a jock, working out with eight sets of barbells he keeps around the world and in warmer climes often running three miles a day. For several years in the 1970s he worked toward a berth in Olympic sailing competition, a desire that was stimulated by his coming fiftieth out of sixty boats during a race in Kingston, Ontario. ("It was a phenomenal blow to my ego.") Systematically, he began to learn sailing all over again; within three years he became North American champion in the Tempest class and seventh in the world. He dropped the sport cold after deciding to expand his business into the U.S. market.

As a teenager, Peter worked summers as a carnival age- and weight-guesser ("You chat the women up and feel them up, pat them on the ass"), lifeguard, supermarket stockboy, pipe-line worker and for two $25 weeks as a labourer in a sports-wear company where his mother operated a sewing machine; the poor-boy-turned-multi-millionaire likes to point out that he's now more than a peer of the man who hired him and his mother.

After high school Nygard was seduced by the ambience of

campuses as he rode in a friend's sports car on a cross-continent trip. Two years at a junior college in Minneapolis convinced him that the humanities courses were a waste of his time and that he should study business. He attended the University of North Dakota because it was the closest college with a business-administration course. He was a straight-A student and during his term as president of Delta Sigma Pi, his branch won a national achievement award. Two years before graduating in 1961, he began going to job interviews for the practice. He ultimately chose the job with the least pay but what he thought was the most opportunity: a management-trainee's position with Eaton's in Winnipeg.

He started at $390 a month in the food department, stacking cans on shelves. With his usual self-confidence, he was feeling superior about his skill and speed in picking up two cans at a time in each hand. One day the department manager watched him and said: "You think you're doing well? Watch this." And he grabbed four cans in each of his huge hands and stacked them faster than Nygard could. It was a small lesson, but the cocky business-administration grad decided that he had to set himself even higher standards. He later moved to Eaton's catalogue-sales department, where he began to reveal a side that is almost as ruthlessly hard on other people as it is on himself. His major headache was dealing with the $20 million worth of catalogue items returned each year. As supervisor of employees who had to unwrap the returned goods and refund money to customers, he set up incentive systems, displayed production charts and consulted with some time-and-motion experts. When he identified the slowest employees, he would call their names over an intercom and ask them to come to his office. A poor producer knew why he was being paged; Nygard's point was to humiliate the employee. Eventually he became home-furnishings manager for seventeen small Eaton's stores in Saskatchewan, Manitoba and northwestern Ontario. He opened four new stores, renovated five others, all the while learning how to run a business. Doug Bishop, then catalogue-sales manager, later to become manager of Eaton's Polo Park store in Winnipeg, remembers the time Nygard opened a home-furnishings store in Dauphin, Manitoba. "I don't think before or after we had a store-opening as smooth. He documented everybody's responsibility right down to the minute it opened. He was very demanding. Although people rebelled at first, they began to respect him."

Inevitably, Nygard had to leave Eaton's. "Peter was a runner," Bishop says. "He was probably too fast for us. You earn your pips in this company over a long time. Peter couldn't have waited that long." Whenever Nygard was asked what he wanted out of business, he'd reply, "Equity" — a piece of the action.

His chance came in 1966 on the night he dated Miss Sweden. "People say: 'You're lucky.' Luck is the crossroads of opportunity and preparation," Nygard says in his best high-school-speech delivery as he delivers one of his homilies, feet propped on his light oak desk. "You've got to expose yourself to opportunity." Eaton's was holding a Nordic promotion in Winnipeg, importing the Misses Sweden, Denmark and Finland. Nygard, who spoke Finnish, was asked to be their escort at the Governor-General's Ball, the highlight of the Winnipeg social season. He and Miss Sweden had stayed up till 6 A.M. and he had barely fallen asleep when the phone rang. It was a corporate headhunter. "Peter, you've got an interview."

"Like hell," Nygard retorted.

"It's this Jewish guy who's in the *schmata* business." The rag trade. The garment industry. "He's doing about $800,000 and he's looking for a sales manager."

It was the worst job offer he'd ever had in his twenty-five years. And the timing was ghastly. Here he was, a Finnish-Canadian boy just fallen in love, and his friend the head-hunter was asking him to leave her to apply for a position with a swatch-sized garment company.

"Give me half an hour." It speaks volumes about Nygard's lifelong priorities — business first, personal relationships second — that, reluctantly but dutifully, he went to the interview. He would lose Miss Sweden forever. (She left him a note: "Peter. It was nice. Goodbye.")

The headhunter had told him that Nathan Jacob of Winnipeg's Jacob Fashions was looking for a sales manager. "Listen," Nygard told Jacob at the interview, "let's get this straight: I'm not interested in a sales-management job. I want to be general manager."

"That's exactly what I'm looking for," Jacob said. He was elderly, without sons to inherit the business, and enough of a maverick, as Nygard says, that "he would hire this gentile boy from the retail business for a predominantly Jewish business."

The Manitoba garment industry dates back to the late nineteenth century, but the first real factories — high-volume tailor shops — began to flourish in the early 1900s under Anglo-Saxon owners who employed many Jewish immigrants with Old Country experience. Over the years, these workers became employers. During the 1940s the industry's emphasis shifted from work clothing to sportswear and in the next decade they focused on merchandising and sought international suppliers.

Nathan Jacob's company, however, was small and unsophisticated, selling only $800,000 worth of blouses and some sportswear. He needed some young energy. "What does it take?" Jacob asked Nygard.

"Only one thing: equity."

They agreed that after a year's trial the young man could buy into the company. He started December 1, 1966, and a month later Jacob learned that he had cancer. In June 1967, Nygard bought a 20-percent share for $45,000 with a borrowed $8,000 as cash payment, with the rest to be financed out of future earnings. In October Nathan Jacob died. Over the following seven years Nygard bought out the estate to become the sole owner of Tan Jay International, which he had named for a line of Jacob's clothing (it became Nygard International in 1985). Working sixteen hours a day, giving up all outside interests, he began educating himself in the garment industry. Among his first shrewd discoveries was that he could best his competition by aiming at a different market: "Everybody advising me said that half the population was under twenty-five and you've got to be selling to that postwar baby-boom market. I cleverly figured out that if half are under twenty-five, half will be over."

Researching the tastes of the older, cautious woman, he interviewed store buyers and concocted a scheme to interview the customer herself. On his clothing tags he included a brief questionnaire that asked the purchaser her age, occupation, size, fitting problems ("how does this fit?") and requested permission to send her a fuller questionnaire. There was an extraordinary 15-percent return on the twenty-five thousand tags, Nygard says; Tan Jay sent the respondents gift pens to fill out the second survey — and half of those questionnaires came back completed. Analysing them, Nygard found "there was a tremendous need for the missy fit, the customer who'd have to buy a pant in one size and the top in another. And they were always sold as outfits, not separates. We learned of the need for coordinates, mix and match. The customer wanted more choice. We also learned of the desire for knits, with their comfort, washability and easy care. At that point there was no wash-and-wear polyester."

Tan Jay took off as the polyester era began and those inexpensive synthetics, together with an emphasis on coordinates and a conservative style, kept the company aloft. When miniskirts were the young woman's passion, Tan Jay gave its customers a skirt that veiled the nature of the mature knee; it sold well in spite of scepticism from the major stores' buyers. "The small stores loved us," Nygard recalls. He refused to go along with the usual wheeling and dealing in the industry, where every price was endlessly negotiable. After researching what his customers really wanted, costing his products out just under his competitors, he never budged on price. He shipped on a first-come, first-served basis.

What has become the thirty-eighth biggest Manitoba-based company was built on three lines of women's off-the-rack clothing. Nygard ignored current styles to concentrate on a conservative rejigging of last year's fashions: the medium-priced Bianca line, the cheaper Tan Jay series stocked in major department stores, and the budget Jay-Set that sold steadily in shops like Leeson's Ladies Wear of Unity, Saskatchewan, until Nygard dropped it recently. In 1980, as his customers matured, Nygard brought out a new line called Alia, better-styled and higher-priced.*

Peter Nygard was as exacting with his office employees as with himself. As one of his secretaries remarked: "Mr. Nygard has a saying that a good secretary is always at the office longer than her boss. What that means is that when he's in town, I put in about sixteen hours and when he's away something like ten hours a day." His Winnipeg management staff knew that every Tuesday night was reserved for a meeting that began at seven and could last until after eleven. Salesmen filed weekly sales reports on every style of clothing Tan Jay produced, rating how style, size and colour sold on a scale of one to four. Based almost entirely on those sales reports, a management committee worked with a couple of pattern designers who — well, "designed" isn't the right word — who *restructured* the current season's styles for the following season's markets. So a grey-flannel jacket with patch pockets that sold well might resurface, indistinguishable except for inside pockets. "We cater to Miss Canada, a middle-of-the-road customer," Murray Batte, the executive vice-president (now Canadian president), would explain to visitors. "She's not interested in the latest thing. She may wear it next year." The designing, which has since become more sophisticated, is now done in the company's office in Montreal, the Canadian fashion capital.

By 1976 the total trade that Jacob Fashions had done in a year — $800,000 — was about the same amount of business that Tan Jay did with Eaton's Winnipeg stores alone. The

---

* Nygard International now offers five lines: Tan Jay Classics, which is the traditional sportswear; the higher-fashion Tan Jay International sportswear; Alia, related separates; and the highest-fashion lines, aimed at the career woman — Bianca, and Bianca-Nygard, which is, in the industry's precious jargon, free-time wear.

company went international (with offices in Hong Kong and Taipei) when Nygard realized that importing often made more economic sense than manufacturing.* By the beginning of the eighties, all of its shirts and sweaters — 35 to 40 percent of its business — were imported. "If they can make them cheaper, let them do it," he would say of his oriental subcontractors. Murray Batte would add, "We can tell the government it can't put a freeze on imports to Tan Jay because everything we bring in coordinates with something we produce here." That attitude did not endear Peter Nygard to his competitors, who were importing less — possibly for patriotic reasons, but more likely because they hadn't been aggressive enough in the Orient. He continues to be critical of any quota system. As he told *Manitoba Business*: "Instead of the present policy, Canadian garment-makers should stick to segments of the market where they can compete effectively and do well. They should be given domestic preference in these segments and the opportunity to compete in the entire North American market [Tan Jay does about 35 percent of its business in the United States]. Imports, meanwhile, should be allowed in quota-free in their segments of the market."

Nygard has been an exporter to the States for a dozen years, but it wasn't until 1977 that he became serious about the market. Seeing his Canadian sales stabilizing at an unusual growth rate of ten percent, Nygard had begun looking south for his next $50 million in sales. His first major American venture was a disaster. Looking for a launching vehicle, he took over the Susan Thomas Vivo clothing division of the Genesco Corporation of New York. From the beginning, the operation was wracked with problems. Nancy Ebker, the clothing division's president, launched a $20-million lawsuit after Nygard fired her and two of her managers (Nygard counter-sued and won the case). He closed

* He had made his first buying trip to the Orient at the encouragement of Nathan Jacobs. "I really stepped out. I thought I was making the biggest purchase of my life: I bought a hundred dozen white turtleneck polyester sweaters. My heart was in my throat, having bought them on spec. I ended up selling about five million of those in the next ten years."

the division in August 1978, absorbing a substantial loss —
how substantial he won't say.

He continued to be aggressive about the vast American
market as his Canadian operation experienced a slump in
demand for his moderate-priced missy lines; women were
buying high-style jeans, sportswear of better quality or, if in
cheaper fabrics, of higher-fashion detailing. He bought a
cluster of three buildings in Los Angeles and has since turned
two of them into factories. In the last three fiscal years, sales
in the States have grown from $7 million to $40 million to the
$50 million he anticipated for 1985-86 (half of which was sold
by the beginning of 1985). Most of his business life centres on
Los Angeles now; he comes to Canada to attend merchandising strategy sessions and board meetings. While president
Murray Batte handles the Canadian operations, Nygard concerns himself with overall corporate development and policy-
making, oversees the Orient end of the business and
negotiates the major fabric-buying.

His company weathered the recession through textbook
methods: turning merchandise around faster, cutting inven-
tories and tightening up on credit. In what was a far less conventional move, he consciously reduced sales by $10 million,
deciding to avoid those retailers who were bad risks. All of
this helped reduce accounts receivable by $2 million and in-
creased his profit margin.

The Manitoba garment industry, meanwhile, survived the
downturn with only a failure or two. Unlike Ontario and
Quebec manufacturers, who have 87 percent of the trade,
many of Manitoba's clothing manufacturers are young and
enterprising, like Nygard, and acutely aware of their unlikely
geographical location, so far from major population centres.
Their factories — larger and more economical to run than
those in the East — have introduced more than $100 million in
new technology in less than a decade.*

---

* Two years ago, Manitoba had as many pattern-grading and -marking computer
installations as Quebec and Ontario combined. Of the three computer-cutting
operations currently in Canada, one is in Manitoba, owned by Westcott Fashions
Limited, which has had an in-house computer since 1974.

In his Winnipeg plants Nygard installed computers that
grade and mark patterns into thirty-two sizes instantly, a process that once took a month. Instead of employees having to
arrange pattern pieces on material laboriously, the system
plots the pieces in an arrangement that makes the most efficient use of the fabric. By the end of 1985, he expected to
install new equipment that would provide a computer link
between Montreal and Los Angeles, at a cost of $400,000. The
computers would store their designs and patterns for instant
retrieval and establish quality control by guaranteeing con-
sistency. Nygard says computers will not displace existing
staff but will reduce the hiring of new employees. The
disbelieving International Ladies' Garment Workers Union
took him to the Manitoba Labour Board in 1985, which
ordered his company to compensate eighteen workers who
had been laid off illegally, give the union $100,000 and pay a
fine of $4,000.

Peter Nygard isn't used to that sort of failure. He has won at
most everything in his life, at no great cost to himself. The
people around him who have suffered the most from his competitive, fanatical focus on business are women. * In his early
thirties he was married for three years to a blonde Tan Jay in-
house model named Carol, for whom he bought (though he
never lived in) the former Gilbert Eaton manse on Winnipeg's
Old-Money avenue, Wellington Crescent. "She wanted a nice
little house," one of Nygard's friends says. "Of course, he
overdid it." The friend remembers Carol's telling him that
Peter wanted to marry her, "But he wants it clearly understood," she told him, "I'll have only six percent of his time."
Six percent. Peter Nygard wasn't kidding. They were married
anyway, and divorced, and there were no children.

---

* In his years of growth, his paradoxical attitudes toward female employees would
show in many ways. He embraced in-house models with a familiarity that went
beyond the usual boss-worker relationship, yet he promoted his secretary, a
mother who was separated, to the position of personnel manager. His enthusiasm
for womankind continues at forty-four; three times during a brief telephone conversation, he invited — sight unseen — a young woman researching some basic
facts for this book to come and stay at his place in Los Angeles.

Along with male buddies like Fred and John Craig Eaton and David Soul, the Hutch of TV's "Starsky and Hutch," he enjoys the many women in his life: "Always. Only second to my number-one activity which has been sports or studying or work. . . . The women issue has created more jealousy in my life among men — more than sports ever has. Can't live without them. . . . As a matter of fact, I hardly ever break up with them anymore. I just have more of them. I'm not jealous. I must create an environment where they prefer my company. I really go out and spoil my women; I say I'm going to make it difficult for the next guy to top this. And that is my sense of security. It's not only buying them up. They have to enjoy your company. There's a certain air of excitement I create because I'm always on the move."

Yet if he can't live without women, he has made it clear that he never intends to live with any of them in a marriage. "Fortunately, at a very young age, I got totally in tune with myself. My mind and my body are very much in harmony. I've got complete freedom. I'm not married and running around with other women. My whole attitude is that I really can't tell a person that I'll live with her happily ever after." In fact, all that any woman should reasonably expect — if she rates him on past performance — is six percent of the precisely apportioned life of Peter Nygard.

Ed Alfke — King of The Wrecks

In the winter of 1975, all Ed Alfke wanted was a reasonably priced, dependable car to get him to the beach where he could learn how to surf. He and his wife, on their first vacation together, had come to Hawaii from their home in Kamloops, British Columbia, and for the first time in his life the twenty-five-year-old Alfke had rented a car. But the new car from a local company kept stalling and when he returned it in disgust, the advertised $9.95 daily rate proved to be — counting all the insurance and gas and mileage costs — about $30 a day. He exploded with anger. "Take your damn car back!" he told the owner. *"To hell with you."*

Alfke kept watching for a cheap car to tote his surfboard during his last week on the island. After three days of looking, off and on, he spotted a rusting old Buick Skylark on a service-station lot. A classic clunker, the Buick was waiting to be rejuvenated and sold for about $300. He convinced the Filipino garage-owner to let this crazy Canadian rent it for $5 a day. *Why the hell can't I?* His security was a $100 credit-card charge which would be cancelled if Alfke brought the car back in a single piece. He did — and paid the owner a reasonable $20 for renting his improvised beach buggy for four days.

It was on the Wardair charter back to Vancouver, when Ed Alfke told his seatmates what an interesting deal he had made — and heard their encouraging responses — that Rent-A-Wreck was conceived. The idea, which no one in Canada had thought of before, was simple: rent well-used yet clean and reliable vehicles at much lower rates than the Big Four — the American-owned Budget, Hertz and Avis and the Canadian-owned Tilden — could rent new ones.

In less than a decade, Alfke turned that desperate solution to his holiday predicament into a $5-million personal fortune built on a flourishing international franchise system, based in Vancouver, that has revenues of about $50 million a year from its fleet of at least five thousand used rental vehicles in 150 franchises. Rent-A-Wreck and some of its smaller imitators have bitten a 20 percent chunk out of the rental business once enjoyed exclusively by the new-car companies. The upstarts still have some distance to go: Budget Rent a Car, the largest in Canada, has double the number of cars in up to two hundred franchises. But the profits of new-car agencies in this country are slender because prices — held down by the aggressive competition of Budget in particular — are pegged much lower here than in the United States. Tilden, for instance, has earned a net profit above 5 percent on sales only three times in more than half a century. In contrast, Rent-A-Wreck's net profit has never been under 5 percent and currently runs above ten. During the recession, not only did Ed

Alfke's business survive, it inevitably thrived with its cut-rate prices during the thorniest years of the downturn: in 1982, for example, twenty-five new locations opened. The number of locations has doubled since then. In the last five years the turnover of franchise-holders has been only 4 percent.

Rent-A-Wreck Systems Limited now has seven franchises in England, 12 in the United States and 131 spread across Canada, from Victoria to St. John's. In this country the franchises offer cars, vans and trucks — few if any of them real wrecks — for $8.95 to $16.95 a day (the average for a car is $10.95), plus $5.95 for $250 deductible insurance and seven cents a kilometre. Or a customer can lease a car, with sixteen hundred free kilometres, for $299 to $499 a month.* In the United States and England the used-car franchises run under the less tacky name of Practical Rent-A-Car. But in 1985 Practical also began to be known in Canada as the name of Alfke's venture into the new-car business. It was a surprising tactic, encouraged as much by automobile manufacturers eager for his trade as it was by the growing need to furnish his own fleet of used cars for Rent-A-Wreck.

An unequally unexpected development in the brief career of this thirty-five-year-old entrepreneur — who since boyhood had considered himself an island, alone and apart — has been the serious consideration he has lately given to taking his corporation public or bringing in partners to enlarge his capital base. The fact that he would even entertain the uncomfortable, notion of sharing his sole proprietorship with others is due in large measure to amiable nagging by a man nearly three decades older, the former chairman of the huge multinational

---

* Comparable weekday rates for new cars at Hertz and Tilden are $23.95 a day, including two hundred free kilometres. Hertz charges 12 cents for every extra kilometre, Tilden 10 cents. The Hertz price includes insurance with $1,000 deductible; an extra $7.50 buys zero deductible, which Rent-A-Wreck doesn't offer. Tilden's includes $750-deductible insurance, with a further $6 for zero. The presence of Rent-A-Wreck has diminished the profits of even such lower-priced new-car rental agencies as Budget, whose British Columbia manager has admitted that when Alfke's franchises have opened near his, he has been forced to drop prices: "If Rent-A-Wreck rents out thirty cars a day, ten or fifteen of them might have been mine."

resource company, Cominco. Nearing retirement age, Gerald Hobbs is now a director of the B.C. Telephone Company and sundry financial institutions, a governor of the University of British Columbia, and an unpaid member of an informal board of four impressive advisors that Ed Alfke has imaginatively set up to offer him their counsel in running Rent-A-Wreck. The others are Al Kohler, until recently executive vice-president of Midas Muffler in Canada, Hans Hartwig, vice-chairman of Western and Pacific Bank, and a senior American executive in the transportation field whose management contract precludes identifying him. Gerald Hobbs, who has not yet met the other three advisors, is mightily impressed with the young man who approached him through a mutual friend in 1984 and asked him to be his business mentor. "Ed Alfke," he says, "is an extraordinarily ingenious, able and unusual young man in that he has the modesty of spirit to recognize that although he's a very creative guy, there are those things he doesn't know or there are people who have greater experience."

What Ed Alfke doesn't know, he'll tell you about. Although a sense of modesty does not obtain in most Western entrepreneurs, he displays a matter-of-fact, unsettling style. Real men don't eat crow, but Alfke has no qualms about castigating his teenaged self: "I was an asshole." More to the point, he says of those so-recent years when he was creating Rent-A-Wreck: "We did everything wrong." At times, he confesses, "I've been totally depressed and scared to death." For a banker's son who grew up to be a businessman, Alfke candidly admits to a shaky foundation in figures, having done poorly in high-school mathematics and failing economics in his half-year at community college. His relentless sobriety of speech and manner — he cracks no jokes and rarely relaxes — belies his boyhood hell-raising and goofing-off, which became worrisome enough for his parents to board him at a disciplined private school in Victoria for a year.

Today, he retains his modesty in the way he lives. Certainly as a specimen of the West-Coast millionaire species, Alfke is letting down the side somewhat. He may dress for the role in

French stretch cords, striped shirt open to the second button, exposing the unavoidable gold chain, and an Ultrasuede jacket. ("I buy these at cost from a friend in Montreal; I don't pay retail for anything.") He has a surfer's blond hair, a full russet beard and a plump nose with a ski jump. His slight five-ten, 160-pound frame is well-tended. But this is no playboy. Since 1980 he has been married to his second wife, Deborah, a woman of model-like beauty — with china-doll black hair and ivory complexion — who works with him as a company accountant. They live in a comfortable but not ostentatious house in Vancouver's pleasantly bourgeois Dunbar district where their leisure is seldom more exciting than cycling and walking the English setter. (Alfke also snorkels and skis.) "He's probably a tough guy to get to know really well," says a banker friend, Tom Sutton. "Certainly he tries his darndest, running around in his Corvette, to give the appearance of being a very outgoing, easy, carefree kind of guy." In fact, Alfke has long since sold his sports-car collection, the '56 and '64 T-birds, the '65 Corvette Stingray, '66 Thunderbird, modified '71 Corvette and the de Tomasa Pantera, an exotic Italian two-seater designed by an Argentine racing driver (his wife found it too bumpy a ride).

He acts about as carefree as Job. Until recently, he routinely put in 110-hour weeks, a consuming way of life he fed with his ferocious energy. He believed he had to be everywhere, know each franchise-holder's every problem. Typical was the complaint of one of his franchisees, Neilly Robertson of Thornhill, north of Toronto: "Ed has to learn to let go a little bit," she said, "and let other people assume some responsibility. He's going to be his own worst enemy. He can't work twenty hours a day, seven days a week." Only in 1984 did Alfke hire a marketing director, who works out of Toronto, and a year later he was actively seeking a general manager to relieve him of some of the burden of detail that he despises. Constant criticism like Neilly Robertson's helped convince him that he had reached the level of his competence as a manager. "I learn better when you place a two-by-four across my head with velocity," he says.

Growing up in the fifties and sixties, Ed Alfke wore a chip that size on his shoulder. He marvels now at the boy he was, a stubborn, unstable loner. His Dutch-Canadian father was a manager for the Canadian Imperial Bank of Commerce during the boom years in the northern British Columbia communities of Peace River and Dawson Creek. A stalwart of the community, Alfke Sr. was president of the Chamber of Commerce, the treasurer of the United Church. Ed's mother, of Irish stock, was an active volunteer for the Ladies Auxiliary, and both parents were ardent, competitive curlers. Because his only brother was nine years older, Ed was raised like an only child — a mouthy, spoiled child whom his mother over-protected. Being the son of a banker in small northern towns helped distance him from other kids, and from the first, he felt he was different: "I've always known since I was young that I would do more than most people, that there was something unique in me." He sees it in mystical terms: although not particularly religious, he believes in a God and maintains that there has always been a protective someone looking out for him — "the good Lord, guardian angels?"

His abrasive nature was a way of insulating himself from people he'd just as soon avoid anyway. He found his self-expression in competition — solo sports. In his teens Ed was a ski racer in the British Columbia Interior, swam and played water polo. But he was undisciplined in school and almost everything else. In Grade 11, after a spate of Saturday-night fistfights and tickets for speeding through Dawson Creek on his motorcycle, his father decided that he could use some straightening out at University School in Victoria, which was run in strict British style with weekend detentions and bamboo canings. He was forced to study for the first time — a two-by-four was figuratively placed across his head with velocity — and the spoiled loner had to learn how to live with eleven other boys in a dormitory. His temper involved him in several fights; one of them, in which he put the teeth of a school rugby star through the boy's lips, did not endear him to the other students. Yet even though the school refused to accept him back for Grade 12, he looks back on that year with fondness. "I think I probably liked the discipline; it gave me the first glimmerings of realization about myself."

But back home, he only squeaked through his final year of high school. Unfocused, he decided to attend a new junior college in British Columbia's Okanagan Valley where, as a self-styled left-wing radical caught up in the rhetoric of the late sixties, he found himself standing up at a students' meeting to criticize the college facilities and being elected student-council president. "It was like a light got switched on," he remembers. "I was absolutely amazed at my leadership and didn't know what to do with it. Almost like now, I guess. I seem to lead people by my personality." Organizing a sit-in, the students marched on the college president only to discover that he agreed with most of their demands. Emotions spent, his interest in studying on the wane — he got only 38 percent in economics — Alfke quit college after only six months to work in the laboratory of a pulp mill in Prince George, where he learned to distrust unions. *

In 1969, after only half a year in the mill, he quit again to join his older brother in running a steakhouse in Prince George. Ed, deciding he wanted a share of the place, sold his Harley-Davidson motorcycle for straight cash and did some creative financing. He borrowed money from a finance company, ostensibly to buy another Harley, and then offered them his motorcycle as security — neglecting to tell them that he had already sold it. Then he borrowed more from another finance company and took all his money to a bank, where he borrowed the balance. Within forty-eight hours, he had raised a total of $15,000 to buy 50 percent of his brother's restaurant, an investment that went to pay off his brother's first partner.

---

* Like so many entrepreneurs. "I used to run between points," he says, "and the union stewards told me to slow down. I was doing an hour's work in twenty minutes. I was resentful of that. The union's attitude just stunk: 'Don't work too fast,' they said. The featherbedding is so blatant. . . . The unions stopped me from getting ahead. That's what so many people fail to realize: that a union will protect you to the point where you *cannot*, much less don't *have* to, do any work, and by that you can't excel if you want to. . . . This business is such that we wouldn't get unionized."

For the next three years, Ed put in 120 hours a week in the steakhouse, washing dishes, cleaning up and cooking. The experience was to change him from a radical who labelled his family "the plastic fantastic society" to a workaholic who embraced capitalism to support a new wife and baby daughter. As the pressure increased, his relationship with his brother began to deteriorate. In the last year of their partnership, when Ed was chef, he was forever at loggerheads with his manager brother over his lax control of costs. When they finally sold out, there was enough money for Ed to pay off his loan, which gave him the beginning of a track record with the bank, and a meagre $10,000 profit.

In 1973, with that profit, $12,000 from his father-in-law and a loan from the Royal Bank, he opened a clothing store called Jean Jungle in the south-central B.C.-Interior city of Kamloops. Alfke had bought the franchise from a young Prince George couple, Brian and Darlene Spooner, who had just started what would become a chain of profitable basic-jean shops across British Columbia. "Ed was a bit of a hothead," says Darlene Spooner. "He wasn't very well-liked. He talked about himself a great deal; he made a habit of telling people how great he was." Yet she recalls him with affection as an exceptional salesman and a good motivator of his staff. The showman within, which Alfke had discovered at junior college, resurfaced in retailing; customers were buying his enthusiasm as much as his clothes. Within six years he had franchises in four towns, but by then he'd lost interest in the clothing business. The Spooners would phone him at noon to find he was still at home in bed. They finally bought him out, and no hard feelings remain on either side: Alfke now speaks of Brian and Darlene Spooner as the most ethical people he has ever known, a couple whose search for self-improvement (among other things, Darlene used to travel around with an Emily Post book on etiquette) had a profound influence on him as a businessman.

During those years with Jean Jungle, Ed Alfke was Joe Entrepreneur, investing in a small construction company with his brother (and making no money on it), a travel agency that for a time was acting as the only Canadian organizer of trips to China (he sold his half-share for $80,000) and a skateboard shop (which gave him a nice cash flow). Money wasn't his motivation; as Darlene Spooner says, "He's insecure so he tries to work it out in different ways. He seems to have a drive for recognition more than money." Alfke agrees: "I enjoy very much being a leader; I enjoy the recognition. I'm never satisfied: I always want it bigger, better, *more*. Money always comes with doing a job well, and I like all the things money can buy, but I have no exotic tastes." But at that time Ed Alfke was experiencing the worst period of his young life. His marriage was crumbling and he was drinking heavily to subdue the guilt he felt. "I made a lot of money in the retail-store business," Alfke says now. "I bought a 450 SL [a Mercedes-Benz sports car] and I went crazy for a couple of years, spent a lot of money, lived very high and damn near died of ulcers." (The interesting fact about his ulcers is that, although they never had him near death, they were bad — yet he suffered them so silently that the Spooners were never aware that he had the condition.) At the height of his unhappiness, in the winter of 1975, he decided to decelerate for three weeks and took his wife on holiday to Hawaii. It was the butt-end of their marriage. At nineteen he had wed his college sweetheart and she had worked as a waitress with him in the steakhouse. The long hours and the togetherness contributed to their breakup six years later, as did what he calls his total lack of awareness of other people's feelings. "Our marriage was a running gunfight," he says.

But when he came home from his Hawaiian vacation with the concept of renting used cars, Alfke was as excited as a sixteen-year-old learning to drive. As far as he knew, nobody in the world had ever thought of the idea before. * Car-dealer

---

* Alfke now acknowledges that used cars were for hire in Florida as long ago as the Second World War, when new ones were not to be had. But he prefers to scoff at published reports that a Los Angeles car dealer named Dave Schwartz was renting old cars in an organized fashion in the early 1970s. Alfke's touchiness may have something to do with the fact that by 1977 — a year after Rent-A-Wreck's birth in

friends did their damndest to discourage him: "The maintenance will kill ya, Ed." But at a bar one night, a beery
Australian who heard about the idea stood up and toasted
him: "The birth of a new company, Rent-A-Wreck. Alfke,
King of the Wrecks." He had a name; now he needed money.
At first his banker, Tom Sutton of the Royal's main branch in
Kamloops, just laughed. "First of all," Sutton remembers, "the
name just turned me right off. And I didn't think it was all that
good an idea." As Alfke recalls their meeting, the banker told
him: "This is a Looney-Tune idea. But you're good for
$15,000. On a personal note."

It was the autumn of 1976. Alfke and his wife were
separated (she has raised their daughter, now in her mid-
teens), and he was ripe for an adventure. With Dale Granger,
a 10 percent partner who had owned several Hertz franchises,
he launched Rent-A-Wreck in the corner of a used-car lot on
the outskirts of Prince George. They had five cars, worth $300
or less, all of them old crocks of more than 100,000 miles,
which they rented for $10 a day and ten cents a mile. "Dale
had a lot of borderline customers at Hertz and they were
perfect candidates for Rent-A-Wreck then — guys known
around town — a little 'iffy,' but basically okay people as long
as they weren't drinking."

Merely on word of mouth, the business blossomed from the
start (in numbers of customers, if not in profits). Unfortunately, the partners had shamelessly stolen their ideas from
the Hertz rental system. Following its standards for
maintenance on new cars didn't work with cars that were on
their last wheels. Like Hertz, they accepted anyone as long as
they had cash or a credit card, without taking into account
their reliability. As the partners were to discover, Rent-A-
Wreck had to screen its customers because used cars can't take
the beating that new ones can. While their gross revenues

Canada — Schwartz was publicizing his own franchise system in the United States.
It too is named Rent-A-Wreck, although the two companies have no links with and
no love for one another. Alfke still smarts at the year it took his lawyers to trademark the name in Canada. "We could have trademarked it in the U.S. too," he says
regretfully, "but we weren't smart enough to do that."

grew, they had no net as their badly selected and under-maintained cars continued to break down. For six months they had no book-keeping system in place and, when they did get one, realized that they had lost about $20,000.

After another few months, they began to attract a more stable blue-collar customer who was fascinated enough with the craziness of the concept to come in with his broken-down Rent-A-Wreck junker on the back of a tow truck and be willing to wait a day if necessary to pick up a replacement. The Prince George location grew to fifty cars (Dale Granger sold his share in 1978) and a Datsun dealer paid Ed Alfke, the sole owner of "the Rent-A-Wreck franchise system" — a rather grandiose name for one guy and a bunch of old cars — $3,500 for the rights to open in Kamloops. By then, Alfke had decided to move the concept and himself to Vancouver, where the novelty value was enough to create instant customers on well-travelled West Broadway. Without even a sign in place, on the day he opened in 1977 with twenty-six cars, he was sold out.

Yet problems continued to dog him. Although he was now paying $500 to $700 a car, the big-city wholesalers sold the boy from the sticks a crop of lemons. And his relationship with his bank had soured. Despite the nearly $200,000 invested in the business by then, he seriously considered abandoning it that first year. The first Vancouver banker he dealt with, at a branch office of the Royal, had no confidence in Rent-A-Wreck. Alfke limped through that year and even sold three franchises in other areas of British Columbia. When he finally transferred to the Royal's main branch in the city, he was dealing again with Tom Sutton, who showed him how to draft an impressive borrowing proposal to keep Rent-A-Wreck afloat. It was a turning point in the company's fortunes. With bank financing supporting him, Alfke was able to entertain some of the many requests to franchise Rent-A-Wreck. Beginning to realize his own limitations, he brought in an accounting firm that helped him design a financial-reporting system that would grow with the company. Franchising consultants Robert Harris and Associates of Toronto offered solid advice: for instance, don't grow so fast that the system's infrastructure collapses. ("We limited our growth to 100 percent a year — period," Alfke says. "We will double in size each year and that's the end of it.") New franchise-holders themselves added their expertise: one with administrative experience in the air force further streamlined the accounting system; another who was a car dealer shared his knowledge of buying and selling used vehicles. (As a result, cars were costing more but lasting longer.) Alfke himself developed an effective classroom franchisee-training program with a proper operations manual. Eventually he felt confident enough to cancel agreements with two operators who failed to meet his maintenance standards.

Along the way, Ed Alfke was maturing. Developing the social skills he needed in a people-focused business, and learning to subdue the temper that had led him into scraps as a teenager (the understanding of his second wife, Debby, helped him control it), Ed Alfke was taking pleasure in the leadership role he had assumed as the creator of an accelerating business. "I am the result of my work as much as vice-versa," he says.

By the end of 1982, five years after its birth, Rent-A-Wreck had two thousand rental vehicles earning more than $10 million in revenues a year. The eighty-six franchisees had paid anywhere from $10,000 to $25,000 to buy in, depending on the size and location of their operation, and $20 a month per car in royalties to support the system (they now pay 6 percent of revenues per car). * At the time, Ed Alfke — worth at least $2 million — was working out of an ugly little office around the corner from his own rental agency in the low-rent east end of Vancouver. "This place really cranks out a lot of money," he liked to say of the location, which then had a fleet of more than a hundred vehicles. "I mean, this gives me $100,000 cash a year after my wages, which are quite substantial. And I feed

* Start-up costs vary, of course, but when a former Xerox manager opened a franchise in Richmond, his launch cost $200,000 (three-quarters of it back-financed) for franchising fee, inventory and office space and equipment. He ran a fleet of 45 cars; his income equalled expenses within six weeks.

all that into the systems company for its growth and development." But because he was spending half his time away from the location — "and our system doesn't allow absentee ownership" — he has since sold it to two businessmen who in their first four months turned a profit of $70,000. He now entertains prospective franchise-holders on the upscale west side of the city in more presentable quarters softened with greenery and adorned with watercolours by the popular Vancouver artist Markgraf.

"The rule of thumb," Alfke explains, "is that you're going to make about $1,000 a car per year profit. That's after bank and wages. So if you run fifty cars, you make fifty grand, more or less." A franchisee buys a car for between $3,000 and $4,000, which is the wholesalers' range of prices to dealers. But not just any car: "You watch incidence of repair, cost of repair, time allotted and return on investment. And then each individual car will stand up at a different rate than another one. We've done all the power-train [drive shaft, clutch, transmission, differential] statistical work. We know you should buy a this instead of a that. For instance, a Pinto will last an awful lot longer on the fleet than a Maverick will, simply because Mavericks tend to loosen up a great deal quicker." Alfke says a car should stand up about a year.

Each vehicle will likely sit idle one week out of four, he estimates, so the franchisee can expect an income of about $500 per car per month. Direct monthly expenses are $120 a car for insurance, $20 in systems royalties, and an average $60 in maintenance, which includes a thorough washing, vacuuming and vinyl cleaning after each rental, as well as mechanical servicing and road-testing every three thousand miles. This totals $200, leaving a margin of $300. After fixed costs — rent, wages, advertising — the remainder is gross profit: about $840 per car per year. After about a year's use, though, the car is sold to the public through signs on the lot or newspaper ads. If it costs $3,000 from the wholesaler, it's actually worth $4,000 retail. Take off $900, the standard, annual 30 percent depreciation for a car that's older than three years. The vehicle could still be sold for $3,100, making a further $100, and yielding a total gain of almost $1,000.

In a twelve-hour-a-day, six-day-a-week, two-week session in Vancouver, franchise-holders are trained by Mary Jane Hlynialuk, who used to be Vancouver city manager for Hertz. Among many other lessons, she teaches franchisees how to buy cars, and they attend a car auction with an experienced buyer. Afterwards, a field-support staff (British Columbia's thirty-two franchisees have four operations supervisors in the field) keeps them current with a catalogue of vehicles to buy or avoid, based on in-house mechanics' reports of durability. They learn the daily-accounting system, which usually requires a book-keeper half a day a month to summarize, and receive an encyclopedic operations manual. Franchisees also get on-location training in qualifying customers — that is, deciding which ones to trust their cars to. Here the science ends and the art begins. Unlike Hertz or Tilden, where a valid credit card guarantees virtually anyone a vehicle, Rent-A-Wreck must sift its customers. "First impressions of the customer are the biggest factor in qualifying," says Mary Jane Hlynialuk. "We note his appearance, his dress, his attitude." A driver must be twenty-one, and if paying with cash instead of a card — and about one-fifth of Rent-A-Wreck's customers do — must have a job. The rental clerk will verify employment and perhaps pose other questions, for example: "Do you own that house?" The cardless customer leaves a deposit of between $100 and $300. No one can buy zero-deductible, as at the new-car companies. "If you're going to drive my car," Ed Alfke argues, "you should invest a little bit in my fenders." And if a customer has three problems in a row with its cars, Rent-A-Wreck asks him politely to take his business elsewhere.

While the requests for franchises are constant, Alfke remains cautious about the character of the people applying; he tries to weed out the hobbyists. One day a middle-manager from IBM came to see Alfke. Tall, nicely tailored in a three-piece navy-blue suit, he said that he was thinking of selling his house and buying a Rent-A-Wreck franchise with his wife. Talking to the IBM manager, Alfke asked whether the fellow might be making a mistake in considering a franchise. "When I look at you," he said, "when I see a sophisticated blue suit, expensive shirt and silk tie, it's got to make me wonder: Do you want a Rent-A-Wreck?"

Certainly many well-bred people do. Bolton Agnew, a young gentleman from a good family in England, came to Canada to make his fortune and, discovering Rent-A-Wreck, pressed Alfke for half a year to open a company in England, which had no competing used-car rental agencies. Alfke was reluctant because a previous attempt had gone nowhere. In 1984 Agnew became a director and general manager of the British operation, a joint-venture partnership named Practical Rent-A-Car, which within six months had seven franchises in place. Another director is a Canadian retired in England, Henry Williams, who has an Order of the British Empire and learned about Alfke when he was visiting Edmonton and hired a Rent-A-Wreck.

Under the Practical name, the company has been operating in the United States since the early eighties, when Alfke sold franchises in Tampa and Sarasota, Florida; by mid-decade he had another three in that state and seven more in major cities between Pittsburgh and Anchorage. Growth has been slow south of the border: "We're being too quiet and staid for the American market, where it's fiercely competitive," Alfke explains. Researching the field in 1985 from regional offices in Pittsburgh, Seattle and Laguna Beach, the company was rewriting its marketing plan for a more assertive American push; until then, it had advertised its existence only through large regional papers.

Even in Canada, Rent-A-Wreck has not displayed any real marketing pizzazz. Until early in this decade, Ed Alfke was always adamant about national advertising: Rent-A-Wreck simply didn't need it. His franchisees disagreed and insisted, at one of their two owners' meetings each year, that the company launch an ad campaign on radio, billboards and in newspapers ("Good cars . . . cheap"). Then they opposed his decision to handle the campaign from Vancouver. Franchise-holder Neilly Robertson of Toronto was one of his critics: "What the hell do they know about our advertising problems here?" But she adds, to Alfke's credit, that he has since admitted, "I'm wrong. I tried to do it all and obviously I made a mistake." The TV advertising, until recently, consisted of insipid and cheaply produced commercials featuring the stilted Alfke. Since then, it has graduated to more exciting graphics, at the suggestion of the company's new vice-president of marketing, based in Toronto.

Hiring a vice-president was a giant step for Ed Alfke, the stubborn loner, who was finally learning to share the business he created. Now he was saying: "I need a general manager here. I'm not a professional enough manager for an operation this size. I lack follow-up and control. I have promoted myself to my level of incompetence." By the end of the decade, he hoped to bump himself upstairs as chairman and hand the reins over to a chief operating officer.

Realizing that he was an entrepreneur and not an administrator, he began seeking counsel, which led him to the unusual concept of a board of advisors, comprising men more experienced in business who would be willing to guide him simply for the pleasure of playing the mentor's role. Of the four he chose, Alfke consults most often with Hans Hartwig of Western and Pacific Bank and Gerald Hobbs, a director of several large corporations. "Ed Alfke," Hobbs says, "is a superb salesman and he's very creative, but he doesn't like sitting behind his desk to look after administrative matters." In his regular visits with Alfke, Hobbs has been badgering him to either make Rent-A-Wreck a public company or take on partners to increase his capital. "There are always opportunities that present themselves where you need some money," he advised.

One of those opportunities arose in 1985, before Alfke had decided to go public or get partners. With the consensus of his franchise-holders, he opened Practical New Car Rental as a low-priced new-car rental agency in Canada that would operate out of existing Rent-A-Wreck franchises. On the surface, it seemed somewhat absurd. Why would a man who had built his success on used cars muddy the waters by going up against the Budgets and Tildens? There were logical reasons. The number of used cars is declining every year; many Canadian vehicles are now sold across the border (with no duty levied) because of the strong American dollar. Buying his own factory-fresh vehicles for Practical would provide him with a steady flow of used cars for Rent-A-Wreck. Hungry new-car manufacturers, meanwhile, were very supportive of Alfke's plan to rent out their vehicles, offering him a line of credit to buy their products. In the end, he borrowed $10 million from the Western and Pacific Bank and the Bank of British Columbia to buy 1,000 Tempo LTDs and vans from Ford Motor Co. of Canada.

But beyond the logical reasons for moving into the new-car business was another, born of rebelliousness. Nobody, least of all the Big Four rental agencies, would have ever suspected the King of the Wrecks to storm their domains in such a frontal attack. Never, in their worst nightmares, had they reckoned on Ed Alfke's telling them again: *"To hell with you."*

4

The
Entertainment
Entrepreneurs

They are originals. Unencumbered by tradition, forced to assume high profiles because they compete for business in provinces with a small population base, the entertainment entrepreneurs of the West are singular capitalists. No one quite like them exists in Eastern Canada; no one there needs to. In satisfying pleasures, in supplying leisure activities, these Westerners often become as well-known as the products or services they provide. And in doing so, they have influenced and redefined the shape of entertainment enterprise throughout Canada.

The West's entertainment entrepreneurs are the businesspeople who become financially involved in the diversions that sweeten our lives. The four we profile on the following pages embrace a broad spectrum of entertainment, from rock music (Bruce Allen) to restaurants (Umberto Menghi), to lovemaking (Gary Hooge and Brenda Humber). They are characteristic of their kind: the capitalists involved in the Western entertainment scene are themselves theatrical and flamboyant individuals. They act out their roles as if they were on stage, or they seek and reap as much attention as the customers they're supposed to be serving.

Consider Bruce Allen of Vancouver, the manager of the multimillion-dollar group Loverboy and the swiftly rising young rock star Bryan Adams. Until recently he thrived on his image as a brawling monster of a man, unpredictable and given to verbal and physical violence. His self-propelled legend as a rascal developed a decade ago, when he was managing Bachman-Turner Overdrive, which was becoming the most commercially successful rock band ever to come out of Canada. A typical incident: headlining a concert in Illinois, BTO was waiting for a warm-up act called Brownsville Station to finish its encore. When the audience kept shouting for more, Brownsville's leader, Cub Koda, brought the group on for another song. As Koda was about to go back on stage, Bruce Allen punched him in the nose and knocked him down a staircase. "I said *one* encore."

In his notoriety, Allen is unique in this country and perhaps in North America. Certainly no manager has ever been celebrated in the lyrics of a song, as he was in Bachman-Turner Overdrive's "Welcome Home": *So glad we left the prairie city/And now we're living on the coast/We went and got ourselves a manager/We all think he's the most.* The rock-attentive public knows his name in a way they don't know the identities of music managers in Eastern Canada. None of them would seek as much attention as their clients; none has Allen's ego. Nor do they have his success. Bruce Allen's peers recognized his remarkableness in 1984: in a vote by American radio programmers, promoters and managers, he was named Manager of the Year.

As extraordinary in Canada as Bruce Allen is in music, Umberto Menghi is in restaurants. The East has a couple of restaurateurs whose names might be recognized by the man in the street — George Cohon of McDonald's and John Arena of Winston's in Toronto. But neither has anywhere near the overwhelming public presence of Menghi, who from his Vancouver base runs eight good restaurants on the West Coast, including two in Seattle and one in San Francisco, and a new publicly traded chain of fast-food pasta shops.

Umberto — few bother with his surname — is one of only two restaurateurs in the country to have had his own television series (the other is a fellow Vancouverite, Stephen Yan, whose "Wok With Yan" has been a fixture on the national CBC network). In fact, Umberto has had two TV series. For one, he surrounded himself with beautiful models, whom he hugged and kissed on camera, flattering them outrageously. His producer, Clancy Grass, called him "the James Bond of cooking," a strained comparison that gains most credence through Umberto's fondness for fast cars, which include a Ferrari, a Lamborghini, a BMW, a Mercedes and a Lincoln limousine. He is also the author of two successful cookbooks.

Two other entrepreneurs specialize in an unusual type of entertainment business. They run a thriving chain of Love Shops in Western Canada. Gary Hooge, (Hoagy, as in Carmichael) and his wife, Brenda Humber, share some of the common characteristics of Menghi and Allen. Like them, they have had the vision to move into the States, recently starting a franchise operation aimed at the American market. They also do not shy away from publicity: Brenda Humber is the performing half of the couple, ever ready to discuss sex and The Love Shops in front of university classes, on television, or before a city council that wants to raise her business-licence fee to $3,000 from $30.

But what make them most similar to the other entrepreneurs in this category are their uniqueness and the influence of their activities: nothing exactly like The Love Shop existed in Canada before one opened in Calgary in 1973. There were tasteless sex shops that dealt in plastic-swathed porn magazines, slot-machine nudie movies and crude adult novelties. No one had thought to tart up these shops with subdued lighting, expensive-looking wall coverings and showcases that featured sexual aids as if they were pieces of jewellery. Certainly no one ever before considered training salespeople to offer thoughtful sexual advice to confused customers. Since The Love Shop surfaced, others like it have appeared — Lovecraft opened in Toronto a year later — and offer some of the same tastefulness, if not the same sexually-trained staff.

Hooge and Humber remain the originals. They and Umberto Menghi, and Bruce Allen, along with many others like them in the West, are creating new standards of performance in the entertainment industry in Canada.

Brenda Humber and Gary Hooge
— The Mom and Pop of Sex

In a career-information booklet that they now distribute to people taking a staff-training course, Gary Hooge and Brenda Humber confess: "We assume most people entering the program have about as much information about sexuality as we did when we started, which was next to none." This husband-and-wife team in their early forties run a Mom-and-Pop operation, sharing the burden of a business, living and working together night and day. But they are clearly opportunistic, having created a $1.8-million-a-year business based on a chain of four retail shops and two franchises in Western Canada. They continue to concern themselves with growth as they begin expanding into the United States.

Their home-office store, The Love Shop, sits on a respectable downtown stretch of Vancouver's main thoroughfare, Granville Street. In its brightly bedecked windows, amid the sheer lingerie and elegantly packaged vibrators, signs announce A Journey of Discovery "for loving explorers who reap greater happiness from the discovery of new and exciting pleasures they can share with each other." Inside, this attempt at a high-minded tone is maintained, with mixed success. The atmosphere is half sultan's tent, half erotic art gallery. Draperies swathe the ceiling, Persian rugs adorn the floor. The feature lamp is Tiffany-like, much of the furniture heavy, dark, antique. Sepia posters of Mae West and her maxims ("A hard man is good to find") vie for wall space with display boards of crotchless panties. There's a rack of conventional, Canadian-made lingerie, nothing over $100. Customers are greeted by lush Muzak and a nice young man in his mid-twenties who quietly asks if this is their first time in the store; if it is, he points out the information cards by each of the products, which are individually displayed on illuminated teakwood counters like pieces of sculpture. The products, perched near the front, range from Emotion Lotion in several flavours, including blueberry pie (with a handy box of Medi-Wipes beside the sampler bottle), to Angel's Delight, an egg-shaped vibrator which, when "placed in the vagina and left there during intercourse . . . transmits waves of exciting pleasure to both" (a convenient rheostat control allows one to dial the vibration level of one's choice). Near the back are the somewhat hard-core goods: the foot-long vibrators and penis extension sleeves that look like instruments of warfare; the $88.95 Fantastica, a strap-on vibrator realistically shaped like a penis, designed to be worn by a woman or man; and the panties for men, some in the shape of rabbit heads, with long pink ears and a nose-shaped pouch. There are vibrators in the shape of pandas and bumpy-textured Lust Fingers, but the only blatantly tacky product, the one that smacks of a sleazy sex shop, is Mister Peter, an ice-cube mould in phallic form.

Some of the essence of the couple who created this sexual wonderland is contained in the catalogue they offer for sale at the store. Not many catalogues can be sold for $3.95, but then, not many open with a tasteful line drawing of a nude man and woman looking wonderfully sated after a bout of love-making.* Printed in elegant brown on heavy cream paper, *The Love Shop Gourmet Lover's Guide & Catalogue* has a seemly style about it when not peddling product; there's not a snigger in its 106 pages. As well as describing merchandise, it presents a small library of books that roam the amatory reaches, from *Liberating Masturbation* to *The Outer Fringe of Sex*. It also serves as a short course on matters sexual, a sort of Honest Sex 101: a debunking of sexual myths, clinical descriptions of the male and female bodies, discussions of the nature of human sexual response and contraception methods, a dissertation on normal sexual dysfunctions, a defence of masturbation, even a simplistic essay on achieving the ideal sexual relationship. If the information and prose feel slightly dated, there's a reason: Brenda Humber and Gary

---

* Not many sales catalogues are as much fun to write as this one was. Its authors took themselves, their products, and perhaps a hundred books on sex and loving to a cabin at Banff for a week of in-depth research. "Hey, Gary, maybe we should try this," Brenda would say as she read about a promising sexual variation or pondered the instructions for a Vagiring or an Analator.

Hooge are graduates of the let-it-all-hang-out sixties and they composed the booklet back in 1975. That was only a year after Nancy Friday's *My Secret Garden* explored women's most intimate sexual fantasies and Erica Jong's *Fear Of Flying* introduced the world to the zipless fuck. And 1975 was not that long after the work of the American sex researchers Masters and Johnson had reached public attention.

The catalogue, since used as a supplementary text in a human-sexuality course at the University of Calgary, has sold 137,000 copies, which attests to its popularity as a self-help manual. Yet it generates only about $20,000 a year in mail-order sales. The unexpected reason seems to be that lovers want to choose their toys in the flesh, so to speak, to visit a shop in person and ask the advice of a sales staff trained to field the most delicate inquiries discreetly, acceptingly, *amorally*. Customer surveys show that half the clientele is female, about 90 percent are people in long-term relationships, and most are married couples in their thirties to fifties. So it is precisely that non-threatening, low-pressured personal approach, in a comforting atmosphere, that has helped make The Love Shop so successful in Victoria, Vancouver, Edmonton, Calgary, Saskatoon and Winnipeg.

Less than a decade ago, Hooge and Humber faced unemployment and pauperdom, at a time when they were expecting the first of their three children. Now they enjoy upper-middle-class wealth and a lifestyle that allows them and their two sons and a daughter a live-in housekeeper, a Volvo, a Porsche and a Mercedes, vacations in Europe and Mexico, and a charming old house on the expensive waterfront of West Vancouver's Cypress Park.

Their stores alone have grossed well over $2.25 million in pre-recession years (although only $1.5 million in 1984), with the worst rate of return being 35 percent on invested capital and the best double that figure. Then there's the Lover's Wear Party, based on the Tupperware model (and known colloquially as the Fuckerware Party). This home-sales spin-off, operating for five years, generated about $250,000 in 1984 from the marketing of lingerie, lotions and sexual aids in places as divergent in style and setting as the Northwest Territories and Texas. The parties — 70 percent of them attracting groups of women, 30 percent couples — may open with the sales representatives briefly attempting to dispense sexual wisdom (such as the nature of physical responses in men and women) but eventually move on to the real reason the party-goers are in attendance: to ogle and purchase the products they've usually only heard of before. The hors d'oeuvres and drinks usually loosen women up enough to model the lingerie and both sexes to buy more than they had intended. The parties also have the sweet side effect of stimulating shop sales by as much as 50 percent.*

Because of the success of the original stores, Love Shop franchises were an inevitable outgrowth; the first were in Saskatoon and Victoria. In 1985, after two years of learning the applicable laws in thirty-two states, Hooge and Humber launched their American franchising operation in Los Angeles at the annual trade show of the International Franchise Association. Their franchising fee is $15,000 per store, with royalties of 10 percent of sales, but they are seeking operators to take over whole regions of the United States; even before the trade show, potential investors had expressed interest in the California and Louisiana regions. Their lavish full-colour franchising brochure both tantalizes and cautions prospective owners: "Of course, you will be professionally trained in customer communication skills as well as product and sexuality knowledge, but most important, you must also bring to The Love Shop the desire to enrich the lives of others."

The desire to become entrepreneurs has certainly enriched the lives of Hooge and Humber who, like so many self-made Westerners, emerged out of the unlikeliest of circumstances to create their business. She was a cheerleader from Red Deer, Alberta, who became a psychiatric social worker because she felt misplaced in her own life and learned only a few years ago

---

*Shop sales average $27 per customer, the parties about $20 higher because of the relaxed home setting. But the profit margins are lower: "In a shop," Hooge says, "you can generate $30,000 with two people, but to do that in parties would take six to eight people" — who take a 25 percent commission on everything they sell.

that she had been suffering from an energy-sapping thyroid condition since the age of sixteen. He was a black-leathered teenage motorcyclist from a strict Mennonite family in Winkler, Manitoba, who later struggled through studies leading to an MBA only to discover a few years ago that his problems in learning had been caused by the word-blindness of dyslexia.

Brenda Humber, an only child, grew up amid entrepreneurs. Both of her grandfathers owned meat businesses and invested in real estate. Three months before Brenda was born in 1945, her father died in the Second World War. Her mother raised her, until the age of eight, in the quiet Calgary home of Brenda's approving grandparents. Then her mother remarried and the family moved to Red Deer, where Brenda's stepfather ran a jewellery store. While he came from a Victorian-style family, he too seemed warm and accepting of her. About the only early sexual memory Brenda has is of Mrs Humber and her friends trading off-colour jokes. In her early teens Brenda was one of the better athletes in town and a popular student. Yet there was something amiss. When she was fifteen, her stepfather's store failed; the Humbers were no longer one of *the* families in Red Deer. About that time, too, Brenda developed an undiagnosed thyroid condition (as doctors would discover two decades later). She gained twenty pounds and the good athlete inexplicably became a perpetually tired teenager who couldn't stay awake in class; her grades declined. Inside, she felt odd, disconnected.

She continued to do well enough in school to get into the University of British Columbia where, to sort out her confusion, she took psychology and sociology. Then, degree and $500 in hand, she went to Europe for two years. It was the sixties, and London was swinging. Just to keep herself charged, to counter the draining effects of her low thyroid output, she sought out excitement. For a while she worked as a croupier in a Soho club. Later she and a girlfriend hitched aimlessly around the continent in their miniskirts. When they ran out of money, Brenda wound up alone in Germany for six months, sponging off friendly families and (without a Teutonic word in her vocabulary) collaborating with a young German man in translating American Western novels. Back in London, she was shamed by a visiting aunt into getting serious and taking a social-work job in a borough health department. But after about a year she realized that her take-home pay would never be more than a pittance; reluctantly she returned home.

In Calgary she became a psychiatric social worker in a provincial mental-health clinic. She learned how to inverview people skilfully, a boon for her eventual work at The Love Shop, and she learned that the paycheque she received every two weeks appeared to have no relationship to the amount of work she had been doing during that time. "That was the thing I loved about getting into business," she says now in typical entrepreneurial style. "You could count how well you were doing at the end of every day."

At the clinic Brenda worked with a woman psychologist who during the summer of 1969 invited her to a pool party. There she saw the psychologist's brother poised on the diving board: long, slender, with curly brown hair, a leanly attractive face and a cleft chin. *That's the man for me!* she thought. He was Gary Hooge and he wasn't the least bit interested.

At twenty-seven Hooge had done his own European trip and had had an affair with a Danish woman. "Her judgment of whether she went to bed with me had only to do with whether she liked me," he remembered. "It had nothing to do with the games we were playing in Canada." It was a maturing experience for a small-town boy who until then had been involved with only three women over ten years in relationships he now thinks of as mini-marriages. Born in Hague, Saskatchewan, he'd grown up in Winkler, a solidly Dutch and German Mennonite community in southern Manitoba. His father's family believed in hellfire, brimstone and hard work. Yet though there were taboos against most everything pleasurable — dances, movies, even track and field — Gary felt a deep sense of loving family. "You always knew you could do almost anything — kill the Queen Mother — and they would take you back," he recalls.

His father was an influential farm-community capitalist

who introduced two- and three-day dry-cleaning service to fifty towns, in competition with a major company that was offering one- to two-week service. In most of those centres he also ran the Sears mail-order outlets and his own finance company and took over a bakery that delivered goods on both sides of the nearby American border. For a while he was mayor of Winkler, a commanding presence in the town.

When Gary rebelled, it was in a typically pacific Mennonite manner.* He had become an adolescent pool shark who did poorly at school in a town where education reigned supreme. In his mid-teens he bought himself a Triumph 650 and donned leather; with his lean face he looked remarkably like his hero, James Dean. But the gang he hung around with never got into fights when its members hulked around the big city of Winnipeg; brawling wasn't part of the Mennonite character. Hard work was, however. Gary's father would give him money for musical instruments, but not for a motorcycle. So from the age of ten, and all through his rebellious years, Gary worked hard in the sugar-beet fields, a general store, a butcher's shop and his father's bakery. Like Brenda, he was a strong athlete, excelling on a Grade Nine softball team that won the Manitoba men's championship.

His teachers recognized his intelligence and chastized him for what they saw as his contempt for learning. Reading had always frustrated him; he never willingly attempted to wade through anything but prescribed textbooks until he was well into his twenties. Although he could understand individual words, he couldn't string them together into comprehensible sentences. He felt somewhat stupid; his elders considered him lazy. When Gary failed Grade nine, his father said: "Why the hell don't you quit school? Why are you wasting your time and our time?" He sent his son to St. John's Ravenscourt, a private boys' school in Winnipeg, which was like trying to survive in the rarefied air of another planet. The students

*Mennonites, a sect of Protestant Christians that began in Switzerland in 1525, have endured constant persecution for their refusal to bear arms, persecution that led them to leave Russia after the revolution and settle in large numbers in the North American Midwest.

came from wealthy families, the school discipline was militaristic, and to a Mennonite, used to the gentle and protective ways of his family, the boys themselves seemed sadistic. Although they weren't any more aggressive than most teenagers in a private-school setting, Gary found the fights among the boys and the occasional swatting he got from the teachers so unnerving that he fled the school one wintry night and slept in a bus shelter.

His parents brought him back home, but when Gary was in Grade ten they decided that small-town Winkler was bad for him and his younger sister, who also had taken to riding with motorcyclists. In 1957, in an astonishing act of love, their father sold his businesses and moved the family to Saskatoon in the hope that they would escape what he considered their undesirable influences. Gary was sixteen, and scared. His high school had just opened and its team of strong teachers insisted that he couldn't be on the basketball team unless his average was sixty. He tried to learn, a stranger in a strange land (when a Joe Cocker song of that name came out later, he claimed it as his own). No one knew he suffered from dyslexia. Yet through a Mennonite-bred persistence he came close to the required average, close enough to make the basketball team, where he shone.

During the summer he worked on construction jobs, which convinced him that he didn't want to be a labourer all his life. His family had raised him to feel good about himself, he had a knack of taking the lead in any group, and his listening skills were well-developed. So, seeing that the students around him were aiming for university, he managed an average that squeaked him into the faculty of commerce at the University of Saskatchewan. He chose commerce only because it had no second-language requirement. There, Gary got lucky. The school was noted for its accounting program — a course that frustrated him, but would prove valuable in his career — and the faculty was strong in the areas of personnel and organizational behaviour, which he enjoyed. Although his agony over reading continued, he learned to closet himself in a dark room and read under a single focused light, with no distractions to interrupt his concentration; later, he began reading aloud so he could hear the words. Even though it might take him ninety minutes to read twenty pages, he persevered. Largely because of his skill in verbal problem-solving, he became one of a few students to whom the dean of commerce taught private, master's-level courses in his home.

After getting his bachelor of commerce with a hard-won C-plus average in 1964, Gary Hooge started a two-year executive-training program with the Hudson's Bay Company in Edmonton. It was there that he had his first sweet taste of entrepreneurship. One summer The Bay sent him to the mountain resort town of Jasper to manage an exclusive men's shop in a lodge. He thrived on the independence. Back in Edmonton that fall, he grew so bored that he quit The Bay three-quarters of the way through his training to help run a small department store his father had opened in Melfort, Saskatchewan. For half a year, he put into practice the efficient inventory-control system he'd learned at The Bay.

He had applied, meanwhile, to several universities across the continent for admission to graduate school to study organizational behaviour. After only a brief stay at Berkeley — (in the tempestuous mid-sixties, the San Francisco university was in a state of siege that unsettled the peace-loving Hooge) — he entered the University of Oregon's master's program in business administration. He did well only on those courses that depended less on learning through reading than on listening to good lectures.

The most inspirational lecturer was a professor of marketing, an expert in entrepreneurship named Norman Smith. A former Calgarian, he had put himself through the University of Alberta by setting up student sales teams to peddle light bulbs door to door; later, he had the profitable Western-Canadian distributorship for a baby's chair that was also sold to housewives. As a professor, he had his own active marketing consulting firm on the side, the profits from which allowed him to drive around campus in a gold-coloured Jaguar. Gary Hooge was one of many students he hired to take gingham-painted trucks around Oregon to do consumer research for a bread company which, under Smith's guidance, would increase its sales from $2.8 million to $20 million.

Norm Smith remembers Hooge as a student who would ask dumb questions. "I really love dumb questions because it shows that somebody has the guts to say he doesn't understand or that it doesn't make sense to him. That's creative." What the professor never knew was that his student was also struggling to make sense of everything he had to read. One day, in conversation with a fellow student he'd seen breezing through a book, Hooge learned about a reading laboratory at the university. When tested, he found his reading was at the Grade eight level; his comprehension was about 30 percent. He signed up for a reading course that changed his life. In two months his speed increased nearly twentyfold and his comprehension climbed to 85 percent. That year he became an A student and won a scholarship. It was nearly two decades later, when his elder son was diagnosed for the same condition, that Gary Hooge finally realized he had dyslexia.*

In earning his MBA, he wrote one of his best papers for Dr Smith, on the importance of cosmetics in the male and female roles. The marketing professor found it insightful and later, at a Christmas get-together, asked Hooge: "Have you ever thought of going on for a Ph.D.?" Overwhelmed, his student cried.

Full of confidence, hankering now to be a college professor like his mentor, Hooge applied for a teaching position at a junior college in Medicine Hat, Alberta. In 1967 the province was lavishing money on post-secondary education and was hungry for administrative talent. The college at Medicine Hat

---

*Dyslexia is a developmental learning disability. It is independent of intelligence or memory and it relates to the acquiring of reading and spelling skills, and not to the breakdown of existing skills, as may happen after a brain injury. Currently popular theories suggest that dyslexia results from a retardation in the general development of language and that because it tends to run in families, as it has in Gary Hooge's, its basis is genetic. No two cases are exactly alike; a person is considered dyslexic if there is a discrepancy between intellectual level and performance at reading and spelling. While some dyslexic students lose all self-esteem and become extreme introverts, many more persevere, as Hooge did, and pass postsecondary exams even after a history of low-grade passes.

was just opening and Hooge was to be more than a teacher; that summer, he had to design the two-year diploma program in business-administration and advertise for students. Within the year he had set up similar departments at colleges in Grande Prairie and then Red Deer where, at twenty-eight, Hooge became the head of the business department.

A year earlier, in 1969, he had gone to Europe on a five-month vacation, had his affair with the sophisticated Danish woman, and came home with a disdain for games-playing North American girls. Late that summer he escorted his psychologist sister to her staff party at a government guidance clinic in Calgary and met Brenda Humber. Although they danced that night, Hooge showed no interest in the twenty-four-year-old with the high forehead, wide mouth and thin lips, whose handsome face today is a rough draft of actress Meryl Streep's. She was interested in him, however, and invited Hooge to the clinic's Christmas party. This time he fell in love with her and after a year of commuting they moved into a house in Sylvan Lake, a resort area near Red Deer. Brenda got a job as a social worker with alcoholics among the criminally insane at a mental institution eighty kilometres away in Ponoka. They married in December 1971.

Their sex life flourished ("It was fantastic," they both recall), but for the first three years the rest of the relationship was stormy. She cooked and cleaned while he merely criticized, wondering why Brenda wasn't as efficient as his Mennonite mother had been, forgetting that his mother had two maids. "We'd fight," Gary says, "and the ducks would lift off the lake." Over time, Brenda began to learn how to handle conflict, which had always been a problem for her, and Gary became less critical.

"The aim of dealing with conflict," they would write later in their *Gourmet Lover's Guide*, "is not for one partner to win and one partner to lose a competition. Rather, the aim is for the relationship to win. When the relationship wins both individuals are stronger."

Other problems surfaced. Brenda hated the coldly bureaucratic way in which Ponoka handled its patients. Suffering migraine headaches, she left to join a guidance clinic in Red Deer. Gary became involved in faculty-association politics, eventually becoming president of the province-wide association. They were strife-filled years at Red Deer, as the top administration fought the staff and students over the way the institution would be run. For one thing, the top brass told Hooge that he was jeopardizing the college's provincial-government grants because he wasn't passing enough students. Hooge was simply applying marketing principles he had learned from Norman Smith: you create a product that's good for the consumer — in this case, the student — rather than one that serves the interests of the supplier, the government. He and other faculty presented their case to the Department of Education. In the ensuing battle, the government purged the college's president, vice-president and board of directors. Hooge was caught in the crossfire. "I was politically naive," he says now. "The Department came in and said, 'Yes, you won, but we don't like shit-disturbers.'" After five years as a department head, he was fired in 1972 and, he claims, blacklisted.

Gary Hooge illustrates a couple of classic maxims about the entrepreneur that bear noting. For five years he was an academic and like bureaucrats anywhere, he had to be a team man; when he showed any brilliance of ideas his superiors considered him unsound and eventually fired him. Though true entrepreneurs can't bloom in the cool, arid environment of most government work, they can suddenly flourish once they move outside to the hothouse atmosphere of private enterprise. As Edward de Bono, the British management consultant and definer of lateral thinking, has pointed out, "I have seen civil servants become opportunity-seeking and even entrepreneurial once they have left the service." The other general truth that obtains in Hooge's case was neatly summarized by that American chronicler of economic policy, George Gilder, when he wrote that entrepreneurs are more likely to find inspiration in a pink slip than in a promotion.

After he was fired Hooge couldn't find a job, and his wife was pregnant. They moved to Calgary, where she rejoined the guidance clinic to work in family therapy. Rather desperately, Hooge considered starting a restaurant but realized it would take $100,000 and they had only $3,000, his pension money from the junior college.

Early in the summer of 1972, they were visiting a friend who was just back from Europe with a catalogue from a chain of successful German sexual-aids stores. Gary and Brenda pored through the catalogue separately. He was talking about it with his friend when Brenda approached and said, "That's it!" Gary needed no convincing: he'd already decided that it was a unique concept for Calgary; he would open Calgary's first sex shop.

Brenda was involved from the beginning, and her presence would change the store's character into more of a love shop. Five months pregnant, she approached a bank manager for a $4,000 loan — supposedly to furnish the baby's room. ("I didn't think too much about it," she says. "That was a means to an end, and I've never been one to follow all the rules.") They now had $7,000. With his MBA and fabricated but convincing financial and cash-flow statements as ammunition, Gary convinced a second banker to lend them another $7,000 (this time to launch "a sensuous novelty shop"). He got the money with little discussion.

Picking items blindly from the German catalogue — "what's an Asia Love Ring? Let's have four of those" — they ordered about $3,000 worth of stock. When it arrived, mostly without instructions, they had a pleasant time learning about products like Come Too (R.S.V.P.), a lotion which, when "gently massaged on the female erogenous zones, quickens secretion flow and heightens orgasmic responses", and the Sextra, worn at the base of the penis, which offers double duty: fitted with soft air-filled nodules that provide a woman a little extra stimulation, it also prolongs and firms her partner's erection.

Then, out of the blue, Gary was hired by the City of Calgary as a management consultant on organizational behaviour. A couple of months later, their first son was born. By that time Gary had found a $500-a-month storefront in the downtown across from the Establishment-frequented Palliser

Hotel and was in the middle of furnishing it, nights and week-ends. Considering the Calgary of 1973 an ultra-conservative city, he designed the space on the model of a discreet jewellery store, showcasing only one of each product. He named it The Love Shop, swathed it in plants and placed the more graphically sexual products at the back of the store, where a large styrofoam heart bore a message straight out of the sixties: *We Wish You Love.*

All this time, he had been wondering who would run the place. Brenda — demonstrating the same streak of adven-turousness she used as a croupier in Soho and a translator in Germany — volunteered. Her first assignment was braving the moral guardians of the police department to get a business licence. City hall's licensing staff, when they heard what kind of shop she was opening, sent her with babe in arms to see a sergeant in the morality squad. He peppered her with ques-tions, among them: "Are you now, have you ever been or do you intend to be a prostitute?" She got the licence.

Gary ran a teaser newspaper campaign with small ads that said only: "The Love Shop is coming." That was enough to en-tice a TV crew and newspaper reporters to the store before opening day. They found a new mother, a former social worker, busily stocking the place with vibrators and dildoes, lingerie and massage lotions, while her baby gurgled beside her. The strategy had changed: because Gary was working for the city, Brenda would be identified as the owner of The Love Shop, a decision that also had the side effect of making the whole venture more respectable.

The resulting publicity was a windfall. On opening day in mid-November, a crowd of sexually curious Calgarians had lined up around the block. The store became so jammed that Brenda had to push some people out the door. They were all buying. The $3,000 worth of stock that she and Gary had thought would last four to six months was gone within the first week. Brenda's mother, originally outraged at the nature of the store, was soothed by her friends' reactions and came in to help. For six months, the couple didn't eat a meal at home. Gary would arrive from work at 4 P.M. and stay till 9 P.M., then drive to the airport to pick up more stock. After a month, he quit his consulting work with the city to go full-time into the new business. Brenda, still nursing, had two shifts of babysitters at the shop. Still suffering from thyroidism, she would take a nap whenever she sat down.

Brenda and Gary discovered a clientele that in many cases was sophisticated enough to explain to the store-owners how to use some of the more exotic products. When an initially cautious Brenda dared to emerge from behind the safety of the till, her social-work skills surfaced. She began asking customers about their sexuality and was astounded at how open they were within the store. "Peoples' sex problems were easily solved: 98 percent was lack of information or having the wrong information," she says. "Everybody was trying to achieve what might be impossible and they were feeling so inadequate." It was then that the concept of a thorough staff training program began to grow. Her display of interest in customers also proved to be an intelligent marketing move.

The only public fuss arose when the university newspaper learned that a police sergeant was visiting The Love Shop regularly to make sure no lascivious products were being peddled. Brenda and Gary had humoured him, keeping under wraps such provocative items as two balls on a string — Duo Playballs — which Japanese women use as vaginal stimulators. The university paper photographed the morality cop in his office with a men's-magazine centrefold on the wall.

Morality became an issue only once more, when Gary asked a bank for a loan to open a store in Edmonton in February 1974, three months after the Calgary shop had begun. Brenda's mother had given the couple $20,000 worth of Canada Savings Bonds to finance the Edmonton operation, which Gary decided to use as collateral for a loan. The Royal Bank refused him, without telling him why. "It's because of the business, isn't it?" he asked the bank manager. "Yes," the manager said, "we don't want to get involved in a sex business." Gary tried several other banks before approaching a friend, a major Calgary developer, who referred him to a banker he knew at the Toronto-Dominion. Gary got the money. The opening of the Edmonton store was a repeat of Calgary: people angrily banged on the door at 8 A.M., and although the owners thought they had ordered enough stock this time to last three to four months, it disappeared in less than a week.

With shops in two cities, eventually a manager running the Edmonton operation, Hooge and Humber began to experience growth problems. Stock control was one concern; they were forever behind in their orders. Gary fell back on what he considered to be the best retail buying system in the world: the Hudson's Bay model. Using a variant of the department store's business and stock-control systems, he generated enough cash flow to repay the Toronto-Dominion three months after taking out the loan.

This turned out to be a mistake, because the couple started having cash flow problems again. "I had assumed the best way to establish my line of credit was to pay the bank back instantly," Hooge recalls. "It was naïve of me. I didn't realize that the money for opening a business was one thing in the bank's eyes and a line of credit for operating was a different thing." Despite the modest credit line, they were emboldened by their experience in Alberta to move temporarily to Winnipeg, along with Brenda's mother and their year-old baby, to open a Love Shop there in November 1974. This time they had no brushes with the law, having asked the Winnipeg police to check with their counterparts in Alberta.

Now with three stores, they knew they were stretching themselves: whenever they had to leave a location in the hands of staff, sales would drop. Training competent managers was the answer, but Brenda Humber didn't want to settle for simple sales training. With her background as a social worker, she had determined within the first few weeks of The Love Shop's existence that it took a special kind of salesperson to handle the clientele.

Today, their training course is based on studies Brenda did at the National Sex Forum in San Francisco, a major North

American sexual-training centre that grew out of the desire of three Methodist ministers to deal with the city's large homosexual community. The Love Shop course is held twice a year in Vancouver, where Gary and Brenda moved in 1977.* It brings together potential owner-operators, store managers and staff, Lover's Wear salespeople, and the occasional interested party willing to part with a $2,000 outsider's fee. Although the trainees pay nothing, they do have to sign an agreement that, if they quit or get fired from their staff jobs with The Love Shop within a year of taking the program, they'll pay the company $500. They also complete a lengthy non-disclosure and non-competition contract; among other things, they must not reveal the Hooge organization's marketing research nor any information contained in manuals about suppliers, product knowledge, sales strategy, procedures and policy, and training.

The program itself is a strange stew of spicy sex and meat-and-potatoes salesmanship, all of it flavoured with little sprinkles of altruism. In its scope and unblinking seriousness, it demonstrates the difference that makes The Love Shop an upright virgin in a world of slatternly sex shops. Just the pre-work activities that trainees must accomplish before showing up for the course are sobering: an estimated sixty hours of tests ("The primary reaction to sexual stimulation in the excitement stage is . . . ."), the completing of a sexual-history questionnaire, the writing of a personal sexual narrative, and the reading of two articles and five books, including *Male Sexuality* and *Guideposts For Effective Salesmanship*.

Only then can candidates take the two-week training program in Vancouver. The seminar leader is Donna Du Bois, The Love Shops' director of operations, who takes trainees

---

*Vancouver proved to be a more sophisticated location. It already had a shop called Ultra Love, which was slightly down-scale from The Love Shop. When Hooge and Humber held an erotic art show to publicize their opening, fewer than a hundred people bothered to attend during its two-week run. Their lone problem in Vancouver occurred in their fourth year there when city hall tried to clean up Granville Street by increasing the business licence of adult-entertainment shops to $3,000 from $30. Humber appeared before city council to lobby successfully against the increase. "We're running a church over here," she told one reporter.

through a sales technique developed by behavioural scientist and management consultant Robert R. Blake and psychologist Jane Srygley Mouton in their *Guideposts* book, a best-seller that motivates with such jargon as "needs analysis" and "establishing expectations." Their system weights concern for the customer as highly as the concern for making the sale, or as the Hooges have put it in their warm, fuzzy way: "Selecting the best solution for the customer's situation will ensure an enriching experience for the customer and a rewarding experience for the Customer Counselor." Done properly, it will also increase their sales commissions.

Brenda Humber herself takes the prospective customer counselors through the Human Sexuality study that's designed to rid them of their inhibitions and make them properly amoral in their handling of customers. Some of it is dryly academic, but the most interesting section is story-telling time, when they swap personal sexual histories and usually discover that, Hey! they're fairly normal, after all.

After sessions on product knowledge, they role-play selling situations in front of video cameras and go on location at the Vancouver store for in-shop familiarization. Successful sales candidates then have about a two-month breaking-in period at their home stores, where as first-level Customer Counselors they can earn $14-$19,000 in salary and commissions.

Among those who have taken the course is Gary Hooge's marketing professor, Norman Smith. Hooge had visited the University of Oregon as a successful graduate and spoken to Smith's class, and in 1981, when Hooge and Humber were first deciding to franchise in the United States, the entrepreneurial professor became financially involved in The Love Shop. He spent three months taking the training program and working in the Vancouver store. But the move south stalled. "Things were a little tight in Canada at the time and the costs of moving down here were pretty expensive," Smith says. Eventually he sold back his shares to his partners.

The marketing professor points out that the plateau Hooge and Humber found themselves on is a natural stage for entrepreneurs: "One author calls it getting through the knothole, as you figure out how to really start expanding. It takes a great deal of capital to expand and you have to be willing to give up something. That's not easy to do for an entrepreneur." He remains convinced, however, of The Love Shops' soundness and can foresee a time when he'll again be involved, perhaps in the push into the States the couple began in 1985. "Gary and Brenda have done it almost perfectly. From a marketing standpoint they have differentiated themselves from sleazy stores; they moved into a marketing niche. The whole mores of our culture have changed amazingly but there is practically no training on human sexuality. Very few males, for instance, know how a woman has an orgasm. And an individual can go into a Love Shop and get some very good counseling, as good as they might get by going to a sex therapist who will charge them $50 to $100 an hour" — a generalization that is enormously biased by his earlier financial interest in the business.

Smith sees Hooge's management weakness as one typical of the sole proprietor: an unwillingness to yield enough control, to delegate authority — in effect, to be enough of what he terms the opportunistic entrepreneur whose company will continue to grow. In marketing, he says, neither Hooge nor Humber have recognized the need for consistent advertising, which they should now be doing to distinguish themselves from the inevitable competitors coming on the scene. They would also profit from a basic marketing study of both their customers and those people who wouldn't be caught dead in the shops. "Maybe Gary's retailing background with the Hudson's Bay is something he should fight. He's focusing only on inventory control instead of taking a broader view of the total marketing program."

A married couple who quickly became much more opportunistic entrepreneurs than the limited craftsmen of Norm Smith's theory, Brenda Humber and Gary Hooge continue to run the business together as a team. She has invested the stores with a respectable image through her professional training, while he brings his management-organization skills. It took them a few years to overcome the competitiveness that can develop between husband and wife in the same business (they used to have battles after he'd try to second-guess her while she was doing TV interviews). She discovered that she was good at teaching, handling the media and in-store selling; she's overseeing the U.S. franchising sales. He specializes in all the business systems and the location and design of the shops. Supportive, respectful of each other's opinions, they have an easy relationship. Early on they developed a system to handle the home/work tensions. They refuse to discuss business before arriving at work in the morning and after a certain hour at night. "When you hit that front door of the office, the personal stuff stops," Gary says. "We never take the argument into the office," Brenda adds.

While she works in the office three days a week, she no longer has to take catnaps. In 1981 a doctor finally told her that she had been a victim of thyroidism since her teens, and prescribed medication that has restored her energy. "When we first lived together, Brenda would sleep every opportunity she got," Gary recalls. "And, coming from my German background, my attitude was that this was 'English'. Yet I could see the energy she was putting into things as we were starting the shops."

With the help of a housekeeper, she melds her business life with the mothering of their three children, sons aged twelve and eight and a daughter aged four. "I have tremendous freedom to reorganize my life depending on the needs of my family." As she speaks, Brenda is sitting in the living-room of their old house, the fireplace fat with crackling logs. It's a wild day on the West Vancouver waterfront and the waves crash over their front yard. She talks about the children and the effect The Love Shop may have on their lives as they mature. Either the stores become so well-known that people realize they are respectable places, she muses, or she and Gary may have to find another business. "The fact is, we own a 'sex shop' and my expertise is in sexuality. I hope my kids aren't going to suffer because we're taking this open approach."

Though they're attractive people, neither of them reek of sexuality. They dress stylishly; they speak thoughtfully. They grow a garden. There's a sandbox in the backyard, a trampoline perched beside a hot tub in the front. Their house is littered with photographs of their kids. For a couple who make their living selling Pleasure Balm and Penis Extender Vibrators, Brenda Humber and Gary Hooge have managed to remain a resolutely middle-class Mom and Pop.

Umberto Menghi — The Prince of Pasta

By any standards, the opening night of Umberto's Restaurant should have been a disaster. A few hours earlier, Umberto Menghi had hocked his wrist watch for $200 to buy lamb and fresh pasta. The menu was limited to Tortellini alla Panna, Costate d'Agnello, salad and one of the best wine lists in town; unfortunately there was nothing in the cellar. As customers trickled in, he greeted them effusively, escorted each to a table and then asked for money — in advance. Most considered turning tail and heading for a more established kitchen, but Menghi's sincerity assuaged their suspicion. With the cash in hand he tore down the block to buy wine and liquor. Once the customers were seated, relieved of their money and propped up with drinks, they noticed the other service was a little slow. Menghi and one waiter were doing everything from cooking and serving to washing up.

At first, there were audible grumbles about the confusion and delays and people began to think about take-out to salvage the evening. Then the food arrived and they were hooked. It was all new to Vancouver — pasta made that day, lamb cooked rare with a subtle Dijon mustard and vermouth sauce and crispy vegetables. Loosened up by the feast, everyone began to enjoy themselves. Some even cleared tables, ferried food back and forth and, in evening finery, helped out in the kitchen. What should have been a career-ending disaster became a giant party. When it was all over, in the wee hours, an exhausted Menghi asked people to ante up what they felt the evening was worth — he'd lost track long before anyway.

The take was $5,000, the year was 1973. Umberto Menghi was twenty-seven and he was on his way.

A decade later, Menghi at forty is amused by the near-disaster, re-interpreting the confusion as a bonus that added to the atmosphere. Menghi can afford to be amused: his eight restaurants gross more than $15 million annually. Profitable sidelines include *The Umberto Menghi Cookbook* (Talonbooks), a 45,000-copy bestseller, and the 1985 release, *Umberto's Pasta Book*, (David Robinson/Whitecap), which sold 6,000 copies in its first week; commercial endorsements on television and in magazines; and two syndicated television cooking series, one of them filmed aboard the Love Boat. Menghi has also bestowed his sauces and homemade pasta upon the gourmet-to-go crowd with Umbertino's, a chain of shops which is being franchised across the country. His eye on even bigger prizes, Menghi has moved into the competitive American dining scene, with two restaurants in Seattle and another in San Francisco.

Each restaurant has a distinctive ambience and decor. Il Giardino is lively and fun, a beehive of activity; stepping inside is like joining a party in progress. Al Porto, right beside Vancouver's business hub, is cooler and more casual. (The Seattle and San Francisco restaurants are similar in design and atmosphere to Al Porto.) Il Caminetto in the ski resort town of Whistler, B.C. exudes après-ski cosiness with tanned faces and tired bodies relaxing by the fire.

Beside Menghi's business triumphs are social ones which have placed him at the centre of Vancouver's small, select circle of people who really count, those whom society columnist Valerie Gibson has dubbed "the Who." Business and financial leaders such as Peter Brown, former chairman of the Vancouver Stock Exchange, call him a close friend and he hangs around with the likes of singer Tom Jones, who dines with Umberto just about every night he's in town.

He courts the financial élite aggressively and with calculation. He'll organize extravaganzas for movers and shakers such as oilman Bob Carter, who paid him $1,000 a head to celebrate the 1979 signing of one of his deals. It was a bac-

chanalian feast, a cross between ancient Rome and Hollywood, held at his elegant, expensive Il Palazzo. The numerous
courses were highlighted by fresh goose liver pâté, flown in
from France that day, consommé garnished with flakes of
18-carat gold (Menghi swears that he caught one guest carefully inspecting his urine between courses), and for the entrée,
an entire wild baby boar, deboned and stuffed with chestnuts.
The service was part of the entertainment. The wild boar was
brought flaming through the darkened restaurant accompanied by an opera singer. The service was exquisite . . . and
why not? There was one waiter for each of the thirty guests.
That evening is firmly lodged in the annals of West Coast
lore, growing larger and more lavish with each telling.

Menghi rightly figures that if he satisfies the Bob Carters
and Peter Browns, the lesser but aspiring movers and shakers
will be quick to follow. Part of Menghi's courtship is strategy
and part is because he genuinely likes and identifies with his
clientele. For the wedding of fellow restaurateur Bud Kanke's
daughter, Menghi stood in pouring rain for hours to set up
two oil drum barbecues and roast an entire lamb as a surprise
addition to the party.

Menghi moves in and out of this circle with such ease that
few significant events are complete without him. One dark
and stormy night, when the Dom was flowing as fast as the
big talk, Tom Jones's manager, Gordon Mills, challenged
Menghi to a snooker game, the best of five. There was no
table to be found, so Menghi chartered a helicopter for
$15,000 to fly the thirteen people three hundred miles to
brother-in-law Jean-Claude Ramon's 320 acre Osoyoos
Ranch. (Those who made the trip marvel that no one was
killed by a ricocheting champagne cork.) Menghi won
$50,000 with a last-ball victory and capped the escapade by
sending his limousine ahead of the helicopter with a load of
extra champagne and food.

Another reason the business community likes and respects
Menghi is his wicked sense of humour, which amuses while
stating unequivocally that Menghi is their equal. One

businessman thought he was being funny by loudly and repeatedly referring to Menghi's restaurants as pizza joints. When he asked for a special spread to impress important New York clients, Menghi sent out for pizza and paraded it around the restaurant, on a silver platter, before setting it down in front of the devastated businessman and his highly amused clients.

On another occasion, hearing that Bob Carter's wife, Sheila Begg, was eating dinner at La Brochette, a French restaurant in Gastown, he sent a team of waiters in tuxedos equipped with silver service to serve a full meal complete with champagne and dessert. "My wife thought it was great," remembers Carter. "But the owners went crazy and wouldn't give the glasses back." Carter turned the tables later when he was eating at Umberto's. Feigning inability to find anything interesting on the dessert menu, he sent his chauffeur over to La Brochette for four chocolate mousses. "Umberto came in later and acted like he thought it was really funny. But he told me if I did it again, he'd kill me. I believed him," says the six-foot-five, 250-pound Carter, who looks like the sheriff in a Western movie.

Over the years, a few businessmen have become enamoured enough of Menghi that they've become his partners — though, at his insistence, very silent ones. In Vancouver he owns Umberto's, La Cantina, Il Giardino and Al Porto outright. He owns 60 percent of the Whistler restaurant and 40 percent of the land it sits on. Peter Brown owns the rest as "a combination of investment and fun." Menghi owns 50 percent of Umberto's in Seattle. David McLean of the McLean, Hungerford and Simon law firm is Menghi's 50 percent partner in the San Francisco restaurant. (Umberto also gets a management fee that amounts to 42 percent of the profits.) McLean, who ate regularly at Menghi's restaurants, courted him as the prime tenant in Hudson House, a burned-out hull of a building that he renovated in Gastown. "I thought having Umberto in the place would establish it as a high-quality building, which in turn would make it easier to lease," says McLean. The strategy worked to perfection with Al Porto in Vancouver, so McLean and his group decided to try it with their 1.5 million-square-foot development in San Francisco's financial district. The partnership is ideal, because McLean limits himself to reading the financial statements and Menghi wouldn't have it any other way.

Menghi has been his own man since he was twelve. Stifled by his close-knit Florentine family, he ran away from home. He took shelter in a nearby pension with a trattoria, where he worked as a cleaner and dishwasher and became quickly entranced by the excitement and vivacity of the restaurant — he was gone a month before his parents hauled him back. The love affair continued and though his family, wealthy property owners, heartily disapproved, he returned to work in the trattoria every summer. By the time he was fifteen, his goal was to own a restaurant. His parents, hoping the whole thing was a youthful infatuation, were aghast. Little Umberto was to become a priest or, at the very least, a professor of art history like his older brother. (He also has two younger sisters, who are in the textile business.) Menghi solved the dispute by running away again, this time to a government-sponsored restaurant school in Rome. For three years, he alternated six months of study with four months of work, learning every conceivable facet of restaurant operation from washing floors to keeping the books.

After graduating in 1964, eighteen-year-old Menghi left home for good. His first job was in France, where he worked as a glorified busboy and waiter. There was a stint in Switzerland and also on the Isle of Jersey where, with a canny eye on the future, he began to learn English. He soon slipped into England without a permit and, in turn, landed jobs at a little pub in Basingstoke and at the prestigious Savoy and Hilton Hotels in London. The goal of owning his own restaurant, never far from Menghi's mind, grew with each position. At every stop, he ingratiated himself with the often irascible head chefs by working extra unpaid shifts in the kitchen. He was voracious for information, absorbing every tidbit and storing it away. "I was fortunate," he says. "I was able to work for some of the best chefs in Europe. I idolized them and I worked so hard that they took the time to talk to me, pass on their experiences, their recipes and some of their cooking secrets." The extra work also got him the best waiter stations and, not incidentally, the most tips. In 1967, feeling British Immigration breathing down his neck, Menghi had to make a change. Reluctant to return to Italy where mandatory military service would shelve his dreams for several years, Menghi went to see a Canadian immigration official he had dated a few times. "She managed to get me a permit to go to Canada in two weeks because Expo [67 in Montreal] was coming up." The well-travelled twenty-one-year-old next found himself at the posh Beaver Club in Montreal's Queen Elizabeth Hotel. And then, in 1968, when Expo ended, and there was an over-supply of waiters, he discovered Vancouver.

Menghi's West Coast début was hardly portentous. Stepping off the train flat broke, he had to sell his camera and raincoat to buy food. "It was the first time I was scared of sur-viving; of having enough to eat," he remembers. But within a month he found work as a waiter at the Panorama Roof of the Hotel Vancouver and began sizing up the city. "I was learning," says Menghi. "I was studying the style of Van-couver people; how they walk, how they think and how they live." He came to the conclusion that the free-and-easy lifestyle of the West-Coast city disappeared when the natives went out to dine. "There was no life or movement in the restaurants," he says. "They were dead." Italian cuisine was nothing short of a scandal. "I've never seen such food in Italy," he states disdainfully. "Pizza, chicken cacciatore, and meat-balls. No finesse. The same old stuff every day — tomatoes, tomatoes, tomatoes." Mainstream food was even more of an abomination to Menghi's delicately tuned palate. Steak and lobster, fried chicken and burgers, burgers, burgers. Yet Menghi saw Vancouver as "young, fresh and growing" — just what he'd been looking for. "I knew it was a place where I could set a trend."

The Coast may have been ripe for the picking, but Menghi's first two attempts were dismal failures. Roaches (1969-70), a combination coffee shop/deli near the University of British Columbia, was one too many in an already crowded area. Besides, his accountant told him the deli was spending $2.75 for a meal the customers were getting for 45 cents. He lost $1,500 on Roaches. Umberto aimed for a more sophisticated clientele with Casa Nova (1971-72), an Italian restaurant. Menghi put his savings of $2,000, his 50 percent partner mortgaged his house for $8,000 and they borrowed $15,000 from the bank. Accounts differ, but most observers claim the partnership ended with a bitter falling-out because Menghi was developing a personal following. He emerged from both disasters penniless but unchastened. In fact, he arrogantly enlarged his aspirations. "In a short time I will have three or four restaurants," he told disbelieving friends — the same friends who were lending him money for rent and food. What they didn't know is that the experiences taught Menghi that *one* critical lesson about financial control. "Partners are fine, but they must be silent — very silent," he states emphatically.

Menghi, not one for wallowing in misfortune, always looks to the main chance. Even as Casa Nova was going under, he had his eye on a location for his own restaurant, a distinctive yellow Victorian house only a few blocks from downtown in Vancouver's historic and then dilapidated Yaletown. To finance the project, he spent a frenzied seven months selling sweaters door-to-door until he had signed orders and sales totaling $40,000. Then he went to the bank and borrowed $35,000 on the strength of the orders. The fact that the bank manager had been a regular customer at Casa Nova was a deciding factor for the recently penniless restaurateur. Refurbishing the old house, once a dress designer's shop, took every penny he'd raised, even though he did most of it himself. On opening night, he desperately needed a good take.

It was 1973 and the place was called Umberto's. The $5,000 pot was far more than even Menghi could have hoped for.

Vancouver loves a legend, even if it is only a one-night flash in the pan. And after the spontaneous party, word spread; the restaurant was full the next night and lineups soon appeared as Umberto's became the place to eat. (There must be a thousand people who claim to have been there that first evening.) Within a year, Menghi had paid off the bank, bought a house, got married and purchased his first Ferrari. In the space of ten years, he's gone through a Lamborghini, a BMW and a Lincoln limousine and currently, he's on his third Ferrari, a $100,000 fire-engine-red GTS 308.

Most of Umberto Menghi's empire evolved through carefully calculated steps and through his own brand of gut-level analysis. Yet it was a bit of serendipity that precipitated his rise from restaurant owner to restaurant mogul. One day in the summer of 1974, the owner of the store next to Umberto's had the bad grace to tow away Menghi's Ferrari from where it was illegally parked. This infuriated Menghi so much that he borrowed $200,000 from the bank and promptly bought the building out from under the offensive neighbour. The lineups at Umberto's hadn't slackened, so Menghi turned the shop into La Cantina, the first Italian-style seafood restaurant in the West, with more than thirty fresh dishes each night.

The expansion bug bit Menghi hard, but he was also shrewdly aware that he was on the right track. In 1976, he spent $350,000 to design and build Il Giardino (The Garden) on a vacant lot on the other side of Umberto's. It's a perfect replica of a Tuscany farmhouse with open-beam ceilings, lots of elbow room, French doors, throw rugs and bright colours. The authenticity even extends to cracked and uneven plaster walls and worn red ceramic floor tile. Il Giardino, specializing in game and fowl, remains one of Vancouver's most unusual restaurants, enjoying laudable longevity in a city that loves surf and turf one night and vegetarian bistros the next.* It is also Umberto's personal favourite. When in town Menghi can invariably be found there eating a late lunch of reindeer

---

* A Vancouver businessman was so taken with Il Giardino, he commissioned architect Werner Forster, who worked with Menghi on the original, to create a $1-million, 5,000-square-foot replica for his home.

pepper steak while signing cheques, interviewing, being interviewed, meeting suppliers, interrogating his accountant and
otherwise taking care of his domain.

Il Palazzo (1978) has been Menghi's only loser since the
birth of Umberto's, but it is certainly the city's most elegant
failure. Opened during the pre-recession salad days when
prosperity seemed endless, Il Palazzo was Menghi's dream of
bringing cultured dining in the classic style to Vancouver. It
sank for the same reason that brought the Queen Mary to
berth as a California side show — it was too expensive even
for well-heeled patrons. The distinguished and formal setting
was complemented by impeccable food and service that
encouraged diners to eat with leisure and digest over long conversations. Menghi spent $750,000 turning the majestic old
Victorian bank into his palace. It is a sumptuous setting with
deep coral walls, marble ceilings, and a three-hundred-year-
old Russian chandelier. As the *pièce de résistance*, Menghi
turned the bank's massive vault into a bar. A sleek black Lincoln Continental limousine picked up the real and pretend
gentry at their homes, until Umberto got fed up with the gentle folk commandeering the car for turns around Stanley Park
and ripping off the television. The final straw came when one
pillar of the establishment urinated in the back seat. Il Palazzo
made money until the recession caught up with it, discouraging all but the fattest expense accounts from the $50-per-
person tabs for delicacies like pheasant in white juniper sauce
and salmon with Asti Spumante and truffles. Menghi stub-
bornly kept Il Palazzo going, varying the hours, soliciting
weddings, changing the menu and finally bringing in a partner, but nothing could make The Palace a winner. Finally
Umbertino's, the public company of which Menghi holds 27
percent of the shares, took over Il Palazzo's lease. It now
serves as the company's commissary and headquarters.

Although the prospect of uncertain times and the sting of Il
Palazzo's downturn would prompt most people to retrench,
Menghi did an about-face on luxury and in 1979 invested
$500,000 in Al Porto in Gastown, a larger, more impersonal
and lower-priced establishment than his other restaurants. In

1981, Whistler, an uncomfortable and dull village with splendid skiing, suddenly exploded into two mountains, Whistler and Blackcomb, making it one of the biggest winter resorts in North America. Included in the metamorphosis was an ultra-trendy instant alpine town, and Menghi opened Il Caminetto (The Fireplace) right in its heart. And, just as he turned his restaurants into the meeting places of the city cognoscenti, so Il Caminetto has become the gathering spot for "the Who" at Whistler.

Menghi's next step was his most daring. For years he had seen the United States as a logical place for expansion; in 1982 he took the plunge with Umberto's in Seattle, one of the rare occasions when Canadians have exported restaurants south of the border. Opening night at the Seattle Umberto's featured twenty-five hundred guests. But Menghi didn't forget his Vancouver friends. The day before the official opening, he flew down five hundred for free food and champagne. The first Seattle restaurant was so well received that Menghi opened another in 1983 and then one in San Francisco in 1984.

To put Menghi's accomplishments into perspective, consider the old saying, "If you want to throw away money, open a restaurant." Ninety percent of those who do are stony-broke within five years. Everything can be right — location, management, capital — and you'll still lose your savings, home, family and the shirt off your back. All it takes is a slight misjudgment of the public's current whimsy, like opening a sushi bar just as pasta fever strikes. Those who make money in the restaurant game usually blend the lowest common denominator of taste with well-scrubbed cleanliness and overfriendly service. ("Hi, I'm Bill! How are you folks!") In such cases, profit is more intimately associated with the economies of scale than with any seduction of the tastebuds.

Finding a restaurant that combines classic service with exquisite food and a healthy bottom line is rare. Running a group of eight quality restaurants, each with a distinct menu, atmosphere and identity is remarkable. And a Canadian who successfully breaks into the U.S. market with this combination is unique. To achieve all three in slightly more than ten years is the culinary equivalent of discovering the double helix.

Ultimately, Menghi's success has less do with shrewd financing or innovative décor than with food. His trademark is Florentine cuisine; it's something you don't get tired of. It relies on fresh ingredients enhanced by subtle sauces; no cute formulas, no unnecessary ingredients. There is only one constant: Menghi does love pepper — red, black, green — as a seasoning, in a marinade or as the basis for a spicy sauce. Typical entrées: Pernice Ripiena Arrostita, deboned partridge stuffed with wild rice and roasted with grapa; Costate di Renna, roasted rack of reindeer with loganberries; and Calamari Ripieni, squid stuffed with prosciutto and herbs baked in wine. Most of his pastas are rich with Romano, Parmesan, wine and whipping cream, and he likes to stuff them with the unexpected: cannelloni with crabmeat and spinach or ground reindeer meat.

Because subtle sauces don't camouflage a dish the way sugary tomato concoctions and heavy dollops of garlic do, premium quality ingredients are crucial. From the first, Menghi hectored a small-time Vancouver food importer, Jose Valagao, into ordering then unheard-of delicacies. Valagao was extremely dubious about Menghi's shopping list. No one else in town wanted Parmesan fresh from Italy, truffles, reindeer meat* or saffron at $1,200 a pound. What's more, Menghi demanded credit. But Menghi was so convincing and so confident that Valagao took the risk. Today, his Continental Importers is the West's largest supplier of specialty foods to restaurants, grossing $6 million, and Menghi is his single largest customer. "Umberto is still a very difficult man to deal with," Valagao admits ruefully. "He always wants the best and he'll embarrass you in front of everybody if he doesn't get it." In fact, Menghi is so lacking in trust when it comes to food, he insists on preparing and eating, with Valagao, any new product before accepting it.

* When Menghi finally talked Valagao into ordering the succulent reindeer meat it was on the condition that he supply no one else in Vancouver for six months; by that time its value as a novelty was gone.

Typically, Menghi's personality inspires both fear and respect in business colleagues and employees. He is enormously charming, exuding the love of life so necessary to those who peddle good food. The flip side of his charm is a tough edge, so rapier sharp it borders on meanness. If Menghi is a fanatic about food quality, he is a martinet about the deportment of his staff. He believes that a bad encounter with a waiter will do as much damage as a poorly prepared meal. In the early years, the casual Canadian attitude to work infuriated him to private tears. "I couldn't understand why people were so stupid." On occasion he has pummelled a particularly sloppy waiter, and he has faced lawsuits for wrongful dismissal. But he has mellowed somewhat since realizing the problem is his own demanding personality that set himself as the standard. "To begin with, I wanted to make them all like me. I learned that I have to give my staff as much attention as I give my customers. I praise them when they do good, but when they do bad, I let them know fast!" Attention, Menghi-style, is unexpected cameo appearances at his restaurant when his façade of bonhomie hides the fact that he misses nothing. Every night he's in town, he makes the rounds of his restaurants, checking everything minutely: tasting each sauce as it simmers; crisply telling the chef exactly what's wrong or nodding if it meets his standards and then moving on; checking levels in the icemaker; adjusting light and sound levels; pausing to show a busboy that he's turning a corkscrew three turns too far; and commenting favourably to a receptionist who has changed her hairstyle.

While Menghi may have evolved a more relaxed attitude to his staff, he is still capable of drastic action when something displeases him. One day in 1982, he found the staff at Il Palazzo bickering and the work well behind schedule. It was thirty minutes before opening, with ninety-five reservations on the books, but he fired the lot, except the chef. As customers arrived, he explained what had happened and offered to supply the food for nothing if they bought champagne. Another spontaneous party erupted, reminiscent of his 1973 opening, with customers waiting on tables and helping out in the kitchen. That night, Il Palazzo sold $7,000 worth of champagne.

When Menghi is annoyed, his eyes — described as seductive by many women — turn positively reptilian. Employees may not enjoy working for Umberto, but even when he's not there they perform with the precision and gusto of a crack military unit.

Despite his well-established image as a flamboyant, gregarious Latin, Menghi isn't a natural charmer. As a boy, he despised having his cheek pinched or being fussed over, and even now he doesn't like being touched or having his personal space invaded. But Menghi is a master at secreting his true feelings behind an ebullient façade, a lesson he learned as a young immigrant. His first Canadian job, at Montreal's Queen Elizbeth Hotel, began miserably. Trained in the European mould of the cool, aloof and thoroughly professional waiter, he was baffled by easy familiarity. "I didn't enjoy being a waiter there at all. I saw other waiters, not a third as accomplished, receiving a far better response from customers and management. They were joking and talking with the customers, so I worked hard to relax a little, to laugh and brag about my experiences."

The rehearsals paid off. These days, Menghi enters his restaurants with the panache of a beloved Broadway star sauntering through Sardi's on opening night, dispensing *bons mots*, hearty back slaps and hugs to his eager customers. The less-restrained follow his every move, while those more conscious of propriety spy with subtle flicks of their eyes, silently wondering whether he'll stop and chat. Menghi has a rare ability to make each guest feel remembered and important. So convincing is he no one ever suspects that his remarkable memory for names is carefully augmented, at each stop, by a briefing from the maître d' and careful study of the reservation book. But for all his mass appeal, courtly old-world charm and Latin-lover looks, Umberto Menghi is essentially a private man. Vancouver *Sun* columnist Denny Boyd, who knows virtually every other shred of gossip worth mentioning, laments, "I don't know anything about his love life. He doesn't mix business with pleasure." Menghi's charisma is such that relatively casual acquaintances feel close to him.* So carefully does Menghi shield his real private life that many of his close friends didn't realize until months after the fact that in 1983 he'd separated from his wife of eight years — the childless marriage a casualty of his dedication to business.

Even his recreation time is losing out to ambition. When Menghi came to Vancouver he, like many other European children who grew up on a diet of "Gunsmoke" and "Bonanza," was enamoured with an image of frontier life. Menghi and brother-in-law Jean-Claude Ramon (a squat, frog-like, fun-loving man and a fellow restaurateur who started Vancouver's La Creperie and L'Orangerie) indulged their John Wayne fantasies by driving all night to spend their weekends riding and roping with Williams Lake cowboys in British Columbia's interior. As they became more prosperous, playing cowboy meant annual week-long hunting trips into the rugged Chilko Lake area, 150 miles north of Vancouver. "It's so exciting," Menghi chortles. "Sighting with binoculars, wearing bandoleers full of bullets. We'd only use three bullets the whole trip, but it was so much fun." They slept under the stars and travelled, "like the old days, on horse with a guide and packhorse." Cowboys of yore, however, didn't stuff their saddlebags with a full formal dinner setting, lamb medallions, duck, caviar, pâté, fine cheeses, vintage wines, liqueurs and, of course, a good cigar to round off a rugged day in the saddle. Menghi relaxed fully on these outings and the high jinks were endless. One evening, while telling tall tales, Ramon bet that Menghi couldn't jump over the campfire while smoking his cigar and holding his full liqueur glass. He cleared the fire with plenty to spare but forgot that it had been built right on the edge of a mountain lake. Menghi talks fondly of these outings, but always in the past tense. There's been no time for cowboys since 1982.

* Menghi likes to tell a story to illustrate this phenomenon. One evening at a party, he was cornered by a society wife who regaled him with inside information about her close friend Umberto Menghi.

In 1984, Menghi took the first step to making his name synonymous with pasta around North America by forming a public company, Umbertino's, initially capitalized at $2 million. He owns half the shares. The franchise operation will provide take-out and delivery pasta, featuring Menghi's sauces. Six franchises were planned for Vancouver by the end of 1985, with feelers coming from as far away as the Orient. In addition to bailing Menghi out of Il Palazzo and providing him with a $60,000 annual management contract, Umbertino's has paid $115,000 for "development assistance given by Umberto Restaurants Ltd."

Gnawing at the edge of his empire are persistent rumours that rapid expansion is diluting the Menghi magic. Ann Hardy, once an unabashed promoter, began suspecting in the 1982-83 edition of *Where To Eat In Canada* that his food and service are not up to earlier standards. Even staunch friends can hardly believe his pace. "I sometimes think that he's spreading himself too thin," admits Denny Boyd. The July 1983 edition of *Equity* magazine was headlined "The tables turn for Mr. Menghi — Umberto in trouble. $10 million will fix it." There's no hint of any money troubles in the text of the story itself.

Menghi reacts angrily to such comments. "My food is better than ever," he says vehemently. "The quality of the ingredients is better, and the cooking is better now that I'm not around all the time to make the chefs nervous." As for the critics, he once gave them the royal treatment; for the important ones, he'd go down to the market and select the freshest and choicest ingredients, choose the perfect wine and cook and serve the meal himself. He figures that the Ann Hardys are simply miffed that he's too busy to cater to them now. "I just don't have time to sit around, bullshit and buy drinks for those people any more," he says.

Menghi believes that the recession has made him a better businessman. Gross sales did drop 12 percent in 1982 to $6.8 million, but this figure is misleading; Il Palazzo alone was down 40 percent. Overall, Menghi's sales declined less than his competitors' did. But the fall in revenue did teach him a lesson: it goaded him into controlling his inventories better and forced him to unload the limo and chauffeur. Restaurateur Bud Kanke, an accountant by trade, sees the improvement: "He's evolving nicely as a businessman."

Menghi has also been careful not to fall into the trap of duplicating a successful restaurant or simply making it larger. He has worked hard to develop a clientele that appreciates the opportunity to eat at a distinctly different Menghi creation every night of the week. This strategy meant that Menghi realized less profit in the short term — the capital cost of building a new restaurant is greater than enlarging or cloning an old one — but it enables him to retain the public's fickle loyalty. And in the end, that's precisely the commodity Menghi's empire is built on.

Bruce Allen — The Raging Bull of Rock

The ten men garbed in their best California Casual were spread around a capacious table in the private dining-room just off the president's office at A&M Records in Los Angeles. The luncheon meeting that fall of 1982 had been called ostensibly to talk about marketing a young singer from Canada, a twenty-two-year-old named Bryan Adams, who looked like a sweet-faced high-school punk in blue jeans and sneakers. Adams was there along with his manager, Bruce Allen, and Allen's New York lawyer. Allen was in Sergio Valente jeans and cowboy boots. Handsome at thirty-seven, except for a nose as thick as a prize-fighter's, he had a high forehead haloed by soft silvering hair and a bald spot growing in back. Allen was a well-established talent manager from Vancouver whose latest group, Loverboy, was selling millions of albums in North America for another company, CBS. For this meeting, a founder of A&M, Jerry Moss, had assembled the Canadian president of the label and five divisional heads in sales and promotion. Moss — the M of A&M (his co-founder was the pop trumpeter Herb Alpert) — was warm and welcoming. But Bruce Allen was there under false pretences. He had no intention of talking about marketing, as he'd suggested to the president from Canada, who had set up the meeting. He was angry because he believed that A&M had badly mishandled Bryan Adams' first major album of his own well-crafted songs, an album that had produced two hit singles yet had had dismal sales.

After opening pleasantries, Jerry Moss asked Allen: "Where do you want to start?"

"Well," Allen replied with the directness of a rabbit punch, "I want to get off the label. I don't think you can do the job."

For long, weighted moments, Moss said nothing. Then he erupted. Standing up, his six-foot-four frame hulking over Allen, he yelled: "Listen, asshole, you're not getting off the label. And I'm going to prove to you that it's better than CBS. You deliver me a good album and you'll sell as many records here as anywhere else."

After further roaring back and forth, Allen agreed to give A&M another chance. He left with his lawyer and Adams. The Canadian president stayed behind, only to arrive in the parking lot a few minutes later to inform Allen that Jerry Moss had excoriated him for allowing Allen to embarrass Moss in front of his staff. The president warned Allen: "Don't ever set me up like that again."

At the time, Bruce Allen had no regrets. He had stage-managed the entire scene with a script that had only two possible denouements, both of them favourable: Moss could either release Bryan Adams from the label, as Allen wanted, or he could be humiliated into promising the record company's fullest financial and promotional backing, as Moss did. Allen and Bryan Adams went on to fulfil their end by delivering a good album, *Cuts Like A Knife*, which — with the active marketing of A&M — ranked in the Top 10 of every year-end poll of North American record sales and airplay in 1983.

Not until months later would Allen admit to himself that he

wasn't proud of what he had done to Jerry Moss. "Jerry is a classy, classy individual," he said, "and I didn't like having to get in the gutter with a guy like that."

It was an unguarded and uncharacteristic admission from a man who had built his career on prodding and pushing people until they danced to his music. Variously nicknamed The Godfather, Mighty Mouth and The Kingmaker, the forty-year-old Bruce Allen lives up to all the expectations you might have of a pugnacious and powerful figure on the North American rock scene. He has become a millionaire whose management firm and booking agency, in which he is a fifty-fifty partner, earned $1.5 million after expenses in 1984 (when his top act, Loverboy, holidayed for most of the year). The albums of Loverboy and Bryan Adams regularly hit platinum in the United States, which means a million units sold — with about $1.16 per album going to the artist. In all, Loverboy has sold more than ten million albums around the world and in a single year, 1983, grossed $46 million. In 1985 Adams's third album, *Reckless*, soared to the Top 10 of the American record charts with the speed of an Exocet missile.

That year Allen was also responsible for the creation of the recording "Tears Are Not Enough," produced in Toronto to raise money for starving Ethiopians. The idea originated in England and was repeated in the United States. One of the American organizers, composer-arranger Quincy Jones, suggested a Canadian version to record producer David Foster (formerly of Victoria), who works with such acts as Dolly Parton and the rock group Chicago. Foster went to the only person in Canada who he knew could stage-manage the event — Bruce Allen. Bryan Adams helped write the lyrics and Paul Dean of Loverboy was among the musicians involved in the final recording and video sessions, but it was Bruce Allen and Loverboy co-manager Lou Blair who coordinated the extraordinary coming-together of fifty of the nation's leading entertainers. Allen got on the phone and within a few days, through his persuasiveness and authority, convinced other managers and their artists across the country that it would be a first-class production to which they should donate their time and services. When they arrived, a sign at the studio entrance requested, "Please check your egos at the door."

Three years earlier, the rock artists managed by Bruce Allen Talent had been the most prominent among the frontline troops of a Canadian assault force that began to invade the American pop market. "There was an incredible interest in Canadian music there for the first time in ten years," recalls Larry LeBlanc, a veteran music journalist in Toronto. "And it started with Loverboy. Without them nobody would have given a damn about what's happening up here." He believes Bryan Adams will be even more successful: "He's got the looks, the songwriting talent, the singing ability — and he's young. The record companies in the States think he's the greatest thing since God."

Until Adams came along, Bruce Allen moulded his properties like pieces of plasticine, dictating what clothes they wore, which songs they sang, how many hundreds of one-night stands they had to do. A rock band's personal manager is its umbilical cord to success. He's often the person who discovers the act in the first place and finances their early existence. It's he who then cozies up to the record companies in Toronto, New York and Los Angeles, trying to convince them to sign the group to a recording contract. In many cases, it's he who goes into the studio with the band and guides them to a more marketable sound. And after he begs the record companies for enough advance cash against royalties to finance a promotional tour and schedules the dates with local and national concert promoters (who charge an average commission of 10 percent), it's always the manager who takes his group on the road for the first time, arranging their meals, transportation, accommodation and recreation while calling in every favour he can to have them interviewed by radio stations and the rock press. In between, he must hold the hands of the band members and blow their noses.* Allen cynically

---

* Sid Bernstein, the New York manager of such rock acts as the Young Rascals and the Bay City Rollers, says the responsibilities of the role include "being a nurse, being a doctor, being a philosopher, being a psychiatrist, being a banker — if you

packaged such groups as Prism and the Powder Blues Band and, more recently, Loverboy. He was particularly ruthless with Prism, which enjoyed moderate American success during the late 1970s. As owner of the band's name, he didn't hesitate to replace the lead singer when the other musicians wanted a change in direction and, when those same band members decided to quit because they didn't like the new singer either, he replaced them with four pickup musicians whom he paid by the week.

But with Adams and a new band called the Payola$, he has let them be more themselves. In the case of Adams, it's because the young singer most closely resembles the entertainer that Allen himself always wanted to be. Instead, he became a manager, but one who would be nearly as well-known as his artists in some circles because of his reputation as the Raging Bull of Rock. He has been notorious as a verbal and physical brawler since the early seventies when he built his first big international band, Bachman-Turner Overdrive, on a combination of screaming, bullying and obsessively hard work. It is a performance carefully calculated to make him as important as his acts, to glorify Bruce Allen, who never had the talent to sing or dance but longed to be up on the stage like his lifelong idol, Elvis Presley.

For a decade and a half Allen has been Canada's most successful rock manager, a machinegun-mouthed, vulgar showman. His success is all the more remarkable because of where it happened. In Western Canada rock acts have had difficulty attracting the attention of the Toronto-based Canadian music industry. As a result, by the time they come to national prominence they are more polished than their counterparts in the East. A factor in the predominance of Western rock artists on the international scene is that, with such a small population base in their half of the country, they have to look beyond their borders to make a living. Tom

---

can afford to be one — being a friend and an ally, their wise man, their medicine, their public-relations man, their troubleshooter — and, above all, a manager has to understand the group."

Harrison, the well-connected rock critic of the Vancouver *Province*, says: "Western Canadian acts get signed because they've put a lot of time and effort into the broadest possible middle ground of commercial acceptance." He affectionately calls Bruce Allen Mr Lowest Common Denominator, a manager who, "after he's said his piece at 120 decibels, will listen."

Listening or talking, Allen has seldom let his guard down long enough to admit his own deficiencies of character — as he did in discussing his treatment of Jerry Moss — or to forgive others their shortcomings. From his early teens his life has been a battle between security and independence, seeking after people who won't desert him, wanting to remain endlessly loyal to them — but abandoning them the moment he thinks they've failed him. Sometimes his actions sound defensible, as when a long-time friend of his, who had helped him during his career, attempted a financial scam in a deal in which Allen was an investor. Despite the friend's support over the years, Allen allowed him no chance to apologize, refusing to let any of his calls get through his switchboard; as far as he was concerned, the man was dead. Other actions seem more callous, as in his relationship with his ailing mother, whom he loves but visits perhaps once a month. She was always a woman of fierce independence, a quality he shares, but for many years she has suffered from multiple sclerosis. "I admire her, but I don't think about it. You know what? It kills me to see my mother that bad. I couldn't stand to see her with a cane. I don't like going to big events and pushing her in a wheelchair." He is cold-blooded in discussing his character flaw. His attitude is "If you're not perfect, go somewhere else."

There have been only five women who figured romantically in his life and it wasn't until his fortieth birthday that he married one of them in 1985: Jane Macdougall, an elegant-boned, well-bred twenty-eight-year-old disc jockey on CFOX, a Vancouver rock station. Macdougall was the only one who refused to live with him. "I won't be your flavour of the month," she said throughout the five years she dated him. For someone in his business, with its opportunity for an endless orgy with wall-to-wall groupies, all of his relationships have been astonishingly long-term; the only exception was the Black Velvet Lady in British liquor ads, who lasted only six months.

In spite of his deep-seated desire for security, Bruce Allen postponed marriage because of his dread of being disappointed by the people he wants to love and trust. In his eyes, the first person to fail him was his father. A marine engineer, he would be away at sea for months on end and, during his concentrated time at home, would overcompensate by bestowing too much attention on Bruce and his younger brother. Bruce can't recall much about his father now: does he remember the fact that they bought an Elvis album together simply because he's such a Presley fan or because it was a nice time with his dad? In 1957, when Bruce was twelve, his father went for a medical examination and the doctor told him he'd live to be a hundred. The next day, he collapsed on a ladder and died. Bruce, shocked, was also enraged — furious that his father had left again, this time for good. He went to school that day, told no one what had happened and was angry when the principal called him out of class and then announced to his classmates what had happened. For the next few years, whenever Bruce had to fill in school forms that asked for his father's name he refused to write "Deceased." In his own coarsely colloquial way, the grown-up Allen summarizes the twelve-year-old's reaction: "You died. You pissed me off. Now fuck you."

His mother, never considering welfare, went to work to support the family. She wanted no help. In her last two years as a public-health dental assistant, when she was in a wheelchair, the dentist rearranged his offices so she could continue and collect her pension. Bruce, who is so much like her in character, was her problem child, a teenager who would get into fights and ignore his school work. Growing up as a lower-middle-class kid in the Dunbar area of Vancouver, he attended the up-scale Prince of Wales high school, where he responded to the other students' comfortable lives with contempt and hidden envy. A good runner who held a British Columbia record in the half-mile, he refused to train with the rest of the track team, working out instead at the Vancouver Olympic Club with the likes of Harry Jerome, and getting his satisfaction in beating all of his teammates. His running career ended suddenly the day he set an unofficial Canadian record in a qualifying heat, but was disqualified for a technicality. His coach, when Bruce solicited his support in appealing the decision, replied: "Don't ask me to look after you. You're not a team player, anyway." Allen never ran competitively again.

At the start of the sixties, Elvis Presley symbolized the rebelliousness of rock 'n' roll. Bruce wanted to be him. * "If I had my choice right now," the forty-year-old Allen says, "I'd like to be as big as him. I'd like to be Bryan Adams." As a boy he had to be content winning elocution contests and in his teens with being a school-dance disc jockey. He was dating Jeani Read then, a clever girl who would grow up to become a columnist on lifestyles for the Vancouver *Province*. They went together eight years, until he was well into his twenties; Read believes Allen has always preferred feminine companionship to the male-dominated rock world he lives in. Once during his teens, to avenge an insult to Jeani, he took a tire iron to a boy; although he broke no bones, Bruce was charged with assault and got a suspended sentence.

Abandoning school before graduating, Bruce built truck bodies at a Kenilworth factory while racing stock cars with moderate success on the weekends. But Jeani Read's intelligence spurred him to continue his education at a catch-up college. There, he organized a floor-hockey team that wore black hoods so nobody would recognize its members as they played the game like violent street-fighters. At twenty he began approaching local bands to play at the college. It was a first step toward his career, which became firmly launched in 1967 when a friend told him about a good English-style rock group called Five Man Cargo that needed a manager. He convinced

---

*· Today, the bookcase in the living-room of his 4,100-square-foot house holds little other than Presley records and biographies. He has made a pilgrimage to Graceland, the late singer's lavish Memphis home, and a Presley photo has a place of honour in his office.

the band to let him handle them, although because he knew nothing about the business, he took only a 5 percent management fee. He learned quickly, using Five Man Cargo as leverage to set himself up as a booking agent. In return for placing this hot new group in their clubs, he demanded that club owners give him exclusive rights to book all their local acts. Several agreed; it would cost them nothing because Allen got his percentage from the bands for arranging the bookings. He hand-crafted these groups into slick purveyors of Top 40 tunes, adjudicating every song they sang, every move they made. By this time he was at the University of British Columbia, where he was half-heartedly taking labour economics. But capitalism beckoned — he was earning $40,000 a year when he dropped out of third-year university.

Within a year he was managing six bands and booking seventeen clubs. Sam Feldman, a former night-club doorman and bouncer, was handling three acts. After a half-hour meeting in 1971, they became partners and their string of exclusive contracts with clubs rose quickly to twenty-three. They were Day and Night. Feldman had a good business head and looked after the details, Allen was a sharp negotiator and a high-profile promoter. Feldman was as calm and controlled as Allen was overheated and outrageous. And Bruce Allen was already into his manic mode, screaming instead of speaking, kicking over a garbage can instead of debating a point. ("A lot of it," Feldman remarks, "is personality defects that he prefers to paint with a positive brush rather than correct.")

Allen had always prided himself on his independence. He refused to drive his mother's car. He kept his paper route until he was eighteen to earn enough money to buy an old Monarch. And now he was proving that he could succeed as a freelance talent agent. Yet for all his professed desire to do things on his own, he craved security, continuing to live in the basement of his mother's house until he was twenty-five, still dating his high-school girlfriend, Jeani Read.

"Then, of course, Randy Bachman walked in the door in 1972," Allen recalls. In fact, he went to Grande Prairie, Alberta, purposely to meet Bachman, where he was performing with his new group, Brave Belt. He had been a guitarist in a Winipeg band, The Guess Who, that had become an international supergroup. But Bachman was a Mormon and the drugs and dollies of life on the road with The Guess Who had offended his sensibilities. When Allen met him, the rock singer who had tasted the sweetness at the top of the charts had lost his record contract and was looking for more work. "If you move to Vancouver," Allen told him, "I'll work for you fifty-two weeks a year." When Bachman's brother, who was managing him, decided to stay in Winnipeg with his family, Randy asked Bruce Allen to handle him.

"Randy, how can I manage the band? You know more about the business than I do."

"Don't worry," Bachman reassured him. "I'll stay beside you and show you the ropes." It was easier to have even an inexperienced manager deal with the booking agents and record companies than it would be for Bachman himself. He offered Allen 20 percent. Allen said he was worth only half that; only near the end, when they parted five years later, had the management fee risen to 15 percent.

At first the slogging was achingly slow. Allen was, as he always is in business deals, inhumanly persistent. The band made an album which their manager tried to sell to twenty-six different companies; all of them passed on it. The Guess Who was still the Canadian champ among rock groups; Bachman was only a tenth-ranked contender. BTO added three new songs to the album and twenty-five of the labels passed again. But Mercury Records bit this time and Bachman prompted Allen, who was green but always game to talk, on what to say in signing the deal with the company in New York. Mercury released the album in 1973 under the group's new name, Bachman-Turner Overdrive.

Bachman, desperate for a comeback, knew the record wouldn't go anywhere unless BTO went on the road in the States for the full 183 days a year the American government allowed the group to work there. Beginning that June, Allen accompanied BTO on every date as they bounced around the States on a madman's itinerary, racing to wherever the album happened to be hot that week. Flying the quartet into the nearest big city, then driving them the rest of the way — often up to five hundred miles overnight — Allen was learning the business from Bachman. Learning the importance of the press, and how to manipulate them away from in-depth interviews with a Mormon rock singer who derided the sinful ways of his fans. Learning never to carry needless grudges against people with whom he had to continue doing business, no matter how much he would have wanted to cut them dead if he didn't need them.* And learning how to cut deals, although in those early days BTO was working for only $150 to $500 a night.

Mercury was subsidizing the tour with advances against the band's royalties, and when the album started to stall at sales of 120,000, it wanted to take BTO off the road. Allen asked his Mercury contact, Lou Simon, for a shortfall to cover losses. Simon refused. "Okay, I'll make you a deal," BTO's manager told him. "Make the money half-recoupable. We'll pick up the difference ourselves and I'll pay it in cash."

"If you lose $40,000, we only have to pay you back $20,000?" Simon said. "Well, you want to do that, go ahead."

But when the album started to do well, Allen asked Simon to repay him the $20,000 that Allen had spent himself. Simon refused: "You made the deal." †

---

* A competitor, such as another rock agent, was different. He was quoted at the time as saying that you had to "grind" a competitor. "You have to kick him, especially when he's down," he said. More recently, Allen has modified his stance a little: "You really have to push for your deals hard, but you have to know when to stop."

† There was an interesting sequel to this which pitted the moral Randy Bachman against Allen and the other three members of the band. In 1976, Allen had an audit done on BTO's finances and found that Mercury had overpaid the group by $96,000 and would probably never discover its mistake. While the band voted three-to-one to keep the money, the dissenting vote was Bachman's. Allen argued: "Think of all the money Mercury Records have ripped off of guys." But he finally informed Lou Simon and other Mercury executives of the overpayment and was astonished when the company told him that because he hadn't fought about swallowing the $20,000 in 1973, BTO could keep the $96,000.

By 1974, a year after their first album was released, Bachman-Turner Overdrive was on its way to the largest international music success a Canadian group had ever experienced. They would sell ten million records and gross $33 million. And rampaging around North America with them was Bruce Allen, whose performances were the equal of any on the stage. One night in North Carolina, when BTO was at the summit of their success, police began moving in to arrest a fan who had bared her breasts and was dancing with the band. Allen turned off the stage lights and when somebody grabbed his shoulder, he swung around and punched a face. It was a policewoman and her nose was bloodied. As a contingent of police waited for him outside the dressing room, Allen hid in a large guitar crate that was forklifted onto a waiting truck. At a concert in Los Angeles, when a group called Jo Jo Gun were the opening act for Bachman-Turner, Allen told their manager to have them finish in fifty minutes to avoid overtime charges for the stage crews. They were still playing after fifty-five minutes. "We're going off when we want to," their manager said. "You're going off right now," Allen insisted, pulling the plug on the band's equipment and then pitching the manager off the eight-foot-high stage.

For a long time on the road, Allen had slept every night in the same room with Randy Bachman ("the last voice that talks to Randy wins the argument," Allen said later). Eventually his sway over Bachman ebbed as the band's accountant, Graeme Waymark, exerted more influence on their leader. By 1976 BTO was receiving increasingly bad press as they spent more time worrying about their personal financial statements than they did about their music. Their albums began to sound like copies of one another and sales dropped from three million to half a million. And in 1977, in a move that Allen blames on Waymark, Randy Bachman announced that he was going on his own as a solo act.

Allen was devastated. Together he and Randy had built one of the most lucrative rock acts in the world. Suddenly Bachman was abandoning it all. Because he was taking Graeme Waymark with him, he was also abandoning Allen, who refused to work with the accountant anymore. Bruce Allen walked away to pick up the pieces of the group, which stayed alive as BTO for another two years, with little success. Bachman failed too in his attempt to go it alone. Allen has never forgiven Bachman. When his fortunes started to soar again a few years later, and Bachman was trying to make a comeback, Allen used a radio show he was doing to denigrate him. "I went out of my way to hurt him, to make sure he didn't come back." Since then, he says, Bachman has asked him to manage him again. "My heart tells me to do it," Allen says, "but my head tells me not to. People don't change; Randy Bachman knows it all." He did attend the last night of a recent BTO revival at a Vancouver night-club; he says it had him in tears.

In its five successful years, Bachman-Turner Overdrive had earned about $1 million in commissions for Allen and his partner, Sam Feldman. "One of the reasons we didn't make as much as we could have," Feldman says, "is that Bruce cut what was a very low-ball deal [with Bachman]." Not only was the partners' percentage on BTO's earnings only 10 percent, for most of the band's life they didn't have any piece of the revenue from publishing rights, which can account for a third of a manager's royalties from his artist. Because BTO wrote its own songs and published them, it received the approximately 40 cents an album that goes to a song's writer and publisher — money on which Allen and Feldman didn't get a commission until near the end. After it was all over, Allen had the $40,000 Excalibur that BTO had given him and the $800,000 house he'd bought, with its swimming pool and a view of the Vancouver waterfront. But the partners dropped some of their profits into bad investments — a mortgaged fishboat owned by a client of Graeme Waymark's, and an apartment building, which Feldman spent an inordinate amount of time managing in a desperate effort to save their assets. If they hadn't finally sold the building, he says, they would have gone bankrupt. Because Waymark had got them into the deal, they launched a $270,000 suit against the accountant; he settled out of court for about $140,000.

During the next two years, Allen and Feldman — never close friends — were drifting further apart as Bruce's rages boiled over more violently. He had no hit group with whom he could spend his days on the road, away from the office. "The focus was on the booking agency again," Sam Feldman says, "and the agency is more of a team effort. The amount of bad-mouthing from a partner was just intolerable." Allen also alienated their employees with his Tartar's temperament. "Democracies don't work in this business," he would yell, swearing at his underlings for any peccadillo. Occasionally his secretary took to slipping Valium into the Cokes that Allen drinks at the rate of a case a day. The staff began to lobby Feldman. As Allen tells the story, Feldman announced to him one day: "Bruce, it's over, I don't want to work with you anymore. And I'm going to take the staff." Feldman insists that he said employees should be allowed to make their own choice, and proposed that the partners split up the company, with him taking the booking agency and paying Bruce about half the profits, until such time as one of Allen's groups became successful. Borrowing $5,000 to open a new office, Feldman left, and the staff went with him.

If Allen had felt discarded by Randy Bachman's abrupt leave-taking, the wholesale desertion of his partner and employees was almost more than he could handle emotionally. He learned that one of the women who'd been with him almost from the beginning had been one of the instigators of the walkout. Much later, he would admit, "You start looking at yourself as a human being; it made me reexamine how I treat other people." But at the time, he felt only anger and bitter resentment.

He was wracked by the two conflicting emotions that have bedevilled him all his life. One was to turn his back on Feldman forever, and certainly in the years since he has seen his partner only a few times a year, in lawyers' or accountants' offices. He didn't congratulate Sam on his marriage, didn't send a gift when his child was born. The agency, however, represented a small refuge for Allen. "When the groups aren't around, that agency pays my salary: I make $50-$60,000 a year from it. Am I going to throw that away and bet on a Loverboy hitting, bet on a Bachman-Turner coming along? That's my security." There's something deeper, though, that Allen mentions almost as an afterthought. "Maybe, emotionally, or security-wise, I need Sam Feldman." *

At the depths of his self-doubt, Allen found himself another partner, another act. Even before the break-up with Feldman, he had heard of a group managed by Lou Blair, a six-foot-five, three-hundred-pound operator of Calgary's Refinery night-club. Allen never was high on the prospects of the band's founding members — guitarist Paul Dean of the Streetheart group and lead singer Mike Reno of Moxy — who were getting on in years for rock musicians. But Blair wanted the experienced Allen's help and persisted until the day he not-so-casually played a new Dean/Reno tape on a car stereo while driving around Palm Springs with Allen. A song called "Turn Me Loose" convinced Allen to become co-manager of the group that became Loverboy.

In a way, it was Bachman-Turner Overdrive all over again. Loverboy was a quintet that played safe, mainstream rock. As the rock journal *Rolling Stone* would say of the band, "They were savvy enough to know that records are marketed like hosiery." To be marketed in the United States, however, demanded a new Bruce Allen that was much more subtle than the old BTO model. Trying to impress Columbia Records, the American parent of the Canadian company that produced Loverboy's first album, Allen had the group do a concert for Columbia executives visiting Toronto. The concert was a disaster: the band wasn't ready, people walked out and the

---

* Feldman now manages his own popular groups, such as Doug and the Slugs and the Headpins, and the partners' biggest arguments concern the non-interest-bearing loans they advance their groups. Of the roughly $400,000 that was out in loans in 1985, Allen had advanced only $35,000 of it to one of his groups, the Payola$. Feldman admits, "It's not right and I hate it," but points out that he used to be on the other side of the arguments when Allen's groups, Prism and Red Rider, had loans outstanding. In what must be a bitter pill for Feldman, some of the staff that left with him have returned to Bruce Allen, among them the man who runs the Bryan Adams tours. Allen found it easier to forgive them than his partner; besides, he says, "you feel like a winner when you take someone back."

Americans expressed their displeasure. In desperation, Allen and Blair took them out for dinner. During the next two and a half hours, Loverboy's managers said not a word about their band or even the record business. Although Allen knew virtually nothing about the subject, they talked fishing with one of the executives, who let it be known he was a keen sports angler. At the end of the evening, he told Allen: "You know, you've got a good track record and I've had a real good time tonight. . . . I'm going to tell everybody back there to say this thing tonight was great, and we're going to put the album out. You get the band in shape to go on the road, and if you back me up, you're going to have a hit."

Allen and Blair sent Loverboy bouncing around the continent, wherever their album was becoming popular — about 250 concerts in that first year. The co-managers* used their own money to pay some of the touring expenses (which eventually totalled $12,000 a night) to show the record company that they were cutting costs. When the first album survived through the Christmas season of 1980, Columbia began to promote it actively. Loverboy was launched. Allen and Blair toured them throughout the United States, Puerto Rico, Europe, the United Kingdom and Japan, and did a $1-million deal with Nissan-Datsun to promote Loverboy on a Canadian tour and underwrite an hour-long television special that was syndicated across the country. The Japanese car company spent $60,000 in promotion costs in Ontario alone; the managers estimated that the advertising for the tour was worth nearly $1 million. The impetus for the promotion came from the company's Toronto ad agency, looking for a splashy way to introduce Nissan's new Sentra model, which was aimed at the same sixteen-to-twenty-four-year-old market to which the rock group appeals. Originally, it was to be a one-shot concert in Vancouver, but Allen convinced the company

---

* Allen describes himself as the merchandiser half of the management team while Blair oversees the creative side, going into the studio with the musicians. Allen says, "Lou looks at my braggadocio, my hype and my ability to motivate as a positive; he has enough confidence to let me be me."

to finance the TV show and a tour coast-to-coast, allowing Loverboy to visit some of the smaller cities it otherwise couldn't afford to play.

Normally, rock groups have to front all the expenses of touring. Bruce Allen insists that Loverboy be cost-efficient and yet the band often tours with two custom-designed buses that can cost $360 a day each and three semi-trailer trucks — to tote the sound system, lights and some relatively restrained stage equipment — that cost $425 apiece, in addition to gas. For one concert at the Coliseum in the band's home base of Vancouver, Loverboy might gross $175,000 (fourteen thousand tickets times $12.50). But the Coliseum might charge the band rental of $35,000. Ushers cost extra ($2,000), as do union stagehands ($5,000), additional security guards ($2,000) and police ($2,000). Crews, stagehands, security and the band members have to be fed ($3,000 a day), tickets printed ($900), commission paid to ticket agents ($10,000), and advertising disseminated ($15,000). The local promoter gets his fee, which can vary widely ($18,000-$20,000 a night is not high). And Allen and Blair take their 17.5 percent management fee. All of which might leave Loverboy with $45,000 or so, to split five ways. * There are, however, other goodies. Allen learned his lesson with Bachman-Turner Overdrive in not sewing up decent percentages of all the spinoffs a rock group generates. He and Blair set up their own company to merchandise all the Loverboy paraphernalia peddled at their concerts: from $1 souvenir buttons to $20 nylon tour jackets. In one long tour, gross sales totalled $7 million U.S., 25 percent of it going to the group, 10 percent to Lou Blair and 10 percent to Allen and Feldman's company.

While Loverboy took a year off to recharge physically and musically in 1984, Bruce Allan was thriving on his latest discovery, Bryan Adams, a kid he had kicked out of his office the day he met him in 1980. Adams was a prodigy who at sixteen joined a once-popular Vancouver group, Sweeney Todd,

---

* Lou Blair does point out one obvious benefit from touring, however: "We sell thirty-thousand to forty-thousand more albums a week when we're on the road than when we're not."

and when the band failed within a year he composed the music in commercials for such stores as The Bay. He was still in his teens when he met local songwriter Jim Vallance; together they wrote tunes for two of Allen's acts, Bachman-Turner Overdrive and Prism. Adams showed up with a tune called "Let Me Take You Dancin'," which had sold 250,000 copies as a disco hit. Allen took him in hand and within seventeen days had him record his first major album for A&M (an earlier, badly produced album had only negligible sales). *You Want It, You Got It* was the product that Allen accused A&M of not promoting while he'd had Adams on the road as an opener for such first-run bands as the Kinks, Foreigner and Loverboy. When A&M Records released his next album, *Cuts Like A Knife*, a music video for the title song became a hit on MTV, the American all-rock television channel. Elaborately produced video versions of pop songs had suddenly become one of the best methods of marketing an act, and Adams's video — which showed the leather-garbed singer in an empty swimming pool into which a sensual woman dives — became a *cause célèbre*, drawing the wrath of *Rolling Stone* as an example of the exploitation of women in rock videos generally and by MTV specifically. The album itself spent two months among the U.S. Top 20. In late 1984 and 1985 his *Reckless* went even bigger, faster, becoming the number-one album throughout North America.

"What you see on stage is Adams," Bruce Allen says. "There's no packaging. All I have to do is get him seen. My job is positioning him." Manager and artist have yet to sign a contract for the 15 percent that Allen has of Adams. "You're a man of your word and I'm a man of my word, so why do we need a contract?" Adams said. Allen, believing he had finally found someone he could trust, agreed. In 1982, he was calling his protégé his personal retirement plan. "He's closest to what I could have been if I could have sung. He's the closest to Elvis. When he hits that stage, he does everything I would do if I had been there."

Allen often speaks as if he were Adams's surrogate father. Unless he changes his mind, that will be the closest to fatherhood he intends to get. He has no plans for children. "In my business I deal with kids all the time and with musicians — they're kids. I watch kids who come to our concerts, coked-up fifteen-year-old girls. I don't want to come home and deal with more kids."

Allen has a comfortable enough environment in which to raise a family. He is married to a woman he trusts and is house-proud. He has nearly $2 million in term deposits as a financial cushion, as well as two internationally acclaimed acts earning more millions for him. Other income is derived from his investment in two Vancouver night-clubs, his promotion of a pro wrestling circuit that's appealing to teenage fans, and his management of Canadian Dale Walters, the 1984 Olympics bronze medallist boxer turned professional featherweight. Yet Bruce Allen goes on talking about all the reasons why he doesn't want children — his age, his lifestyle — never mentioning that he was a child once and that his father failed him. "You died. You pissed me off. Now fuck you."

5

The Tomorrow Traders

The tomorrow traders buy, sell, trade, manufacture and unabashedly use an intangible commodity — the future. The two men in this chapter, financier Donald Cormie and scientist John MacDonald, were selected because they are elbows-deep in something that affects every aspect of our lives — high technology. MacDonald designs and manufactures devices of the future and Cormie develops them and bends them to his will to make his financial empire operate more quickly, more efficiently and thus more profitably. They are not victims of change, they are the change-makers, and they've become millionaires as a result.

Today, "high tech" is a cliché used to describe everything from office décor to banking, but its pervasiveness cannot be overstated. Its grip on our society is evident in a few statistics. In British Columbia, the total sales of the electronic manufacturing industry in 1984 overtook those in fishing — one of the big three resource-based industries that have traditionally fueled the West Coast economy — to become the province's fifth largest sector. In 1947 the first television set was sold in North America; just thirty years later the average household owns two, at least one of which is colour. In 1964 there were five hundred mainframe computers in Canada; today sixteen thousand are in use. In 1982 fewer than one million homes had personal computers; the figure has doubled in three years and is climbing by 50 percent annually. Not only are

MacDonald and Cormie part of this new world, but they are the very people who are making it possible — indeed inevitable. Cormie's application of science and computer technology to all his enterprises, from ranching to finance, are unprecedented. Technology is so essential to Cormie's business and is pushed by him to such extremes that he often finds that the specific piece of equipment he needs does not yet exist. When that happens he doesn't give up, he simply builds it — in house. The creations of Vancouver's MacDonald Dettwiler bring us clear pictures of the surface of Saturn and make it possible for people to see things they'd previously only dreamed of seeing.

There's so much talk of the future in everyday life that most of us believe we are already firmly ensconced in the era depicted in *Star Wars*. But we suffer anomie and insecurity when the unfamiliar tentacles of what futurist Alvin Toffler has called the electronic revolution penetrate our daily lives. Both Toffler and sociologist Charles Reich have written of the isolation and apathy that afflict people when incomprehensible technology appears to control their lives. It's an old theme, but we feel it even more acutely today because, despite an argot peppered with high-tech buzz words, change is accelerating and we feel ever less in control. As soon as we grasp one new development, another radical change shoves it aside. It is almost impossible to keep up. Just as we begin to understand automatic bank tellers, chequebooks become totally obsolete as retail stores begin to debit our accounts and charge cards directly with the push of a button. By the time most people develop a passing familiarity with computers, voice synthesizers will allow even illiterates to talk to a dressed-up microchip and perform orally many complex functions that now require a keyboard operator. So although the future swirls around us like an ever-present fog, few feel comfortable, because they cannot see their feet as they walk through it.

The tomorrow traders can't always see their feet either but for them, the uncertainty and novelty of the future is an expressway, not an obstacle course. They aren't necessarily clairvoyant, although John MacDonald comes as close to it as the legendary sibyl, but they are completely unawed by the unknown.

Of all the entrepreneurs in this book, the tomorrow traders are the most vulnerable. If things go wrong they have no familiar cave to retreat to, no tried-and-true commodity to fall back on until cash flow recovers. In fact, one of them, twenty-four-year-old Steve Buchan, went bankrupt just as this book was entering its final stages. Buchan chewed and clawed his way out of a Montreal boys' home to form his own computer-retailing business when he was eighteen. By the time he was twenty-three, he was a paper millionaire. But a combination of toughness learned on the street and a gift for salesmanship wasn't enough to keep him solvent in today's vicious retail computer market. And John MacDonald was on the edge of bankruptcy with the FOCUS project, a state-of-the-art flight-analysis system for commercial airlines that does everything but fly the plane itself. He couldn't retreat when his staff told him the system was unworkable because his business was based on being a pioneer in information systems. If he couldn't make FOCUS work, he would be no different from an ordinary manufacturer who turns out essentially the same product year after year — and his pride is in being a man of the future.

The vulnerability of tomorrow traders also lies in the sheer pace of technological change. Not only must they feel comfortable dabbling in the esoterica of digital gadgets but they have to be quick enough on their feet to drop one product at the right time and pick up another. For five years, Steve Buchan, a young man with an intuitive grasp of how a computer operates, made those lightning adjustments while computer companies disappeared as fast as they opened their doors and product lines changed almost overnight. In the end, he got caught with a large inventory of virtually unsalable models that had been hot items two months earlier.

The pell-mell pace of the high-tech field makes the tomorrow traders vulnerable for a third reason: gambling on the future is the hairiest bet to make. Everyone, for example, must eat. Whether the latest food fad will seduce the public palate is a risk a food manufacturer takes — but at least he's risking an unknown commodity in a known environment. Cormie and MacDonald daily risk new commodities in completely untried environments. Cormie, for instance, has no way of knowing if people would use banking services that allow the instantaneous transfer of money from coast to coast — he must create the system and invest his money first. And there are failures — MacDonald Dettwiler still services the only four purchasers of the company's ill-fated attempt at producing minicomputers for business.

For every tomorrow trader who makes it, there are myriad wonderful inventions and their creators who have fallen by the wayside. One of Canada's finest inventors and clearly a man of the future is Vancouver's Bill Cameron. He has patented over seventy inventions and techniques, yet none of them have become a successful business. He was the first to develop the revolutionary all-plastic ski, which was being manufactured by a Japanese firm. Then along came an even better idea — the German-designed foam-core model, which made Cameron's creation commercially obsolete. There are thousands like Bill Cameron, armed with farsighted developments that rarely get past the prototype stage.

The pace of the electronic revolution is forever subjected to hyperbole, but a few examples serve to show how unrelenting the change is in Cormie and MacDonald's world. The cost of sixty-four thousand bits of dynamic computer memory (64 K) was $5 in 1982. By the end of 1985, bits cost 2 or 3 millicents each, or $1.28 for 64 K. By 1990 64 K will be available for 60 cents — about 1 millicent per bit. Gallium arsenide, one hundred times faster in the transmission of information than silicon, will soon make current modems, which can send up to 2,500 words a minute, seem as slow as a carthorse on the highway. Voice synthesizers, until now cumbersome and expensive, have overnight begun to transform the computer relationship into two-way communication. In 1982, Texas Instruments and General Instruments began making thumbnail-sized silicon syllable makers, the key element in voice synthesizers, costing under $15. The syllable makers use stored raw sound data to construct exact sounds and reproduce authentic-sounding voices. And, once we can talk to computers, the last obstacle to their universality will be gone.

It's hardly surprising that the tomorrow traders who thrive on the future occasionally forget the requirements of the present. As entrepreneurs, they are the least well-rounded of the Money Rustlers. MacDonald learned a nearly fatal lesson when he assumed that mastery of the esoterica of space-age communication is enough. He now ruefully admits he doesn't have nearly the same head for business details that he does for digital circuitry and remote sensing. Just as everything was going under, business skills were imposed upon him — and now he concentrates on science and selling, the areas in which he excels.

Cormie, however, is an exception. He's so firmly anchored in the basics of his legal training and the fundamental lesson of thrift he learned as a boy that he can conjure up the technical genie and bend it to his will without straying beyond the boundaries of sound business practice. Rather, he uses his servant to redefine those boundaries.

The tomorrow traders are vitally important Money Rustlers. Not only are they absorbed by the technolgy of the future, but they are financially ambitious. If they weren't they would be academics or hobbyists, not entrepreneurs contributing directly to the economy. They are also crucial to national confidence, because men like John MacDonald and Donald Cormie laugh in the face of our insecurities about high tech. MacDonald has demonstrated that Canadians can compete as equals of the electronic giants and Cormie shows business the direction it must take to remain competitive. The two men wrestle the future to the ground. They are the daring cowboy capitalists that easterners like to think inhabit the West, but in this instance they are true pioneers, not just showmen.

Dr John S. MacDonald — Mr Wizard

There's a little piece of John S. MacDonald's genius everywhere, from Pouch Cove, Newfoundland, to Malaysia, from planet Earth to outer space. MacDonald, 49, is a scientist, a technician whose projects are integral to the exploration of space and the digital control of satellite ground stations. His life is filled with extraordinary creativity and is spent in engineering fields so esoteric that only a tiny percentage of the population can even understand what he is doing, let alone how he is doing it.

But in over three decades of scientific tinkering, his most notable and painful creation is not another space-age gizmo with a barely comprehensible seven-word title; it's a company. MacDonald's walls are festooned with pictures and mementos telling the story of MacDonald Dettwiler (MD for short). The company sometimes grew in spite of him from a $48,000-a-year basement operation started in 1968 — almost lost to bankruptcy twice — to a $29 million-a-year miniature technical giant, competing successfully with IBM, 3-M and other monoliths. A hand-lettered certificate dated January 25, 1982, and signed by Columbia shuttle astronauts Joe H. Engle and Richard H. Truly, lauds MD's contribution to the exploration of space.

As John MacDonald likes to tell it, his life is one fortuitous quirk of fate after another. "I've got horseshoes up my ass," he's fond of saying. He earnestly talks as if serendipity magically lifted him from a life of blissful mediocrity in Prince Rupert, British Columbia, where he was born in 1936, to a doctorate in engineering from the Massachussetts Institute of Technology, and then whisked him up the pinnacle of technical wisdom to his lofty position as one of Canada's most respected technical gurus.

As the multi-millionaire founder and chairman of the board of MacDonald Dettwiler, he can be forgiven for thinking his career is garnished with luck. It's a long way down from up there, and he and his family would have been perfectly content if he had ended up driving a truck. His grandfather came to Canada in 1911 to work on the Grand Trunk Railway as a brakeman and conductor. His father Neil, a male nurse at a mental hospital in the Outer Hebrides, left Scotland for Prince Rupert in 1928, on the eve of the Depression. Perhaps a little of the MacDonald luck was poking through then, because while everyone else was losing jobs, Neil MacDonald found one as a steward on a lighthouse tender; by the end of his career he had risen to the position of captain of a Fisheries Patrol Boat. Alice, John's mother, a third-generation Canadian, moved to Prince Rupert when she was three. Neither parent had any particular interest in or aptitude for science.

Chance, according to MacDonald, first interfered one day while he was doing what every kid in Prince Rupert did, whiling away time. He was idly firing a balsawood airplane into the air with a slingshot, watching it soar to its zenith, spread its wings and then glide on air currents to the ground. But air currents are unpredictable and it plopped down on the roof of his next door neighbour, George Daniels, who owned an electronics shop specializing in building, renting and servicing fishboat radios. Daniels was furious at the interruption when MacDonald pleaded with him to retrieve the plane. He cussed and bitched but grudgingly got the toy off his roof. "Of course, it landed on the roof again," laughs MacDonald, "and he was even more upset the second time, so I thought I'd better quit." Daniels wasn't angry enough not to chat, however, and he took MacDonald down to see his basement. "That was the beginning! I became fascinated with these radio telephones. I started helping him and he taught me how to drill chassis, do wiring and gave me books on them." That encounter unlocked the gift that is the foundation of MacDonald's success — an aptitude for unravelling technical puzzles. Science is full of Newtonian wizards and prescient discoveries, but MacDonald's brilliance is in tackling problems logically — breaking them down piece by piece, relying on analysis rather than intuition.

The cliché about a kid in a candy shop is particularly apt of MacDonald in those days. Electronics dominated his life; he worked evenings and weekends at the shop and he also took

on freelance assignments, tinkering with the gadgets in his
high school such as the public address system and the
auditorium lighting system. That summer, misfortune dealt
MacDonald another lucky hand. His mentor, Daniels,
developed a heart problem and couldn't make his annual service calls. The sixteen-year-old MacDonald needed no urging
to fill in for his employer and spent a blissful summer hitch-
hiking up and down the British Columbia coast, working on
fish boats and fish packers, installing radios and adjusting fre-
quencies. The next year, a local fisherman's co-op bought a
bunch of war surplus Loran A navigation sets, which they
hoped would allow fish boats to pinpoint their position. It
was a hell of an idea, at a terrific price — unfortunately the
system was designed for World War II bombers, and no one
could figure out how to operate them. After much head-
scratching, the whole lot was dumped in Gordon Daniels's
lap. Just as puzzled as everyone else, he turned it over to his
assistant.

The challenge engrossed MacDonald. He read everything
he could find and fiddled endlessly with the sets until he had
their intricacies mastered. Then he discovered a serious
drawback. The Loran sets operated on a different power
system than the fish boats and in order to make them work,
an additional generator had to be installed in each boat. "You
had a choice," chuckles MacDonald, "either keep the engines
running or flatten the batteries. The wiring on your average
fish boat is a sight to behold. Junctions would heat up like hell
when the Loran was turned on, so there was a danger of fire,
and when it was turned on it'd scream like a banshee." Not a
smashing success, but it was MacDonald's first contact with
digital systems, an area of technology that became a corner-
stone of MD's later success.

"My ambition then was to work for Daniels for the rest of
my life," he recalls. It was his mother, one of the few people in
Prince Rupert with a high-school certificate at the time, who
pushed him a little further. "If you want to do this sort of
thing, don't stop with Gordon Daniels's basement," she
scoffed. "Go to the top; go to university." Among

MacDonald's peers higher education was thought to be a school on a hilltop, but eighteen-year-old MacDonald took her words seriously. In the fall of 1954 he left home for the University of British Columbia and electrical engineering.

He soon discovered that he had the abstract reasoning skills necessary to visualize and understand three-dimensional algebra and to break it down into digestible concepts — to the awe of bewildered classmates who crowded into his informal tutorials throughout his second year. He graduated with honours from UBC in 1959; one of only six out of 260 other engineering students to receive the coveted distinction that year.

Luck has constantly interceded in John MacDonald's life by salting his career with people who have nudged him in the right direction, helping him to unlock his potential. During MacDonald's freshman year, a third-year engineering student who lived in the same boarding-house badgered and belittled him about his rustic ways. "He boasted that he was going to the Massachusetts Institute of Technology," MacDonald remembers. "He let me know that MIT was the top engineering school and there was no way I was ever going to get in. I'd never even heard of MIT, but after the goading I thought well, goddamn it, I'm going to show him." The older student didn't even finish his degree.

The first two summers as an undergraduate, MacDonald returned to Prince George to work for a competitor of Gordon Daniels's who, by this time, had moved his shop to Victoria. His final two summers were spent at Chalk River, Ontario, working for Atomic Energy of Canada. It was an intoxicating era for AECL. The use of semi-conductors in digital circuitry for measuring atomic reactions was just beginning. The corporation was in the forefront of transistorization technology and MacDonald was doing the work. One of his projects was to eliminate the last vacuum tubes in the old-fashioned mainframe computers and to change the system from analog to digital — just the sort of hands-on problem that MacDonald revels in.

Chalk River was also where he met his wife-to-be,

Alfredette, a strong-minded French-Canadian from Ontario. She was working as a security officer at the plant and took her job seriously enough to pull his file and look at it before she agreed to go out with him. "I was curious about him," she admits, "but I wouldn't have gone out with just anyone." The eighteen-year-old Alfredette fell in love with MacDonald, particularly with his "gorgeous, long legs," and married him a year later in 1959. Alfredette and others who met him found MacDonald to be an earnest, studious and quiet twenty-two-year-old who was saved by his Prince Rupert background from the pomposity of the up-and-coming scientist. Alfredette had little notion that the man she was marrying would soon be one of the best technical minds in the world but, even then, she was suffused with unusual confidence in him. "I think I was too young to understand what he was doing, but you always have a feeling about people. I had never been to British Columbia but I knew there were mountains there. I had a vision that all he had to do was hold my hand and we could jump over them together."

The cultural gap MacDonald had found between UBC and Prince Rupert seemed a very small ditch when he arrived at MIT in 1959. "You had to get used to stress if you were a grad student at MIT," remembers Alfredette, "especially if you were from the backwoods." She recalls the terrific pressure to measure up against the student élite, who were skimmed from the top 10 percent of universities around the world, and the professors, who were the men other academics quoted. Those were the days when there was one school of unassailable prestige for every profession; economists went to the London School of Economics, doctors went to Johns Hopkins, artists to the Sorbonne, businessmen and lawyers to Harvard and engineers to MIT. Few people at MIT had even heard of UBC, which was an insignificant school with a reputation for its beautiful campus and salubrious climate. The breakneck pace, frightening competitiveness and rigid intolerance of mediocrity at MIT were a revelation to MacDonald. Even more startling was his early discovery that he was as good as any of his fellow students.

By his second year, MacDonald won the rare honour of being named an instructor in electrical engineering while still a student. Characteristically, in response to this latest accolade he raised his sights only marginally. "My whole ambition was to be an academic and there I was at the top school in the world, teaching." MacDonald might have settled into this career, but another lucky nudge pushed him into the path of M.R. Bose, an instructor on circuit theory. The two men became friends, often talking for hours while the twenty-seven-year-old MacDonald exercised his flair for assembling and diagnosing complicated circuitry on Bose's sophisticated stereo-speaker projects. MacDonald was startled to discover that his new friend's ultimate ambitions lay outside both science and academe. "I saw him start with an idea and build it into a corporation," says MacDonald, "and it didn't look too terribly difficult." One day Bose was "shooting the breeze after class," the next he was in production in a "rinky-dink little plant," and soon after he was running the giant corporation that Bose Speakers Limited is today, producing some of the finest stereo equipment in the world.* MacDonald was to rue his naïve and arrogant observation about the ease of building a corporation. He didn't rush immediately into the business world, but it was always there in the back of his mind.

MacDonald's years at MIT foreshadowed a personal characteristic that nearly sent MacDonald Dettwiler into bankruptcy years later. The brilliant young man was a dilettante, landing like a butterfly on one project, studying and solving the problem and then flying gently off into the breeze. MacDonald wasn't a plodder, as many academics are, content to replicate experiment after experiment, perfecting a different' picayune aspect each time. MacDonald was interested in the big picture and the thrill of discovery. This approach, although an important aspect of the successful business, taken

---

* While the idea of the scholar turned businessman seemed novel to MacDonald, there is a long tradition of MIT instructors going on to form their own businesses. Von Hipple started High Voltage Engineering. Doc Egerton formed Egerton Housemand and Greer. Edwin Land created Polaroid.

to its extreme can be disaster when profit depends on doing the same clever thing over and over. "I become fascinated with something new and go on to it," he admits. An example is MacDonald's pathfinding Ph.D. research in the area of biological interfacing with computers. For his thesis Mac-Donald created a machine that perfectly forged handwriting. Today, Jerry Lettvin, a professor at MIT and one of the foremost people working in this field, believes that MacDonald's thesis was a benchmark. "Other people are just starting to catch up," he points out. It could have been the basis of an illustrious research career; instead, MacDonald dropped it cold.

In the year following his graduation in 1965, MacDonald taught at MIT as an assistant professor* with a Ford Foundation Post-Doctoral Fellowship, before returning to Canada in 1966. It was the beginning of technology's long reign; MIT graduates were in demand and every university was scrambling to jump into bed with science. MacDonald was offered a job at UBC and for the first time his enthusiastic arrogance was heading him for disappointment. "I had this idealistic illusion that through a university like UBC I could create an educational environment that I'd experienced at MIT. There's a fantastic learning-culture that the place has imbedded — the formal delving into a subject to uncover [the] absolutely fundamental [reasons how and why something worked], rather than merely being satisfied with finding an answer that worked." His excitement was doused when he realized that first-year professors, even those with an MIT cachet, had no hope of creating their own private nirvanas. His idea was· soon swallowed up in the small-stakes politics of higher education. †

As always, luck was lurking nearby, this time in the form of

• Among his students were astronauts Buzz Aldren and Tony Engel.

† MacDonald may have been frustrated at UBC but the core 25 percent of MacDonald Dettwiler's technical talent was trained at UBC, and many of its top people were MacDonald's own graduate students.

Swiss-born Werner (Vern) Dettwiler, one of MacDonald's former undergraduate classmates, now working in the university's fledgling computer department. The maths and physics major — "I'm really more of an engineer than anything else" — had been taking on a few consulting jobs in his spare time. Both men had been thinking about something different when MacDonald heard that Lenkurt Electric Limited (now Microtel) was in a jam. "Competitors were coming into British Columbia with computer-based control systems [for remote microwave towers], and they didn't know the first thing about computers, so they were in a box." MacDonald landed the $48,000 contract to design and manufacture the software for the computer-based supervisory-control system. With two other silent partners, they formed a company and tackled the project in a makeshift lab and manufacturing facility in MacDonald's basement, working weekends and evenings while also keeping their full-time jobs at UBC during the day. They developed a program complete with a special language, well before the introduction of the microcomputer, that allowed the average repair person to monitor and adjust equipment and kick in back-up systems, all over the telephone line. The program, called NIPERS, was a tremendous advance, saving thousands of dollars in emergency repairs to remote towers. The next year, Lenkurt sold the system to Iran, and it's still in use in British Columbia today.

From their consulting work, MacDonald and Dettwiler believed there were a great many "things" that needed to be built to satisfy various clients in the technical field. At the time they had no thought of specializing in a particular area. The company was essentially a systems house; they took requests as they came, solved the problem, built a system and moved on. The company wasn't even officially named until 1969, when they incorporated. "We wanted the word 'Western' to be in the title, like Western Digital Systems or Western Computer Systems," says Dettwiler. But every name they chose was already taken. "Finally it got to the point where customers said, 'We want to pay you. Who are you?' so we settled on MacDonald Dettwiler and Associates."

MacDonald was in his element; he was a pioneer in virtually everything the company did. Its later domination of fields like remote sensing, digital data processing, synthetic aperture radar and ground satellite stations happened not because the partners chased after those markets but because MD had the knack of doing things first or better than anyone else. In 1971, with ten employees, MacDonald Dettwiler began to manufacture key components for a federal government ground-satellite station in Saskatchewan. So effective and reliable were the parts that the back-ups have never been used in nearly fifteen years. The company is still the world's leading supplier of those parts. In 1978 MD garnered international attention when it produced a "real-time" satellite image, allowing earth-bound technicians to see precisely what the satellite saw. The image is produced by Synthetic Aperture Radar, which has a lens with an effective radius of thirty-five miles, unhindered by cloud and other weather systems that block a satellite's vision.

MD's FIRE 240, a digital film recorder, is the best in the world for mechanical and digital imaging in black and white as well as colour. FIRE kicked off a string of innovative developments, all of which were remarkable in predicting and filling current technological needs. FIRE 600, designed for the seismographic industry, produces computer images in ten minutes compared to the old chemical system of developing a print, which takes an hour and a half. FIRE 9000 is revolutionizing electronics with its ability to plot circuit boards digitally.*

Until 1978, MD hadn't had an unprofitable year as it grew to ninety employees and grossed $5.5 million. But the unbroken success couldn't continue. In retrospect, it was a stunning achievement that MD lasted so long without serious problems because the cost of developing hardware and software is notoriously difficult to foresee. The company took on

* Robert Heath, an MD marketing manager, predicts FIRE 9000 will be the company's biggest development. One vendor in the United States sells circuit tracking systems to 99 percent of the market but doesn't have this new technology. Heath sees an immediate revenue of $7.7 million from FIRE 9000 alone.

project after project, finished them on time, or just about, and made a little money on most. Overruns on one project were paid from cash advances for the next, a common industry practice. MacDonald Dettwiler had had no outside capital infusion since its inception in 1967, but things ran relatively smoothly as long as the overruns were short and the projects relatively small.

The roots of MD's crisis, which continued from 1978 to 1982 and took the company to the brink of bankruptcy in 1978 and 1981, were deeply entwined in the company's greatest strength, MacDonald himself. MacDonald is first and foremost a creator, a species that views everything in life as a problem to be solved. As with his Ph.D., once the solution is found, the agile, restless mind moves on to something else. A good businessman, on the other hand, solves a problem and then tries to market the solution, with as little modification as possible, and as cheaply, extensively and as profitably as possible. MacDonald derides the process as "churning out sausages in a meat grinder, each one the same."

His first big failure came when he set MD off on a tangent that has since created a whole new generation of young millionaires — microcomputers. A company employee was convinced of the micro's future and MacDonald was impressed enough with his arguments to try for a piece of a burgeoning market. In 1976 MD spent $500,000 to build and develop what would be the world's first microcomputer. IBM came along in 1977 and blew them out of the water with its 4300 series.* MD was clearly ahead of its time, but Mac-Donald now realizes that the idea wasn't enough. "We just didn't have the right [corporate] environment to get into small computers. It takes a different type of culture than we had to do that." In addition to this project, for which they had no contract, MD had about the same amount of money invested in the development of a promising mobile data-communications system.

* MacDonald is proud that they still service the four customers who bought the system, but it is done at a loss, and a good businessman probably would have written off the whole lot.

Eventually, MacDonald looked up from his work bench to see his beloved company teetering on the brink of a crevasse filled with bills he couldn't pay. On the books was a giant multi-million dollar Mobile Radio Data System* job, but the contract wasn't signed and the advance was six months away. The banks weren't prepared to help, either; high tech carries financial clout in the eighties, but a few years ago it still smacked of wizardry in Canada, and was considered something better left to the Japanese, Germans and Americans. Besides, how do you assess an inventory of ideas?

His partners were unwilling to expose themselves to risk so MacDonald, with a net worth at the time of about $300,000 (including his home), gulped and signed a series of loan guarantees totalling $1 million to bridge the cash-flow problems. "I believed we would not fail," he now says of that extraordinary risk. In return, MacDonald demanded and received control; his share went from 33 percent to 55 percent.

He also sold the research and rights of the mobile data and business system to Ventures West, a Vancouver-based venture capital firm for $125,000 and a royalty that stops at $900,000. (Ventures West is already halfway to paying it off.) This bit of technology became the basis of Mobile Data International, a company formed by Ventures West with basically only one product, the MRDS developed by MacDonald Dettwiler. Today, the technology is still a world leader, beating competition from Motorola. In 1985 Mobile Data International will gross about $25 million. MacDonald now understands the value of churning out sausages.

The emergency infusion was only a quick fix; MD was still badly undercapitalized, without sufficient reserves to tide it over shortfalls. MacDonald understood the problem intellectually. "When you bootstrap a company, it's inevitable that someday you must finance it and I have to admit that I should have done it a couple of years before," says MacDonald ruefully. "But you live and learn." However, MacDonald seemed

---

* The MRDS provided a terminal in a car which hooked up to a central dispatch. The system is the basis of most in-car police computers which have proven successful in Canada and the United States.

unable to put this critical lesson into practice and the arrival of another successful project led the way into MD's near downfall. In 1978, Pacific Western Airlines asked the company to design something to relieve the company of its antiquated methods of flight planning, aircraft dispatch and calculation of fuel consumption — all of which was laboriously done by hand. MacDonald's answer, AIDS (Airline Information and Dispatch System), was an elegant state-of-the-art creation that was both compact (relying on microcomputers, not mainframes) and relatively inexpensive — MD quoted $400,000.

AIDS actually cost MacDonald Dettwiler $700,000 to develop. Instead of recouping the losses by putting the successful project into the meatgrinder and peddling it vigorously to hundreds of regional airlines, MacDonald sold an even bigger and better system, FOCUS, designed for larger airlines, to three international airlines. MacDonald estimated that the system would require around $4 million, and he threw in another $1.4 million for good measure. It was an enormous project for a company that was still grossing less than $10 million. "I thought, 'For that kind of money, what can possibly go wrong?' " he says regretfully. "I really figured I was out of the glue with FOCUS. What I didn't realize was that there was a huge gluepot waiting for me." By this time MacDonald was completely out of touch with his cherished workbench, rarely talking directly to technical people and spending the vast majority of his time hustling contracts overseas.* MD was hooked on new contracts, mainlining the advances, rather than building at least a few stable income earners to keep up the cash flow. Today, MacDonald admits this problem and his frantic travel schedule shows that he understood it at a gut level. "My greatest fear was to wake up

* His fall 1984 schedule is a mirror of his travel itinerary throughout the late seventies and early eighties: from September 10 — Boston; from September 18 — Europe, with stops in Switzerland, Amsterdam, Stockholm, Munich and England; from September 30 — Paris; from October 6 — Greece; and back to Vancouver, October 30.

some morning and not have any contracts. So I was out there hustling business. It was almost compulsive."

FOCUS had short-circuited before MacDonald had any inkling of trouble. The project was going nowhere, and it wasn't a matter of being a little behind schedule. He was astonished to discover a virulent debate within the company about whether the whole concept was even technically feasible — an inopportune time for such a debate, considering that the delivery date was only a few months away and almost all of the $5.4 million had already been spent. MacDonald was devastated, but the scientist in him took over and he collected the data. He sequestered himself over Christmas and took on the almost impossible task of mastering a highly sophisticated project with which he had had little to do since its conception. "I familiarized myself with the details of the entire FOCUS hardware system and I came to the conclusion on New Year's Day, 1981, that it was not only technically viable but that there was a very elegant solution." However, there was still a small problem: "I also came to the conclusion that we needed $3 million to finish the goddamn thing." * There was barely enough to cover the next month's payroll. MD had two choices: finish the contracted projects and bankrupt the company or back out of the deals and face lawsuits that would frighten away potential customers and guarantee no bank would take a gamble on a loan. For the Prince Rupert kid, accustomed to solving just about any puzzle that came his way, the dilemma was agonizing. For the brilliant engineer who had loped from MIT into competition with giants like IBM, the sense of failure was humiliating. "It was really the first time he was in a situation where he didn't feel he could do anything," says his wife.

And, as if all MacDonald's bad luck accumulated at once, the federal government really cut the feet out from under him. "I had a deal with the Canada Development Corporation [to bail out MD] that they welched on," he says, his face still flushing with anger five years later. "They led us down the

* In fact, it ended up costing another $5 million.

garden path, telling us everything was okay, then at the last minute the CDC board rejected the deal," he continues, almost shouting. "I didn't know what the hell I was going to do. At that stage, it looked like the whole works was going down the tube." Vern Dettwiler, who'd been out of the management side for years, felt the company was out of control. "John suffered tremendously during that period. I thought his health was in trouble. He would think he recognized what had to be done, we'd have some conversations, make a few agreements, and the next day everything would be turned around."

It is difficult to understand why MacDonald didn't act faster to salvage MD, because he clearly realized that even if he had a good business head he couldn't possibly manage to sell, supervise the creative end of MD and run the daily operation all at the same time. MacDonald's eldest son, Neil*, observes that his father's passion for ideas was worsened by his desire to control everything. "The excitement comes from attempting new projects, but he was trying to do too much. He was filling his platter too full." One close associate firmly believes that MacDonald's wife is to blame, saying that her influence kept him from doing anything until it was too late. Paradoxically, Alfredette's unshakable confidence in MacDonald may have dissuaded him from bringing in help. "John is so honest, but he sells himself short," she says. "He's much more of a businessman than he says he is, but he doesn't like it. Besides, there is only so much time."

Looking back, MacDonald chooses to see Ventures West as a white knight charging in to prevent disaster. In truth, Ventures West had been lurking in the wings, waiting for the other predators to move away from the carrion. In 1982 the company made an initial offer to salvage MD, before the

---

* An ambitious engineer in his own right and, at twenty-three, already a businessman. In late 1984 he formed Condev Biosystems Limited, a bio-resource engineering firm, specializing in manipulating various environmental variables to improve food production in agriculture and fish farming. The company is also involved in food processing and is currently pioneering a mechanical method of shucking oysters.

CDC fiasco, which MacDonald dismissed as being "very clever and very complicated." But he wasn't quite desperate enough to overcome his aversion to an organization so unabashedly in the business of churning out sausages. Ventures West got together with local businessman John Pitts and breathed $6 million into MD on the condition that Pitts* be installed as president. In the end, CDC's betrayal was good for MacDonald. It kept the government out of his business and teamed him up with a very savvy group of people. He sold a few shares himself for cash and ended up with a 20 percent ownership of the company, Ventures West receiving a 33 percent share.

If there was any magic in the decline and salvation of MD it came in the shape of John Pitts, a fifty-seven-year-old nononsense negotiator with a wolf's eye for the jugular. Mac-Donald, whose idea of hardball is a game played with nine men and a bat, was on the sidelines feeling squeamish while Pitts roughed up SwissAir over the FOCUS contract. What he saw helped him put his business career into perspective. "I sat in the meetings and provided information and my guts were going around in circles as he pushed them to the brink," MacDonald reveals. "He told them, 'If you don't do this, MD is going to go belly-up and you'll lose everything you've put in.' That was the tack he used. It was pretty rough on me. I kept jumping up and telling SwissAir that if they went for it, it'd be the best deal they ever saw." SwissAir capitulated, extending the deadline. At the same time, Pitts negotiated a loan extension from the Royal Bank and MacDonald Dettwiler was back in business, running to boost revenue which had not increased from $13 million in 1981. By 1984, sales were up to $21 million, with Pitts confidently predicting $100 million by 1990.

---

* Pitts, who has an engineering degree from McGill and an MBA from Harvard, had a long history of successful investment and management in the forest and electronics industries, buying a major share of Okanagan Helicopters and taking over its presidency in 1971. Okanagan Helicopters' gross revenue rose from $6 million that year to $80 million in 1981, when he was ousted by a sale of the control block.

John Pitts also took the direct approach with MacDonald, telling him "some of your 'highfalutin' ideas have got to go." One of those ideas was MacDonald's philosophy of keeping MD at a distance from military contracts, despite the obvious military applications of its satellite expertise.*

Some suggest that with the emergence of Pitts, MacDonald — although still a multi-millionaire — is now little more than the company mascot trotted out primarily for ceremonial occasions. If so, MacDonald is untroubled by the charge. In fact, he is back doing what he has always loved and done best; developing ideas, seeing them get underway and then chasing down another problem to solve. "He has gone through a two-phase cycle," observes his son, Neil. "There is creativity in a hands-on situation and creativity in pure thought process. During the rough period he was running the company instead of being creative. Now he has the fulfilment of being creative by searching out ideas and thinking up ways of exploiting the company's technical expertise." MacDonald, long revered for his contributions to science, has now become a respected and influential elder in the development of the Canadian high-tech industry.† And, if he no longer owns a majority share of the company that bears his name, the boy from Prince Rupert has the satisfaction of achieving what he always wanted to do — bring a little piece of MIT to Canada.

---

* MacDonald downplays his antiwar feelings, but one of the reasons he left MIT to return to Canada was because of the school's increasing association with the U.S. defence department. "I wasn't rabidly antiwar, I just wasn't comfortable with it." He didn't go out of his way to avoid defence projects but subtly kept them at bay by not installing a high enough level of security at MD. One of the first changes Pitt made was to "harden" the company's security so it can compete for Pentagon contracts.

† He is a member of the Imaging Spectrometer Scientific Advisory Group for NASA's Jet Propulsion Laboratory, the Science Council of Canada, the Board of Trustees of British Columbia's Discovery Foundation, the Board of Management of British Columbia Research and the Board of Directors of Canadian Applied Sciences. He was also on the National Research Council from 1975 to 1978, and on the British Columbia Science Council from 1978 to 1981.

Donald Cormie — The Empire of Thrift

In 1962 Donald Cormie's new ranch was intended as a hobby, a place to relax from the pressures of running Principal Group, an umbrella corporation of primarily financial companies that has mushroomed to $1 billion in assets. Today, the fourteen-thousand-acre Cormie Ranch, run by his twenty-seven-year-old son Bruce and worth over $20 million, * is a working laboratory perfecting computerized genetic selection techniques and space-age breeding procedures. It boasts the largest privately held bull semen bank in the world; Sparky, the only Maine Anjou stud bull to become the U.S. national point champion three years running, and Signal †, a million-dollar Simmental bull with more living sons and daughters (150,000 of them at last count) than any animal in history. Cormie takes great delight in being able to manipulate the sex life of Sparky and his other bulls from a small computer that sits on his desk in downtown Edmonton, forty miles from the ranch.

"I can run ten ranches as well as I can run one and it's all done through this little toy," says Bruce Cormie, patting a compact computer on his ranch headquarters desk. "It does everything but make the coffee and feed the cattle — and we're working on that." There are only fifteen hundred head on the Cormie Ranch, but this is no fatten 'em up and ship 'em out feedlot. The royalty of beef-breeding are raised here, Maine Anjou, Simmental, Polled Herefords and Charolais. Seed stock from these bluebloods are shipped world-wide to enrich beef herds and improve select genetic traits.

Breeding and shipping stock at the ranch is something out of science fiction. Artificial insemination ensures that the

---

* Don Cormie purchased the original seven thousand acres in 1962 for $11 an acre. In 1985 they were worth $500 an acre.

† Signal was never shown but he was declared a leader in four different genetic traits, four years in a row, a feat never accomplished before or since by any bull. Although the bull died two years ago, he still lives on in the semen bank. When he died he left behind over twenty-five thousand vials valued at $5 million.

prize bulls aren't allowed to risk injuring themselves with the real thing. As a technique it isn't so unusual, but frozen embryo transplants * are. "We used to have to rent a 747 and stick all these live animals in it and ship them," says Bruce Cormie. "The transportation costs were a killer and the animals weren't resistant to their new environment." Now Cormie and a staff of experts supervise the removal of week-old embryos from a donor female, with all the genetic make-up intact, pack a thousand of them into a tank two feet high and transplant them into animals as far away as Argentina or Australia.

But Sparky and his 1,500 blueblooded compatriots at the Cormie Ranch are just the most sensational and visible aspects of Don Cormie's empire of innovation. Principal Trust, one of the thirteen companies under Principal Group, † is the fastest growing financial institution in the country, averaging 28 percent annually in its thirty-year history. It is the first and only company in the world where you can buy, add to and borrow from mutual funds via an automatic teller machine. Principal Group also has the first Instanet computer in the country, allowing it to buy and sell stocks as fast as traders on the exchange floor, and the company is so completely computerized that share certificates appear from anywhere in the world via printout.

In addition to its singular technology, Principal has a history of calculated bets against the flow of conventional wisdom. For instance, Cormie decided inflation was ending when economic oracles were saying a double-digit figure would be with us until the year 2000. He knew oil prices had

---

* It is the same technique that led to the first test-tube babies and, even in the cattle world, transplants are still considered pioneer work.

† The group includes subsidiaries ranging from Collective Securities Limited, Principal Savings and Trust, Principal Life Insurance Company of Canada, Principal Investors Corporation [U.S.A.], Principal Certificate Series Incorporated [U.S.A.], Principal World Fund Inc., Principal Equity Fund Incorporated [U.S.A.], Principal Cash Management Fund, Incorporated, U.S.A., Principal Venture Fund Limited, Collective Mutual Fund Limited. There are thirty-six branches from Halifax to Victoria and also in Phoenix, Arizona.

peaked while the provincial and federal governments were still gleefully dividing up imagined profits. And Cormie was certain that the real-estate boom was ending in 1981, even while speculators were scooping up all the land they could. This kind of foresight bordering on clairvoyance, coupled with technology that would be at home on a space shuttle, has made Donald Cormie worth nearly $200 million at the age of sixty-two.

Cormie's business derring-do and creative zeal is surprising, considering the simple Scottish philosophy of thrift espoused by his father, George Mills Cormie. Unlike many entrepreneurs, whose drive to achieve grew from childhood deprivation, Cormie's upbringing, just outside Edmonton, was smooth and joyous. "I had a tremendous childhood. We.* had parents who always encouraged us to do and try things." The close family had a strong sense of achievement and excellence, but the pivotal lesson Donald Cormie learned was thrift. Cormie's father was a Provincial Poultry Commissioner who kept the family accounts in a big black book. Twice a year he gathered the family together and reviewed what their money was doing for them. "Save 10 percent of all you earn and give 10 percent to the church" was his strategy for a responsible and secure life. †

Cormie's early career showed his dedication to excellence and achievement. While at the University of Alberta, he was editor of the *Gateway*, the student paper. He graduated in 1944, second in his class, and won the Judge Green Silver Medal in Law. He graduated from Harvard with a master's in international law in 1946 and then articled with a previous Chief Justice of the Supreme Court of Alberta. Cormie was a partner in the law firm of Smith, Clement, Parlee and

---

* He had five brothers and a sister; one brother was killed during the war and the others are retired, three in Victoria and one in Edmonton.

† Cormie confesses that although he still saves 10 percent, and in fact has never spent a dime of his savings, preferring to borrow against it and repay the principal out of income, the United Church he attends no longer gets another 10 percent.

Whitaker from 1947 to 1953 and in 1954 formed Cormie-Kennedy Law Firm, of which he is still the senior, but inactive partner.

The 10 percent rule has been passed on to his eight children like a dominant chromosome. "My father might pay a dollar for shovelling the sidewalks and at the time that job might be worth 25 cents," says Bruce Cormie, "then he would sit down and say, 'Now Bruce, do you want to spend that money on candy and get bad teeth? Or do you want to put it in the bank so it's working for you when you're in school, when you're in bed, when you're sick?' " The second generation Cormie black book recorded even the most paltry addition of interest; it is Cormie's talisman and he still carries it around with him. The habit is so strong that each of Cormie's children still saves 10 percent. Son Jamie distinctly remembers the unease he felt when, as a newlywed, he was unable to put aside his normal 10 percent for the first few months.

Cormie's personal regimen of thrift, the resultant nest-egg and an idle half-time football conversation laid the groundwork for the formation of Principal Group. It was at an Edmonton Eskimos football game in 1952 that Cormie got talking with his seat-mate, the late Ralph Foster, a dignified former official of the World Bank. The two men were delighted to discover they both believed in saving 10 percent of what they earned. "We thought it might be a good idea to have a business that sold the thrift concept and so the following spring we started First Investors Corporation." Cormie, Foster and several silent partners from Melton Real Estate in Edmonton each threw $10,000 into the pot and formed a company specializing in certificate lending.* The venture came at a perfect time for Cormie. Although he had been practising law for only seven years he was finding the profession a little pedestrian and his creative instincts were already being thwarted. "It was frustrating to act for clients and lay out

---

* Cormie gradually bought out his partners when they died or retired from business and now owns 90 percent.

careful business plans for them which they wouldn't follow. I was dying to try out my ideas."

From the day the first certificate was sold over a kitchen table in Edmonton, Principal Trust (the name was changed in 1959) galloped at growth like an eager foal. Cormie has always been the unquestioned leader of the umbrella Principal Group, but Ken Marlin is its boisterous heart. For the most part, Marlin and Cormie are opposites. Marlin is bluff and hearty, perhaps seventy-five pounds overweight. Where ten concise words will do, Cormie might use five, but Marlin makes a speech.

When he first met Cormie in 1954 at the house of a mutual friend in Saskatoon, Marlin was thirty-one, had four children and was ripe for change. "I couldn't see anything for me ten years down the road," he recalls. Cormie took Marlin a little by surprise. "He was the vice-president of a financial institution and I expected a guy with grey hair and a pot belly. He told me about his dream of a financial institution with money to invest in the West. It really caught my fancy." The relationship was sealed when Cormie learned that Marlin too was a saver. "I'd put away money every month even if other bills didn't get paid." Always a hustler, Marlin was working as a telegrapher-train dispatcher for CPR and, on the side, was doubling his salary by selling Electrolux vacuum cleaners door-to-door.

Cormie had persuaded Marlin to try selling a few certificates and the forms kicked around in the trunk of his car for a week, until one day he stopped for gas and struck up a conversation with a book-keeper who was auditing a gas station. The talk got around to investments and Marlin hauled the forms out of the car. "Frankly, I didn't know what the hell the pitch was. I didn't talk interest rate, term, anything!" he remembers. "I just gave him a testimonial. I was really selling the philosophy of thrift." Marlin sold a $10,000 plan that afternoon and during the next two months, he sold sixty certificates, making more money on commissions than his railroad and vacuum-cleaner salaries put together.

Cormie, impressed with Marlin's results, asked him to take

over the head office and Marlin promptly quit his job, packed up his wife and kids and moved to Edmonton, where he found that Cormie's "vast pool of Western capital" consisted of one employee in a distinctly shabby one-room head office. In 1955, Marlin opened the first Calgary branch and earned his 10 percent share of Principal by financing the forward selling of his salesmen out of his own pocket, over his wife's strenuous objections. "She kept complaining that we were feeding other people's kids when we didn't have much ourselves," remembers Marlin.

Not surprisingly, Marlin and Cormie, both ambitious men, have over the years been at loggerheads from time to time. The most serious falling-out came in 1967 when Marlin began to branch out. "Nine for him and one for me and I was getting frustrated," Marlin admits, referring to the profit split. He started Marlin Travel, * formed a construction company, built condos in Hawaii and purchased a fleet of tour limos in Hawaii. But Cormie is completely intolerant of divided loyalties. "He felt strongly that I shouldn't have outside business interests," says Marlin, whose own response was, "Tell me about it; you've got Cormie Ranch." Cormie wouldn't budge, however, and Marlin, having built up a net worth of over $2 million outside of Principal, no longer felt any need to prove himself and turned over the businesses to his son.

Considering the radical nature of the innovations on the ranch and Principal Group, Cormie's public image is surprising. "Ultra-orthodox and ultra-conservative," is the assessment of Dan Ziegler, business editor of the Edmonton *Journal*. "Cool and very aloof," comments the vice-president of an Edmonton-based bank. But that's just the way Cormie wants it: he uses his staid public façade and his media-shy reputation like a shield to protect Principal from prying eyes. "You like to stay a little quiet until you get a certain size. Once you get over a billion dollars, the environment changes. We've always

---

* Now a thirty-branch Western travel agency.

avoided publicity. Your competitors leave you alone when you're small, but when you get big, they start shooting at you."

Cormie's well-entrenched conservative image overlays a man who is privately amused by the misconceptions about him and who admits he is a closet eccentric. Cormie's conventional persona is so powerful that even the media fails to see the contradiction in its reporting of Cormie's occasionally very outlandish displays. Outrageous behaviour has become so much *de rigueur* among the new Western business élite that hardly a week goes by without some worthy dropping his pants in front of an astonished cocktail waitress or pushing someone into a swimming pool. Don Cormie, of whom no one expects such things, can have a bit of fun, make it seem like a reasonable, proper event, and for the punch line turn a nice profit. In July of 1983 he stunned and titillated the cattle world by auctioning off ten of his prize Maine Anjou heifers at the foot of the marble-and-mahogany staircase on the twenty-ninth floor of Principal Plaza. Attended by the national media and the cattle-buying élite from all over North America, the meticulously planned event went off without a hitch. The elevators were specially slowed and padded so they wouldn't shock the cattle. Normally, cattle auctions show the animals in action, but a canter through the executive offices was a bit too much, even for Cormie, so video cassettes of each one were shown as the heifers went on the block. "We got double what we have ever got at any other sale," Cormie quietly points out, "and there was even a clip about it on TV in Los Angeles!"

Another memorable event was Principal Trust's 1984 Silver Treasure promotion. There were traffic jams in downtown Edmonton as people scooped up silver coins from a treasure chest. The only hitch was that they had to put the money into an account for a month. It normally costs Principal $20 to get one person in the door and opening an account. On a normal day, Principal gets two or three walk-ins a day and the figure jumps to thirty or forty through advertising. Each day the silver scooping promotion ran, Principal got four hundred new accounts at a cost of less than $10 each — the maximum coinage even the largest hands could grab out of the chest.

Cormie also puts on some of the most bizarre in-house sales promotions in the industry. Principal likes to kick off campaigns with a flourish. Champagne breakfasts aren't uncommon, and once an executive rode a horse into a meeting at corporate headquarters to set the stage for a sales blitz. Another time, a diminutive and meticulous twenty-eight-year-old junior executive named Grant Mitchell arrived at a meeting clad in a green tennis shirt, blue bathing suit, and swim fins, and around his neck he wore a garland of sports paraphernalia and beer cans. He looked like the perfect fool, but the campaign boosted sales. "That's the sort of thing admired around here," he says, "having the guts to take a chance." Within two months Mitchell was promoted to vice-president of operations for the entire Principal Group. The company newsletter is full of reports of executives betting cases of champagne over who will win their personal sales derby.

The reason Cormie's public image is so powerful is because it is grounded in reality. A handsome man, just under six feet tall, once slim and whip-cord lean, the years have broadened his frame, leaving it stocky and powerful. He looks like actor Rod Taylor without a smirk. Cormie radiates sombre competence, underlined by the kind of confidence usually only enjoyed by those with inherited fortunes. His calmness inspires instinctive trust. He's the kind of man you'd want in charge during a crisis: the surgeon performing a triple bypass on your heart when the operating-room power fails; the pilot when your plane is hijacked by terrorists; the banker protecting your life savings during a recession. He is studiously the quintessential professional — controlled, highly motivated from within, even a little mean in his single-minded pursuit of achievement. But professionalism is only part of the man and Cormie, in an unguarded moment, refers to it all — from the gold-plated fixtures in his executive bathroom to his one thousand square feet of G.Max computers — as a bit of a game. He calls Principal Group's recently reached $1 billion in assets a magical mark. He playfully toys with the cockpit at his desk, opening and closing his blinds and locking his drawers with the flick of a finger. He confesses that one of his favourite gadgets is a digital bathroom scale that growls "One at a time, please" when he puts on a bit of weight.

The $38-million Principal Plaza confirms the discrepancy between the public Cormie and the private man. Depending on the day and the door you open, a visitor's evaluation of Principal Group could be either that it is an exquisitely design-ed enclave of financial tradition or a freewheeling, hair-down, feet-on-the-table repository of go-getters and tradition-busting upstarts. The décor is stunning. Inset mahogany French double-doors guard the foyer (this is far too grand to call a lobby) on the twenty-ninth floor. St. George and his dragon, the Cormie Crest, are etched into the glass. Mirrors, columns, a graceful polished mahogany balustrade and Italian marble floors turn visitors with business to transact into rubbernecks. Even a pimply-faced courier in a hurry hangs his head back, adam's apple popping, to gawk at the surroun-dings. The broad swooping circle of the receptionist's desk overlooks the city, the Saskatchewan River Valley and the prairie, the kind of view normally reserved for CEOs. And adjacent to her throne, a twenty-foot span of butter-soft suede sofa waits to cushion the tense buttocks of outsiders.

Cormie talks matter-of-factly about the building's utility, but his conventional words can't mask his thrill over his crea-tion and he can't resist showing it off himself. He excuses the massive staircase, connecting the twenty-ninth and thirtieth floors and wasting thousands of square feet of floor space, as a good place to hold a meeting. He talks about the efficiency of the executive boardroom, where a Pope-sized pulpit hides a control panel of buttons that taps the room directly into the master computer, and operates a video-recording system and a host of other communications paraphernalia. Upstairs, in the great hallway on the thirtieth floor, the atmosphere is that of a private museum: heavy, silk kimonos hang from the walls and hand-knotted rugs are scattered here and there. "Everybody collects art," Cormie tosses off, waving his hand at the Emily Carr, Krieghoff, A.Y. Jackson, Lawren Harris and other Canadian paintings hanging above the sitting area in his office. "I mean, that's one thing you do when you have an office." But few go to the trouble Cormie has for a favoured painting. He loves the brooding Lawren Harris so much that he searched out a weaver in Calgary to duplicate the work on three large woven panels hanging in the board-room. He also has a particular fondness for the primitive colours of his Ted Harrison canvas and he can't pass it with-out pointing out — touching the canvas with his thick, power-ful fingers — that it is really a painting of the Cormie Ranch, complete with every member of his family, hired hands and even the resident one-legged dog.

On a whirlwind tour, Cormie's stocky figure hurries from room to room, impatient to get on to his next surprise. Out-side the master control centre, a massive colony of robot-like information storage and data retrieval computers reside in a climate-controlled room. "They're safe in there," he says, tap-ping the bullet proof glass as he marches by. Outside the elevators on the twenty-eighth floor, Cormie bustles across the grey velvety carpet into a small room off a cramped corri-dor where a technician, who looks more boy than man, is elbow-deep in circuitry and computer boards. He is construct-ing an advanced condenser that allows Principal's custom machines to talk with other computers and translate "outside" programs. "We couldn't find what we wanted," he grins with the joyful dedication of a hungry child whipping up a batch of fudge, "so I'm making it."

The few outsiders who know about this work boggle. "What they are accomplishing there is incredible," says Dick McClure, an Edmonton consultant in information manage-ment and data processing. "This isn't even their primary business and they've had very little help from outside. Building their own condenser is unheard of. They're in such a position that no one else can help them write programs." As McClure contemplates the ramifications for computer con-sultants of Principal's self-sufficiency, he adds: "It's both in-triguing and disturbing."

In addition to an in-house computer factory, Cormie is overseeing the development of a sensitive security system that operates by taking pictures, comparing them and, if something changes — like the presence of an unauthorized person — it sounds the alarm and locks all the doors. The system can instantly read an employee's entrance card in Halifax, check back to Edmonton to make sure he's legitimate and then spring the door open. It remembers the last hundred cards, so if the person enters again, the door opens without the checking delay. As Cormie tours the jumbled room where the system is being further perfected, he can't resist touching odds and ends. It seems that it wouldn't take much for him to doff his jacket and start tinkering. Principal's security is so advanced that there are no outside experts who could be hired to run it, so Cormie has a single young technician supervising students, showing them how to wire the board.

But Principal Group has not risen from a small company with assets of $60,000 in 1954 to a diverse billion-dollar empire solely on the strength of a gadget fancier who also gets choked up about a nice bit of brushwork. Cormie has earned his reputation for being a very tough man and the weight of his personality is felt at every level of operations. At a weekly executive sales meeting he discusses an employee with patronizing dispassion and elects not to promote him because a promotion would remove him from a problem job that "he's got to work through for the development of his own character. When he does, he'll be worth a lot more to the company." When it was disclosed that the sales of one long-time manager had slipped drastically, Cormie, with a puzzled look on his face, said, "Gee, he used to be our top salesman," but he doesn't suggest a holiday for him or a man-to-man pep talk. Rather, he quietly orders that an additional manager be placed in the branch, with exactly the same status, to increase competition.

Aspiring employees are often intimidated by Cormie's reputation. All they hear is that Cormie is demanding and relentlessly present in every aspect of his empire, primarily through his own energy but also through five of his children (he has eight) who work in Principal Group.* Cormie knows what people say: "I have a lot of people come in and say, 'I don't think you're the right kind of company to work for. If people don't perform, you don't give them long enough to prove it and hire someone else.' We demand efficiency and if people can't do the job, you get people who can." He shows no false sentiment about firing people. "There are some people who just can't seem to earn their keep. If you keep them on when they are not effective, it dissipates the energies of the company."

In an age of nice notions like employee participation in decision making and in Japanese-style quality circles, Cormie is busy perfecting the reward-and-punishment approach to capitalism. He characterizes his management approach as one that creates a culture in the company that attracts doers rather than bureaucrats.† Salesmen are ranked and their individual sales figures tallied weekly and published for general perusal — not saved for hushed, private meetings. All employees are objectively evaluated in terms of their future worth to the company, weighed against present achievement. Paramount is the belief that if you squeeze hard, and in the right place, performance improves. "If you concentrate on objectives, morale goes up," Cormie points out. "If focus shifts, grumbling begins. It's amazing to see everyone really behind a goal."

* Donnie, 36, works for Principal in Vancouver; Alison, 34, has a Ph.D. in geology and economics from McMaster; John Cormie, a taller, slimmer and slightly gentler-looking version of his father, is president of Principal Trust; Neil, 30, designed the Cormie Ranch security system and has a bachelor's in economics from the University of Victoria; James, always called Jamie, did graduate work in economics at the University of Alberta and is vice-president of investments; Bruce, 27, is the manager of Cormie Ranch and vice-president of agricultural services. Cormie's wife, Eivor, has a bachelor's in economics from the University of Alberta and son Robert, 20, is a third year commerce/law student who works for a local broker during the summer. He is the Cormie family's "designated lawyer."

† Cormie doesn't skimp on the reward side. His employees' salaries are competitive at all levels. And Principal has chartered planes to take deserving sales staff to Paris and the Near East, all expenses paid.

The key group of goal-setters at Principal Group attends the weekly finance meeting, which decides on overall investment policies and then executes them. The participants, Jeff Watters, head of the investment department, James Cormie, vice-president of the investment group, and John Cormie, president of Principal Trust, are all under thirty and uninhibited by the financial power they wield. Laughter is ready, and not just at the boss's jokes. There are no feet on the table, but postures are slouched and casual — rumpling the impeccable three-piece suits adorning this small crowd of lean and sharp achievers. No notes are kept. Cormie demands a free flow of ideas and believes that minutes or other recording techniques discourage people from taking the chance to expound outlandish ideas.* Few greybeards exist anywhere in the company and those that do carefully avoid the role of elder statesman. The youth of the executive is no accident. Cormie grew tired of the old hands' subtle resistance to new ideas and new technology. The result is an organization, even at executive levels, with a mean age under thirty-five — the two oldest people in Principal are Cormie at sixty-three and his 10 percent partner, Ken Marlin, aged sixty-one. "People are most creative in their early thirties," he says. They're also more amiable, more open to change, more willing to pursue his sometimes revolutionary strategies and his desire to reach further and further into futuristic technology.

Most companies crept into the computer age, and banks were among the slowest to change. Principal Trust threw itself at the microchip. "Our on-line system is so efficient that you could deposit $100 in our Halifax branch and half a minute later your husband could draw it out in Victoria," brags Cormie. Then there is the machine that has Canadian stockbrokers up in arms, Instanet. It allows Cormie to buy and sell stock in seconds, bypassing a broker and his fees, tying

* Principal has great informality of manner: everybody is called by their first names with one exception. Donald Cormie is either Mr Cormie or DMC to senior executives and sons. "He deserves that," one secretary told me in explaining the discrepancy.

directly in with the floor of any exchange in North America. Principal Trust is also the first financial institution in the country to go on the American Depository Trust System. "We don't even see share certificates any more. We used to send them by armoured car to Montreal and by bank courier to Edmonton and all that nonsense. Now all we do is get a computer print-out." Principal's tentacles even reach deep into the Royal Bank, which handles its deposits. The bank's computers are tapped by Principal so that Cormie knows the status of every one of his accounts every minute. When millions are massaged daily, an hour's delay in a critical investment is costly.

The formidable security in place and under development implies that there is something worth stealing at the Principal Group. Although Principal stores no bullion — or even vials of semen — on the premises, Cormie is protecting something even more valuable — information. He maintains a Strategic Planning Group that devotes itself exclusively to giving Principal an edge. As early as 1943, when he was a delegate at a UN international conference in Salisbury, Connecticut, Cormie believed that life and business are governed by cycles. He and his staff plot a vast array of statistics, including U.S. commodity prices since 1820, the cost of labour in England since 900 A.D., the history of Dow Jones trading since 1885, the U.S. monetary schedule — to name a few. All these charts are overlaid, adjusted for inflation and then digested by Cormie who, when he travels, * bounces the ideas off others, testing to determine if the conditions shown by his charts are consistent with reality. Once Cormie is satisfied, he announces, "I've done my homework," lays out his plans, and relentlessly executes them. As a result he has a remarkable record of accurate predictions, much of which he attributes simply to smart analysis of historical trends. "If you can see the cyclical

---

* Cormie and his wife are dedicated participants in the Young Presidents' Organization. Cormie was its first Edmonton member. He is also a longtime member of the World Business Council. They have attended almost every international conference held by the two organizations over the past twenty years.

patterns you are much more comfortable about when to borrow and not to borrow. There is a time when it pays you to go into the stock market and when it's a disaster. There are a lot of little signposts; they give you a little advance notice. It's not 100 percent right — you're following a trail." Cormie's ability to follow a trail has powered an incredible 60 percent growth of Principal's total assets from $627 million in 1982 to $1 billion in 1985. During the same period virtually every other financial institution operating in the West was writing down their assets. *

Cormie's foresight has saved the company from more than one disaster. In 1969 Principal was poised to open a life-insurance company to complement its mutual sales. Ken Marlin had visited every branch, tying up loose ends, and had even accepted delivery of the policies when Cormie called a board meeting, announced he'd done his homework and told everyone that the stock market was overheated and that they'd better pull in their horns or lose them. "I had grave doubts and even the directors were saying, 'Holy Christ, what are you doing,' " remembers Ken Marlin. "But once Cormie says, 'I've done my homework', there's no budging him." The life-insurance company was shelved, an austerity program instituted and Principal sold its stock and purchased land. Within six months, life-insurance sales were virtually non-existent and several of the biggest companies in Canada went bankrupt.

Part of the reason for the growth in assets from 1982 to 1985 was Cormie's realization in 1982 that the Canadian dollar, in relation to the U.S. dollar, was going to drop to historic lows. Cormie transferred 70 percent of Principal's

---

* One of Cormie's research coups occurred when he was planning the development of the Cormie Ranch. Research showed that wet years showed up in the area every eleven years. His strategy was to peg those peak water-table years as crop failures and sell machinery just before they happened when prices and optimism were high. Prior to the bad years, the land is put to grass and cattle. As the cattle are maturing, beef prices rise because everyone has sold out of cattle and are planting crops. Then, as the wet years end and machinery, fertilizer and seed prices are depressed, the cattle are sold and the land put back into crops.

assets — cash and stocks into U.S. currency and debts into Canadian money. By 1984 the seesaw of currencies had earned Principal a 25 percent profit, in addition to normal investment profits. And then, in September 1984, Cormie — convinced that the Canadian dollar would return to par — began reversing the process.

About the only place Don Cormie hasn't made his mark is in Ontario — and that's no accident. "We do not want to have our main companies registered in Ontario, because every time we go in there to register, they want us to do something odd-ball," he says with a touch of exasperation. "Ontario doesn't allow you to innovate. We have two U.S. mutual funds, good for sale all over the U.S. We brought those mutual funds into Alberta, British Columbia, Manitoba and Saskatchewan and they accepted it. Ontario had forty-nine objections, of which three were illegal in the States. If we did them, we'd go to jail in the U.S., yet they wouldn't budge. You talk to Ontario officials and they don't even seem to know what you are talking about. They think they've got all the answers in their regulations."

But, not surprisingly, Cormie has a plan. In September 1983 Principal Group quietly bought 78 percent of the voting stock of Bomac Batten Limited (since renamed Principal Neotech Limited), a publicly traded Ontario company with a thirty-year background in the graphics industry and a more recent interest in computerized reproduction. Principal is proceeding slowly ("we like to keep our heads down"), installing their own management team, building up assets and learning the ropes in Ontario — *doing their homework*. And when the homework is done, things are bound to get interesting. Already the stock has tripled in value since Cormie bought it.

Don Cormie has national and international ambitions for Principal Group. Every year he extends the company into another province or another part of the world. And, although being Alberta-based keeps Principal far removed from the central corridors of power in Canada and the United States, he is determined to control his operation from Edmonton. "It's a hard job building a large business in a small place like Western Canada," he admits. "Our business isn't really here anymore, it's all around — down in the United States, off-shore. We're just using this as a headquarters. We've had people trying to get us to move to Toronto, where they claim the environment for big business is better. But I've grown up here and lived here and I figure if [the climate's] not right, why don't we make it right?"